THE EQUINOX PACT BOOK 1: AWAKENING

LEIGH WALKER

AWAKENING

A YOUNG ADULT PARANORMAL ROMANCE

THE EQUINOX PACT BOOK 1

Sign up for Leigh's new release notifications, and never miss a new book! www.leighwalkerbooks.com

THE
EQUINOX PACT
BOOK ONE

LEIGH WALKER

DAYLIGHT

LAST NIGHT I dreamt I was on the island again. I'm down near west beach, at the Tower. It's been a while, but it looks the same. It can't be—I know this. But in the dream, I choose to ignore the facts.

I stand in the field at the end of the drive. The crickets chirp in the high grass as it sways, swept by the ocean breeze. Toward the water the enormous mansion looms, white and empty, its tower outlined against the darkening sky. The waves crash against the rocks. The ocean rumbles, buzzing in my ears.

I want to go inside the house more than anything. I want to see who else is here. But as I start up the steps, something, some dim awareness, tugs at me: *Go back. Leave.* I should never have returned. But in the way of dreams, my limbs are heavy, and I'm slow to follow instructions. The only thing that's fast are my thoughts. They whizz, chasing the truth, reaching for the edge of the memory of what happened to this place. It eludes me, slipping around the corner, just out of reach...

I jerk awake, first stunned by the sunlight streaming through the unfamiliar windows, then grateful for it. In the sun, it's safe to think about the big white mansion on the island.

I turn and stare at the empty space next to me, and my sense of well-being evaporates.

Some things are never safe to think about.

SURFACE

EVEN THOUGH IT was a five-hour drive to Bar Harbor, I wasn't ready when the bus pulled into the station. I peered through the window but didn't see my dad waiting for me. Instead there was my stepmother, Becky, scowling at her phone and furiously texting.

Becky Hale was blonde, tall and slender, her white jeans faux-casually cuffed above her tanned ankles. She arranged her enormous designer bag over her shoulder and pushed her aviator sunglasses up on her nose, while still managing to rapid-fire off a text with one thumb. She didn't look up as the trickle of seasonal workers and tourists spilled out from the bus. Such people were beneath her concern. I grabbed my duffel bag and took a deep breath, preparing myself.

Becky sort of really sucked.

"Hey." She put her phone away and smiled at me coolly, and I was briefly entranced by the sight of her pretty face. She had that effect on people, and I often wondered what her life would be like if she didn't have her looks to mask her personality. "Your father couldn't leave the island—one of the lobster boats just came in." My father ran the co-op on Dawnhaven, and one of his jobs was getting the lobsters weighed and accounted for when the fishermen came in.

"Okay. Thanks for coming." I peered around her. "Where's Amelia?" Amelia, my half-sister, was fourteen and almost as petrifying as her mother.

"She's at sailing lessons."

"Ah." My heart sank. I'd been praying they'd changed their minds at the last minute and sent her to summer camp.

"Is that all you have?" Becky eyed my cheap duffel with disdain.

"Yes." In fact, the contents of my bag were all I had left in the world, but I was not exactly into sharing with Becky.

"Then let's go." She turned on her heel and disappeared into the parking lot.

There was no *How are you doing? Have you eaten?* or *How were the last couple of weeks with Aunt Jackie?* kind of talk from Becky Hale. She did not give a shit, and she wasn't afraid to show it.

I hustled after her. If I wasn't careful, she'd leave me behind and then blame me for it.

———

MOUNT DESERT ISLAND OR MDI, as it's commonly known, is the largest island in Maine. The fact that it's an island used to confuse me when I was little because you could drive there, right across the Trenton Bridge.

Home to Acadia National Park, MDI is comprised of approximately eighteen towns, most notably the famous tourist destination, Bar Harbor. It boasts mountains, forests, quaint towns with New England charm, and the coldest, cleanest, bluest part of the Atlantic Ocean. It's also a playground for America's rich and famous. The Rockefellers once lived on the island, and lots of television executives and celebrities have homes there: the producer of *Law and Order*, Martha Stewart, John Travolta, Susan Sarandon. A famous young actress was spotted on MDI last summer at a wedding. People gossiped that she'd been out shopping in the afternoon before the ceremony, wearing a white tank top with no bra.

Becky drove us to Pine Harbor. From there we'd take

a water taxi to the small island of Dawnhaven, where Becky, Amelia and my dad lived. It had a year-round population of about a hundred, mostly commercial lobstermen and their families. In the summer, tourists and locals alike flocked to Dawnhaven to have dinner at the restaurant and explore the art galleries, gravel paths, rose bushes and rocky beaches.

The ferry parking lot was packed, and the dock was crowded with tourists when we pulled in. They waited for public transportation, the mail boat, which delivered the mail and other goods to Dawnhaven several times a day. The Hales never took the mail boat. If my father couldn't pick her up, Becky hired a private water taxi. My stepmother didn't suffer much. She'd never rub shoulders with tourists and their faux-leather fanny packs and cheap "Maine-Vacationland" T-shirts.

Becky parked her enormous Mercedes SUV in one of the reserved spots and we climbed out. I immediately felt eyes on us. *I know what it looks like.* Some of the tourists stared, probably wondering if Becky was famous or just really rich. With the rap-star-grade SUV, along with the huge designer bag, perfect looks and air of detached superiority, strangers often did a double-take when they saw her.

I was wearing capri leggings, an oversized *Worcester Polytechnic Institute* T-shirt, and five-dollar flip flops from Old Navy. Maybe people thought I was her assistant.

"Grab your bag," she said. "Bud doesn't wait for anyone." She didn't look at me as she spoke. I took my duffel from the trunk, then nodded toward the case of wine and groceries from Main Street Market. "I'll come back for that."

"The crew will get it." She frowned. "Let's go. We have a couple of things to discuss." I followed her down the steep ramp to the dock. There were dozens of boats parked nearby, running the gamut from yachts, to mid-sized sailboats to dinghies. The blue-green water shone in the early afternoon sunlight. Even with all the boats, the water was clean. Freezing, to be sure, but pristine.

Becky swung a long leg over the side of the water taxi, the *Breathless*, and easily climbed on board. Once she'd settled in, she pulled her aviators down on her nose, all the better to narrow her eyes at me. "First of all, you have to get a job. Today. You can't just be hanging around, texting your friends all summer."

"O-Okay." But finding a position could be tricky. Dawnhaven was tiny, with one run-down store and one restaurant. The local kids usually lined up their jobs a year in advance. "I'll see if they still need anyone at the *Portside*."

"They'll hire you if they want my business this

7

summer," she sniffed. "Next thing: you have a curfew. I expect you in our house by ten every night, no exceptions unless you're working."

"Don't worry about it—I don't know anyone on the island. I'll probably be home all the time."

The tiniest crease permitted by Becky's strict Botox schedule appeared between her eyes. "Hopefully you'll stay busy. And I expect you to be on your best behavior in front of Amelia. That goes without saying." Even though she felt the need to say it.

"Of course," I mumbled. Becky always seemed to assume, because of my mother's issues, that I was somehow tainted. Little did she know that I'd never drank a beer or vaped, let alone kissed a boy. I was shunned by the popular group back home; on the weekends, I spent my free time working at a sub shop. I'd been deemed "basic" since eighth grade and perhaps "emo" after my mom died—Lena Harris had caught me crying in the bathroom one day. Whatever. I had one more year left before college, one year with Becky and Amelia, one year of suck.

I just have to make it through.

Bud, the captain of the *Breathless*, nodded to us as he reached the dock. "We'll be going in a minute."

"Thanks, Bud." Becky smiled at him, the faker. Of course, he smiled right back. The tourists watched as

Bud and his crew loaded the groceries and wine into the boat. They were probably trying to figure out if they'd seen Becky in the tabloids.

"Your father will be happy to see you," she said.

I nodded. "Me too."

"He wanted to come and get you." I could tell this was the truth because she didn't seem to want to say it.

"That's nice."

She pushed the sunglasses up on her head and forced me to confront those light-blue eyes, so cold, in direct contradiction to the smattering of freckles across her nose. In the beginning, the freckles had given me hope that Becky might have a friendly bone in her body; they lied. "This is going to be really tough for me, you know."

"I know." I could only imagine the fight.

"I've worked really hard to make sure Amelia has good character. Please don't be a bad influence."

Years of dealing with Becky had taught me that trying to defend myself was a waste of perfectly decent oxygen. "Don't worry. I won't."

"She thinks your mother died from cancer."

The young crewman untied the boat from the dock and hopped aboard. "Here we go," Bud said. He put the boat into drive without preamble.

Becky watched me carefully. "I don't want any mention of what happened. The past is in the past."

I nodded, even though her words cut me. The past, as in my mother, had only been dead for three months. Her death was below Becky's consideration, as was my grief, but I was literally out of options. "Of course. Your house, your rules." She'd been drilling it into me since I was four.

As the *Breathless* navigated out of the harbor, the tourists watched us, their expressions open and eager. Becky's golden aviators were back in place, secured against the ocean breeze. Her white-blond hair blew back from her face as she watched the bay open up, mansions lining each side of the craggy coastline. *I know what it looks like.* But it was so far from the truth that had I been capable, I would've laughed and laughed.

3

THE ISLAND

I WOULD NEVER ADMIT it to Becky, but I loved the island. The way the ocean smelled as we crossed from Pine Harbor to Dawnhaven was my favorite scent in all the world. The land was unspoiled, and the earth smelled the way God had probably intended it: pure, luscious, clean.

We passed two of the neighboring islands, Crescent and Spruce Island, covered with trees and fronted by rocky beaches. I checked on the enormous Osprey nest as we rode by. Easily six feet across, it was situated on top of a tall, man-made tower and had been there for years.

Dawnhaven came into view. First the uninhabited portion, the rocky coastline bordered by the forest, followed by the restaurant, the dock and the bustling

11

co-op, where my father worked, and the lobstermen brought in their daily hauls.

I'd fallen for the island because of my dad. When I was younger, he used to tell me stories about it. "The settlers named it Dawnhaven because of what the Indians told them. It's the easternmost island in the state, so you see the sun come up first. The tribe that lived here, the *Wabanaki*, used to have to first watch. They protected the others and let them know if they saw danger coming from the ocean."

After he and my mother divorced, he moved to the island on a whim. It had been good to him. As the manager of the fisherman's co-op, he knew all the residents. Tall, ruggedly handsome, and always good-natured, the local women loved him. He started dating Becky, they got pregnant with Amelia, and they got married soon after.

The sun was halfway over the horizon now; I basked in the warmth on my face as we neared the island dock. Part of me couldn't wait to see my father, but I'd learned over the years to be conscious of showing too much affection for him. Becky didn't want us to be close. Still, my heart leapt when I saw him waving from the dock. People called him "Big Kyle" for a reason. My father was six-foot-five and had the shoulders of a linebacker. A grin split his face as the boat got closer. I'd pay for it later, but I couldn't help but grin back. "Dad!"

"Hi, pumpkin!" He pulled me off the boat and wrapped me in a hug, engulfing me in his arms. It was like hugging a giant, friendly meat-locker. "Glad you made it safe and sound. Was the bus all right?" I could hear the undercurrent of guilt in his voice, always bubbling below the surface.

"It was fine."

"You girls get some lunch?" he asked.

Becky made a big show of getting off the boat by herself. She whipped her sunglasses off and gave him a look. "No, we did *not*. I had to make it back to pick up Amelia from her lesson. I can't just leave her there."

"Amelia is fourteen, and she has a bike," Kyle reminded her gently. He turned back to me. "Would my beautiful daughter like to get some lunch?"

I couldn't see Becky, but I felt certain she was scowling. I didn't want to start the summer off on the wrong foot. "I'm fine."

Dad's face softened. "C'mon. Let's go get some chowder and a burger. Becky can drive Her Highness home."

Becky stepped forward. "Kyle—"

He gave her a warning look, something he usually reserved for the big fights they had about me. "I'm taking Taylor to lunch. You and Amelia are welcome to join us, if you like."

"Fine." She shrugged as if she didn't care. "You can just load the groceries into the truck, Bud. I'm going to get Amelia."

"All right, Mrs. Hale." The captain tipped his hat.

"I'll see you down there, Kyle. Order me an iced tea, please." Becky put her sunglasses back on and hustled toward the small dock where Amelia took sailing lessons. Of course they were coming to lunch. She wouldn't want us alone for too long, lest the focus be taken off of her and Amelia for a nanosecond.

My dad threw his arm around me as we walked up the ramp, then crossed the field to get to the *Portside*. The island looked just as I remembered. The fields stretched out around us. The dock bustled with activity, kids played wiffle ball down by the beach, the trim white church sat at the top of the road, and the dark-green firs rose majestically into the sky.

"How are you holding up?" Dad asked.

"I'm fine."

"It was nice that you could stay with Aunt Jackie to finish up school." He shot me a look. "Was it okay over there?"

"Are you asking me if she's still drinking and smoking?"

When he nodded, I gave him a patient smile. "This *is* Aunt Jackie we're talking about. But it wasn't too bad." When Aunt Jackie was off her shift at the hospital, she maintained a busy cheap-vodka-and-Parliament Lights schedule, but she wasn't mean. "She said I was welcome to stay."

My dad stopped walking. "Absolutely not. You're not going back down there—your aunt means well, but that's no place for you. I want you out of that city. After what happened..." He shook his head. "And don't say a word about Aunt Jackie's offer in front of Becky, if you know what I mean."

We hadn't had much time to talk about how, exactly, he'd wrangled Becky's permission for me to come and live with them. Although I supposed the fact that he was my only parent left had something to do with it. I swallowed hard. "It must have been...difficult...for her to agree to this."

He started toward the restaurant. "She didn't have a choice."

"I bet that went over well."

"Doesn't matter." His forehead creased. "I guess it took what happened with your mom for me to grow a backbone, but there you have it. I'm sorry, kid."

I opened my mouth but then my eyes filled with tears, so I closed it. I waited for my composure to return and then asked, "Do you think the restaurant's hiring? I need to keep busy."

"Well you're in luck!" My dad grinned, trying to lighten the mood. "One of their little waitresses just got a fancy internship in Manhattan and had to leave the island. I already put a word in for you with the owner, so I think you're in good shape."

"Do they know I've never waited tables before?" The idea of serving tourists and locals alike every night in the busy restaurant was daunting, but it was better than tiptoeing around Becky in her mausoleum of a house all summer.

"They know you're a good kid and a hard worker, and that's all that matters." Dad smiled at me as we reached the pier that led to the restaurant. An art gallery and a souvenir shop shared the landing. A beach, hewn with rocks at low tide, bordered the small wharf on the right. Sometimes when it was high tide, and the bar had been busy, people jumped off the restaurant's roof right into the ocean.

The smell of fried haddock and French fries wafted out from the screen door, and my stomach growled. Dad squeezed my shoulders, and I knew he was happy I'd arrived. "C'mon. The cook this summer is *really* good." A friendly hostess showed us to a table for four by the windows. Even in the early afternoon, the bar was packed. The bartender, who was young and ridiculously attractive, had short dreadlocks, dark skin and a diamond stud in her nose. She expertly poured out a line of tequila shots for a group of lobstermen, not spilling a drop.

"I guess they got a good haul today," I mused.

"Yeah they did. Plus, they go to bed so early, it's about cocktail hour for them right now." Kyle chuckled.

"Hey Big Kyle, you want one of these?" One of the guys held up a shot.

"Nah, I'm still on the clock, Rich." Dad smiled at him. "I'm having lunch with my little girl."

Rich's jaw dropped. "That's *Taylor*? Good lord, when did you get so grown up?" He and the other fishermen came over. "I'm real sorry to hear about your mom," Rich said.

"T-Thanks."

They switched gears easily, chatting and asking how my school year had gone. I hadn't seen any of these men for several years. When I was younger, I spent most Julys on the island. But Becky has said the long visits were "confusing" for Amelia, so for the past few summers I'd just come up for a quick weekend or two.

"God Kyle, she looks just like you," Rich said.

"Aw, that's sweet. You think I look that good?" Kyle laughed.

"*Excuse* me." Becky elbowed her way past the throng of lobstermen to the table, a sulky looking Amelia in tow. "Do you mind if we sit?"

Rich gave her an easy smile. "Not at all, Bec. You enjoy your lunch, now." He and the others made haste back toward the bar as Becky pulled out a chair for Amelia and blinked at her husband. "You want to say something?"

Kyle looked at her, stymied. "Um."

She gesticulated to their daughter. "How about *hello*?"

"Hello Amelia." He smiled at his younger daughter and she smiled back.

"Hi Dad. Hey, Taylor." Amelia was pretty like her mother, with a smattering of freckles, blue eyes, and thick, naturally blond hair that fell past her shoulders. She already had a light tan beneath her white tee and lavender athletic shorts. But pretty as she was, there was something off about her face, a constant sneer around her nose. She looked like she perpetually smelled something sour, like a big clump of used cat litter was somehow following her around.

I made myself smile at my half-sister. *Maybe she's changed?* "Hey. How were your sailing lessons?"

Amelia made a gagging noise. "Terrible. Mrs. Sutherland is, like, the biggest douche."

Hasn't changed much.

Dad went rigid. "Amelia." He kept his voice low, but it was loaded. "Do not speak like that."

Becky came to her daughter's rescue. "Mrs. Sutherland made them tie knots for the past three hours. She's too old to still be teaching—she sucked back when *I* had her. Two grand a summer for lessons, and they're doing knots. It's ridiculous, and I'm totally complaining."

Kyle looked at his wife like she was crazy. "What good do you think that's going to do?"

Becky shrugged, whipped out her phone, and started scrolling. "Did you order me an iced tea?" Her tone indicated she was expecting to be disappointed. Every question, every statement Becky made seemed loaded. It was like walking in an emotional minefield. One false step and *boom.*

"Not yet. No one's been over." Either Kyle had unlimited patience, or he'd learned the hard way that it was easier to play nice.

"Well, since you were so busy socializing, they probably didn't want to interrupt." She didn't look up. "Amelia, posture." But Amelia whipped out her own phone and hunched over it, ignoring her mother's admonition. The two of them didn't say another word as they continued to scroll.

My dad frowned. "It was really nice of you to join us."

"Huh?" Becky looked up, confused.

I was momentarily distracted from the discomfort level at our table by a stunning picnic boat pulling up to the nearby dock. My dad had taught me enough for me to recognize the boat as a Hinckley, a luxury brand made locally on MDI. Its beautiful real-wood hull gleamed in the early afternoon sunlight. A young man wearing a baseball hat and a rumpled white button-down shirt hopped out to tie it up. I caught a glimpse of his face, handsome, with a square jaw. He looked a little older than me, maybe twenty. I didn't recognize him.

Norumbega, the boat read.

I felt eyes on me and turned to find the bartender staring. I smiled but she looked down, fastidiously drying a glass.

"That Champlain kid has his friends living up at the house this summer. I heard there's some weird stuff going on." Becky scrunched her nose and stared out at the dock. "Marybeth said Donnie saw him out on his boat in the middle of the night, doing some sort of chant in the bay. She heard he's running some sort of *cult*."

Kyle let out a bark of laughter. "Marybeth needs to do something besides gossip and host wine o'clock."

Becky stared him down. "This is the first summer

he's ever spent up here, but he doesn't even bother with the locals. He never talks to anyone besides his friends. Not one word. And he has all those strange people coming over, parking at his dock and going up to the Tower. You notice that?"

"Yeah well, maybe he's just doing his own thing. Nothing wrong with that," Kyle said.

"What's a cult?" Amelia asked. "You mean, like, that Leah Remini show?"

"Yes—it's like a religious group, but they're usually smaller. And dangerous." Becky narrowed her eyes at her daughter. "Don't ever join one."

"James is hot, though." Amelia raised her eyebrows as she watched him finish tying the boat. "He's, like, the only guy on this island worth looking at. I don't care if he *is* in a cult, he can recruit me."

"Amelia." Kyle grimaced and looked up at the ceiling, as though he were begging for some help from heaven above.

But Becky smiled indulgently at her daughter. "Oh honey, I get it, trust me. He's handsome *and* he's rich." It seemed like a thinly veiled dig at my father, but again he didn't flinch. "But no cults for you, and no college boys. Now sit up straight young lady, or I am disconnecting the Wi-Fi when we get home."

4

STANDING APOLOGY

THERE WAS nothing worse than being a guest, I decided. I'd never gotten comfortable at Aunt Jackie's apartment, which was cramped and messy. For different reasons, there was no way I'd ever relax at Becky's house.

Still, I admired the cedar shingles and tasteful white trim of the farmhouse-style home as we pulled down the long gravel drive. Becky's house boasted six bedrooms, six bathrooms, two fireplaces, and Viking appliances. There was the new addition of an outdoor fire pit and small, immaculate in-ground pool that no one ever seemed to use.

The inside of the house was pristine. This was no summer cottage with Downeast charm. It was like living in a museum, one decorated in Restoration Hardware. I never knew where it was safe to sit—Amelia had once told me that their throw pillows cost four hundred dollars each. How did my big, rugged father survive here? He was like a bull in an Anthropologie shop.

Becky gave me a different room this time, one that had its own staircase at the back of the kitchen and a private bathroom. I guessed it was originally the maid's quarters, but I didn't care. The room was cheerful, with a multicolored bed spread and paintings of the island on the bright-white walls. I loved it. Maybe I could hide in there all summer and never come out.

But I'd have to leave the safety of my room, and soon. After lunch Dad had brought me over to meet the *Portside* owner, Jenny. She admitted to being desperate for another server and hired me on the spot. My first shift was in an hour, and I had to get ready. Relieved that I'd already met Becky's condition of securing employment, I unpacked my clothes and put them carefully into the dresser. I put on the white polo shirt and black shorts that Jenny had given me, then tied the apron around my waist. The uniform smelled funny, and felt stiff and new, but there was no time to wash it. I pulled my hair up into a ponytail and brushed my teeth.

Becky was in the kitchen when I went downstairs. As soon as she saw me, I could tell that she was annoyed, and was going to be annoyed by my presence all year. Or more precisely, the rest of my life.

"Hey," I said. "I'm heading back to the restaurant. They're going to train me tonight."

Her cool blue eyes flicked over me. "Good luck." Her tone, as always, had an edge of disapproval to it.

My dad stepped into the room and gave her a look. Becky tensed up—she hadn't known he was there. "Hey there," he said to me. "You look ready to go, except— aren't you wearing sneakers for your shift?"

I looked down at my cheap flip flops, cheeks heating. "These are all I have."

Becky *tsked* behind me and my father's jaw went taut. "Honey, can you please lend Taylor a pair of sneakers? You're the same size, if I remember correctly."

"We are *not* the same size."

"What size are you?" he asked me gently.

"Seven."

He turned to his wife. "And you?"

"Seven and a half," she said triumphantly.

"Close enough. Now please go get her a pair, and some socks. She can't be serving food in her flip flops."

Becky opened her mouth to argue but Kyle stopped her with another look. "You have a thousand pairs of shoes. You can spare some for Taylor. I'll take her off-island to get a new pair tomorrow."

Becky stomped up the stairs and my dad shook his head. "Sorry."

I shrugged. "It's not your fault, but I don't want to make it any worse for you."

Becky came back to the kitchen a minute later. She dangled a pair of pristine white, unworn running shoes out toward me like I had the plague and she was unwillingly giving me the antidote. "Your father doesn't need to take you off-island just to go shopping. He has to work tomorrow, and he promised Amelia he'd take her to the beach." She handed me the sneakers. "You can keep these, and the socks. I don't want them back."

"Thanks." Even though what she meant was, she wouldn't want them back because I was going to wear them.

"Now if you'll excuse me, I need to go check on my daughter. She said she has a headache." Again, her tone was accusatory. At me for probably causing the headache, at my dad for not caring enough about it.

Dad waited while I laced the sneakers up. "I'll walk you down to the dock." Once we were outside, he took a deep breath. "You know you have my standing apology when it comes to Becky."

"Yeah, I know." He'd covered for her when I was younger, but there was no disguising her position now.

"I swore I'd never get divorced again, and we have Amelia, so…" He shrugged. "I'm just rolling along."

I nodded.

"I wish she wasn't jealous, but she is. Always has been."

"Of what?" This was the part that really got to me. Becky had everything—she'd already won. "She's jealous of your junkie ex-wife and your daughter you barely see? What's she so afraid of? I'm going to college next year."

"Taylor." My dad winced. "Maybe she thinks it's some sort of a competition between you and Amelia, but it isn't like that. She doesn't understand, I guess."

"It doesn't matter. I'm not mad at you."

"I know you aren't. But maybe you should be. I've tried to keep things on an even keel and that's won out over being a father to you. That's not fair."

"I'm fine. I've always been fine." It was the truth.

He hesitated. "The circumstances are awful, but I'm still glad you're here. I feel like I'm getting the second chance I don't deserve."

"Don't say that." I squeezed his arm. The thing with my dad was, he was a good guy. He capitulated to Becky, but I didn't judge him for that. He was out of his depth. He was trying to be good to Becky, Amelia and me—and even to my mom, back when she would let him help. How could I be mad at him for trying his best?

My mother thought I was naive because I wasn't angry that he'd started a "new" family. But I wasn't and never had been. My mother was the one who'd ended their marriage. And my dad, despite being far away and remarried, had never once let me down. Becky was so wealthy that he didn't have to work, but he still managed the co-op so he could support me and my mom. He faithfully called me twice a week and texted every day. Even though it'd pushed Becky right over the edge, he'd immediately started custody proceedings when things started to go really down the tubes back home. But Mom's final overdose happened before the court date, and then there was nothing left to fight over.

Dad and I had agreed that I was going to spend the last three months of my junior year at Aunt Jackie's, and then I was coming to the island. I was supposed to finish school at Mount Desert Island High, but I didn't know if I could last a whole year with Becky and Amelia, and vice versa.

Dad looked down at the bright-white sneakers Becky had given me. "You don't own a pair of running shoes, do you?"

"No."

"I didn't know—I thought she was using the money I sent to take care of you. But that's no excuse, because it's my job to know." He cursed under his breath. "If I'd come down there more, if I'd been there for you and your mother, things never would've gotten so out of control."

"Dad." I stopped walking. "Now isn't the time to get into it, but even I didn't know what was going on until it was too late." My mother had always had issues, but the abruptness with which the drugs had claimed her was almost unfathomable. It's not like she came home one day and made an announcement: *I tried heroin, and oh fuck, it's game over.* It was just…game over. There was life before heroin, and then there was nothing but heroin, and then there was just nothing.

"The first time I called 9-1-1, I thought she was having a stroke," I said. "I had no idea. She was shaking and her lips were blue. The paramedics gave her Narcan and kept asking how much she'd shot, and if she'd mixed it with alcohol. I had no idea she was using, and I was living with her."

"I can't believe you had to see your mother like that." He sounded like he might cry. He stared out at the water for a minute, collecting himself. "We should get you to the restaurant. I don't want you to be late for your first shift."

"Yeah."

We started walking again and my dad said, "Worcester's one of the worst cities for drugs. I know you'd never do anything like that, but I don't want you going back down there. You've seen enough. You need to just be a kid."

"I appreciate that, but what about Becky? I don't know if she can last a whole year with me. She can barely get through lunch."

"She doesn't have a choice. I'm your father. It's about time I started acting like it."

"Dad—"

"C'mon now." He forced a smile. "Let me beat myself up a little. I deserve a lot worse. And as for Becky, I can handle her."

I wanted to arch an eyebrow, but I instead, I forced a smile in return. "Okay Dad. If you say so."

5

WAITING

I'D HAD a feeling that waiting tables was going to be an unmitigated disaster, and I was right. Jenny, the owner, said I'd be trained, but what she really meant was that I'd be thrown to the wolves and that the kitchen staff would grimace every time I went back there and asked another dumb question.

"You've had a job before, right?" Jenny asked when I turned in my paperwork.

"I worked at a sub shop."

She smiled encouragingly. "You'll be fine," she lied. Then she hustled off to seat yet another party. For such a tiny place, there was no shortage of customers. People drove their boats over from neighboring islands to come for dinner. The restaurant was packed, even on a Wednesday night.

30

Eden Lambert, one of the waitresses, was tasked with showing me the ropes. The Lamberts were the biggest family on Dawnhaven. There were five brothers and three sisters, all married, all commercial fishermen, with at least three children apiece. You could spot them easily by the signature Lambert-red curls. Eden had hers pulled up into a springy ponytail. She told me she was a sophomore at Bowdoin and had spent summers working at the restaurant since she was fourteen.

Eden moved around the restaurant easily, smiling at the customers and joking with the kitchen staff. She made it look easy, but it wasn't. "Draw a grid in your notebook and number the tables," she said. "That way you can keep track of who needs what and where they are."

I started scribbling down the table numbers, but she sighed impatiently. "Are you going to get that new four-top water, or what?"

"Y-Yes." I shoved the little notebook back into my apron and started filling water glasses from the pitcher. There was a large brown serving tray stacked nearby, but I was too scared to carry it. I hand-delivered the water glasses to the table two by two.

"That's going to take a while." Eden looked at me as though I had three heads. "You've never waited tables before, have you?"

"No."

She grimaced. "Meet me here at three tomorrow and I'll show you how to carry drinks on a tray. Otherwise, you're going to be in the weeds with one party. Now just follow me tonight and watch what I do. I'm not going to split my tips with you, though. I'm doing double the work."

"That's fine." Eden clearly knew what she was doing, and I did not. Whatever she could teach me would be more valuable in the long run.

I followed her diligently all through my shift, but still managed to dip my apron in the chowder and get yelled at by one of the line cooks. Eden sent me back to the kitchen to grab an appetizer. I hustled, taking one of the crab cake orders from beneath the heat lamps. "Hey— New Girl!" the line cook roared. Sweat poured down his face as he glared at me from behind the line. "You need a ticket. Do not take a plate without a ticket! You'll screw everything up!"

"O-Okay." I scurried off, vowing to never go into the kitchen again. Unfortunately, Eden kept sending me back there, telling me to get oyster crackers and dressing and ramekins of hot butter for the lobsters. I didn't know where anything was. I kept asking questions, but by the ninth time I asked someone for something, they started ignoring me. "There goes the new girl, again," the line cook muttered. He blotted his face with a towel and sautéed more mussels while I searched desperately for the hot tea bags.

Everyone was skirting the weeds—we had a full house. The wait staff hustled from their tables to the computer to place their orders to the kitchen to pick them up. No one stopped to chat, side-eye was given and there were claims that drinks were being taken from the bar out of turn; it was sink or swim. Thankfully as the hours wore on the crowd thinned out. We stopped serving at nine. I breathed a sigh of relief at eight fifty-five; we'd made it.

But then another party of four sauntered in, and Jenny sat them in our station. My heart sank for a couple of reasons. Not only were we stuck here for the next hour and a half while they ordered, the grumbling, exhausted cooks were going to be pissed and take it out on us. They'd have to reopen the containers of food they'd put away and dirty the stations they'd already wiped down.

To add insult to injury, our new customers were stylish and intimidating—this would be the equivalent of waiting on the popular kids. It was the day bartender with the pierced nose. She wore a hoodie and jeans, looking ridiculously attractive and elegant for someone in a sweatshirt. She and her three friends laughed as they settled in at the table. I recognized one of them as the boy who'd docked the Hinckley boat earlier, the "Champlain kid," as Becky had referred to him. He wore the same white button-down shirt and upon closer inspection, was even more handsome than I'd thought. Another girl, equally attractive, with coffee-colored skin, long black hair and enormous brown eyes, sat on the bartender's right. Across the table was a guy with dark skin, his back to me. His shoulders hulked beneath his *Patriots* #12 T-shirt and his cornrows were fitted with white beads.

"These guys are always together, and they only come in after the place clears out. Everybody else thinks it's rude, but whatever. I told Jenny to put them in my station." Eden reapplied her pink lipstick at the wait station, just out of sight of the customers. "They're big tippers, so please for the love of God do not spill anything on them."

"I won't." I peered around the corner at the table. "She works here, right?"

"Josie, yeah. She also models part-time, in case you couldn't guess. But if you can get past the fact that she's gorgeous and almost completely perfect, she's pretty nice." Eden stuck her tube of lipstick into her apron and smacked her lips. She looked fresh and clean, while my hair felt frizzy, my mascara was probably running, and my skin was damp with sweat.

"The other girl, Dylan, that's Josie's girlfriend. She's from the city—she's a chemical engineering student or something. She's here for the summer and yes, she always looks that good. Patrick is the big guy, his mom's a tech mogul who owns part of the WNBA. She bought one of the island's biggest houses last year. And then there's James, of course. Not like you could miss him. Not only is he hot, he's like, a gazillionaire. His family owns a ton of properties. He's spending this summer out at the Tower."

"The Tower…where's that, again?"

"You know, the big old mansion down on west beach. It has a lookout."

I kept peering at the them from the safety of the wait station. "He's a little young to be a gazillionaire, isn't he?"

Eden sighed. "He's a *Champlain*. You know, like the hedge fund?" When I stared at her blankly, she just shook her head. "Never mind. Are you ready? We need to hustle otherwise the kitchen will lose their you-know-what." She started pouring waters. "Why don't you go ahead and take their drink order? It's the last table, you might as well. It's not like they're going to bite."

"Okay." Still, I hesitated, peering at the table. The guy in the white shirt looked up and our eyes locked. I stood for a moment, deer-in-the-headlights style, my mouth gaping. Then like an idiot I ducked back behind the corner. What did I think, he couldn't see me? Eden watched me then muttered to herself, probably about being stuck with the new (and possibly crazy) girl. I needed to get it together. I got out my notebook, plastered a smile on my face and headed to the table, heart pounding.

I didn't know why I was so nervous. I'd been tiptoeing around the popular kids my whole life. Maybe it was because Josie worked here, and I didn't want to screw up in front of her? *Or maybe it's because that Champlain dude keeps staring?* His eyes were unusual—were they gray? Dark blue? I went to the table and readied my pen. My gaze immediately tracked to his handsome face, a moth to a flame. "Hey."

He raised his eyebrows, a small smile on his face. He had thick, dark hair and one dimple. "Hey yourself."

"How's it going?" Josie asked. When she smiled it showed her perfect teeth and she was even more impossibly gorgeous. "Tonight's your first night, right?"

"Y-Yes." I swallowed nervously. "Can I get you something to drink?"

"I'll have an espresso," Josie said, "and Dylan would like an iced tea. Guys?"

I wrote the order down quickly, petrified that I would somehow mess up their drinks.

"I'll have a seltzer," the boy said. "I'm James, by the way."

I nodded, my cheeks heating. *What's my deal?* "I'm Taylor." He smiled at me and I frowned. He was too handsome to talk to.

"Hey." James leaned closer. "Are you okay?"

I nodded, surprised by his directness and embarrassed that I was blushing like an idiot. I was in the rabbit hole of blushing now. There was no coming out of it. "Yes, of course."

He looked just above my head, an amused expression passing over his features. "You sure about that?"

"Huh? Um, never mind." Discombobulated, I turned to his friend in the Patriots shirt. "Hi, what can I get for you?"

"I'm Patrick—nice to meet you." He leaned forward, a friendly smile on his face. "Could I please have some water?"

"Yes. And it's nice to meet you, too." Anxious to get away from the table, I whirled around and ran smack dab into Eden. I smashed into her tray and sent waters flying everywhere. "Oh my God!"

Eden smiled at me tightly and I could tell that not only was she pissed, she wasn't the least bit surprised. Her polo was soaked; a few ice cubes clung to it. "No big deal. It happens to everyone. I'm just going to go wipe my shirt."

Josie got up and helped clean, stacking the glasses back on the tray and picking up dripping cubes of ice. "This is why I don't get dressed to come here. Jenny never trains anybody on the basics."

"I'm sorry." I leaned down and started wiping the floor.

She looked at me and shook her head. "I saw you in here earlier today. Was that your family?"

"My dad." I kept wiping. "And his wife and daughter."

"Oh yeah, I know that Becky. She's never met a wine pour that's big enough." Josie chuckled. "Your dad's all right, though."

"Thanks." I picked up the tray and we both stood. "Sorry about that. And watch your step."

She smirked. "Oh, I'll be fine. I'm a little worried about you, though."

"I'm good," I mumbled. I bussed the glasses, wondering why everyone seemed to need to get into the new girl's business.

Eden held her hands up as I came back around the corner. "Easy," she chided.

"It was an accident!"

Her face softened. "Oh, come on, I know it was. Waiting on those guys can be intimidating, too, I get it. You go ahead and clean up—I'll take care of them. They're just having dessert. We'll be done soon."

"I can get their drinks," I offered.

Eden's raised her eyebrows. "I got it, really."

I gave her a foul look as I started cleaning the wait station, but I didn't mean it. She'd been tolerating my incompetence all night. I refilled the salt and pepper shakers and restocked the napkins. I wiped the counter and straightened the ketchup bottles. Once everything looked organized, I felt a little better.

The cooks were having their shift drink at the bar, and the one who'd yelled at me waved me over. *Great.* "You do okay tonight, New Girl?"

My shoulders slumped. "Between getting ignored, getting yelled at and knocking a bunch of drinks to the floor, it wasn't so bad."

He chuckled and held out his hand. "I'm Elias, and I'm sorry for that earlier. My bark is worse than my bite."

I shook his hand. "Taylor. And thanks for letting me know."

"We're good, as long as we're clear—do not come into my kitchen and try to take food without a ticket."

"I won't ever do it again."

"See?" He grinned. "You're going to do just fine."

I had my doubts, but my heart lifted as I took off my apron. Eden winked at me while she was drizzling chocolate sauce on a piece of Boston Cream pie. "See you tomorrow at three. Don't be late—you need all the help you can get."

"That's the truth. And thank you."

"No problem."

Embarrassed, I didn't look at Josie's table as I headed to the exit. She called to me anyway. "See you tomorrow, New Girl!"

I heard them laughing as I left, and my face once again went up in flames.

HIM

I MADE myself scarce the next morning until Becky left to take Amelia to sailing lessons. My father went to the co-op at five a.m. every day, so he was long gone by the time I crept downstairs.

The kitchen was immaculate and quiet, and I was glad I'd have at least a little while to explore. I was starving. Becky didn't eat much, and she tried to limit Amelia's snacking, but my dad insisted that they keep real food in the house. I made myself a cup of coffee in the Keurig. I found organic cream in the fridge and dumped some in, then added a heaping spoonful of sugar. Next I took out organic eggs and cheddar cheese and made a scramble, holding my mug and relishing my coffee while the food cooked. There was fresh Sourdough bread—I toasted two slices and then slathered them with butter. When it was all ready, I greedily ate every bite, moaning to myself at how good it tasted.

I never had access to a kitchen like this, to the heavy sauté pans and the gas stove and the freshly crushed pink Himalayan salt. My apartment with my mother had one scuffed pan and our milk always had a slightly sour smell, even when it was new. It was because it was cheap, the skim milk so watery you could almost see through it. Aunt Jackie's fridge was also a wasteland, filled with diet soda and fluorescent yogurts stuffed with so much fake sugar they made your mouth buzz. The Hale double-sided refrigerator was stocked with pure, unadulterated bliss. It made me feel bad for all the crap I normally ate—*this* was real food.

Becky probably had a protein shake for breakfast, as she preferred to save her calories for white wine. She didn't understand what she was missing out on, because it had always been right in front of her face.

Speaking of Becky—I'd dressed in a sports bra and running shorts and laced up the sneakers she'd so begrudgingly bestowed on me the previous evening. I wasn't much of a runner. I actually wasn't a runner at all, but I might as well try it now that I had proper shoes. Plus, I wanted to see more of the island without anyone asking me what I was doing. Running was the perfect excuse.

I made sure the kitchen was spotless before I left, just like I found it, and then made my way outside. I shivered a little even though the sun was climbing in the sky: it was always sweatshirt weather on the island. I glanced at the glistening pool as I passed, vowing to swim in it later. I headed out to the end of the drive, then took a left onto the dirt road. Becky's shoes sure were going to get dusty.

I hadn't spent much time here in the last few years, but Dawnhaven was so tiny it was impossible to forget where everything was. I started to run, first past the road to my right that led to the public beach, then by the makeshift, slightly creepy mini-golf course erected by some of the island's children. A molding teddy bear with one eye peered at me from the eleventh hole; I picked up my pace.

After the golf course came the yellow-clapboard, one-room schoolhouse. The year-round residents sent their younger children there (except for Amelia, who'd gone to a private Montessori school off-island since she was three). Once it was time for middle school, the kids took the mail boat to Pine Harbor and then the school bus to the larger MDI school which went through twelfth grade.

The school yard was abandoned. There was a meager, lightly rusting play-set out front, along with an abandoned basketball court. My dad and I occasionally came here to shoot hoops in the early afternoon, before the mosquitos descended.

Next came the run-down store that doubled as the post office. They usually had a carton or two of milk and a loaf of white bread for sale. Becky preferred to order her groceries from the market in Pine Harbor; they delivered via the mail boat, and notably also shipped wine by the case.

After the store there were a few houses—Bud, the captain of the *Breathless*, lived on the left, and Melinda, who was a poetry professor, had a home decorated with bursting flower boxes on the right. Then the road diverged. If I ran straight, I'd go into another neighborhood. To the left was west beach.

I headed left.

A few lobstermen had homes on this road, but at this hour of the day it was deserted. They'd been out on the water for hours already, and their houses were quiet except for the buzzing of bees in the flower gardens. Woefully out of shape, I was already struggling to catch my breath. I slowed to a walk. The sun shone down on me and for a moment all I noticed was the absence of noise. It was so different from the city. There was silence all around, filling every space, the weight of it pressing against my head.

But the island was deceiving. It always took a while to sense the rhythm of it, to feel how fully alive it truly was. As my breathing returned to normal, I noticed the hum that was all around me. There were bees, grasshoppers, birds, and the sound of the breeze in the pine trees, their gentle sway against each other. The ocean churned in the background, the tide in flux, the waves crashing against the rocks. What masqueraded as silence was actually movement and life everywhere.

I reached the end of the public road. To the left was a private, gravel drive. It led to what I now knew was the Champlain estate, which was bordered by a rocky beach. I'd been down here before plenty of times. Although it was private, tourists and locals alike ventured down to west beach. People liked to take pictures of the mansion, gleaming and white against the sky. Plus, the Champlain property had a clear view of Moss Head, a tiny land mass which boasted a working lighthouse. You could also see the seals out here—they loved the little cove between Moss Head and the island.

Seals were my favorite. I told myself it was a desire to see the wildlife, not to snoop out the Champlain estate, that had me going down the narrow, twisty drive.

Wild rose bushes bordered each side of the pass, their bright-pink blooms a distraction from the mass of furry-like thorns that covered each stem. I hadn't made it far when tires crunched over the gravel, coming from the house and heading my way. *Crap!* I quickly jumped off the path, scraping through the bushes to the rocky ledge above. I'd barely made it as a rusty old truck came bombing around the corner, spraying gravel until its brakes screeched to a stop.

James Champlain peered up at me from the driver's side. "You okay?"

My shoulders and torso were scratched and bleeding. "Yeah. I just got into it with this rosebush." I pointed toward the offending party.

"Sorry about that. I never expect anyone on this road... I should be more careful." He tilted his head, his grayish-blue eyes raking over me. "So, to what do I owe this honor?"

"Oh—I wasn't coming to your house. I was just out for a run and thought I'd check out the seals." I said it so fast, I babbled.

"Everyone loves a seal."

I could tell he didn't believe me, but I nodded vehemently anyway.

He took pity on me and changed the subject. "I was going down to the boathouse for a minute. It's just out past the beach. You want to come?"

"Um." I looked down at myself, my sweaty hot-pink sports bra, orange running shorts and Becky's bright-white shoes. My pale skin was freshly adorned with multiple, bloody scratches. Not my best look.

"I can drop you home afterwards if you want." He smiled. "Just watch the rosebush."

I picked my way down the rocks and climbed into his truck, which had sand on the seats and smelled like chewing gum. James turned to me, his gaze resting just over my head. "You're better today?"

I looked above me, confused, but then his steel-colored eyes were on my face again. "Yeah, I'm good."

"Are you hurt?" He glanced at the scratches, then quickly looked away.

"Not really."

He reached behind his seat and pulled out a long-sleeved blue T-shirt. "Here, you can put this on if you want. It's clean." He inched the truck forward, going slowly now.

"T-Thanks." Confused, I slid the shirt on over my head. It smelled like the beach. "I don't want to ruin your seats."

"Oh no, it's not that. It's the blood. I'm actually a little squeamish." He chuckled.

"Oh. Sorry."

He shook his head. "You don't need to apologize on account of those bushes. Those suckers'll get you every time. Are you sure you're all right?"

"Yeah, thanks." Now that he was closer, I could see big, pale biceps peeking out from beneath his plain white tee, and the bottom of an intricate tattoo. His chest was larger and more muscular than I'd guessed. I really wished I'd taken a shower.

"So Taylor." He gave me a friendly smile. "How do you like working at the restaurant?"

"It was fine, except when I was spilling things or annoying people."

"I know you spilled things." He laughed. "But you also annoyed people?"

I nodded. "I asked too many questions. Actually, all I *did* was ask questions, and then I spilled things. So, I'm not off to a great start, but it'll get better. I'm meeting Eden before my shift tonight and she's going to help me learn to balance things on trays."

He shot me a quick glance. "Good luck."

"Thanks, I need it." We reached the end of the drive and he eased the truck out onto the road, driving about five miles per hour, the accepted speed limit on the island. "What about you? Are you working this summer?"

"Something like that. I'm actually doing something for my father."

"Oh, is your father here, too?" Eden had said he was here alone.

"Not this summer." James frowned and watched the road. "But I expect he'll check in on me eventually."

"Do you come here every year?" I asked. "I haven't seen you before."

"No, I don't. Sometimes I come in the winter when no one's around, but this is the first summer I've spent here. My family's busy so we don't get out here very much. It's a shame, really. The house just sits there. What about you?"

"This will be the first summer I've spent here, too. My dad's lived here for years, though. With my step-mother Becky and their daughter Amelia. You know the Windsor estate?"

"Down by the Gallery? Yeah, I know it. That's you?"

I nodded, even though it would never be mine.

He navigated the truck past the post office, the school, the mini-golf course. "What are you, seventeen? You'll be a senior this year? Where do you go?"

"I'll be eighteen in September. I'm supposed to go to MDI High for senior year," I mumbled.

He glanced over at me. "And you don't want to?"

I shrugged. "It's fine. I'm looking forward to college. What about you—are you in school? How old are you?"

"Twenty-one. I'm taking classes here and there, but mostly I've been working for my family."

"Do you like that?" He'd asked me a lot of questions, I figured it was fair.

"Not all the time." He laughed. "It's like anything, I guess. Has its good and bad parts."

"What sort of work is it?"

He half-frowned. "Hmm... I guess it's really about checks and balances."

I shook my head, confused. "Does that have to do with finance?"

"Sometimes." He didn't offer more as we drove slowly down the road that led to the public beach. There were cottages, along with some larger homes, and bikes were parked off to the side. We passed several long boathouses, some of which doubled as summer residences, until we almost reached the end of the road. I'd never been down this far before.

James parked in front of an enormous, brand-new building that extended out onto the beach. It was shingled, with a metal roof, solar panels and a new-construction smell. It looked like a mansion. "Here we are."

"This is your *boat*house?"

"Well, we use it for other things." James smiled. "Come on inside, I'll show you."

TAKE MY WORD FOR IT

JAMES HOPPED out of the truck, undid the latch and opened up the barn-like door. I'd never been inside a boathouse before, but this one had to be unique. The first part of the enormous structure had a concrete-pad floor and the ceiling soared above my head. There was a fifty-foot sailboat parked inside. *Mia*, the glossy letters read across the back. I didn't have to know much about boats to understand that it had cost a small fortune.

Eden's words came back to me: James was a gazil-lionaire. He must have been. If his family didn't even spend time up here, but had two enormous houses on Dawnhaven... I couldn't wrap my brain around that sort of wealth.

I walked past the *Mia* to the far end of the building. Its floor-to-ceiling windows faced the beach, and an Lshaped couch with cozy throw pillows was positioned to enjoy the view. There was a massive fireplace made from natural stone, and a full kitchen lined the wall. A string of white lights blinked above the cabinets, one small bohemian touch.

"Your boat must be very comfortable here."

"Ha ha."

I turned to find James watching me, again looking just slightly above my head. I hesitated, unsure if there was something different about his eyesight or his vision, not wanting to ask and make him uncomfortable. But then he looked at my face again and I wondered if I'd been imagining things.

"So, let's sit for a minute." He motioned toward the couch. "Want some water?"

"Sure." I settled into the luxurious cushions and looked around some more. The coffee table was littered with cards and an abandoned game of Scrabble. "Do you hang out with your friends here a lot?"

"Sometimes. We prefer the Tower."

"I'm sure it's nice." If it was nicer than this, it must have been incredible. There was a private, unobstructed view of the beach. The tide was out, and the dark sand stretched down, turning to multicolored pebbles. "This place is beautiful—so's the boat."

"Thanks." He handed me the water and then sat at

THE EQUINOX PACT BOOK 1: AWAKENING

the opposite end of the couch. "It's named after my great-grandmother.

"Cool. Hey, what about your other boat—the Hinckley? I saw you dock it the other day. It had an unusual name."

James smiled. "*Norumbega*. You have an excellent memory."

"What does it mean?"

James looked out at the water. "Norumbega was the name of a mythical city. The first European explorers who came to this island were searching for it. They believed it had pillars of gold and overflowing riches."

"They thought it was real?" I asked.

James nodded. "It actually appeared on some early maps. Some of the explorers got the Indians who lived here to help them look for it. They never found it, of course. So the explorers came back here. They took over the island, and the whole island of Mount Desert, eventually."

"So why did you name your boat after the city—if that's an okay question to ask?" I'd no idea if I was being inappropriate. I'd never had the occasion to ask a really rich person why they named their boat a certain way.

"It's okay." His quick smile warmed my insides. "My father named the boat. He said he felt like he'd discovered that magical place when he came to MDI for the first time. He's loved it his whole life."

I smiled back. "That's nice. I love it here, too."

James looked slightly above my head again. "You sure about that?"

"Yeah. Hey, what're you looking at?" I peered above me, scanning for whatever it was that kept drawing his attention.

James's gaze was directly eye level when I stopped. "I have some vision issues."

My face grew hot. "I'm so sorry."

He shrugged a big shoulder. "Don't be. It doesn't bother me when people notice. It means they're paying attention."

I nodded, still uncomfortable. "Where do you live when you're not here?" I asked, anxious to change the subject to just about anything else.

"We have a house in Washington State. I spend some time there, and Hawaii, too. And Martha's Vineyard."

"Oh. Wow." I braced myself, waiting for him to ask me the same question. My answer would be pale in comparison.

"What about you?" James asked.

"I'm from Worcester." I smiled. "About as underwhelming as you can get."

"Not really." He smiled. "The first American Valentine's Day cards were designed in the city of Worcester."

"Really? Is that true?"

James shrugged. "If you can trust Wikipedia."

"Huh. Maybe it's more interesting then I give it credit for."

He briefly glanced above my head again. "You don't like it?" James asked, even though it sounded more like a statement than a question.

"It's dirty. And crowded. So no, I guess I don't like it much."

"Sounds fair." He put his feet up on the coffee table. "How come you're living up here now?"

I took a deep breath. I'd been rehearsing how I'd answer this for the past three months. "My mom died this spring. So now I'm living with my dad."

"Aw, I'm sorry." James's shoulders slumped. "I hadn't heard about it."

"I wouldn't expect you to know." I shook my head. "My dad's pretty private." *And Becky doesn't like him to talk about me.*

"Are you close to him?"

"Yes, very much so. He's a great guy." James's gaze drifted back above my head, but this time I didn't bother looking too. "Trust me, I'm telling the truth."

"What?" His eyes snapped back to my face.

"Oh, I don't know why I just said that!" I shook my head. "I felt like you were double-checking me, or something."

"Taylor... Huh." He stared at me, his mouth agape. "That's an interesting thing to say."

I winced. "Yeah." An awkward silence descended on us. When he still didn't say anything, I panicked. "Um, that was really dumb of me. I should probably go."

"Hey, it's okay—"

"Like I said, I'm really sorry. I'm just babbling." I stood up and my knee banged the Scrabble board, almost knocking it over. "I have to do some chores before my shift. Thanks for having me!" Before I could say anything else crazy or break something, I fled. I couldn't get out of there fast enough.

"Okay, see you." James didn't sound alarmed, at least.

Once I made it outside, I cringed. *Way to go.* I started running, because I literally wanted to run away. *Idiot idiot idiot.* The hot guy tells me he has vision issues, and I go weird on him. The thing was, he kept looking above my head—like he was looking *at* something. But it was probably lazy eye. *Dear earth, please swallow me whole.*

I heard a car behind me. I wildly thought of sprinting away, but I'd only make a bigger ass out of myself when I collapsed fifty feet down the road. James's big old pickup came even with me and he smiled, flashing that dimple. "Hey. Since there's nowhere to run—ha ha—can I at least drive you home?"

"Yeah." I slowed to a walk, then stopped. "I'm really not much of a runner." I climbed into the truck, unsure of what else to say. "Listen, I'm really sorry about that. I don't even know—"

"Nah, it's fine." The muscle in his jaw worked as we drove down the street, and he was quiet for a minute. "You noticed something that a lot of other people don't. My vision issue, I mean."

We turned the corner, past the row of high hedges, and pulled down Becky's long drive. James parked in front of the house. He sat there for a second, looking straight ahead. "Don't get out, okay? I want to tell you something."

"O-Okay."

"You thought I was checking on something, and you were right." He turned to me and I was forced to confront his high cheekbones, full lips, and those piercing, steel-colored eyes. "People don't always say what they mean."

I nodded, waiting for him to continue.

"So when I was looking above your head like that, I was reading your aura. I wanted to know if you really liked your dad."

"Um." I gripped the door handle. "My aura?"

"Yeah, it's like a smoky swirl of color. It hangs out above your head."

"My head." I looked up. "There's colored smoke above my head."

"That's what I'm doing when I look at you like that—seeing what your mood is, and if it matches what you're saying. After a while I won't need to look anymore. I'll be able to tell by the sound of your voice."

When I gaped at him, he continued. "It's not just you. I can do it with everyone." His dark-gray eyes looked up, just above my head again. "So I can tell without you saying anything that you think I'm a freak, and that you'd like to get out of my truck now."

"I don't think that," I lied.

James smiled as he brought his gaze to meet mine again. "Okay Taylor, I'll take your word for it. See you around." I took that as my cue. I let myself out and ran into the house.

By the time I looked back outside, the truck was gone.

8

SHIFT

"WAS THAT JAMES CHAMPLAIN?" Becky's whole face creased in disbelief as she stared out the window.

"Yeah. He gave me a ride home from my run."

She whirled and inspected me. "Since when do you run?"

"I have for a while."

Becky might not read auras, but she didn't believe me. She looked me up and down, suspicious. "Those shoes are ruined."

I reached down and wiped off some of the dirt. "I'll clean them."

"Why'd James Champlain give you a ride? He's been here for months and I've never seen him talk to anyone."

I shrugged. "He saw me out on my run and I think he could tell I was getting tired. Plus, he was at the restaurant last night. I spilled a bunch of drinks when I was waiting on his table and I think he felt bad for me."

"Ah, okay." Finally, an explanation she could make sense of. "You didn't tell him what I said, did you?"

"That he's a cult leader?" I blinked at her. "I would never repeat something like that, Becky."

"Good. It wasn't meant for your ears, anyway." She adjusted her bangles against her bony wrist and headed back to the kitchen. "I'm going off-island for yoga. When Kyle's finished at the co-op, he's taking Amelia to the beach for some one-on-one time." She said this pointedly, so there was no mistaking I was not allowed to encroach. "What're you going to do?"

"I'm working." After last night I was pretty sure I hated waitressing, but just about anything beat hanging around the house. I would ask for every double shift that existed from now until the end of August.

"Okay, see you." Satisfied things were in as much order as she could manage, Becky disappeared.

Now if only *I* could. I sought refuge in my room, taking a quick shower and changing into clean sweats. I grabbed my uniform and threw it in the washer, along with the sports bra and running shorts. I inhaled the scent of James's blue T-shirt again and decided not to wash it.

Let it serve as a memory of my strange morning.

I couldn't believe James said he'd been reading colored smoke above my head. What was weirder was that I almost believed him. He'd seemed capable of sensing my mood, and whether or not I meant what I said. It was some sort of parlor trick; he must be really good at reading expressions and voice inflections.

But why would a guy like James make up something strange like that? Was it for attention? How much extra attention did a gazillionaire with great hair and a fifty-foot sailboat need?

I decided to push it out of my mind for now. I knew from experience that sometimes, people did shit for literally no reason other than to mess with you.

All the more reason to keep to myself.

"OKAY—HOLD the stand in your right hand, tray on your left shoulder." Eden smiled at me. "You can do this!"

I scowled. "Is it true the kitchen staff is putting money on whether I drop everything?"

"Don't worry about that. Focus on what's important: do not look at the drinks." Eden shook her head, her red curls bouncing back and forth. "If you look, you spill. Just watch where you're going and you'll be fine."

I doubted that, but I hoisted the tray up over my

shoulder anyway. There were six small glasses of water on it. I prayed I wouldn't trip and send them flying everywhere.

"Now just walk over to the table and put the stand down. That's right, open it up," Eden encouraged.

I somehow jerked the metal serving stand open with one hand. Then I bent my knees, grabbed the tray with both hands and shakily put it on the server.

"See? There you go!"

I heard cursing and saw Elias and one of the other cooks watching from the entrance to the kitchen. Elias handed money to the other guy, then shrugged at me. "It's nothing personal, New Girl."

"Yeah right." Josie gave Elias a look as she slipped behind the bar. "You've been talking about how much money you're going to make all day."

He grinned as he headed back into the kitchen. "Day's not over yet."

Josie eyed my tray. "It looks like you did okay."

"Yeah—better than last night anyway."

"Just wait until someone orders a martini." Josie chuckled as she tied her apron around her waist. She started taking drink glasses out of the small washer. "Then you're screwed."

Eden saw the look of utter horror on my face and

patted my arm. "I'll help her. You'll get the hang of it, eventually."

"How long did it take you?" I asked.

She shrugged. "A summer or two. No big deal."

I groaned.

"Let's go read the specials board. C'mon." Eden hustled off to the kitchen.

"So... I heard you saw James today." Josie put more foggy glasses on the bar to dry. "How was that?"

The thing about the island? Everyone knew everything.

"Good." I nodded jerkily. "He showed me his boathouse."

She arched an eyebrow. "He said you were out near the Tower, looking for a seal."

"Yeah, right. I love them." I laughed, a braying, awkward sound.

"I can take you out on the water there sometime, near Moss Head. They like to hang out in the little cove. I have a Kodiak. Maybe we can go tomorrow."

"Oh, wow. Thanks, I'd love to."

Josie flashed her brilliant smile. "Sure thing, New Girl. Good luck tonight."

I headed back to the kitchen where the chef told us the specials, which included two new appetizers and three new entrees, all replete with special sauces, herbs and allergen warnings. I scrambled to copy everything down from the board, praying that most of the customers simply ordered dock-burgers and left it at that.

We started to prep the wait stations, filling the water pitchers, stuffing sugar packets into their ceramic holders. As we prepped, my mouth went dry—I was dreading our first customers. Eden had announced that I'd have two tables all to myself tonight.

"You'll be fine." She held up her hand as if to swear by this. "It's only two tables—a two-top and four-top, right next to my station. I can help you anytime you need."

"I feel like I might throw up." I clutched my stomach.

"Just take it easy, and remember, don't look at the drinks when you're carrying them!"

I went back into the kitchen and stared at the specials board again.

"New Girl, why do you look green?" Elias asked.

"I have my own tables tonight."

"Is that right?" He smiled at me gently. "You're going to be fine."

"Um... I sort of doubt that?"

"Hey, I saw you with that tray today—I lost money because you had such a steady hand. And you've sworn on your life that you won't take food without a ticket.

You're in good shape! Even if your customers hate you, you'll be all right with the rest of us, I promise you that."

"Thanks. That makes it better." A little.

I went back out to the wait station. Eden was re-applying her lipstick, two of the other girls were organizing the supplies near the coffee maker, and the male servers were folding napkins and talking about where they'd gone wake-boarding that morning. No one seemed nervous. It was a typical day at the office for them. For me, it was the beginning of an ulcer.

There was already a pretty good crowd at the bar. The fishermen were having a few beers before they went home and went to bed at seven-thirty. There were some other customers, an older, preppy couple with matching fleeces and two young women nursing Cosmopolitans. *Please God, don't let any of my customers order a Cosmopolitan.*

Jenny sat the first table at five o'clock sharp. Thankfully, it went to Eden. I watched as she went to the couple, took their drink order, then swiftly and efficiently entered it into the computer. To me it seemed like a miracle, but she looked as though she was bored stiff. "I can't wait till it gets busy—I need to make money."

"Yeah." I needed to make money, too, but I was still petrified.

I felt eyes on me and turned to see James taking a seat on one of the barstools. He looked handsome in an olive hoodie and a pair of dark jeans. "Hey Taylor." He jutted his chin toward me and my stomach flip-flopped. "Hope you have a good night tonight."

"T-Thanks."

Eden watched this exchange with interest. "What's up with that? He doesn't talk to many people."

I shrugged. "He's just being nice because I made such a mess last night."

"Huh." Eden nudged me. "Hey, looks like you've got your first table!"

I watched as Jenny steered a well-dressed elderly couple to my two-top. I sent up a quick prayer. *Please don't let them order martinis.*

I uncapped my pen, took a deep breath, and headed over.

"Good evening, young lady," the man said. "I'd like a dry Manhattan, and my wife would like an Old Fashioned."

"Great! I'll be right back with those." I fake-smiled so hard my face hurt. I had no idea what these drinks were. I scrolled through the computer, finally finding them and entering them into the system. Then I went to the bar and waited.

The drink pick up was right next to James.

"So." He played with his coaster as his iced tea left a condensation ring on the counter. "Nervous?"

I glanced up over my head, then smiled at him. "What gave it away?"

"Ha. Actually, it was your posture. And the scowl."

I couldn't help it—I laughed. "My table ordered two drinks and I don't know what sort of glasses they come in." Josie mixed whiskey and vermouth with a dash of something from a small bottle labeled *Bitters.* I watched, relieved, as she poured it into a rocks glass and garnished it with an orange peel and some cherries.

But then she started mixing another drink and put a martini glass on the counter. My heart sank.

"Ah, I see what's going on here," James said. "The dreaded martini glass."

I blew out a deep breath as Josie poured the cocktail and then garnished it with a lemon twist. "Pray for me."

"I'm on it." James smiled.

I put the drinks on a small tray and Josie gave me a thumbs-up. "You got this, New Girl. Just do not look at the glasses."

I licked my lips. "O-Okay."

She and James smirked at each other as I raised the tray up over my shoulder and did not look at it. It was a short trip to the table. I walked slow, so slow. When I closed the gap, I gingerly put the tray on the table—a no-no, but I did it anyway—and didn't look as I picked up the martini glass and put it in front of the woman. It didn't splash. I put the rocks glass in front of the man. "Almost." He smiled as he switched the glasses, not spilling a drop.

"Sorry about that. Would you like to hear the specials?"

"No." The man smiled kindly, and I knew that he knew I was nervous. "We're each going to have a cup of chowder, and then the dock-burger medium-well. Sound good to you?"

"Yeah. It really does."

Things got better after that, meaning that Jenny didn't seat me another table until my two-top had their coffee and paid the bill. They tipped me twenty percent. James had dinner at the bar, chatting with Josie and otherwise keeping to himself. Eden's station was full, which suited her perfectly, so I helped her get waters and ramekins of butter and anything else she needed.

Then Jenny sat a four-top in my station. My stomach dropped as my dad, Amelia, Becky, and her friend Marybeth took their seats. I didn't know Marybeth well, but the disapproving once-over she gave me indicated she'd heard plenty about me from Becky. My dad wore a crewneck sweatshirt, and Amelia was in a fleece and flip flops, but both Marybeth and Becky were a little dressed up. They wore white jeans, expensive-looking sweaters, and lots of hippie, beaded bracelets. They had identically lush eyelash extensions; they looked like twins except that Becky was blonde and Marybeth had wavy chestnut hair. I swallowed hard as I headed to the table, clicking and un-clicking my pen.

"Hi pumpkin," my dad said, beaming. "Thought we'd come and see my favorite waitress for dinner." Becky gave Marybeth a look, as if to say, *see what I have to deal with?*

Amelia blinked up at me. "You know how to wait tables?"

"I'm learning."

"Ooh, can you serve me champagne?"

"Amelia." Dad looked as though he might smack her. "She'll have an orange soda, thank you. And I'll have an IPA. Becky? Marybeth?"

"I'd like a glass of the South African *Sauvignon blanc*," Becky said immediately. "Actually, make that a bottle. That bartender is a cheap pour. Marybeth, does that sound good to you?"

"Yes, but I'd like to start with a Cosmopolitan. Can you please ask Josie to use fresh lime juice? The bottled stuff has too many preservatives."

"Sure." I smiled at them then headed straight for the computer. It just figured Marybeth would have to order a drink like that. The idea of spilling it all over Becky's white jeans held some promise, but then again, I had to live with the woman for the next thirteen and a half months. Not that I was counting.

Again, I waited at the bar next to James. Josie scowled as she read the ticket. "Fresh lime juice? Let me guess, that Marybeth doesn't want the bottled stuff because it's not 'healthy.'" She started squeezing limes into a drink mixer, muttering to herself. "She'll shoot filler into her lips and glue some dead mink's fur right next to her eyeballs, but no bottled lime juice."

"That's your stepmother—the blonde?" James peered at the table, a small frown creeping over his features. "No wonder you don't like her."

Had I said I didn't like her? I couldn't remember. "She's not that bad."

He sucked in a deep breath. "I beg to differ."

"Based on what?"

He jerked his chin in Becky's direction. "You know."

Josie eyed us with interest. "Really, James? You're telling the new girl all your secrets?" She opened the bottle of wine for me, bless her heart, and put it on the tray.

He shrugged. "Not all of them."

Josie raised her eyebrows and went back to pouring drinks.

James smiled and his dimple peeped out. "You're not wrong about your stepmother, you should know that. Not that it's going to make you feel any better."

"No, it's not." I put the Cosmopolitan on the tray and it splashed a little. "But I appreciate it all the same." Feeling strangely buoyed by James's diagnosis of Becky, I headed for the table, not looking at the drinks even once.

9

YOU'RE WELCOME

RANDOM THOUGHTS SWIRLED the next morning as I brushed my teeth. Perhaps they weren't that random, after all; they kept circling back to James.

Josie knew about his aura reading, that was clear. But did she believe it was true? And what did he mean, he hadn't told me all of his secrets? What else could there be?

I puzzled the possibilities as I crept down the stairs. My dad had already left for work and I didn't want to risk running into Becky and Amelia. But Kyle's voice drifted from the kitchen, and I stopped when I got close enough to hear what he was saying.

"She's working, she's doing her own laundry, she's making her bed and keeping the house clean—I'm not sure what you're complaining about." My dad sounded angry.

"She was with that boy yesterday—he dropped her off here. And I saw him at the bar last night talking to her. She hasn't even been here a week. I don't want Amelia exposed to this kind of stuff."

"What stuff?"

"Boys. Sex. Drinking."

"Getting a ride home isn't sex, and working at a bar isn't drinking. You're reaching. Taylor's a good kid. She hasn't even been here for three days. Give her a freaking break—and me, too. I only came home for my phone charger, not your drama."

"I knew this was going to happen." Becky sounded close to tears. "She is going to rip this family apart."

"Jesus. You're unbelievable, you know that?"

"See?" Becky started crying. "This is exactly what I mean."

Kyle sighed. "I have to get back to work. We can talk about this later. Please calm down—if Amelia sees you crying, she's going to get upset."

I heard his footsteps leave the kitchen. The front door closed, and a second later Amelia came downstairs. "Mom? Is everything all right?"

"It's fine." Becky sniffled. "Your dad's just kind of being a jerk."

"Probably because of Taylor," Amelia said knowingly. "He always gets mad at you when she's around."

"Right?" Becky sounded slightly cheered. "I told him that, but he bit my head off."

"Can't she go live with her aunt, or something?" Amelia whined. "I hate having someone else in the house with us. I feel so judged."

"Exactly. And your dad gets in on it, too. It's like he's on her team."

"Yeah." Amelia sounded annoyed. "Why did her stupid mother have to die? It's, like, so unfair. Everybody thinks it's weird that I have some random girl living with me."

"I know," Becky said. "It would be better if she wasn't so…so…"

"White trash?" Amelia giggled.

"Amelia!" But Becky sounded pleased, not scandalized. "Now eat your breakfast. If you have oatmeal, remember, that's it for carbs today."

Amelia groaned, and I crept back upstairs. Before I reached my room I heard Becky say, "Do you want to go off-island and go shopping today? I need to get away from the riffraff."

"Can we get lunch?" Amelia asked.

"We can get whatever you want," Becky said dotingly, "as long as it's not carbs."

I WAITED until they were gone to leave my room. I hated the way I felt—achy inside, stung. Sticks and stones were one thing, but why Amelia and Becky's words still hurt me after all this time, I'd never know. I wasn't going to make it. Forget the school year; I'd never even last through the summer.

In spite of the dull ache inside me, I managed to enjoy my breakfast: coffee, orange juice, and an enormous wild-Maine blueberry muffin that my dad had brought home for me the day before. I slathered it with butter and thought of Becky. She didn't touch butter. I put even more on the second half of my muffin and gloated that although I might be white-trash, I was at least smart enough to eat butter. Could you die from not eating enough fat? I really hoped so. But it seemed more likely that it just turned you into a bitch.

I walked outside, antsy, unsure of what to do with myself. I had hours until my shift. I wanted to go for a walk, but with an island this small, I'd see everyone I knew within two minutes. I could run again, but that hadn't seemed to work out well. I went and sat on one of the lounge chairs by the abandoned pool. Its pristine water sparkled in the morning sunlight and I wished it was hot enough to jump in. I could splash chlorine on the lawn and maybe discolor Becky's lush green grass...

My rather pathetic shortlist of revenge tactics was interrupted by a car coming down the driveway. A cherry-red jeep, jacked up with oversized tires, pulled up in front of the house. Josie hopped out of the driver's side, her bright-white smile a sharp contrast to my dark thoughts. "You want to go out to the Head? The tide's coming in, it's the perfect time to look for seals."

"I'd love to. Let me just grab my fleece." I was grateful for the distraction. Part of me wanted to stay home and sulk, but what would that solve? I threw on my jacket, then went and climbed up into the jeep. It had a brand-new car smell and pristine black leather seats. "This is really nice. I'm surprised you have it on the island." The unspoken rule on Dawnhaven was that everyone drove beaters. Old trucks, rusted minivans, and the occasional retired station wagon were the local staples. You could only drive five miles per hour and all the roads were either dirt or gravel; even Becky drove an old GMC pickup.

"I love my jeep." Josie put it in reverse and backed out. "I can't live without it. Plus, we can take it out on the beach over near the Tower. Don't tell anyone that, okay? The town board would freak if they knew I had my car near the shore. It's not like this is Nantucket, or something."

"What do you mean?"

"Aren't you from Massachusetts?" she asked.

"Yeah."

Josie put the jeep in drive and headed down the main road. "But you've never been to Nantucket?"

When I shook my head, she said, "Everybody lets a little air out of their tires and drives their cars out onto the beach. It's like tailgating—it's fun."

"I'm sure." My summers mostly consisted of hanging out in our poorly air-conditioned apartment. When I got really desperate, I'd head to the Worcester public pool, crowded with small children and their wayward Band-Aids. Although it was also located in Massachusetts, Nantucket had always been out of my reach. I'd seen pictures, of course: the lighthouses, the clambakes on the beach, the really rich people inexplicably always wearing pastel plaid. It sounded mythical and glamorous, a modern-day Norumbega. "I'll have to check it out someday."

"James has a house over on Martha's Vineyard, that's nice too. I actually like it better than Nantucket. It's more chill, you know?"

I nodded, even though I knew nothing of the sort. "So you've been to his house on the Vineyard?"

"Yeah, we went last summer."

"Have you been friends for a long time?"

Josie nodded. "A couple of years now."

"Where'd you meet him?"

She eyed me. "Are we playing twenty questions about James?"

"I just...want to know about him. I don't remember ever hearing about him before." I tried to sound neutral, not obsessed.

"He doesn't get out much." Josie navigated the jeep past the store and the school, turning left to head toward west beach. "But we're having fun this summer. We're making him leave the house every once in a while."

I wanted to ask more questions about him but decided against it. "So, where do you live when you're not here?"

"We're still in New York. Dylan's finishing up school at Columbia."

"Oh. That's nice." I felt way out of my league in this conversation. Nantucket, Martha's Vineyard, Columbia... My world consisted of the sub shop, Walmart, and my dilapidated high school.

"Not really." Josie shrugged. "New York's so dirty compared to here. I don't know if I'm going to be able to handle it when we go back."

We reached the private drive that led to the Tower. Small, rustic cottages dotted the end of the public road. They were so tiny, I wondered how the people who rented them slept inside.

"You ready?" Josie eased the jeep onto the gravel.

"Yeah. Thanks so much for picking me up. I'm excited to go out on your boat. I really hope the seals are out." So close to James's house, I started babbling again. I clamped my mouth shut so I'd stop.

She raised an eyebrow but didn't say anything as we drove slowly around the sharp corners. The rose bushes scratched the jeep as we passed and Josie cursed. After a few twists and turns, the rock ledge on the right-hand side of the drive leveled down. You could see the ocean, the tide rushing in over the dark rocky beach. We passed a Private Property sign carved onto a tree and then the Tower was suddenly before us, enormous, white and sprawling, its lookout jutting into the sky. A few years back I'd done a school project about the mansions in Newport, Rhode Island. The Tower reminded me of them: stone-faced, elegant, impenetrable. I couldn't imagine living in a huge house like that.

"Wow." I gaped at it.

"You've never been out here before?"

"Only to the beach. I've never been this close to the house." The Tower was the sole property on this part of the island; no one was around for at least a mile. The yard stretched out around us, but really, "yard" wasn't the right word—they were grounds. The thick green grass ran up to the rock ledge that bordered the beach. We parked next to James's truck and another car, a rusted old Chevrolet Chevette. Both the old cars seemed out of place parked in front of the stately home. As we climbed out of the jeep, the sound of waves crashing against the seawall boomed.

"I told you the tide was coming in." Josie smiled. "My Kodiak's down on the beach. I just put air in it, so we have to drag it down to the water. You ready?"

"Sure." I glanced at the house. Someone was inside, watching us through the floor-to-ceiling windows, but I couldn't make them out. I followed Josie over part of the rock wall that separated the lawn from the rocky beach. The house and its deck rose up above us. It jutted above the seawall, which was what separated the Tower from the ocean. The wall was made up of huge rectangular rocks, gray and pink, and bordered the house on three sides. From our view down on the beach, the house looked mammoth, a majestic castle rising above the seawall. Planters bursting with flowers and lounge chairs dotted the long deck, which faced the craggy coastline. It was the perfect spot to watch the tide come and go.

James strolled out onto the deck and waved. My heart lurched. I smiled and waved back, then caught Josie staring. "It's a nice view, huh?" she asked.

"Yeah." My heart thudded in my chest. "It's really nice."

10

ONCE UPON A SEAL

JOSIE and I dragged the red-rubber Kodiak to the edge of the water, careful to keep the small motor lifted away from the rocky beach. Josie was wearing waterproof boots, but I only had on my flip flops. I would've been freezing but carrying the boat had me sweating as we passed huge rocks, seaweed and some abandoned buoys that had washed up on shore. Josie buckled her life vest and handed me one. As I clipped it across my chest, I wondered if James was still watching us. I was too embarrassed to look—the thought that he was so close had my heart lurching or thudding, I wasn't sure which.

As the tide rushed in the seawall began to disappear below the water. Once it was fully high tide, I guessed that half of it would be submerged, as would most of the beach we'd walked out on.

Moss Head was straight ahead. It was a small scrap of an island, a working lighthouse its sole inhabitant. To the right, the ocean stretched out; waves crashed against the small stones that made up west beach. Fir trees rose beyond the shore, the forest dark and silent even in the morning sun. To the left of the house there was another beach, all rocks. A large dock jutted into the ocean. Beyond it, the ocean extended to the horizon, as far as the eye could see.

The icy water numbed me to my ankles. "Hop in," Josie said as she started to push the raft out.

I climbed on board and then she jumped in too, grabbing a seat on the small bench opposite me. I faced the house now, there was no escaping it. Smiling, James waved with both arms from the front of the deck. He wore a tight-fitting gray hoodie that showed off his big shoulders. If Josie hadn't been watching me, I would've fanned myself.

Once we drifted a little deeper, the sound of the waves lessened and Josie dropped the motor in. The water swept around us as we headed toward the center of the channel, halfway between the Tower and the Head. "Did you know you could walk all the way across at low tide?" she asked.

I nodded. "My dad's talked about doing it, but we've just never timed it right. Do you guys go over?"

"Yeah, we've done it a few times. You can grab mussels from the rocks out in the middle of the channel. It's pretty cool to eat something you plucked right from the ocean."

"I bet." I smiled as she maneuvered the rudder and brought us to idle in the calmer water. "You seem like you really like it here."

"What's not to like?" She motioned to the big house, the beach and the clear blue sky beyond. "Maine is heaven—I'm starting to think New York is hell. What about you, New Girl? You like living here?"

"I like the island." I shrugged, the memory of Becky and Amelia's conversation rearing up. "I'm not sure it's going to work out, though."

"James won't be happy to hear that."

I looked at Josie, surprised. "What do you mean?"

She cocked her head at me. "You don't need to play dumb. In fact, you really need to be smart about this."

"About what?"

"C'mon. You know he likes you. I almost fell over behind the bar last night when he mentioned his auras. I can't believe he told you that."

I opened my mouth and closed it. I wasn't sure what to say, what she believed.

"I'm sure you think he's crazy—because saying you

can see colored smoke and read people's moods *is* crazy. But James doesn't lie, okay?"

"I didn't think he was lying." I shrugged. "I just didn't think it could be true."

"Put that to the side for a minute." She leaned closer. "My point is, James doesn't open up to people. So the fact that he's telling you things after just meeting you has you on my radar, New Girl."

"Um." I looked out at the dark water swirling around us. There wasn't exactly an elegant way to exit the conversation. "On your radar in a bad way?"

Josie kept staring. "That depends on whether we can trust you to keep your mouth shut."

I blew out a deep breath. "I'm not going to say anything to anybody. It isn't their business."

"I need you to mean that." Josie's friendly smile was nowhere in sight.

"I mean it." My voice came out small. I suddenly wanted to get back to the shore. I glanced at the house and was surprised to see that not only had Dylan and Patrick joined James out on the deck, they were doing some sort of group exercise. "Are they…wait, are they doing *yoga*?"

Josie stopped glaring at me long enough to glance at the deck. "Yeah, those are sun salutations. Dylan's a certified instructor."

"Do they do it a lot?" I was genuinely curious, and also eager to change the direction of the conversation.

"Every morning. James is hardcore about it, says it's good to get into a flow state."

"Huh." I was briefly mesmerized by the sight of him. He'd removed his hoodie to reveal the tank top beneath. His pale muscles rippled as he lifted his arms above his head.

"Back to what we were talking about," Josie said, "hey wait! Look!" She pointed past my shoulder and I turned to find a seal bobbing near us. It's perfect, smooth head gave it almost a human profile, and I could see its whiskers and its large, dark eyes.

"Oh my goodness. It's so cute." Another seal popped up next to it and they hung out side by side, bobbing in the cold water. We watched them for a while. I couldn't tell if they noticed us or not; if they did, they didn't seem at all bothered by us gawking from our raft. They floated in the mellow waves, their big bellies buoying them like life vests. I wondered what they were thinking.

"This place is totally magic," Josie said. "I can't believe we get to see things like this."

"It sure beats Worcester," I agreed. All we had were squirrels with mangy-looking tails and the occasional rat.

We watched them for another minute until first one seal ducked underwater, then the other. I looked out into the clear, dark ocean, but they were gone. "Thank you. That was so cool."

"Anytime." She was quiet as we sat, waiting to see if the seals popped back up. After a couple of minutes, Josie started the motor. "I think they're gone."

"Yeah, they probably saw some fish."

As she maneuvered the Kodiak back toward shore, Josie frowned. "Listen. I need your word that you won't say anything about James."

I held up my right hand. "We don't have to talk about it anymore, okay? I won't say a word to anyone, I promise."

She nodded, concentrating on navigating back the beach. An uneasy silence settled between us as we dragged the Kodiak onto the shrinking coast, the tide crashing up higher and higher. "Let's just get this up by the ledge, then I'll drive you home," Josie said.

"Okay."

"Hey Taylor." James was suddenly above us on the deck, a smile on his face as he leaned his big shoulders over the railing. "Can you come up here for a minute?"

Josie shot me a sour look and I hesitated, but James waved me up. "C'mon. I want you to see the view—If Jo's got stuff to do, I can drive you home after."

We got the boat all the way up, then I climbed over the wall and upstairs to the deck. James still wore his tank top; up close I could see that it was only slightly more alabaster than his smooth skin. The tattoo I'd glimpsed yesterday was now on full display. It was a large, dark outline of a circle. Inside it was another circle separated into four equal quadrants. "That's some tattoo."

"Yeah, thanks—although I'm not sure that was a compliment."

"No, it's beautiful. I've never seen a symbol like that. What's it mean?"

"Let me show you my deck and maybe I'll tell you." He grinned at me and started toward the front of the house. "C'mon, we just saw those seals come up again."

I followed him down the deck, which was the length of the house. I glimpsed inside and saw a soaring ceiling, gleaming wide-plank hardwood floors, dark, fancy-looking furniture, and a huge stone fireplace. The ocean stretched out around us on three sides. The water rushed up, covering the rocky beach that Josie and I had walked out on not too long ago. Now it looked as though we could jump off the deck and swim, even though I knew it was still shallow.

James stopped halfway down the deck. "What's Josie upset about?"

I was about to ask how he knew, but I stopped myself. "She wanted to make sure I didn't tell anyone about...what you told me."

"Ah. She's my ride or die." When he laughed and I didn't, he continued, "Did she threaten you?"

I shrugged. "Not exactly."

"She won't actually hurt you if you tell anyone. She'll just hate you and make your life miserable."

"Great."

"I'm kidding." He nodded toward Josie as she climbed the stairs. "She's calming down. She just wants to protect me."

"From what?"

But he didn't answer. Instead, we reached the front portion of the deck and I was confronted by Dylan and Patrick doing downward-facing dogs on their respective yoga mats. Patrick wore mesh basketball shorts and a yellow T-shirt; a circle of sweat plastered the thin material to his back. Dylan wore black athletic tights with mesh cutouts and a black sports bra. Her hair was pulled back in a high ponytail, and the muscles in her shoulders rippled in the sunlight. She looked up at me and smiled. "Hey Taylor."

She was so pretty, it almost hurt to look at her. "Hey."

I glanced at James, who paid the dazzling Dylan no attention. He waved me over to the railing. "There they are." The two seals had re-emerged on the eastern side of the house and were bobbing in the waves. "Look, one of them has an urchin."

The bigger seal held a prickly black ball. He turned it inside out, nibbling from the tender flesh inside.

"You're so lucky." I glanced at James. "I can't believe you get to see stuff like this every day."

He leaned back against the railing and smiled at me. "Now that we're friends, you can too."

"Thanks." I couldn't help but smile back.

"Want me to give you a ride home?"

"Sure." Was it only yesterday that I'd vowed to keep to myself? I wasn't sure where my resolve had gone, but it was nowhere to be found.

"I can take her." Josie frowned as she joined us.

"I got it, Jose. And you don't need to frown. If Taylor said she won't talk, she won't."

"Talk about what?" Patrick asked.

"Nothing," Josie and James said simultaneously.

Patrick grimaced as Dylan led him into a low, painful-looking plank pose. "You two need to chill," he grunted. "You know we'll find out anyway."

"True." Josie plopped down on the deck and sat cross-legged. She looked as though she had no intention of doing a plank.

"Come on." James put his hand on my lower back and cocked his head back toward the water. "You can come and see these guys whenever you want. Dylan and Patrick, too."

"Ha ha," I heard Patrick say as James led me through the gate and down onto the yard. "I'm just as cute as the seals!"

"Bye, New Girl," Josie called.

"Bye Josie. Thanks again." I wondered what her mood would be later when I saw her at work.

"Don't worry about her," James said. He dropped his hand, and I wished he'd put it back. "She's just testing you."

I glanced back over my shoulder, but I couldn't see the others anymore. "Does she do that to all your new friends?"

"I'm not sure." His dimple peeped out. "I don't make many."

"I feel so special," I joked.

"You should." When he smiled at me, it was like the sun coming out. "Want to see something?"

Before I could stop myself, I smiled back. "Yes."

I followed him across the yard, my eyes tracking the outlines of his pale muscles. There was so much beauty around me—the forest ahead, the lush green grass, the ocean, the stunning house—but I could only look at James. The rest of the world just fell away.

I'd never been in trouble before, but I wondered if maybe this was what it felt like.

11

EDGAR

"YOU GUYS ARE FUNNY," I said. "I don't know too many people who do yoga together every morning. Do they all live with you?"

He shrugged. "Dylan and Josie are staying with me this summer. Patrick has a house on the island, too, but he just ends us crashing with us. It's been fun."

"Have you known them long?"

"Josie, yes. I met Dylan when they started dating a couple of years ago. I just met Patrick last year, but I feel like I've known him for forever." James kept walking, heading toward the tree line. "What about you? Do you have a lot of friends back home?"

"N-No." I'd mostly kept to myself.

"Maybe you'll make new friends up here. Like me." James nodded. "Ah, here we are."

We stopped and he knelt down. There were four rectangular pieces of clear plastic, each about one foot long, jutting out of the ground. They were arranged in a square. Each one of them was filled with brightly colored plastic beads of various sizes, along with a smattering of pastel-colored glass marbles.

"What's this?" I asked.

"This is Edgar's loot." James squinted up into the fir trees lining the edge of the grounds. "I'm going to rearrange some of it and see if he comes out. He gets a little territorial."

I nervously glanced toward the forest. "Who's Edgar?"

James didn't look up as he took two beads from the first container, one from the second, and three marbles from the third. He left the fourth collection intact. He carefully lined the objects in a neat row on the grass. Then he stood up and grabbed my hand, dragging me back a couple of paces.

"Edgar is a crow." James squeezed my hand reassuringly, then dropped it.

"Huh?" But after a moment, a big black bird swooped out of the forest and landed near the containers. Its feathers were dark, inky, so black they were almost blue. It cocked its head and blinked at us in rapid succession. Then it hopped in a circle around the "loot," carefully eyeing the line of beads and marbles laid out on the grass.

It looked up and blinked at us again, as if trying to decide whether we were a threat.

"It's okay, buddy." James's voice was calm and soothing. "Do your thing. I just wanted to show Taylor."

The crow blinked again and then it picked up one bead and hopped over to the first container, inspecting it. He put the bead down and looked at it again, then looked back at the container. He hopped back and took the second bead from the row, working his way down the line.

Then he deposited the two beads back into the first container.

He repeated the process with the second container, depositing the one missing bead back inside. Edgar returned the three marbles to the third container. He eyed the fourth container, blinking at it, taking its measure. Seemingly satisfied, he flew back to the edge of the forest and settled on the grass, watching us.

"He's waiting to see if I do it again." James chuckled.

"Is that… Is he… Is Edgar your pet?"

"Nah, you can't keep a crow for a pet. But he lives in these woods."

"How did you know he could do that?" I motioned toward the loot.

"Somebody left a bracelet out on the beach and the beads came off it. Edgar collected them, he had them in this stash. I watched him for a few days—he kept checking the beads, taking them out and putting them back in. I knew crows could count, so I moved some of them to another place just to see what he would do. He moved the beads back to the first spot, and we've been playing this little game ever since." James watched as Edgar swooped up into a tree. "He likes to keep everything organized."

"Crows can actually count?" I stared at the big bird.

"They have a propensity to gauge volume." James shrugged. "Anyway, that's Edgar."

"Wow. That's pretty amazing." I felt like the crow watched us as we headed to James's truck. "There's a lot of wildlife going on down here. I feel like I've been on safari."

"I'm telling you, it's exciting." He started the truck and then took an envelope out of the cup holder. "This is for you. I was going to drop it off later."

I glanced at it. *Taylor Hale*, it read in fancy script. "What is it?"

"It's an invitation—open it."

My hands were a little shaky as I slid the envelope open.

SUMMER SOLSTICE CELEBRATION
SATURDAY, JUNE 20TH

The Champlain Residence, West Beach
Dawnhaven, ME
6pm
RSVP - Regrets Only

"You're having a party?"

"Why do you sound so surprised?"

"I just thought you sort of kept to yourself, is all."

James shrugged a big shoulder. "I'm not inviting a ton of people. But it's the solstice, the longest day of the year and the true beginning of summer. The Tower's the best place on the island to watch the sun set. I think we should celebrate, don't you?"

I nodded. He could've told me that he wanted to march through the woods, wear party hats and blow on kazoos to celebrate Edgar the crow's birthday and I would've said yes. "I'll see if I can take the night off."

James smiled at me. "I hope you can come."

Trouble, I thought again. I stared at his dimple. *So, so much trouble.*

I SOMEHOW MANAGED to survive my next shift. Josie was cool toward me, but I was so busy I didn't have time to worry about it. I had a lot to keep track of—three of my tables ordered lobster dinners and I needed to locate the bibs, lobster crackers, and wet wipes. Eden had a full station, so I was on my own.

It was a night of firsts. Four of my customers ordered martinis, and I didn't dare look at my tray while I delivered them. I served escargot with snail tongs. I made a frothy cappuccino. I drizzled chocolate sauce on several desserts. I bussed my tables. I did not take food without a ticket. Elias complimented me on picking up my orders on time, and all of my tables tipped me twenty percent.

I was elated, and more than a little exhausted, by the time my shift ended.

"G'night, Josie," I said as I put her share of my tips on the counter.

"Good night, New Girl." She winked at me, a peace offering.

There was a bounce in my step as I walked home. A blanket of stars stretched overhead. I tried not to think about James, but it was impossible. Memories from the morning washed over me—the seals bobbing in the water, James in that tank top, the dark contours of his tattoo against his ivory skin. Edgar the crow. I'd been thinking of the creature off and on all day, how it hopped and carefully inspected each of the tubes, taking stock of the brightly colored treasures. The way it blinked at us and watched us from the tree.

I was about to turn into Becky's drive when a slow-moving truck headed my way, headlights bobbing as it drove over the ruts in the dirt road. James pulled up next to me and rolled the window down. "Hey."

"Hey." I was sweaty and smelled like lobster meat, so I didn't lean in too close.

"I meant to get down here earlier to offer you a ride home," he said. His expression was a little sheepish. "I just wanted to make sure you got home safe."

A hot blush crept up my neck, and I was grateful for the dark. "That's nice. But I'm fine—I definitely feel safe on the island."

"It's safe here. I just wanted to make sure." He nodded, then smiled at me. "Goodnight, Taylor."

"Goodnight." I wondered if he could read my aura in the dark, and then I blushed some more. "Thanks again."

His truck idled in the road until I made it into the house, then the headlights disappeared.

STICKS AND STONES

BY SOME MINOR MIRACLE, Jenny closed the restaurant for a private function Saturday night. I suddenly found myself with the night off, able to attend James's solstice party.

"I don't know who rented the restaurant," Eden gossiped to me that afternoon. With some rare free time, we'd gone down to the public beach and spread out a blanket. Eden had packed peanut butter and jelly sandwiches, chips and seltzers for us. We wore our bathing suits, both hoping to get some sun even though it was breezy and cool.

Eden adjusted the strap of her black-and-white polka dot bikini top. "Whoever it was, apparently they paid in full up front and have their own servers. Normally when people rent the restaurant out for a private function, they ask us to work. But nope, not tonight."

"So what're you doing?" I wanted to ask her to come with me to the party, but I didn't know if I could. Those invites were fancy.

"It's the funniest thing. I got invited to a party at the Tower." Eden pulled an envelope out of her bag. "This was in my mailbox this morning. Wait"—Eden frowned at me—"did you get one? 'Cause I'm going to feel really bad otherwise."

"I did." I breathed a sigh of relief. "I'm so glad you're going."

"Phew, me too! I've never been down there before. And these are *f-a-n-c-y*." She fanned herself with the invite. "Do you want to get dressed and go together?"

"Yes." I was glad Eden couldn't read my aura. I'd be embarrassed to admit how much that meant to me.

We spent the rest of the afternoon at the beach. We skimmed rocks, had a contest to see who could keep their feet in the freezing water the longest, and Eden told me more about Jenny, the owner of the restaurant, and some of the other workers.

Jenny had made a fortune in commercial real estate in New York but had left the city for MDI's slower pace. She'd dated one of the island residents, Melinda the poetry professor, but they'd broken up the summer before. Eden gossiped that Tara, Dwight and some of the other servers partied too much, and that Elias and most of the other kitchen staff rented one big house together. Apparently, their house was party central.

Eden dropped me off on her way home and we made plans to meet up after dinner. I sat out on the front step, carefully wiping the sand from my feet before I went inside. My dad wasn't back from work yet and Becky's truck was in the drive; I had a sour feeling in my stomach as I opened the door.

Amelia was sprawled across the couch in the living room, her face stuck in her phone. "Hey," I said.

She didn't look up. "Hey."

I wanted to sneak upstairs, but Becky waited in the kitchen.

"I heard the restaurant was closed tonight." She regarded me coolly, her hands on her hips. "What're you going to do? Kyle and I were planning to take Amelia off-island to go to dinner with Marybeth and Donnie. I already made reservations."

I knew what she was asking—*do we have to include you?*—so I was relieved to have an answer ready. "Um, Eden Lambert and I were invited down to the Tower. For a solstice party. I heard it's going to be small," I added hastily.

Becky arched an eyebrow. "A *party?*"

Amelia shrieked from the other room, "You got invited to James Champlain's party? I want to go!"

"Absolutely not," Becky called to her. She frowned at me. "This is exactly the sort of thing I was hoping to avoid this summer, Taylor."

"I-I know. I didn't expect to be invited."

"Well, you must've done something." She made it sound like it was a very bad thing, whatever it was.

It was not in my nature to be cunning, but a strategy dawned on me. "I don't have to go—I could go to dinner with you guys instead. I don't want to be any trouble."

"No it's fine." She didn't want me going to parties, but she *really* didn't want me encroaching on their night out. "Just be in by curfew."

I nodded. "I will, I promise." Relieved to get away from her, I retreated upstairs.

Amelia stormed into the kitchen once I'd gone. She was so loud, I heard her from the top of the stairs. "How did she get invited to that party? Those guys don't talk to anyone, and now Taylor-Trash is getting the red carpet rolled out for her?"

Becky snorted. "Oh honey—don't be jealous. There's no red carpet. A boy like James Champlain only wants one thing from a girl like Taylor."

"Ew," Amelia said. "He's going to catch her cooties."

"Probably. But at least he's rich enough to get them fumigated," her mother replied.

I'D SMILED at my dad when he got home from the co-op. Like a robot, programmed to be a good girl, I'd said all the right things. Yes, I had a good day. Yes, I'd be careful at the party. You guys have fun at dinner.

But a hole—dark, pitted and hot—gnawed at my chest.

Taylor-Trash. Cooties. Fumigated. I didn't want to let what they'd said get to me, but I still felt a physical ache. I wondered if Becky or Amelia would ever know how much it hurt to have someone say things like that about you. How it made you doubt yourself. Because if they felt that way, maybe it was true.

It didn't matter. I shoved the incident from my thoughts, determined to have fun with Eden. I walked slowly to her house, trying to talk myself into a better state of mind. The Lamberts' home was a white farmhouse with spruce-green shutters, traditional, neat and plain. Dozens of lobster traps were stacked in the yard. Both of Eden's parents were commercial fishermen; they fished the local harbors year-round and were known as two of the hardest working people on the island.

"Hey." Eden opened the screen door before I even knocked. She eyed my outfit—flip flops, cutoff jean shorts and a flannel shirt. "Is that what you're wearing?"

"Um…"

"C'mon." She waved me inside. "I have a dress that'll fit you perfect." She turned inside the house and hollered, "Mom, Taylor's here! We're just gonna go and get ready!"

"Have her come in here and say hello," her mom hollered back. "I made crab cakes!"

Eden rolled her eyes and motioned for me to follow her through the cluttered, colorful living room, down a narrow hallway to the kitchen at the back of the house. "Hey there, Taylor," Mrs. Lambert said. She pushed an errant red curl off her forehead and surprised me by pulling me in for a hug. She smelled like laundry detergent. "It's so nice to see you."

"Hi, Mrs. Lambert."

"Ugh Mom, you don't have to man-handle her." Eden waved her mother off me. "Do we have to eat right now? We need to get ready."

"Sit down and have a crab cake. I know once you get to that party, all you're going to be doing is gawking." Mrs. Lambert shooed us toward the table, which had fabric placemats on it and a stack of newspapers piled on one end. She put on an oven mitt, whipped open the oven and grabbed the crab cakes, talking while she served us and poured us each an iced tea. "They haven't had a party down at the Tower in *years*. Do you girls need a chaperone? 'Cause I'd love to see it!"

"Ugh Mom, *no*. It's Josie and James and all their rich, super-model friends! I can't bring my mom." Eden giggled.

Mrs. Lambert sat down with us. "Can you at least take some pictures? Please? I haven't been down there since Nelson had that rager in the eighties. Now *that* was a party." She sighed. "You fools are probably just going to stand there, look pretty and take pictures for your Facebooks."

Eden snorted. "Only dinosaurs are on Facebook, Mom."

"Right, right. You'll post to your snap-talker, or whatever that thing is." She waved her hand. "Enough about all that. How are you, Taylor? How do you like living on the island this summer?"

"It's good." I had a bite of crab. "This is delicious, Mrs. Lambert, thank you."

"You come over here and eat anytime. I know Becky doesn't cook much." Mrs. Lambert frowned, looking like she might have more to say on the topic of Becky, but she held back. "Eden tells me you've gotten friendly with the Champlain boy?"

I glanced at Eden, who was giving her mother a death stare. "Did she? Um, yeah. He seems nice, but I don't know him very well."

Mrs. Lambert nodded. "Well people talk, you know. You can't go for a swim around here without everybody knowing about it. I've heard some things about him, but I think he's a nice young man. Seems to be, anyway. Nelson never brought him up here when he was younger. He's a damn fool, if you ask me."

Eden blinked at her. "Nelson Champlain's a fool, mom? I'd like to be a fool like him and go jump in my ocean of money."

Mrs. Lambert's nostrils flared. "Who abandons a house like that? It's been sitting there for too long—it's a shame. The only person who's been in there for years is the caretaker."

Eden sighed. "They have, like, *ten* other houses. At least. I don't know—if I was a gazillionaire, I'd probably mix it up, too."

"I'm just glad that they're finally using it. It's about time there's some life down there."

Eden made a face at her mother. "I'm sure they're thrilled that you approve."

"Ha ha. Don't be fresh, young lady. Excuse us, Taylor.

My daughter comes home from college and thinks she's smarter than me."

Eden rolled her eyes and I laughed. "No worries, Mrs. Lambert. Thanks again for the crab cake."

"All right girls. Finish up and go get dressed. Then I'm taking a picture for the Facebook!"

13

A CHANCE

"Your Mom's nice," I told Eden.

"Try this on." She handed me a cute multicolored striped dress. "And thanks. My mom's great, but she's a lot. She's got something to say about everyone."

"But she didn't say anything bad."

"Wait till she has a glass of wine." Eden's eyes widened. "She has opinions. Lots of them."

"Ha. Well, at least she means well." I held up the dress against me. "You don't think this is too much?"

"Um *no*, I do not. It's a cotton dress, Taylor. That and a little mascara will go a long way."

"I don't usually wear dresses." But there was no use arguing. Eden insisted I put it on, then she brushed out my long hair and put mascara and a little bit of lipstick on me. When she'd finished, she stood back and rubbed her hands together. "Voila! James is going to freak!"

"Eden, it's not like that." But I smiled when I caught my reflection in the mirror. I was pretty much crap with makeup, but Eden had made me look pretty, not too made up. I looked just like myself but with a few improvements. "Thank you."

"You're welcome." Eden smiled. "And you can swear up and down that 'it's not like that,' but I heard from a reliable source that James checked on you last night when you got done with your shift."

"Who told you that?" Mrs. Lambert was right—you literally couldn't go for a swim around here without everyone knowing about it.

Eden laughed. "I saw him, silly. I left right after you."

My cheeks blazed. "Just because he was checking on me doesn't mean anything."

"Yeah, yeah, yeah. But he didn't check on me, and as far as I know, he didn't check on anybody else." She dug through her crowded closet. "I'm just saying, he likes you."

"We'll see." I tried to sound nonchalant.

She held up a white eyelet dress and a jean jacket. "D'you think I can wear this?"

"I think you'll look really pretty in that." I smiled at my friend.

Mrs. Lambert wouldn't let us leave without a few pictures. She dragged us out onto the front lawn; Eden put her hand on her hip and lowered her chin, and I mimicked her. We both smiled, and I felt a flash of happiness.

"You girls look pretty." Mrs. Lambert beamed at us. "Have a good time tonight."

"Thanks again, Mrs. Lambert." Eden might be embarrassed by her, but I enjoyed her mother's warm attention.

We took Eden's truck. Her curls bounced as we drove over the chunky gravel on the way to the Tower. "Are you nervous?" She checked her lipstick in the rearview mirror. "'Cause I am."

"Sort of." The rose bushes scraped the sides of the truck and my stomach flipped. "Do you know who else is going to be here?"

"Uh-uh." She shook her head. "I figured you'd be invited, but I wasn't sure about who else. I didn't want to hurt anyone's feelings by asking."

"It'll be fine. Josie will be here, and Dylan, Patrick…" I swallowed hard as we drove further, and the Tower's grounds opened up. There were tons of cars in the lot. Several boats were tied up to the dock, including Josie's red Kodiak. "Um, and lots of other people."

Eden parked the truck and gaped at the rows of cars

and the crowd of people on the deck. "Where did they all come from? This has got to be everybody on the island. C'mon, I don't want to miss anything." She grabbed my hand and we bravely marched up to the deck. Reggae music wafted from the house. We had to wedge ourselves onto the platform, which was filled with people laughing, talking, and enjoying the view of the ocean. I recognized Elias and several of the other kitchen workers at the opposite end of the deck. He waved at us. "Hey Eden, New Girl—over here!"

We worked our way through the throng until we reached them. Elias carefully held his red plastic cup steady as he hugged each of us. Then he motioned out at the crowd , the ocean, and the house. "Have you *ever* seen a party like this? I feel like Martha Stewart threw this thing together!"

Martha Stewart lived nearby, in Seal Harbor. "Is she here?" Eden excitedly scanned the crowd.

"No, I don't think so. But just look at this place." Elias leaned back against the deck. "It's magic."

From the safety at the edge of the crowd, I got a good look at the festivities. Fairy lights were strung the length of the deck, and "chandeliers" made from fresh flowers hung at equal intervals. There was a giant banquet table set up against the house. There were pitchers of punch with sliced oranges, peaches and apples inside; tall, clear-blue glasses of water garnished with herbs, and wine buckets made from ice with colorful flowers frozen inside. Rows and rows of appetizers and desserts were set out, along with an enormous cake covered with multi-colored berries and flowers. The spread was chic, elegant and earthy. It had likely cost a small fortune.

"Do you want a drink?" Eden asked.

"I'll have some water. Do you want me to go get it?"

"I'll go." She bravely adjusted her jean jacket. "Wish me luck."

She waded into the crowd and Elias nudged me. "Someone's been looking for you."

"Who?"

He nudged me again, then jerked his chin in the direction of the entryway. "Our fearless host, that's who."

James was standing in the doorway, scanning the crowd. When his gaze found me, he smiled and waved. I smiled and waved back.

"I would go and say 'hi' to that hot man if I were you." Elias fixed his hair, but as he had a shaved head, it didn't do much. "In fact, if you don't make a move, I will."

"How do you know he was looking for me?" I asked.

"Because he asked me if I'd seen you." Elias rolled his

eyes. "And now he's standing there, waiting for you like a fool."

"I-I'll go over." I nodded my head jerkily.

"That's it, New Girl—you go and get it. Thank God you don't have to carry a tray tonight."

I maneuvered my way through the crowd to James's side. He wore a white linen shirt, open at the throat, and a pair of khaki shorts which showcased his muscular legs. "Hey."

"Hey yourself." He grinned at me. "I'm glad you made it. Otherwise all of this would've been for nothing."

"Aw, c'mon." I blushed at his teasing words. "You're celebrating the solstice, remember?"

"I just needed an excuse to get you back down here, is all." He shrugged, but he didn't stop smiling. "Can I get you a drink?"

"Eden's getting me some water."

"All right. I need to find another way to be of use, then." He scratched the back of his neck. "Would you like to see the house?"

"Sure." I looked around for Eden, to make sure she was okay. She was chatting to several people at the bar, a big smile on her face.

James tracked my gaze. "I can tell she's happy. She'll be fine until I bring you back." He held out his arm for me, and my heart thudded as I took it.

"So who are all these people?" I asked him.

He shrugged. "I don't really know. Josie invited everyone."

The music was louder inside, and while it wasn't overwhelming, the house was. I tried not to gape at the heavy, antique-looking furniture and original oil paintings hanging on the walls. The ceiling soared above us. I glimpsed the kitchen, which looked like it was straight from an architectural magazine. "It's a beautiful home," I said lamely. But it wasn't a home. It was a mansion.

"It's a little museum-y, if you ask me." James shrugged. "I've been thinking about redecorating. Maybe some beanbags. And a leather couch, because I'm always spilling my drink." He chuckled, then stopped when he looked at me. "What's going on, Taylor?"

"N-Nothing." That wasn't exactly true; I was in culture-shock. I'd known he was wealthy, but inside his home—one of his ten homes, if Eden was correct—it became clear to me that James was from a world so far removed from mine, it was like another stratosphere.

Our apartment back in Worcester consisted of a Goodwill couch that smelled like smoke, and a kitchenette with a tan, chipped linoleum countertop. I didn't even have a bed frame. If I was out of place in Becky's house, I was completely out of my league in James's. I thought about what Amelia had said earlier: *Taylor-Trash.* She wasn't exactly wrong.

"Hey, c'mon. Let me show you my favorite spot—it's quiet." James grabbed my hand and led me through a door and up a flight of stairs. I only glimpsed the second level of the home, catching a flash of a mandarin-colored couch that probably cost more than a year of private-college tuition. We ascended the narrowing stairs to a third level. I was breathing hard by the time we reached the door at the top.

"This," James said, "is the Tower." We climbed up into the empty room. Its gleaming, dark hardwood floors were bare, and windows lined the walls on all four sides. The ocean spread out before us, a clear, dark blue-green. The tide was coming in, and the channel coursed between the Tower's seawall and Moss Head. A coastal wind blew by the windows, waves crashed against the beach, and chimes of reggae drifted up from the kitchen. Still, it was peaceful up there. We could see out in every direction, the ocean in front of us, the beach to our sides, the grounds and the forest behind us.

"This is amazing." For some reason, it made me feel sad.

"Thanks?" He glanced at me. "You don't sound happy about it. What's going on?"

There was no use lying to him. Either he could read

my aura, or he could hear it in my voice. "I'm just a little overwhelmed, I think. I've never been in a house like this before."

"It's just a house."

I went and stood next to him at the front windows. We watched the water churn and swirl below. "Easy to say when it's *your* house."

"Fair enough." He gently nudged me, then nodded his chin in the direction of the view. "But what makes it amazing doesn't have anything to do with the house itself—it's out there. And that's got nothing to do with me." He smiled. "So don't hold it against me, okay? Give a guy a chance."

I laughed, but my cheeks burned. Did he really want a chance? A chance with me?

"I'm so glad I came up here this summer." James stared out at the ocean. "I wasn't sure if I'd like it. But it was the right choice—I know that now. I'm glad you're here, Taylor."

"T-Thank you." I nodded, still blushing. "Me too."

"Yeah?" His dimple peeped out.

"Yeah."

We stayed like that, staring out at the mesmerizing water. And for the first time in a long time, maybe in forever, I felt something bubble up in my chest.

I wasn't sure, but it felt suspiciously like hope.

14

SOLSTICE

Josie and Dylan pounced on us when we made it back downstairs. "There you are," Dylan said, "everybody's been looking for you!"

James smirked. "Really? Who's been looking for me?"

"Me." Josie put her hands on her hips. She wore a fitted white crop-top and a matching gauzy skirt. To stand near her was to be humbled.

"And me." Dylan was no less dazzling. Her dark hair cascaded in waves past the spaghetti straps of her patterned sundress.

"I figured, since I don't know anybody else here." James nodded toward me. "I'm taking Taylor out to watch the sunset. Want to come?"

"Oh *no*." Dylan winked at him then made a kissing face. "We don't want to disturb you."

Josie chuckled. "Hey, Taylor. Cute dress."

"Thanks. It's Eden's."

"Nice." She looked from me to James, sizing up our proximity to one another. "We'll just leave you two alone. Go on and enjoy the view—it'll be romantic."

James briefly stuck his tongue out at her. "Gee, thanks." He grabbed my hand and pulled me through the throng of people out on the deck. Eden was already perfectly positioned to watch the sunset. She leaned against the railing, surrounded by a knot of young men which included Patrick.

"Hey Taylor!" Her eyes almost popped out of her head when she saw that James was holding my hand. *Oh my God!* she mouthed.

"Hey." I gave her a death-stare similar to the one she'd given her mother earlier and she burst out laughing.

"Here we are." James maneuvered us into the one remaining spot by the railing, a few groups away from Eden and Patrick. "We should have the perfect view." But he wasn't looking at the horizon. He was looking at my face.

"Yeah." Embarrassed, I turned and looked out at the water.

He shook his head, chuckled, and released my hand. "Sorry about that."

"Y-You don't have to be sorry." I didn't dare reach for his hand again, even though I missed it against mine.

We stood next to each other, watching the sky. The afternoon's clouds had blown out and the sun was large and bright as it headed toward the horizon. There was laughter and chatter all around us. "So James... I've never been to a solstice party before. Tell me what we're celebrating."

He nodded toward the sun. "It's the longest day of the year. It's the start of summer, and the beginning of the season of bounty."

"Bounty." I raised my eyebrows. *"Bounty?"*

He laughed. "Hey, I told you that I don't get out much. I guess my reading vocabulary sounds weird in the real world."

"I'm just teasing you. I don't get out much, either."

He motioned to the throng of people all around us. "You don't like parties?"

"It's not that I don't like them." I could count the number of parties I'd been to on one hand. "I just haven't really been to many."

"Because you were busy back home?" He watched my face carefully.

"Yeah." I turned back toward the sunset. The sky became streaked above us, hues of indigo, purple and pink chasing the setting sun. "This is incredible. Do you watch the sun set every night?"

"Yep." He leaned over the railing. "And I get up early and watch it come up. I don't want to miss it. You can't beat the view—it never disappoints."

People crowded closer around us, taking pictures of the sky and raising their glasses in a toast. James and I were pressed together, shoulder to shoulder. Having him so close made me shiver, and I prayed he didn't notice. The sun started to drop; it happened slowly, and then all at once. Pink scaly clouds chased the light. The colors in the sky were so beautiful, so extraordinary, they were almost impossible to believe.

"This is it," he said. "Here we go." The sun was huge in the sky. It began to dip below the mountains on the horizon. Red hues joined the blues, pinks, and purples; it was a riot of color for the grand finale. Once the sun passed from view, whoops and shouts erupted from the crowd. Someone cranked up the music. People drifted back toward the bar, and someone popped open a bottle of champagne. James and I stayed where we were on the railing, watching the sky. I couldn't get over what I'd just witnessed.

"I've never seen a sunset like that before."

He grinned. "Then you should come back tomorrow."

I smiled, but I didn't know what to say.

"Hey James, can you help me out?" Patrick stuck his head out of the house, a sheepish expression on his face. "I think I broke the water machine."

"Yeah, I'm coming." James looked at me. "Will you be all right?"

"I'll be fine." I motioned vaguely to the groups of people standing near me. "Me and all my friends have catching up to do. Plus, I can look for seals."

He chuckled but gave me a long look before he left, disappearing into the crowd.

"*He*llo." Eden immediately appeared by my side, delivering my long-awaited drink. "Oh my God, tell me everything—*what* is going on with the longing looks and the hand-holding? I thought you said he wasn't into you!"

I laughed and had a sip of water. "Who says he is?"

"You might be the worst liar I ever met." She crossed her arms against her chest. "Now tell me what's going on, or I won't help you when you're in the weeds at our next shift. And you know you're going to be in the weeds!"

"Ugh. I don't know what's going on. That's the truth, okay?" I kept my voice low. "I like him. I don't know if he likes me."

"Trust me, he does. I can see it from a mile away. It's

intense, the way he looks at you. Like, this is no summer fling for him. I can tell."

"Hey Eden, New Girl—you want to dance?" Elias called as he made his way into the house. He snapped his hands above his head and swayed his hips in time to the music. "Let's go!"

"Um, no thank you!" The only thing worse than waiting tables was dancing, as far as I was concerned.

"Wait for me, I'm coming!" Eden handed me her red plastic cup. "Hold my beer—just kidding, it's water. I'm driving, remember?" She winked at me. "And don't worry, I'll send Prince Charming back out for you."

"Eden don't—" But she was gone before I could finish my admonition. She joined Elias and he grabbed her hand, laughing and twirling her as they entered the house.

I leaned against the railing, watching the party as it moved inside. The music got louder, and the house started to throb with the beat.

"Why aren't you in there?" A guy I hadn't seen was suddenly beside me, clutching a red plastic cup. He was maybe in his late thirties, with thick, curly hair and a somewhat rumpled appearance, as if he'd napped in his clothes. He wore glasses, a faded fatigue jacket, ripped jeans and low-top sneakers. His breath wafted past me, reeking of whiskey.

"I'm not really into dancing." I smiled at him politely. On a scale of one-to-ten, he was probably a six drunk. Depending on how full his cup was, he'd be an eight in no time.

"Aw, c'mon." He had another sip from his drink and ever so slightly swayed on his feet. "A young girl like you? You should go for it. Boogie." He raised his hands in the air, dancing in place.

"I'm going to pass, but thanks."

"That's a shame. You should loosen up, girlfriend. C'mon, I'll show you." He took a step closer but James was suddenly in between us.

He frowned at the guy, then glanced at me. "Everything okay, Taylor?"

"Yep. We were just talking about dancing."

James raised an eyebrow. "Do you want to dance?"

"No. No I do not."

"Ah, but you should. I told her she should! And here's why—back me up on this, my dude." The drunk guy seemed to warm to his topic. "When you're young, you should try new things, am I right?"

James resumed frowning.

"C'mon, work with me here. The point is, it doesn't matter if she can't dance, 'cause she'll still look good! Gotta take advantage of that hotness while it lasts." He peered around James and pointed at me. "It's fleeting, all of it. Youth is fleeting. Hotness is fleeting. The opportunity to dance at a party like this is fleeting. You gotta own it while you can. And you should smile, girlfriend. There's nothing to be scowling about with a face like that."

"Huh, that's an interesting position." James realigned himself between the drunk guy and me. "But do you want to know what *I* think?"

"Not really." The guy took another ill-advised sip. "I was just hoping the hot girl would listen. Take in my hard-earned wisdom, you know what I mean?"

"Yeah well, humor me." James's smile was icy. "Here's a little wisdom for you. I think people—men, in particular—should stop telling women what to do. And they should stop commenting on their looks and telling them to smile. It's obnoxious. Not to mention patriarchal."

"Oh Christ. Here we go." The guy scoffed, then chugged from his cup. "You know, this is exactly what's wrong with the world."

James took a deep breath, and I had the sense that he might be counting backwards from ten. "What's that?"

"You and your god-damned knee-jerk censorship." The guy's voice grew louder. "People literally can't say *anything* without the PC-police coming out gangbusters. How can you even have a freaking conversation anymore? All I said was, the hot girl should go dance while she can. She should dance while she's young and pretty and people want to watch her. That's, like, a *compliment*."

"I don't really think it is."

"Oh of *course* not. Anything I say you're going to turn against me. Somehow I'm the villain because I'm a dude."

"That's not what I was say—"

"I was only talking to this girl." The guy raised his voice and several people turned to stare. "I was *talking*— not offending, not groping, just *talking*—and then you swoop in, protector of the deck, and start throwing the patriarchy around. Which you and I both know is a big act so you can get into her pants. The fact that it'll probably work makes me sick!"

"It might be the Wild Turkey that's making you sick," I offered. "Just a thought."

"You two are killing me." He drained his glass.

James stood up taller, the outline of his big muscles visible under his shirt. "I think you should do yourself a favor and go home."

The rumpled guy's shoulders sagged. He seemed suddenly deflated, a balloon whose hot air had escaped with his rant. "Aren't you taking this protector of the deck thing a little seriously?"

"It's my deck. I do take it seriously."

The guy cursed. When James took a step closer, he said, "All right, all right." He set his empty cup on the railing, then unsteadily climbed down the deck stairs.

"He's not going to drive, is he?" I asked.

James seemed to relax a little. "Nah, I saw him walking down here from one of the cabins. He's on the island with some of his buddies for guys' trip, I heard them talking." We watched as he disappeared down the drive, his steps uncertain over the large gravel rocks. "He's in rough shape. Nighty-night."

"Thanks for the rescue." I nudged him. "He was pretty harmless, though. Until you got him going about the patriarchy."

"Ha, yeah. Sorry about that. Pet peeve of mine."

"The patriarchy?"

"Older men hitting on younger women. Or anyone hitting on you, I guess. I didn't like it." James shook his head. "I saw his aura when he was getting close to you… I didn't handle myself well."

My insides warmed. "You were fine."

"In my defense, I could also tell he was drunk. I just wanted to make sure you were okay."

"I forgive you, Protector of the Deck." My phone buzzed and I grabbed it, turning off the alarm. "Oh crap. I have to get home before curfew. I need to go get Eden."

"She's inside, dancing. Why don't you tell her I'll take you home?"

"But it's your party."

"I won't miss much." He shrugged. "I'd like to take you."

"Okay. Let me just go and find her." The party had mostly moved inside. The reggae was gone, replaced by a popular dance song, and a heavy bass thumped throughout the house. Eden was easy to spot—she whirled in the middle of the packed dance floor in the living room, red curls flying. Patrick laughed and caught her. They threw up their hands and kept dancing together.

"Eden!" I maneuvered through the gyrating crowd. "Hey."

"Hey!" Eden pulled me in for a hug. "D'you need to get home? I'm coming."

"No, it's okay—James said he'd take me."

Patrick grinned at the news and Eden gave him a quick smile, then turned back to me. "You sure? 'Cause I don't mind at all. Really."

"I know." I could tell she meant it. "Have fun and be safe, okay? See you tomorrow."

She gave me one more squeeze and released me. "See you tomorrow." She whooped as Patrick grabbed her hand and twirled her around.

I winnowed my way back through the dancers, but someone caught me by the wrist. Elias stopped dancing long enough to size me up. "You leaving, New Girl?"

"Yes."

"Is that fine man driving you home?"

I laughed. "Yes."

He released me. "This just keeps on getting better and better, doesn't it? See you tomorrow!"

"Okay, see you." I went back out to the deck, grateful for the quiet and the cool evening air. I was warm inside, happy that my friends were having fun, happy that I suddenly *had* friends. There was a smattering of stars in the sky, just becoming visible. The sky was so beautiful it made my heart ache. My dad was right. The island was a magical place.

James waited for me, his tall outline visible in the fading light. "You ready?"

"Yeah." I felt it again—that hope bubbling up. I tried to not be afraid of it. "Yeah, I am."

15

RING A DING DING

JAMES HAD STASHED his truck in the woods, so it was easy for us to get out. We caught a glimpse of the drunk guy down by the cabins. He didn't look up from his hammock as we bounced by, easing off the gravel and onto the paved road.

"He looks like he's about to pass out."

"Yeah, he's all done." James gave me a quick look. "How did you know he was drinking Wild Turkey?"

"I read his cup's aura," I joked.

"Ha-ha. No, really. How did you know?"

"Um, the same way I knew that if he finished his drink, he was going to be sloppy drunk. Plus I smelled his breath." I shrugged. I had a lot of experience sizing up how compromised people were. "It's one of my more practical life skills."

He nodded but didn't say anything else as he drove five miles per hour toward town. When we pulled into Becky's house, all the lights were still off. "Looks like you beat them."

"Yeah." I breathed a sigh of relief. "Now I just have to get to bed before they get back home."

"Is it that bad?" His tone was light, but I knew the question was serious.

"Nah." I turned to him and smiled. "Thanks for having me tonight. It was a great party."

He smiled back. "I don't even like parties, but I had a good time."

"Me too."

There was an awkward pause, so I opened my door. "Thanks again."

"You bet."

Right before I went inside the house, James called, "Hey Taylor?"

"Yeah?"

"Do you want to hang out tomorrow?"

I smiled. "I'd like that."

"Good." I caught a flash of his dimple as he backed the truck out.

And then I went inside, floating on air.

Ding-dong.

I sat straight up in bed, confused. It was pitch-black except for the small sliver of light coming through the window. "Hello?"

There was no answer, only a deafening silence.

I must've been dreaming. I laid back down, but just as I was about to drift off, I heard it again: the doorbell. *Ding-dong!*

I looked at the clock on my nightstand: two-fifteen a.m. Who the heck would ring Becky's doorbell at 2:15 in the morning? I panicked, thinking of the party. I wondered if anyone had gotten so drunk that they'd wandered down here and were looking for me. James wouldn't do that, and neither would Eden, but there were so many people there...

I checked my phone. No texts, no calls.

I threw on a sweatshirt and tiptoed down the stairs. They creaked, but when I made it to the kitchen, it was deathly silent. I'd heard Dad, Becky and Amelia come in earlier, so I knew they were home. Maybe they hadn't heard the doorbell?

I held my breath, listening. Nothing.

But then I thought I heard something outside, a scraping, or perhaps a rustling. I crept into the living room and tried to peer out through the windows, but there was only darkness.

Someone knocked on the door and I jumped sky-high.

Rap, rap, rap.

"H-Hello?" But no one answered. I wanted to run and get my dad, good old Big Kyle, because he was scared of nothing and would promptly beat the crap out of anyone who tried to get in the house. But if I got my dad, I'd wake up Becky, and what a shit-show that would be...

I tried to clear my head, but I heard something outside again. Was it whispering? I couldn't be sure. I crept closer to the door, listening, my heart thudding in my ears. *Okay Taylor.* I licked my lips. *There's nothing to be scared of on the island.* My dad had always said it was the safest place in the whole world.

It's probably someone who's lost, or drunk, or most likely both. I could run back to my room and hide, but I'd just be petrified up there, wondering what was going on.

Rap, rap, rap. Softly, so softly I might've imagined it. "Who's there?" I whispered.

But no one answered. I opened the door a crack, securing my weight behind it in case whoever it was tried to push their way in.

There was no one on the front steps.

It was a new moon so there was barely any light. I cautiously looked around to make sure no one waited to spring out at me. But the steps and landing were empty. I crept outside, squinting to try and see the length of the yard in the darkness, waiting for my eyes to adjust. Then I saw something—a flash of long hair, dishwater blond, as a pale figure streaked across the lawn toward the trees. There was something familiar about the form. But that was only the crazy talking, the fear, my brain trying to make sense of the incomprehensible…

"H-Hello? Do you need help?" I called, but it—she, I felt certain—was gone. All I heard was a rustling in the trees.

"Taylor." James was suddenly right next to me, gripping my hands.

"Oh!" I jumped back, almost falling off the steps, but he caught me.

"Are you all right? What did you see?"

"N-Nothing." I shook my head, confused. "Did you ring my doorbell?"

"No, of course not." James pulled me protectively against him and scanned the yard. "Whoever it was, they're gone. Go inside now and lock the door. I'm here. You're safe."

"What? I don't understand what's going on. What're you doing down here in the middle of the night?"

He squeezed me. "I was just checking on you."

"Why?"

"Shh." He leaned closer and pressed a finger to his lips. "Your dad's coming. Go on inside. I've got things covered out here, I promise. We'll talk tomorrow."

James disappeared into the shadows just as my dad stuck his head out the door. "Taylor? What the hell's going on?"

"I don't know." I wrapped my arms around myself and ran for him. "I don't know if it was just a bad dream, but I thought I heard the doorbell ring. Did you hear it?"

"No, I just heard you out here. C'mere kiddo. You're shaking." He pulled me inside, turned on the lamp and peered at my face. "You okay? Tell me what happened."

"I promise Dad—I wasn't drinking or doing anything tonight."

"I know that, honey."

"O-Okay." I nodded shakily. "I went to bed before you got home, and then the doorbell just woke me up. It rang twice. I went outside to see who it was but there was no one there." That wasn't the whole truth, but as I didn't know what the thing was that I'd seen, or understand what James was doing in my yard at two in the morning, I didn't know what to say.

Kyle glanced at the door. "I'm going to go out there, just to take a look."

"No Dad, it's okay. I'm pretty sure I just had a nightmare. Don't go outside, okay?" I gripped his arm. "I feel safer with you in the house."

"I never do this, but..." My dad locked the front door. "Peace of mind, okay?"

"Okay. Love you, Dad."

"I love you too, honey. Go and get some sleep, I'll wait for you to go up." He kissed the top of my head, then stood watch at the bottom of the stairs until I made it to my room.

"Thanks Dad." I pulled the covers up to my chin and listened as he went through the kitchen and climbed the other set of stairs to his room. My room was quiet, still. The incident had been disturbing, but I felt strangely calm. James was outside the house; my dad was inside. Both of them would look out for me. I was safe, protected.

I rolled over and fell into a deep, dreamless sleep.

16

INTRODUCTIONS

AMELIA WAS right in my face the next morning. "Oh my god, how was the party?"

"Good. The sunset was incredible."

"Um…yay." She scowled. "How many people were there?"

"I don't know. About fifty?"

"I can't believe I missed it—this sucks so hard!" She gave me a quick once-over, taking in my faded leggings and oversized T-shirt. "What did you wear?"

"Eden lent me a dress."

She arched an eyebrow. It didn't matter how much money the Lamberts earned from fishing, or what competitive college Eden attended. They were considered below Becky and Amelia's standards. "I bet that was something."

Becky sailed into the kitchen, her hair freshly blown out. She wore a white linen tank top and lots of gold bangles, and her tastefully applied makeup sparkled in the sunlight. "You made it home on time last night, correct?"

"Yes." I held my breath, wondering if my dad had told her about the doorbell, but she didn't say anything as she made herself a coffee.

Amelia scrolled on her phone. She didn't glance up at her mother when she said, "Taylor said there were *fifty* people at the Tower last night."

Becky's eyes widened. "That's a lot. Did some of them park at his dock?" she asked me.

"Yeah." It was weird a sensation, having information that they wanted.

"And I got stuck going to dinner with you guys," Amelia grumbled. "*So* not fair."

Becky didn't say anything. She started flicking through a catalog as she had her coffee. After a minute, I backed out of the room. "Well, see you guys."

"Taylor, hold on." Becky motioned for me to come back. "I'm having some friends over this morning, and then we're heading to the club. What're you doing today?"

What she meant was, will you be skulking around

while I have my rich friends over? "I have plans with James." My face reddened.

Amelia actually looked up from her phone, impressed, and Becky crossed her arms against her chest. "Really?" It was more of an accusation than a question.

"Really." I straightened my spine. "Is that okay?"

Becky's eyes widened, as if she were surprised at my directness.

"I won't go, if there's something else you want me to do, or if you're not comfortable with it." Her house, her rules.

Becky looked momentarily taken aback. "Just let your father know where you are and what you're doing."

I nodded. "Okay. I'll try to be out of your hair before your friends come over."

She frowned as I walked up the stairs. "Why's she sucking up?" Amelia asked, once I'd reached the top of the stairs.

"I'm not sure." Becky sounded troubled. "But it can't be good."

JAMES TEXTED ME, saying he'd be down in a little while if I was still up for hanging out. *Yes*, I texted back. I wanted to get out of the house before Becky's petrifying squad of rich ladies came over.

I quickly took a shower and got dressed. Jean shorts and a button-down shirt were okay for a day-date, weren't they? I had no idea. But I brushed my teeth and put on some mascara, because at least I knew those were socially acceptable things to do.

I didn't eat breakfast. Not only because Amelia and Becky were still downstairs, but because I was suddenly nervous. James and I had the whole day to spend together. I wondered what his explanation would be about last night...

I heard a car in the driveway and sprinted down the stairs. But my heart sank. It was Marybeth and two of Becky's other friends. I hung back in the safety of the stairwell landing as they came in. Sylvie was a stylish woman with short silver hair and an oversized croc-odile tote. Gina was tall, curvy, and had a mass of black hair worn long past her shoulders. Becky air-kissed each of them. "Mimosas, ladies? The water taxi's not taking us across until ten-thirty, so we've got plenty of time."

"Sure." Sylvie smiled.

"None for me." Gina pursed her lips. "I'm fasting until noon."

"Still doing the intermittent-fast thing, huh? Do you

think it's actually doing anything?" Sylvie sounded skeptical.

"It's scientifically proven to work." Gina scowled at her. "I haven't lost pounds, but my clothes fit better."

"I'd love a drink, but no juice, please." Marybeth winked at Becky. "My skin can't handle the sugar."

"I keep telling you to do that colonic cleanse," Sylvie tsked. "It would help with those under-eye bags, too."

"So I heard the party at the Tower got pretty wild last night," Marybeth said, deftly steering the conversation away from her under-eye bags and the questionable effectiveness of Gina's fasting.

"There were more than fifty people there," Becky said, her voice becoming animated. "Taylor went. She said some of them drove their boats over from Pine Harbor."

"Taylor went to the party?" Sylvie asked. "You mean, Kyle's daughter?"

"Kyle's *other* daughter." Becky cleared her throat.

"Ah, my bad. Sorry." Sylvie didn't sound sorry.

"Yeah, she's actually has plans with James Champlain again today—that's why I had you come over a little early. You might get to catch a glimpse of him. Although I'm not sure what he's doing, hanging around with Taylor so much," Becky said.

"I'd say it's pretty obvious." Marybeth chortled. "He's

a handsome boy, she's a pretty girl..." I couldn't see Becky's face, but something must've pulled Marybeth up short. "Not as pretty as Amelia, of course."

The sound of another car came down the drive. I peered around the corner and saw James's rusty truck. I took a deep breath; there was no way out except past Becky and her friends. Time to go and face the firing squad.

"Hey Becky, my ride's here." I smiled at her as she and her friends looked me up and down.

"*That's* what you're wearing?" Amelia came out of the kitchen and popped her earbuds out.

"Um..." I glanced down at my button-down shirt. "Yes?"

Sylvie, Gina and Marybeth watched us with interest. Then James knocked on the door. "I'll get it!" Amelia screeched and raced passed me. She smoothed her hair before she threw the door open. James stood on the front step. He flashed a megawatt smile at her. "Good morning. Is Taylor here?"

"Oh, hey." Amelia sounded bored, but she tossed her hair again. "Yeah, she is."

"Great." James blinked at her. "So... May I come in?"

"Sure." Amelia stepped aside.

"Hey James! So nice to finally meet you." Becky

sprang into action, followed closely by Marybeth, Sylvie and Gina.

"Hi, Mrs. Hale. It's nice to see you." The other women introduced themselves and James shook their hands. "It's nice to see you, too."

I stood back and watched as they crowded around him, a mass of perfect hair, unnaturally smooth skin and luxurious fabrics. The women seemed thrilled with James—it was likely a combination of his big shoulders, strong jawline, and staggering family fortune. There wasn't a hint of concern about him being a possible cult-leader.

James smiled patiently as they interrogated him.

"I knew your father years ago, back in the day. How is he?"

"How's your mother, James? We haven't seen you all in decades!"

"The new boathouse is to *die* for. I'd love to know who your designer was, we're thinking about updating ours! Want to give me a tour sometime?"

"How's the Tower? Are you planning on opening it up? I know the Friends of the Island are looking to hold their annual fundraiser someplace new this year..."

"I'll have to talk to their board about that," James said patiently.

"Oh, you can talk to me about it!" Becky said brightly. "I'm the chair."

"Great. I'll check in with my parents about hosting the fundraiser. And they told me to send their best to everyone—they're sorry they haven't been up here in so long."

"I always enjoyed your father," Sylvie said. She made the word "enjoy" seem somehow inappropriate.

But James didn't miss a beat. "You still would. He hasn't changed much."

"Well, we're just so glad that you're using the house this summer!" Becky beamed at him. "And I don't think you've met my daughter yet. Amelia, this is James. James, Amelia."

James formally shook her hand. "Amelia."

She turned scarlet. "Hey."

James caught my eye. "Excuse me, ladies. I'm here to pick up my friend. Hi Taylor. You ready?"

"Yep." I forced myself to join their group and smile. No one pounced on me with questions, and no one shook my hand. *Thank God, right?* "Bye everyone. Nice to see you."

They murmured goodbyes, then watched us as James gently steered me out of the house, opening and closing the front door for me. I'd no doubt that they gawked out the windows as he opened the passenger-side of the truck and waited until I climbed in.

"Well, that was... A lot." He smirked as he eased the truck backwards down the drive. "What a pit of vipers. Did they even say anything to you before I got there?"

"No, but in their defense, I *was* hiding out on the stairs." I sighed. "That's just how they are. They're busy day-drinking and one-upping each other, then they're going to the club for the day."

"The Haven Club?" he asked.

"I think so."

He frowned. "You've been coming up here all these summers, and they've never taken you to the club?"

"No." I shook my head. "I don't really think I'm club material."

"I beg to differ," James's voice was soft. "So hey— what do you want to do today? I was thinking we could take my boat out."

"I'd love that. The Hinckley?"

"Ah, that's my girl." His dimple peeped out. "I love a woman who knows her boats."

I giggled. "That's probably the only kind I know."

"And it's the only kind I drive. So see? It was meant to be, Taylor." We drove down to his boathouse and he parked out front. "It's docked down here."

"Okay."

He glanced quickly above my head. "So you're really okay, even after your morning with the vipers?"

"I'm used to it. Plus, I'm tougher than I look," I said. Now that I'd escaped the house, Becky and her friends were no longer my concern. My thoughts shifted to the night before, and I wondered when James would be ready to talk about what had happened.

We were quiet as we walked down his long private dock, taking in the view of the island from here. You could see the town dock, the co-op, and the island. It was a beautiful morning, warm and clear. The water sparkled in the sunlight. The *Norumbega* waited at the end of the pier, its navy hull and polished wood interior glowing.

When we got to the boat, James tossed the bumpers inside the cabin and motioned toward the rear knot. "Can you untie that?"

"Sure." I took the thick rope between my hands, happy to be of use. I untied the knot and carefully coiled up the rope, then handed it to James. We climbed on board and he handed me an orange life vest. "Aren't you going to wear one?" I asked.

"Nah."

I dutifully clipped mine on, then sat on the comfortable blue-and-white striped built-in couch. Up close, the Hinckley's glorious details revealed themselves. At the front of the boat—the *bow*, my dad had taught me—there was the steering wheel and two captain's chairs, covered by a hardtop. Where I sat in the back, the *stern*, there were two built-in couches, two built-in chairs, and an enormous cooler. The floor of the boat was immaculate, and the cabin had touches of beautiful hard wood. The blue-and-white fabric covering the chairs and couches tied everything together. It was a hell of a boat, even though technically it was a yacht.

James started the motor and gently pulled out into the harbor. "Do you want to come up here while I drive? You can be my co-captain."

"Yeah." I went and sat next to him. We waved at the fishermen who passed us as we carefully navigated around the boats docked in the harbor. "Where are we going?"

James shrugged. "I thought we could just circle around. We can go by Spruce Island and Crescent, and anywhere else you like."

"Sounds great."

I had a million questions to ask him, so many things I wanted to talk about, but for a few minutes I just soaked in the scenery. It was so gorgeous. From out in the water, you could see that each of the islands was covered with trees. The water was a deep, clear blue-green. There wasn't a cloud in the sky.

"Do you want a jacket?" James asked. He wore a heavy hoodie.

"No, I'm good." I smiled at him.

"Good." He drove the boat down in between Crescent Island and Dawnhaven, leaving the busy harbor behind. It was quieter out here. James slowed the Hinckley down to a crawl and we watched the islands as they passed. "So last night…"

"Yeah, we should talk about that." I hesitated. "Why were you down at my house?"

His expression darkened as he steered the boat. "I guess I have to ask you something, first."

"Okay…"

"Do you believe what I told you? That I can read auras?"

I answered before I could think it through. "Yes."

He glanced at me. "Really?"

I pointed above my head. "Double-check me." I wasn't sure when I'd accepted his strange talent. But James seemed like an honest person to me. I didn't know if it *could* be true that he saw auras, but he absolutely had an uncanny knack for reading people. In any event, I believed that he believed it, and that seemed like the most important thing.

"Thank you," James said. "It's not the sort of thing that's easy for me to talk about. But I trust you. And also

I think you get that—that some things are hard to talk about."

"Oh yeah." I laughed even though it wasn't funny. "I get that."

"So last night..." The muscle in James's jaw jumped. "I heard something. And I just had a feeling—I was just worried about you."

My brow furrowed. "You heard something from down at the Tower?"

"Sort of." His eyes darkened. "It was more of a feeling, I guess."

"Did you drive your truck down to Becky's?" I wasn't sure why I was asking, but I hadn't seen it.

"It was parked down the road." He didn't look at me.

"Oh. I didn't hear it, is all."

"Yeah, well." James took a deep breath. "So that feeling I was telling you about? It's sort of like the auras. Sometimes I just get feelings, pretty intense ones. And I've learned that it's important for me to follow my gut."

"So when you were worried about me last night, you wanted to check on me. Even though it was two a.m."

"Yeah, I thought I should." He blew out a deep breath. "Can you tell me what happened? Why were you outside?"

"I don't really know. I woke up because I thought I

149

heard the doorbell ring. Then I figured I was dreaming, but when I started falling back asleep it rang again."

James nodded, waiting for me to continue.

"I went downstairs, but nobody else was up. Then someone knocked on the door, so I opened it—but there was nobody there. I mean, I *thought* I saw someone..." I shook my head as if to clear it. "But I didn't. I couldn't have."

"Who did you think it was?" James asked quietly.

I looked up at his handsome face. I didn't say anything for a full minute. Then: "My mother. I thought... I thought I saw my mother."

17

A DIFFERENT LIGHT

BUT I HADN'T SEEN my mother, of course. She was dead. My mind had just been playing tricks on me.

James stopped the boat and took my hands. "Aw Taylor, I'm so sorry."

"D-Don't be." To my utter horror, my eyes filled with tears. "I was just dreaming. It didn't mean anything. I'm not crazy."

"Hey, hey. I tell you I can read auras and have premonitions, and you're worried that I think *you're* crazy?" He squeezed my hands. "Taylor, look at me."

I raised my eyes, fighting the tears with everything I had. "What?"

"You just lost your mom, right? It's normal for stuff like that to happen."

"Delusions and hallucinations?" I asked. "That's normal?"

James's expression softened. "Dreams are normal. Feelings are normal. Being sad is normal."

I withdrew my hands from his and stiffly nodded. "I know."

"Do you want to talk about what happened to your mom?" he asked gently. "You don't have to, if you don't want to."

"I don't want to." My voice was hoarse.

"Okay. I understand." He put the boat back into drive and focused on the water, giving me some space.

I waited for a few minutes, torn. I wanted to tell him what happened, but it was hard to talk about. When he wasn't looking at me, I said quickly, "She overdosed." The words came out flat but rushed. "She was a heroin addict."

He reached back over and gently took my hand. "I'm so sorry."

"Thank you." The tears abated, and I felt a little better since I'd said it out loud. At least he knew. "But please don't tell anyone. Becky doesn't want word getting around."

At that, James scowled a little.

"My mom always had problems, but it was mostly drinking." My voice sounded funny to my ears. "This past fall, a lot of her friends started using. A couple of them died. I think she just gave up."

"So you lost her suddenly," James said.

"Yeah." I swallowed hard. "It was pretty fast."

He nodded. "It makes sense then."

I jerked my head at him. "What does?"

"That you thought you saw her last night—it hasn't been that long. You have to give yourself a break, give yourself some time to heal." He shot me a quick look. "Just because Becky wants to act like it never happened, like it's something you can keep tidy and put away in a box, that doesn't mean you can feel that way. It's your mom."

I stared out at the water. "I thought I made my peace with it."

"It can sneak up on you." He squeezed my hand again. "Sometimes when we lose somebody like that, I don't know. It's hard when you don't get to say goodbye."

It sounded as though he knew what he was talking about. "Did... Did you lose someone?"

"My brother." He gripped my hand. "It was a couple of years ago."

"I'm so sorry." I'd never heard about a brother.

"I'm sorry, too." But James smiled at me. "It was tough. There was a time not that long ago when I felt pretty lost. But it gets easier. Not better, but easier. You know what I mean?"

"I think so." I nodded. "Yeah, I do."

We spent the next hour driving around Dawnhaven and Spruce Island. I glimpsed parts of each island I'd never seen before, which was pretty cool. We circled back into Hart Sound. Both of us were quiet, but it wasn't uncomfortable. Being surrounded by so much beauty lifted me out of myself, and I felt relieved that I'd told James about my mother.

We passed the Osprey nest and he pointed to it. "D'you see him?" The giant bird was perched on the edge of the platform, surveying the activity beneath it.

"He's huge! He could give Edgar a run for his money." I hadn't seen the bird in years. It was magnificent, with a white body, a black-and-white marked face, and enormous black wings.

"Did you know he's twenty years old? Somebody told me that—one of the fishermen, I think."

"Twenty, huh?" I marveled at the big bird as he disappeared behind us.

"Hey, are you hungry?" James asked. My stomach growled before I could answer. "I don't have to read your aura for that." He laughed, then turned the boat east.

"Where are we going?"

"Want to try the Haven Club? They have killer burgers."

"Um…the Haven Club, as in the club that my stepmother and her viper friends are at?"

"The very same. Don't worry, it's pretty big."

"I assume you know that you have to be a member to get in there?" I asked.

"You assume correctly." James grinned. "My father has a legacy membership. We're in for like, I don't know. A hundred years?"

"You have a one-hundred-year membership." I shook my head. "Of course you do."

"I'd never been there before this summer." He shrugged. "I really don't know what the big deal is. The pool's freezing. The burgers are good, though."

James maneuvered the boat into Crowley Cove. The town proper was one of MDI's wealthiest. I glimpsed the rooftops of several enormous estates near the shoreline, but the properties were hidden, surrounded by the privacy of tall fir trees.

James pulled the boat up to a floating dock and a valet helped him with the bumpers.

"Good afternoon, Mr. Champlain. Nice to see you again."

"You too, Eric. How are you?"

"Great, sir." Eric grinned at him. "Want me to keep the boat here, or are you staying for the afternoon?"

"We're just having lunch. See you in a little bit."

James helped me off the boat, then led me up a steep ramp to the club. "Before I forget, we aren't allowed to have our phones out."

I blinked at him.

"Yeah, it's a rule. For privacy, or something." He didn't let go of my hand as we reached the top.

"Wow," I said. I didn't have access to a better word than that. The Haven Club was situated at the top of a rolling hill, dotted with fir trees; Hart Sound stretched out beneath us in an incredible view. The club itself was grand and austere, with an old-world charm. An Olympic-sized pool greeted us, surrounded by bright-white lounge chairs with green umbrellas. One lone woman, wearing a bright-yellow bathing suit and a swim cap, dutifully swam laps. There were several sunbathers lounging in the chairs, their designer sunglasses firmly in place, icy drinks within reach.

The club's gray-stone building was enormous, with grand arched windows and massive white shutters covered in ivy. Outdoor seating covered the patio; older men in sports coats and women in flowery dresses sat in pairs and groups, eating lunch.

"Um....I think we're underdressed."

"Nah, c'mon. You look great. Don't worry—it's just lunch."

I might've imagined it, but everyone stared when we walked up. The members were pedigreed enough to keep talking, but I felt eyes on us, curious ones. I tried unsuccessfully to tuck my shirt into my shorts. James seemed completely at ease, even with everyone staring at him, as we headed past the pool toward the restaurant.

"Hi Amelia," James said.

I hadn't noticed my half-sister, who gaped at us from her lounger. She wore a black bikini and an incredulous expression. "Taylor?"

"Hey." I smiled. I never knew what to say to her. "Cute suit."

"Um, does Mom know you're here?"

James calmly smiled at her. "She will in a minute. Nice to see you."

"Yeah..." She watched, dumbfounded, as James led me away. A host wearing a suit and tie appeared out of nowhere. "Mr. Champlain, it's lovely to see you. Table for two?"

"Yes, please. And when you have a minute, can you send Carl over? I need to speak with him."

"Of course."

The host led us past the precisely groomed guests.

These people were seriously well bred—no one batted an eye at me in my jean shorts or James in his hoodie. Of course, they'd probably heard the name Champlain, or perhaps they already knew who he was. I glimpsed Becky and her friends. They seemed stunned to see us, but Becky recovered quickly and gave James a friendly smile. Thankfully, we were seated on the opposite side of the restaurant, at a private table overlooking the sound.

I glanced at Becky, who was having a furtive discussion with her friends, most definitely about me and James. "What's her aura say?" I asked.

James raised his eyebrows. "You sure you want to know?"

My shoulders slumped. "Maybe not."

Our waiter came and we ordered without even looking at the menus, two iced teas and two burgers.

"Back to Becky." James shook his head. "Don't let her get to you. She's not someone… Ah. I don't know how to say this without sounding like a jerk."

"By all means, go on."

James glanced at Becky and gave her a megawatt smile, which she returned. "She's not someone who's aware that there's anything going on except what's right in front of her face."

My brow furrowed. "I don't understand."

James sighed. "It's hard to explain. But Becky's someone who is hyper-aware of herself and her own thoughts. And she's aware of Amelia. There's nothing else for either of them. Everything else is either an obstacle or blurry."

"You mean she's self-obsessed?" I asked. I could've told him that. "You can read that in her aura?"

"Yeah, but it's not just that. It's like she can only hear her own thoughts—she's out of touch with everything else because it gets blocked out."

"Okay…" I wasn't sure I understood, but our food arrived. We were both too hungry to talk. Becky and her friends intermittently stared at us, but I tried to ignore them. Lunch was incredible; apparently rich people had the very best of everything, including burgers and herbed French fries.

We were almost finished when an older man in an expensive-looking suit appeared at our table, his silver hair glinting in the sunlight. He beamed at James. "Good afternoon, Mr. Champlain. We're so pleased you've come back to join us. How are your meals?"

"Excellent, Carl." James put his napkin down. "Thanks so much for making the time for me."

"Your family is very important to the club, sir. We're thrilled that you're spending some time with us this summer. What can I do for you?"

"This is my friend, Taylor Hale."

Carl swept into a bow. "It's a pleasure, Ms. Hale. Any relation to the Dawnhaven Hales?"

"Yes, Kyle's my father." I smiled at him and prayed he didn't mention Becky, who was currently staring at us.

"Lovely to make your acquaintance." Carl's smile was refined but seemed sincere.

"Taylor's the reason why I asked to see you," James said. "I'd like her added to my membership. And also, her friend Eden Lambert. Please add her as well."

Carl's smile widened. "I'd love to. We'll be so pleased to have more young members, it really livens the place up."

"Perfect." James flashed his dimple. "Carl, one last thing. Please send a bottle of your best champagne to Mrs. Hale's table, and put their meal on my tab."

"I'll see to it at once." Carl was gone immediately in a flash of navy suit.

"So...I'm a member now?" I gaped at him.

"Yep." He ate his last fry. "And Eden, because I know her family has a boat and she can drive you over here. You two seem like good friends. It's always more fun to hang by the pool with a good friend."

My gaping was redirected to Becky's table. Their waiter had brought over the champagne and showed them the label. I thought I heard Marybeth squeal, but I couldn't be sure.

"You sure know how to make a girl's morning."

James stared. "You're the only girl that matters."

I nodded toward Becky's table. "They seem pretty happy with their champagne."

"I've charmed a snake or two in my time." He grinned. "You ready to get out of here?"

"Sure."

When we stood, he reached for my hand. We stopped at Becky's table on the way out. "Enjoy your afternoon, ladies."

Becky beamed up at him while the other ladies smiled worshipfully. "Thank you so much for lunch, and also for the champagne. It's my favorite."

"Anytime." He flashed them the dimple.

I thought I heard Marybeth sigh, but I couldn't be sure.

GLIMPSES

AFTER JAMES BROUGHT ME HOME, I changed into my work uniform and brushed my teeth, then pulled my hair up into a high ponytail. I wanted to get to work before Becky and Amelia got back. I didn't know what they'd ask me, or how they'd treat me, and I didn't want to find out.

I hustled down the drive but something dark glinted in the corner of my vision. I stopped. "Edgar?" A crow peered at me from one of the trees at the edge of the lawn. Was that him? If yes, what was he doing all the way down here? Frowning, I practically ran into my dad once I rounded the corner.

"Hey honey." His face split into a grin. "I'd give you a hug, but I smell like a lobster pound. You going to work?"

"Yeah. Hey, thanks again for getting up last night to check on me. I was pretty freaked out."

"I wanted to talk to you about that, and a couple of other things…" He took a deep breath. "But you have to get going?" He sounded hopeful.

My stomach twisted. My dad never was a really big talker, so I knew whatever he needed to say probably wasn't coming from him. "I have a minute."

He cleared his throat. "So, Becky's been texting me. She mentioned that you're spending more time with the Champlain kid. He took you to lunch today, right?"

News sure traveled fast around here. "Yep."

"Do you like him?"

I nodded.

"So…" My dad looked pained. "Is he your boyfriend now?"

"Um." My cheeks heated. "We're just hanging out."

"Yeah see, that's the thing." He scrubbed a big hand over his bristly hair. "Becky's worried that means something it probably doesn't."

I raised my gaze to meet his. I felt like I might throw up from embarrassment, but I said, "Dad, I haven't even kissed him or anything. We're just getting to know each other. He's nice—we're friends."

"Okay honey." But Kyle looked pained. "She's just

worried about Amelia getting the wrong idea, or something."

"Right. She's always worried about that."

"She asked me to tell you… Um…" His cheeks turned ruddy. "No friends in the house if we're not home."

I crossed my arms against my chest. "I can't have Eden over?"

"No, that's fine," he said automatically.

"So no boys in the house is what you meant."

"Honey, I trust you. You know that." His shoulders slumped. "I'm sorry. You don't deserve to be cross-examined like this."

He wasn't actually accusing me of anything, but I still felt like I might cry. "It's okay."

"I really wish I didn't smell like chum." He forced a smile. "You sure look like you need a hug."

"I'm fine. I should get going, though."

"Have a good shift. One last thing—you didn't hear any more noises last night, did you?"

I shook my head.

"Okay honey. Me either." Dad patted me on the shoulder. "Must've just been a bad dream. See you when you get home, okay? I love you, Taylor."

"Love you too." I swallowed hard as I stomped down the road toward the dock. *Fucking Becky.* How did she make me feel so slutty when I hadn't even kissed James, let alone anyone else?

The restaurant was empty; Jenny hadn't opened for brunch. Josie looked up from the bar and frowned. "What happened to you?"

"My step-monster." I shrugged. "She hates me."

Josie arched an eyebrow. "She doesn't like anybody except herself."

"Yeah well." I pulled my apron around my waist and tied it tight. "She likes James."

Josie snorted. "All the rich ladies like James. They think he's the second coming."

"Thanks for inviting me to the party," I said, anxious to change the subject. "It was fun."

"You and James seemed pretty cozy."

"M-hmm. Did people stay late?"

She shrugged. "We kicked them out around midnight. I was glad James had the restaurant closed this morning, though—it still would've been too early."

"*James* had the restaurant closed?"

A funny look crossed Josie's face. "You know what? I need more limes." She hustled for the kitchen.

What she said confused me, but I focused on filling the salt and pepper shakers. I was no fan of waitressing, but I felt grateful for the busy hours that stretched out before me. Work meant I didn't have to be at Becky's house, and she couldn't accuse me of sleeping around while I was at the restaurant. At least I didn't think she could—I probably shouldn't put it past her.

The cooks set up the kitchen; I could hear Elias singing as he did his prep work. The rest of the waitstaff trickled in, and the hard-core fishermen who worked Sundays started to fill the seats at the bar.

Eden was one of the last to arrive. She made a beeline right to me. "Hey! Can I tell you—I just got the *craziest* email!"

I stuffed more sugar packets into my ramekins. "What was it?"

Eden started organizing the fake sweeteners, lining the little yellow and pink packets up in a neat row. "It was from the manager at the Haven Club. He said I had an honorary *lifetime* membership, courtesy of a certain Mr. Champlain!"

"Yeah." I nodded. "Cool."

"Oh boy—I knew it! You got one too." Eden chuckled. "There sure are perks to being a gazillionaire's girlfriend's bestie."

"I'm not his girlfriend."

She smiled slyly. "You keep saying that, and yet, the perks keep rolling in."

"How did things go with Patrick last night?"

Eden's crafty smile disappeared, replaced by a smooth mask. "Fine."

"You didn't feel a love connection?" I eyed her. "I thought maybe that's what I was seeing when you were dancing with him."

She cleared her throat and tossed her hair. "A lady doesn't kiss and tell."

"Ooh, you kissed him?"

Her cheeks turned a little pink. "Don't you have water pitchers to fill, or something?"

"Already filled them." I waggled my eyebrows at her. "So I have plenty of time to listen to details."

Eden's cheek flushed more deeply as Patrick, James and Dylan ambled into the restaurant. "I have to go read the specials." She zipped off before I could pester her further.

James and the others took a table in the bar and he nodded to me. I grinned back until I caught Josie watching us. She leaned over the polished wood and said, "You know, he never used to come in here that much. Must be something on the menu that he *really* likes."

"The chowder?" I asked.

"Nah, I think it's the New Girl."

Following Eden's lead, I said, "I need to go and check the specials."

But Elias was waiting for me when I went back into the kitchen. "How'd it go with Daddy Warbucks last night?"

"You're funny."

"No, I'm serious." He eyed me over the line. "I saw you on his Hinckley today! What's going on?"

Of course he'd seen me on James's boat. Everybody on the island knew everything. "He took me out for a ride, and then we went to lunch."

Elias fanned himself. "Did he happen to wear a tank top?"

"No, he wore a hoodie—now stop pestering me!"

"You're blushing, New Girl!" he called as I fled the kitchen.

I'd never been so glad to see two new tables in my section. I dove into work, happily taking orders and not looking at the drinks when I carried them on the tray. My two tables became four, and before long, my station was full. To my surprise, I managed okay. I didn't take food without a ticket, and I didn't get into the weeds even though the restaurant was packed.

"We have an hour wait—for a Sunday, this is great." Eden carried an enormous tray filled with lobster dinners. "I'm going to make enough money to pay for all my books before July Fourth!"

I wanted to ask about her books, and more about Patrick; I wanted to go and see James to say hi. But I was so busy I couldn't do anything but work. The time flew by. Eventually I noticed James and the others leaving their table. He held up his hand to his ear and mouthed, *I'll call you.*

I nodded and mouthed back, *Okay.* We grinned at each other like idiots for a second.

As they headed for the door, another knot of customers filed in. It was the curly-haired guy from the party and his friends. James eyed him with disdain. The guy nodded at him but kept a wide berth. James shot me another look and I mouthed, *It's okay.* Then one of my customers motioned for me and I had to go.

I was dimly aware of Drunk Guy and his friends for the rest of my shift. They'd taken over James's table in the bar and were drinking endless rounds of craft beer. Their conversation seemed boisterous but harmless. They blended in with the other customers without issue, and after a while, I forgot all about them.

Eventually, the restaurant started to quiet down. The two parties I had left paid their tabs and were lingering over dessert and coffee. I untied my apron and made quick run for the bathroom. There was no ladies' room inside the restaurant. We had to use the public restroom at the beginning of the dock, so I hustled down the pier. The art gallery had closed, and the fishermen had all gone home for the night. The bathrooms were empty. I moved quickly, anxious to get back and clean up my tables.

Back on the pier, I noticed my shoe was untied. I bent to tie it—when I stood back up, I was face to face with Drunk Guy.

"Oh!" I took a step back. "I didn't see you there."

He smiled, but it wasn't a nice smile. "I see your reaction to me hasn't improved any."

"It's nothing personal. You just startled me." He was only about a three drunk, but his mood seemed sour. "I have to get back to my tables now."

"Of course." He moved out of my way, but I could feel his eyes on me until I reached the restaurant.

I cleaned my station and started cashing out. His group was one of the last ones to leave. Luckily, Drunk Guy didn't look at me again. I'd probably imagined how close he'd been to me on the pier. Still, I made sure he and his friends were long gone before I went home.

"Do you want a ride?" Eden asked.

"Sure."

Tired from our long shift, we were both quiet as she

drove me to Becky's driveway. "Just one question," I said before I hopped out. "Do you like him, or not?"

"Patrick?" Eden yawned. "Yeah I like him. But I'm not taking it too seriously. My boyfriend and I are taking a break this summer, but he's still going to be there when the fall semester starts."

"You have a boyfriend?"

"You said only one question." But she smiled at me. "But yeah, we've been going out since my freshman year. I told him I wanted to date other people this summer, though."

"How come?"

"Taylor Hale, that's three questions."

I opened the truck door. "If I pack you a sandwich, will you tell me at the beach tomorrow?"

"Ha, bribe me with food—you already know me too well." She grinned. "But sure, I'll tell you all about it. As long as you promise to talk about James!"

She waved and drove off before I had a chance to object. I started to make my way down the long driveway. My limbs were tired, heavy from the long, physical shift. Waitressing was harder than it looked—it was a workout, cardio *and* weight training. Those heavy trays were no joke! I was going to have legitimate biceps by the end of the summer.

I'd just made it past the pool when I heard something. A rustling, then a splash.

"Edgar?" I called. *Did crows even swim?* No answer.

"James?"

I held my breath. The silence was deafening.

Until something splashed in the pool again, louder this time.

19

RUN FOR IT

I stood, frozen in place.

"Nice pool."

I recognized the voice—Drunk Guy's voice.

"My dad is six-foot-five, and he has a gun." My words came from old habit, cultivated by years of living in a rough neighborhood.

"Good for him." The light coming from the house was bright enough that I could see him climb the ladder and stand on the lawn. Drunk Guy was in all his clothes, dripping wet. He reached out toward me. "Come here."

"No." I needed to run, but my legs were lead. I couldn't move.

"I said, *come here*." Drunk Guy's voice sounded different. It was deeper and slightly slurred—he'd passed the three-drunk mark and was headed for double digits.

"And I said no." Why did the front door seem so far away?

He started to shake, a violent shiver. "D-d-don't say n-n-no to me."

Serves him right. It was freaking freezing on the island at night and the fool had jumped in the pool with all his clothes on. *I hope he gets pneumonia.* But his shivering didn't stop—it turned more spastic, his whole body violently shaking. He looked like he might be having a seizure.

"Hey. Are—are you okay?"

"N-n-n-n-o." It came out a high-speed stutter. *"N-n-n-n-n-o."*

I didn't know what was happening to him. If this was a seizure, it was a terrible one.

"Hold on, I'll get help." Seeing him like that somehow got my legs moving. I wasn't even sure if there was a doctor on the island, but my dad could do something. I raced for the door but somehow Drunk Guy was already on the step in front of me, blocking my entrance.

"Let me get my dad. He can help you."

"N-n-n-n-n-n-o." He was sopping wet, every inch of him shaking. Water droplets from the pool spewed out from him as if he were a sprinkler on speed. I'd seen my mother have a seizure, but this was different—Drunk

Guy moved so fast I couldn't make out his face. His head jerked crazily and his body was spastic but somehow, he still managed to clench a hand around my wrist.

I tried to duck around him, but his grip tightened. He dragged me down the steps. I wanted to scream *No!* I wanted to yell *Dad!* But it was like I was in a nightmare, the kind where I couldn't find my voice. Time slowed down, and I could only gape in horror as he dragged me out onto the lawn.

"C-c-c-c-c-come w-w-w-w-with m-m-m-m-m-me." He headed toward the woods, his hand like a vice around my wrist. I dug my heels into the grass, but he was unnaturally powerful—even as he convulsed, he pulled me behind him with ease. He must have been on drugs, something awful.

We reached the darkness of the tree line. I did *not* want to go into the forest with him. I yanked my arm, desperate to break free of his crazy-strong grasp. "Help." My voice was a croak, but at least it worked. *"Help!"*

Drunk Guy kept dragging me.

There was a burst of light from the trees, sudden and illuminating. *Lightning?* I looked up—a blanket of stars and a cloudless sky stretched above us. Another flash of bright-white light lit the forest. Drunk Guy stopped walking, but he didn't stop shaking. He tightened his grip around my wrist.

We stood, the forest dark again. But then brilliant-white light blazed inside the trees again. Something crashed out of the woods, exploding directly into Drunk Guy's chest and sending us both flying. "Oof!" I landed flat on my back, the wind knocked out of me. I turned to see Drunk Guy sprawled next to me, but it took a full minute for my brain to process everything else.

What I saw didn't make any sense.

James straddled my attacker as he convulsed beneath him. But there was something weird about James—he had light all around him, like he'd been struck by lightning and was still conducting the electricity from it.

He had his forearm across Drunk Guy's windpipe, pressing it into the ground.

"James, don't." My voice was so hoarse it didn't carry. "James!"

Drunk Guy convulsed beneath him, flailing his arms, and James eased up a little. My attacker took a breath in —a painful, desperate sound.

"Taylor." James's voice was calm, a wild contrast to his glowing appearance. "Get inside the house. Lock the door. Nothing's going to happen—I've got you." He leaned down and got into Drunk Guy's face. "One word about the patriarchy, and I'm gonna crush your throat. Got it?"

The only answer was his spastic movements.

I sat up a little. James was no longer glowing. Had I imagined it?

"Go inside. *Now.*"

With one final look at them, I fled.

I'd never been so happy to be in Becky's house in my whole life.

———

SLEEP WAS out of the question, but so was sneaking out. I waited for a minute, pacing my room, hoping that James would text me or something. Was he still out there? What had happened? Was he safe? Had he hurt Drunk Guy or let him go? Was Drunk Guy still convulsing? I peered out my window, but it faced the back yard and was useless.

I paced some more, then gave up and snuck out to the landing. I held my breath and listened, but it was silent. I crept down the stairs under the guise of getting a glass of water. If I woke Becky up, she'd be pissed, but getting water after a long night of work wasn't something she could really punish me for.

I didn't turn the lights on as I went and stood in the living room, peering through the windows. I blinked at what I saw. *Maybe I'm dreaming?*

I had to be. None of this could be real.

James was back in super-conductor mode, a bluish-white light surrounding his body. I watched, jaw gaping, as he leaned over Drunk Guy and appeared to give him mouth-to-mouth resuscitation. Light from James's mouth traveled into my attacker's mouth. It filtered down his body, which slowly stopped jerking then came to rest. James stopped giving him CPR. He hung his head over the body, his hands held together as if in prayer. After a minute, Drunk Guy shot to his feet. He jerkily walked down the driveway, away from the house. Gone were the seizure-like movements, but his gait was unnatural, as if perhaps he were sleepwalking.

I wasn't sure if he was okay, but I was sure happy to see him go.

James put his hands on the ground. It looked as though he were feeling around for something. All of a sudden tracks lit up in the yard—they had to be mine and Drunk Guy's footprints. I could see where I'd dug my feet in the grass in an attempt to escape. The area near the forest, where they'd struggled, lit up with the same bluish light. After a second, the light seemed to get brighter, then it went out.

A still-glowing James got up and made his way over to the pool. He put his hands on top of the water, and then all at once the pool flashed with a bright light. The light faded, just as the glow around James receded. He walked down to the edge of the driveway and looked around, then bent over something.

My phone buzzed in my pocket.

All clear, he wrote. *See you tomorrow?*

I blinked at my phone. *Sure,* I texted back. And then, because I couldn't possibly think of anything else I could do besides go crazy, I went to bed.

20

AS IF

THE NEXT DAY dawned bright and sunny. Puffy white clouds dotted the sky, and the green grass swayed in the breeze.

Becky's lawn looked as though nothing unusual had happened on it recently. But for the second night in a row, there'd been a disturbance in the yard. A weird one. And for the second night in a row, James had come down to protect me.

I peered out the window, clutching my coffee. I could see Edgar—at least, I still thought it was Edgar—perched in a nearby tree. I had the strange sensation that he was keeping watch, but that was crazy.

There was a lot of crazy going around.

James had sent me a text first thing that morning. *Want to go wake-boarding?*

Sounds fun, I texted back, as if this were in fact a normal day and we were in fact normal people. I wanted to ask if he would be glowing during our outing, or rescuing me from anything, but I decided it was best to save these questions for later when I could look him in the eye. I had zero idea what his explanation was going to be. I half-hoped he'd tell me that I was nuts, that none of what I'd witnessed ever happened.

Amelia slunk into the living room in her sweats and scowled at me.

"Hey, Amelia."

She laid down on the couch, not looking at me.

"What's the matter?"

Amelia promptly started scrolling through her phone. "Mom's making me do extra sailing lessons." She looked up briefly, just long enough to give me an accusatory look. "She doesn't want me with time on my hands, hanging around the house."

I smiled. "She probably just wants you to enjoy your summer."

"She probably doesn't want me around *you*." Amelia frowned at her phone as if it had somehow wronged her. "Maybe if you weren't so busy ho'ing around, I wouldn't have to be in sailing-lesson hell."

"I-I'm sorry?"

Amelia snorted. "No you're not. I saw you yesterday

at the pool with James. You're, like, *such* a wannabe. A guy like that's never gonna actually date you. He's just going to bone you and toss you aside. But you were holding his hand in broad daylight like you're his girl-friend—when we all know you're a skank. Everybody was laughing at you and all you did was smile. You're such a fucking idiot."

I took a step back—I felt like she'd slapped me. "Amelia. You're fourteen. You shouldn't be talking like that."

"Shut *up*." She glared at me. "This is my freaking house. Do not tell me what to do in *my freaking house*."

Becky suddenly appeared from around the corner. "What's going on in here?"

"Taylor told me to shut up." Amelia's lower lip quivered.

Becky whirled on me. "Taylor?"

"Um… That's not exactly what happened." I opened my mouth to say more but the doorbell rang.

Becky narrowed her eyes at me. "You are *not* saved by the bell. Hold on a minute."

James stood at the door, wearing board shorts, a tight-fitting tank top, a sweatshirt tied around his waist, and a dazzling smile. He held out a bouquet of wild roses to Becky. "Good morning, Mrs. Hale. These are for you, fresh from the side of my driveway."

"James, thank you." Becky's tone was a one-eighty; she was as nice as organic Whole Foods pie. "Come on in." She turned back to us and smiled—a cue. I would not be punished in front of James.

Even Amelia had put her phone down and was on the verge of looking pleasant. These people! For some reason, their two-facedness bothered me more than the verbal whupping I'd been getting.

"So," Becky said. "What are you two up to today?"

James went and stood next to me. He didn't have to say a word; I could tell from his expression that their politeness wasn't fooling him. "Well, I wanted to know if it was okay if Taylor came out in my boat today. I'm taking some friends wake-boarding and I thought she could try it."

Becky beamed at him. "Sounds great." She probably hoped I'd break my neck and drown.

"You have the night off, don't you Taylor?" he asked me.

"Yes."

"Would you like to go to dinner with me?"

I nodded as Becky and Amelia stared. "That'd be great." *Get me the hell out of here and never bring me back.*

James turned back to Becky. "She's working so much, I thought it would be fun to take her to Bebe's. Have you guys been?"

"We just went two nights ago—it was excellent. Definitely make a reservation."

"Will do." James flashed them both a megawatt smile. "I think we're going to stop by the co-op to check in with Mr. Hale, too. I haven't met him yet. I want to make sure he's okay with me taking Taylor off-island tonight." He cocked his head at me. "Is there anything you want to talk to your dad about?"

Amelia stiffened, which made me smile. "I'll have to see if anything comes to mind."

I would never rat her out because it would hurt my dad, but I'd love to make her a little paranoid. Maybe next time, she'd keep her foul mouth shut.

"We should get going—Josie's waiting down at the boathouse. Mrs. Hale, Gina wanted the number of my architect. Want me to text it to you?" He whipped out his phone, they exchanged numbers, and James pressed *send*. "Also, I asked my dad about the Friends of the Island benefit. He said he'd be honored to host it at the Tower."

Becky's eyes shone. "Really?"

"Yeah, he said it's a great cause. Just let me know the date—I'll make sure we have enough staff to help out."

Becky gushed so hard at James for a full minute that I had to tune her out. "Taylor," she asked, breaking my reverie, "don't you need clothes for tonight?"

I had on James's T-shirt, a pair of jean shorts and a bikini. "Probably. Is it okay if I come home later to change?"

"Um, you live here," Becky reminded me. "Of *course* it's okay."

"O-Okay." Her shift in tone toward me was so abrupt, it almost knocked me off balance. I accepted James hand as he led me out. "Thanks guys. See you later."

"Bye!" Becky called brightly. Of all the fakers, Becky was the fakiest. *Of* course *it's okay.* As if.

21

SHOCK AND AWE

"So." James pulled the truck down by the co-op and parked it. "What the heck was going on in there?"

"Amelia is upset with me, I guess."

He turned the truck off, waiting for me to go on.

"She thinks her mother's putting her in more sailing lessons because I'm a bad influence."

James blinked. *"You're* the bad influence? If you could see Amelia's aura, you'd know who was the troublema—"

"James." I took a deep breath. "Amelia's hardly the issue we need to be discussing. What… What happened last night? What was that? I feel like I'm going crazy."

"You're not." He gripped the steering wheel and stared out into the field. "But… Can we baby-step this?"

I raised my eyebrows. "Huh?"

"I mean, can we just have a normal day?" He gave me a hopeful look. "If I promise to tell you more later, over dinner tonight, can we just hang out with our friends today and have fun?"

The offer was appealing, but I wouldn't be able to function until dinner unless I knew something, anything. "I need something—one thing to hold me over. I can't get last night out of my head." I put my hands on my face, as if it could block out the mental image of Drunk Guy seizing in front of me.

"Okay, okay."

I peeked at him from between my fingers. "Can you tell me what that light was? Where it came from?"

"Me." He scratched at his collar bone. "It's mine."

"More than that—I need more than that." I dropped my hands into my lap. "What does it do?"

He sighed. "Sometimes I use it to clean things."

"What?" But I wanted to laugh: all I could picture was the feather duster from *Beauty and the Beast*, a magic cleaning aid.

"You were in the house watching me, right?" he asked. "Remember when I used my light on the tracks in the yard, and on the pool?"

"Yeah."

"I was cleaning them."

The image of the animated feather duster dissipated,

and all I was left with was the crazy. I turned and stared at him. "You were cleaning Becky's pool with your magic light."

James sighed. "You know when the pool people come over, and they shock your pool?"

"Not everyone has a pool," I reminded him.

"Fine. But the cleaning companies do what's called 'shocking' the pool—it eliminates the algae and bacteria."

"So you shocked Becky's pool with your magic light to clean the algae out of it in the middle of the night? After you fought Drunk Guy and almost killed him?"

"I didn't almost kill him." James's knuckles whitened around the steering wheel. "But if he'd hurt you..."

"What was wrong with him?" I asked.

James shook his head. "I'm not sure."

"Tell me more about the cleaning. Or the shocking. Or the whatever."

The muscle in James's jaw went taut. "I told you that sometimes I get feelings about things, and about the auras... Sometimes, a person or a place give me a bad feeling and they can give off an aura. So after Adam did that last night—"

"Wait—who's Adam?"

"The guy who attacked you," James said patiently. "He left his mark all over the yard and the pool, like an aura. I wanted to erase it. I don't want anything like that, like *him*, close to you ever again."

I sighed. "I still don't understand."

James stared straight ahead. "I don't expect you to. It's complicated. It's a lot."

"Okay…" I didn't have to read auras to tell James was really uncomfortable. "So you don't want to talk more about this until tonight?"

"We've kind of been through a lot in a short period of time." He glanced at me. "Maybe some normalcy would be a nice change of pace."

"I can't argue with that." I leaned back against the seat. "But I do have two requests."

"I'm all ears."

"First of all, you never told me what that means." I nodded toward the tattoo on his shoulder. Now that I was face-to-face with his bicep, I wanted to know more about the unusual symbol. "Second of all, I forgot I asked Eden to go to the beach with me today. Can we invite her out on the boat?"

"Patrick already did—she'll be at the boathouse when we get there." He smiled. "And about this…" He traced the dark outline of his tattoo with his finger. The circle held four equal sections, divided around a cross. "It's a Native American symbol for balance. The four quadrants represent the four seasons and the four elements."

"So what's the cross mean?"

"I don't think it's a cross in the religious sense," he said softly. "It's more of an intersection."

"Okay..." I looked at the heavy lines of the tattoo, so dark against his pale skin. "So what does it mean to you? Why'd you get it?"

"It represents balance, and the intersection of that balance. That's important to me."

I stared at the tattoo, my gaze trailing to his handsome face. I should think that James was a poser, a faker. I *should* think he was crazy or feeding me lines about shocking the pool and his earnestness about his Native-American balance tattoo, or both. Instead, I believed him.

I shook my head. "I don't even know what to say to you."

He smiled. "You missed me?"

I sighed. "I did miss you." There was nothing I could do about the truth.

We sat in the truck, the sun warming our faces. The air between us became heavy, a weighted blanket of feelings. James turned toward me, tucking my hair behind my ear. He leaned closer. Our faces were inches apart. I stared at his eyes, that steel-gray blue, and the hard line of his jaw.

Right past him, through the driver's side window, Drunk Guy—Adam—ambled down the drive.

"Oh!" I pulled back. "He's okay!"

James looked at him. "Ah, there he is, the douchelord himself. C'mon—I want to check something." We both hopped out of the truck. Drunk Guy took a stagger step back when he saw James.

"Hey Adam," James said.

Adam gave him an uneasy smile. "Hey, Protector of the Deck."

James motioned toward the town dock. "You taking the mail boat off?"

"Yeah." Adam scrubbed a hand over his messy, thick curls. "I'm heading home."

"You're leaving already?"

Adam nodded. "It turns out that island life's not for me. My buddies are going to stay for a couple of days, but I need to get back to the city."

"Okay man. Take care." James nodded to him, then held his hand out for me. As I took it, Adam gave me a quick once-over, but he didn't say anything.

I searched his face for evidence of what had happened last night, but he appeared fine, if a little tired. "Hey."

"Hey." His voice was neutral, and he looked at me as if he'd never seen me before. "See ya. Take care, guys."

We watched him start down the pier and I turned to James. "He didn't recognize me."

James smiled and squeezed my hand. "Good."

"Did you shock him, too?"

"Something like that."

"So he doesn't remember anything about last night?" I asked.

James shrugged. "Doesn't seem like it."

We watched as he sauntered down the pier, holding his bag over his shoulder. "Is he going to be okay?"

"I think so. It's Adam's lucky day, I guess."

"How'd you find out his name?"

"I did a little research." James shrugged a big shoulder. "Hey, are you okay to duck in and see your dad? I haven't met him yet. I feel bad stealing you away again when he doesn't even know who I am."

"Sure." But as we held hands and headed for the co-op, my stomach tightened.

"What's the matter, Taylor?"

I didn't have to ask how he knew. I stopped walking. "My dad's the one who told me about Becky. That she's worried I'm being a bad influence on Amelia."

"Because you're spending time with me?" he asked.

"Because she thinks we're sleeping together," I blurted out.

"I see." James didn't let go of my hand. "What does your dad think?"

"He doesn't think anything."

"Okay." James tugged me closer and leaned down. "Well, *I* think that Becky shouldn't talk like that about you, and she shouldn't make your dad the bad guy."

I nodded. "I agree."

"I'd like to meet him," James said. "But if you're not comfortable yet, I respect that."

"No, let's go. Since we're hanging out, I know he'd like me to introduce you. It's not like we're sneaking around."

James looked down at our hands, which were entwined in broad daylight at the most public spot on the island. "No, it's definitely not."

I straightened my shoulders as we headed down to the co-op. It was a long, one-room building filled with lobster tanks and scales. Below the office, submerged beneath the pier, were more holding tanks for the lobsters. Once the hauls were weighed in and tracked, they were divided into shipments. Then the crustaceans were put back into the tanks in the cold Maine ocean, where they would await their fate.

The bell chimed when I opened the door. "Hey Dad."

My dad worked alone, and at this early hour, the co-op was empty. Big Kyle wore a large, stained apron; he tapped something into the computer at the desk, a stubby pencil behind his ear. "Hey honey. What a nice surprise." When he looked up, he did a double-take.

"I wanted you to meet James."

James stepped forward and shook my dad's meat-paw of a hand. "It's nice to see you, Mr. Hale."

My dad scanned him from head to toe. "You too. I heard you're going wake-boarding?"

I shook my head. "Wow, news travels fast around here."

Kyle held up his cell phone. "I can't get away from this thing. Becky pings me all day long. I also hear the Friends of the Island benefit's going to be held at the Tower." He eyed James. "So you're all over my radar this morning."

James cleared his throat. "Hopefully that's okay with you."

"Well, that depends." My dad's smile wasn't his normal, friendly one. He was definitely sizing James up. "What are your plans with respect to my daughter?"

"Dad!" I wailed, embarrassed.

But James smiled. "I wanted to ask if it was okay if Taylor came wake-boarding with me and a few friends today, and also, if you're comfortable with me bringing her off-island for dinner."

Kyle eyed James. "You have a captain's license?"

"Yes, sir."

"And do you drive your boat responsibly?"

James nodded. "I do. I'm not a fan of people drinking and then driving their boats, either. It's so dangerous."

"But will there be alcohol on your boat today?" Kyle asked. "I've seen that cooler."

"Yes sir. My friends are twenty-one and they packed beer. But I won't touch any because I'm driving."

My dad looked at me. "Taylor?"

"I don't drink, Dad."

He nodded. "Well, I guess I can't argue with any of that. But James, will you make sure my daughter's safe out on that wakeboard? And please have her in by her curfew tonight."

"Dad, I'll be fine."

"I won't let anything bad happen to her, sir, and I'll have her in on time. You have my word," James said

He and my dad stared at each other for a beat.

"Then I guess I can say it was nice to meet you." It still wasn't my dad's best smile, but it was something. It was a start.

22

WAKE ME UP

"Whew." James actually waited until we were back in the truck to grab my hand again. "You're dad's intense."

"You think?" I glanced back at the co-op, where Kyle was waving to us from the door. "I always think of him as laid-back."

"Not when it comes to you." James squeezed my hand. "He loves you so much, Taylor. He'd do anything for you."

My cheeks heated. "I know."

James's boathouse was literally around the corner from the co-op; we made it in no time. I recognized Josie's jeep and Eden's truck, both parked out front. The sun shone above us as James took my hand again and we made our way down the dock to his boat. Eden, Patrick, Josie and Dylan were already on board. The music was turned up; their laughter and chatter floated up to us.

"Hey guys!" Dylan said once we joined them. "We're going to have so much fun." She air-kissed me and then both Patrick and Josie hugged me. I felt as if I'd passed some kind of test. James started the boat, his friends crowding around him, as Eden and I took the back couch.

"I'm so glad you're here," I said. "But I forgot your sandwich!"

She laughed. "It's okay. Did you see that cooler? They packed lobster rolls. Like I said, there are *perks* to being your friend."

I giggled then asked, "Are you on a date?"

Her eyes glittered with mischief. "Are you?"

"I'm pretty sure I am, yeah. James just met my dad."

"Wow." Eden looked impressed. "He survived Big Kyle *and* Becky? He might need a Medal of Honor."

"My dad's not bad."

"No, he's awesome—that's not what I meant. It's just that he looks like an NFL player. Any guy who dates you has to be pretty brave." She nodded toward James, who steered the boat into the harbor. "He seems pretty secure, though."

I laughed. "You think?"

Josie came back and offered us drinks. True to my

word, I had water while Eden and Dylan had spiked seltzers and Josie and Patrick had beers. We sat in a circle while James drove the boat past Spruce Island, heading out into open water.

Patrick smiled at me warmly. "So Taylor—I feel like I don't know that much about you."

"Maybe because James is obsessed with her and keeps her all to himself." Josie popped a grape into her mouth and offered some to the rest of us.

"Ha. I think it's more because there's not much to know. I'm here for the summer, and then I'm going to start MDI High."

"Do you guys move off-island in the fall?" Patrick asked.

"No. Becky, my stepmother, doesn't like living on the mainland. They go down to Florida for a couple of weeks each year, though. Her family has a place there." Or so I'd heard.

"Wow." Patrick looked impressed. "Not many people stay on Dawnhaven—my mom says she can't even handle June here because it's too cold."

"Yeah, but you're from L.A. Trust me, it's not that bad." Eden grabbed a grape. "We live here year round. All my aunts and uncles do, too."

"Yeah, but your family fishes." Patrick turned back to me. "Does your dad work at the co-op all year?"

"Yep. They stay open."

"I never thought about it. I can't imagine being here with snow on the ground, taking the mailboat to school." Patrick glanced at James. "But now I know why James is talking about staying after we go back at the end of the summer."

My heart skipped a beat. "Huh?"

"Shut *up*, Patrick." James gave him a dirty look.

"Oh boy." Patrick cleared his throat. "In other breaking news, maybe the ice and snow aren't *that* scary. I'm thinking about transferring to Bates."

Eden, who was a sophomore at neighboring Bowdoin, almost spit her seltzer out. "Really?"

He eyed her. "Don't go freaking out, Red. They have a better philosophy program than UCLA. It's just something I'm thinking about."

"Maybe you should be thinking about what you can actually *do* with a philosophy major instead of who has the best reputation," Eden offered.

Patrick laughed. "Spoken like a true finance major."

"What about you guys?" I asked Dylan and Josie. "What're your plans?"

"I have one year left in my program. I don't know what we're going to do after that." Dylan looked at Josie. "What do you think?"

Josie shrugged. "After living up here, I think Manhattan's a shit-hole. Can you get a job in Maine?"

Dylan stroked her long dark hair and looked out at the mountains. There was nothing but nature in sight. "Maybe. Is there any place to work around here as a biomedical engineer?"

"Portland," Eden said.

"Hmm." Dylan sounded optimistic. "Something to think about."

"Excuse me for a sec." I went up and joined James at the wheel. His cheeks were ruddy, and I wondered if it was from the wind or something else. "Everything okay?"

"Yep."

"Are you actually thinking about staying up here after summer's over?" I asked, careful to keep my voice low.

"Maybe." He watched the water.

"What's it depend on?"

His gaze flicked to me and then away again. He frowned. "On whether or not that makes me a stalker."

"You're not a stalker." Much to my surprise, I leaned up and kissed him on the cheek. His skin was smooth and cool beneath my lips. "I should be so lucky."

He turned and gave me a look that I physically felt, deep and low in my belly. "I'm the lucky one, Taylor."

THE EQUINOX PACT BOOK 1: AWAKENING

"Hey lovebirds," Josie called, "are we going to wakeboard or what?"

"Yeah." James's smile was so deep, his dimple peeked out. "Sure thing."

WAKEBOARDING WAS TREACHEROUS BUT FUN. Both Josie and Eden could do tricks; Dylan, Patrick and I shared a more "hanging on for our lives" kind of style. Josie went first. In her black bikini with her perfectly toned muscles, she made standing on the board look easy.

It wasn't. I fell three times before I was able to hold onto the rope, arms shaking, as James gently pulled me around the bay. I happily gave up my spot to Eden, who surprised me by being able to do tricks, like jump the board over the wake. "Woo hoo!" Patrick yelled.

Eden grinned at him and he grinned back.

"Looks like you're not the only one on the love boat," Dylan said.

I smiled painfully. "Ha. Yeah." Maybe I could get more awkward, but maybe not.

"C'mon, New Girl." Josie zipped up her sweatshirt and wrapped a towel around her. "Tell us what's going on."

"Um... James and I are going to dinner tonight."

"Ooh." Josie leaned forward. "Bebe's?"

"Yeah. Have you guys been there?" What I wanted to ask was, had James taken anyone else there?

"Yeah, we went a couple weeks ago. James said it seemed like the perfect place for a date. I guess he's finally got someone to take." Josie eyed me. "He's going all out for you. I guess he's even letting that Becky have her fundraiser down at the Tower?"

"That's what I heard."

"I bet she's sucking up to you," Josie said.

"Not really. I'm not exactly her favorite."

"Yeah, but she wants this gala bad—I heard Marybeth talking about it at the bar. All those rich ladies want to get down to the Tower and snoop. They need hobbies."

I raised my water to her. "I'll drink to that."

Eden climbed up the ladder, a huge smile on her face. "You guys, look—we've got company!" She pointed to the wake behind the boat, where three porpoises crested.

"Oh my god!" Dylan shrieked. "It's Flipper!"

The porpoises bobbed behind us, their snouts intermittently breaking the waves. I'd never seen one up close before; its smooth gray skin caught the sunlight and water sprayed from its blowhole before it went back beneath the water.

I glanced at James. He'd turned from the steering

wheel and was watching the porpoises, and us, and me, with a huge grin on his face. I grinned back at him. That's when I realized what had been bubbling inside my chest. It wasn't just hope.

It was love.

23

YOU

WE ENDED our day with plans to do it again, hopefully later that week. James dropped me off at home, vowing to be back in an hour. "Reservations are at six," he said. "Is that okay?"

"Of course." But suddenly I was worried about what I was going to wear. Maybe Eden would let me borrow her dress again...

There was an awkward pause—James looked at me and I looked at him. "O-Okay. See you in a little bit." I jumped out of the cab before I did anything dumb, like wait like an idiot for him to kiss me.

He grinned as he drove off, and I started counting the minutes until I'd see him again.

"There you are." My dad smiled at me when I went through the door. "Did you have fun?"

"It was great. We saw three porpoises!"

"That's awesome, honey."

The house seemed unusually quiet. "Where are Becky and Amelia?"

"Off-island getting pedicures," he said. "What time is James picking you back up?"

"Soon—our reservations are at six. I have to call Eden, I need to borrow a dress from her."

"I thought that might be an issue. Bebe's is kind of fancy, at least for MDI." He sheepishly handed me a bag. "I went over to Pine Harbor and got you something to wear. Becky and Amelia shop at this place all the time."

From the scented paper inside the bag, I pulled out a very pretty, and very proper, black dress. It was short but not too short, with cute ruffle detailing on the chest. It was a label I recognized, a brand so expensive I'd never even bothered to look at it. There was also a pair of gold sandals inside, size seven.

"Aw Dad." My eyes filled with tears. "I've literally never had a dress this nice before."

A dark look crossed his face. "That's a shame—and it's my fault."

"No, c'mon. I'm only saying: I love it. Thank you so much."

"You're welcome, honey." He gave me a quick hug

and kissed the top of my head. "Now go on and get dressed. You don't want to keep a guy waiting."

"Does this mean you like him?" I asked.

"I didn't say that. How old is he, by the way?"

"Twenty-one—only three years older than me. So if he was still a senior, I'd be a sophomore." I held my breath, waiting to see what, if anything, Big Kyle would say.

"That's still too old for you." Dad sighed. "But if you have to date somebody, I guess he doesn't seem *that* bad."

"Thanks, Dad." I gave him one last hug before I practically sailed into the shower. I washed my hair in record time, anxious to blow it dry and do my makeup before James arrived. Most of all, I couldn't wait to try my new dress on.

I blew dry my hair and brushed it so it fell over my shoulders. I had some color from being out on the boat, so I took it easy with my makeup. A little mascara, some eyeliner and some lip gloss and I was finished. I eagerly tried on the dress and shoes. The dress was amazing—it was cotton, but it had a certain weight to it that I guessed only money could buy. It fit so nice. I tried on the sandals and they were perfect. When I looked in the mirror, I almost didn't recognize myself.

I took a deep breath as a car pulled into the drive,

then rushed down the stairs. My heart sank as I saw Becky and Amelia getting out of their truck, but it lifted again as James parked behind them. He really was my protector—things felt safer with him around.

"Taylor honey, I'm speechless." My dad put his hand over his heart. "You look beautiful."

"I *love* the dress. It was so expensive, though!" I'd almost fainted when I saw the price tag.

"You deserve something nice. Don't even think about it." Dad opened the door and Amelia, Becky and James came in. James looked drop-dead gorgeous in a pair of dark jeans and a light gray button-down shirt. His hair was still a little wet around his ears and the back of his neck.

Becky was saying something about the gala, but she stopped in her tracks when she saw me. "That's a pretty dress, Taylor!" A brief look of suspicion snuck across her face—perhaps she was wondering if I'd stolen it— but as she was on her best behavior, she quashed it immediately.

I stood there, uncomfortable, as they all stared at me. I wasn't sure, but that might've been the first nice thing Becky had ever said to me. "Thanks."

James shook my dad's hand, then made a beeline for me. "You look beautiful."

"T-Thanks." Being the center of attention was not my thing. "We should get going, right?"

"Yeah."

"Where'd you get that dress, Taylor?" Amelia looked me up and down. "It looks like it's from Aqua."

"I got it for her," Dad said quickly. "Bebe's is kind of dressy, so."

Amelia's eyes almost bugged out. "*You* bought her that dress?"

"Have a good night, guys!" James flashed the dimple as we made our getaway. "I'll be sure to have Taylor back by curfew."

As he closed the door behind us, I heard Amelia's voice rise. "When have you ever bought *me* anything?"

"Honey, it's not like that…"

James shot me a quick look. "You okay?"

"I'll be better when we're out of here."

He threw the truck into drive. "Your wish is my command."

As we pulled down the driveway, I caught a glimpse of Edgar. From his perch, he watched us go, then flew back toward the woods.

THE SUN WAS HANGING low in the sky as we crossed Hart

Sound to Porpoise Harbor. Going to dinner on the *Norumbega* was fun. We waved at the passengers on the other boats, checked on the Osprey as we passed its nest, and saw a crowd having clambake down on Crescent Island's beach.

After parking at the restaurant's crowded dock, we tied up and then headed down the pier to the restaurant. James threw his arm around me and kissed the top of my head, giving me shivers. "I meant what I said—you look gorgeous."

"Thank you. You look great, of course."

He chuckled. "Of *course*."

"I'm really excited about tonight. You're going to answer all my questions, right?"

James sighed and pulled me closer. "If that's what you want."

I nodded, warm but with running chills from being against him. "That's what I want."

There was a well-dressed crowd waiting outside of Bebe's, but for once, I felt like I fit in okay. James checked in with the hostess and she brought us to our table right away. People definitely stared. Did everyone know who James was? They might've, or maybe like me, they were just entranced by the sight of all his handsomeness tucked into those dark jeans.

Bebe's was elegant, with big windows looking out on

the water and dark-red walls. Candles winked on all the tables. The hostess seated us at a secluded booth in the corner, which was perfect for the purposes of my interrogation. Our server brought us water, then menus. I stared at the list of appetizers and entrees feeling more than a little lost.

James reached for my hand. "There's tapas—lots of small plates. Do you want to share some stuff?"

"Sure." But I wrinkled my nose at the menu. What the heck was citrus ponzu or duck confit?

"Is there anything you hate?" James asked, as the server approached.

"Ketchup," I said quickly, "and maybe duck."

James laughed. "We won't have either, I promise." He ordered a bunch of things—lobster *moqueca*, spring rolls, seared yellowfin tuna, filet mignon and two non-alcoholic sangrias.

Then he got back to the very important business of holding my hand. "So Taylor."

"So James."

"You have questions."

"I do." I'd prepared a mental list. "I have a lot of them, actually. Are you up for this?"

He squeezed my hand. "I'm trying to be."

"Thank you." I stared at his handsome face. "I guess my first question is, did you send Edgar to my yard?"

He almost spit out his water. "I didn't see that one coming."

"Well?" I asked. "A big old crow's been out there for days. I can't be sure, but I think it's him."

"It's him." James was quiet for a moment. Then he said, "I didn't send him, exactly. But I thought it would be a good idea if someone was down there keeping an eye on you, and he's been going to Becky's ever since."

I'd vowed to stay calm no matter what, so I played with my spoon while I thought it through. "Are you saying that you have some kind of power over him?"

"Not at all." James shrugged. "I'm saying that he sensed that I was worried, so he went to watch over you."

"Do you have..." I didn't know how to phrase this. "Do you have a special way to communicate with him?"

He leaned forward. "It's not any different than how I communicate with you. You and I use words, sure. But it's more than that. If I felt something—if I was sad or worried—you'd pick up on it, right? Even though you can't read auras, you'd still know on some deeper level."

"Yeah. But... How did he know you were worried about *me*?"

"I don't know," James said. "I think he could just feel it."

The server brought our drinks and we each had a sip.

I'd never had sangria before—it was fruity, a little spicy, and delicious. "I guess what you're saying makes sense on some weird level. Animals are different than people. My grandfather had a dog who could tell he was sick before the rest of us knew. It's sort of like that, I guess? They have intuition or senses we don't have or don't know how to use."

"I think that's as good an explanation as any."

"So my next question—this is just housekeeping, by the way—Josie mentioned something. She said you had the restaurant closed yesterday. Is that true?"

He laughed, but it sounded more embarrassed than amused. "Can I ask *you* a question?"

I nodded.

"Remember when I asked you if I was being a stalker?"

I sighed. "You're not."

He squeezed my hand. "Would your answer change if I told you that I rented out the restaurant both Saturday night for my party and the next morning just so we could hang out?"

I opened my mouth and closed it. James's face fell.

"Don't do that," I said. "Don't look like that. I'm not saying you're a stalker, I'm saying I need a minute to process." Luckily, our server brought fresh bread and butter and the first round of appetizers. I wasn't sure what it was, but it smelled delicious.

The server bowed. "The lobster *moqueca*. Enjoy."

I tried a bite and moaned. "This is insane." James still didn't say anything, and I put my fork down. "The lobster's insane, not you. I don't think you're a stalker, okay? I'm flattered that you'd do something like that to spend time with me. I guess my bigger issue is that I kind of can't believe it."

"You can't believe that I did it?" He sounded confused.

"I can't believe that you did it for *me*." If we were going to be honest with each other, I had to do my part —no matter how painful. "Honestly, I'm not sure why you're making the effort. You could literally smile at any girl and they would want to be with you. All you have to do is flash the dimple."

He flashed the dimple. "Is that working?"

"Yes." I threw up my hands. "That's the whole point. You don't need to close the Portside or take me to a fancy restaurant to impress me—I'm already impressed."

"I'm not trying to impress you." James raised his steel-gray eyes to meet mine. "I'm trying to be with you."

I took a deep breath. I didn't want to think of Amelia's words, but they came back, icy and biting. *A guy like that's never gonna actually date you. He's just going to bone you and toss you aside... You're such a fucking idiot.*

"But why?" I pushed the plate of lobster away, losing my appetite. "Why me?"

"Because you're *you*." James reached for my hand. "Why do you like me?"

"Um, because you're perfect."

"I mean it, Taylor. Is it the dimple?"

"I am sort of obsessed with it," I admitted, "but that's not the only reason."

"Is it my boat?" he asked.

"I also love the boat, but that's not why I like you."

He gave me a long look. "My house? My money?"

I snatched my hand back. "No, of course not."

"So… You like me for me?"

I took a deep breath. "Yes."

"That's exactly why I like you," James said. "I have a feeling you don't see yourself the way I do."

"Maybe not." My cheeks heated. "But I know there's a lot of other girls out there, and plenty of them are from your world. I'm not."

"You are from my world." James tentatively reached for my hand again, then brought it to his lips and kissed it. "And I knew from the first time I saw you, the first time I talked to you, that you're special."

I stared at our entwined hands as he went on. "You

were direct with me in a way that a lot of people aren't. But that wasn't just what I appreciated—it was how you made me feel, from the first time we hung out. You have a good heart, Taylor. One of the best. You've been through so much, but you still have so much love to give. That's a rare gift."

I raised my gaze to meet his. "You can tell that from my aura?"

He shook his head. "I can tell because that's what my gut says, and my gut is never wrong. I'm always looking for signs that the world's getting better. You're a sign—a flashing, neon sign. The brightest I've ever met."

"Me?"

He kissed my hand again. "You."

24

THE MESSAGE

"IT SCARES ME," I admitted, still staring out our fingers laced together. "This scares me."

James ducked his head. "It scares me too."

"It's like, I don't know... Ever since I've been to the island, even with Becky, everything's just been going so good. Ever since I met you." My eyes filled with tears and I blinked them back. "I don't want to get used to things being this good."

"Why not?"

I stared at him. "Because then I have something to lose."

"Ah, I see." He kissed my hand again. "You're not going to lose me."

"That's not exactly something you can promise."

"But that's exactly what I'm promising you."

216

We stared at each other for a beat. The server came, bringing things, clearing things. James and I kept staring.

"You have more questions, I'm sure." James jutted his chin at me. "I'm waiting."

I blew out a deep breath. "What happened last night? What is your…light? Is that what you call it?"

"We can call it a light. I don't really have anybody that I can talk to about it, so I don't usually call it anything."

"Do your friends know?"

He nodded. "Only Josie's seen it, but they're aware." James speared a bite of spring roll onto his fork. "And I don't know what it is exactly. I only know what it can do—some of what it can do, I guess. It might be able to do things that I don't know about yet."

"How long have you had it?" I asked. "Were you born with it?"

"No, I wasn't born with it. But I've had it for a long time—a *very* long time."

When I gave him a look, he sighed. "How are you with crazy? Like, really crazy?"

"I'm here," I said. "I'm here with your aura-reading, premonition-having, crow-herding, light-wielding self. So I guess I'm pretty good with it."

We both laughed.

"Oh hey, wait—someone's coming." James frowned as a well-dressed woman in her forties came toward our table. She was Asian, attractive, with long dark hair and bright-pink lipstick. She wore a colorful print scarf wrapped around her neck several times and large sea-glass earrings. She smiled as she reached our table.

"Are you James Champlain?" she asked.

"Yes. And you are…?"

"Lilly Burke." She shook his hand. "It's a pleasure to meet you—you know my wife, Maeve Burke. She runs the psychic shop in Bar Harbor. She's been out to the Tower a couple of times."

"Oh yeah, I know Maeve. Weren't you guys at the solstice party?"

Lilly nodded. "But only for a minute. Our son called —he couldn't figure out how to turn off the stove when his pizza was done. So it was right back into the boat for us." She laughed.

James scanned the restaurant. "Is Maeve here with you tonight?"

"No, she's not—and that's the funny thing." Lilly smiled broadly. "She and our kids are home. No one wanted to go to dinner but me. I had the *strongest* feeling that I should be here, and now I know why." She turned to me. "Are you Taylor?"

I was momentarily taken aback. "Yes. Hi, it's nice to meet you."

But Lilly didn't take my hand when I held it out. "Can I sit next to you for a minute?" Before I could say yes, she slid into the booth next to me. "May I put my hands on your arm?" she asked.

"S-sure?" I looked at James, but he was watching Lilly intently. She put her hands on my bare arm and closed her eyes.

"Hmm." She opened her eyes after one second but didn't take her hands off me. Then she sat and stared at the table, appearing to be deep in thought.

"Is everything all right?" I asked.

"Oh yes." She smiled again. "I just have a message for you."

"W-what?"

She kept staring at the table, then she nodded her head as if she were agreeing with someone. Finally, she took her cool hands off mine, sat up straight, and looked me in the eye. "Someone's been trying to get in touch with you."

It was a good thing she was sitting on the outside of the booth—I would've fallen out. "I'm sorry?"

"No, *I'm* sorry. I should explain." She shook her head. "I'm a medium. I don't normally approach people like this, out of the blue, but she's been very persistent. She really needed to reach out to you."

I wanted to ask who 'she' was, but I was too scared.

"Lilly," James said, "I think you might need to explain some more."

"Oh, of course!" Lilly laughed. "I always forget that not everyone is used to this sort of thing. I'm married to a tarot-card reading psychic, my wife's married to me, a medium. We freak our kids' friends out all the time."

She smiled at me warmly. "I've been able to communicate to those who've passed since I was a little girl. They've always spoken to me or shown me signs. Sometimes I'll have people come into the studio and I can have a conversation with a loved one for them or send messages back and forth. And sometimes I'll receive communication from the other side without knowing the person they're trying to reach here. Usually I can't do anything about it."

"But tonight you could?" James's voice was gentle.

Lilly nodded. "Like I said, I had this overwhelming urge to come to Bebe's tonight. It was the same way with the solstice party—Maeve and I have three kids, we don't get out much. But I *really* wanted to go to that party! But then our kids called and we had to leave. I felt like I was missing more than just a good time."

She leaned closer. "Taylor, your mother has been reaching out to me."

"M-my mother's dead."

"Oh I know, honey!" Lilly's eyes were sympathetic. "She started contacting me about ten days ago. How long have you been here, on the island?"

I was shaking. "About that long."

"And has anything unusual happened since you've been here? Your mother indicated she tried to reach you."

I nodded. "I thought I saw her the other night after the party, out in my yard. But it was just a dream…"

"Oh, you poor thing." Lilly patted my hand. "It's okay, Taylor. Your mother is okay. Actually, she's great."

"She's *dead.*"

Lilly took both my hands. "True, but she's moved on. There isn't any suffering. There isn't any more pain."

I took a deep, shaky breath.

Lilly squeezed my hands—even if she'd never told me, I would've known she was a mom. "I know she had some trouble while she was still here. That's why she wanted me to tell you she's okay. She's so much better. She wants you to know that nothing hurts anymore, and that she's at peace."

Tears started streaming down my face.

"Oh boy, here we both go." Lilly released me so she

could wipe her face as her own eyes filled with tears. "She wanted you to understand that she knows you're here, and she can tell you're happy. She also said that there are two people around you that you can trust. She said they'll protect you no matter what. Do you know who that might be?"

I nodded automatically. My dad and James.

"Good." Lilly wiped her eyes. "She also wanted to say that she's sorry."

"She doesn't have to be sorry." I shook my head. "It wasn't her fault."

Lilly nodded. "She's a mom, though. Of course she feels that way—she had a lot of guilt, a lot of regret."

"She shouldn't. Tell her she shouldn't."

Lilly closed her eyes for a full minute. When she opened them, she smiled. "She's at peace now—she couldn't move on until she knew you were going to be okay no matter what's coming. She said she wanted you to know that she'll always love you, and that she's always with you in your heart."

"O-Okay." I was grateful we were in the corner booth, because I couldn't get the tears under control.

"Phew, that was a lot! I need a drink." Lilly abruptly hopped up, smiling again. "It was so nice to meet you guys."

"Give my best to Maeve," James said, "and please, come out to the house again sometime soon."

"Sounds great. Take care, Taylor."

Before I could thank her through my tears, Lilly disappeared into the restaurant.

We were quiet for a couple of minutes as I wiped my eyes and got my breathing under control. "I'm going to ask you a stupid question." James kept his voice low. "Are you okay?"

I sniffled. "I have no idea."

He eyed our half-empty plates. "Do you want to get out of here?"

I nodded. James protectively wrapped his arms around me and led me out of the dining room. He paid the bill on our way out and brought me to the boat. My tears had subsided, but I felt like I was in shock.

James maneuvered out into the harbor and started heading home. The light was fading. "I owe you an apology."

"What?" I asked. "Why?"

He watched me, his steel-gray eyes darkening along with the sky. "It's kind of a long story."

"I've got hours until curfew," I said, "and I don't think much more could freak me out tonight."

He kissed the top of my head as he steered the boat toward home. "We'll see about that."

25

WILD WORLD

WE DROVE in silence back to the boathouse. I tried to make sense of my strange encounter with Lilly, but really, what more was there to understand? She had a message from my dead mother.

My mother had tried to contact me the other night. She'd rung my doorbell. *Her ghost rang my doorbell?* I wasn't sure I believed in ghosts, exactly, but her spirit had certainly just spoken to me through Lilly. The craziness continued, but at some point, all my disbelief had gone out the window. James could read auras and had a blue light. My mother had just contacted me at dinner through a medium.

I looked out at the water, the mountains, and the islands. It was so beautiful it made my heart ache. Still, I felt like I was looking at the world with new eyes.

We tied up the *Norumbega* and went inside the boathouse. James pulled a beer out of the refrigerator for himself, a water for me.

"I've never seen you drink before," I said.

"Liquid courage." He had a sip. "Did Lilly upset you?"

"No—but I mean, I had a strong reaction to what she said. It definitely caught me off guard."

"Do you believe her?" he asked.

"I want to. I don't know how this stuff works, but she was pretty specific. I don't think that was some kind of trick—it's too random."

James nodded. "I know Maeve, her wife, a little bit. She's nice. She's come out to the Tower for some of our gatherings."

"What sort of gatherings?"

He shrugged. "Josie and Dylan like to have people over—sometimes we do yoga, other times it's group meditations and chanting. You can tell when you get a bunch of like-minded people together, I don't know, it's like everybody's happy. It's powerful. It raises the vibration. That's what Dylan says, anyway. I think she's right. You can feel it when it happens."

I remembered what Becky had said, that people gossiped James was running some sort of cult. "I heard some of the locals think that's sort of strange."

"Yeah, well." James put his feet up on the coffee table. "I guess it is, if you've never experienced it."

I smiled at him. "I'll come to a group chant sometime. I could use a vibration boost."

"Are you feeling any better?" he asked softly.

"I'm tired, but I feel more like myself. We should get back to our talk, shouldn't we?"

"I guess." James raised his beer to me. "There's no turning back now."

"Before Lilly came to the table, you were telling me something," I said. "You were telling me about your light, and how long you've had it."

"I'll tell you the story. Like you said, you can handle the crazy. But can we do something, first?"

"Sure." But I wasn't prepared for how fast he moved. In an instant, James was kneeling on the floor before me.

He took my hands and looked me in the eye. "I need to tell you a couple of things before I get into my story."

"O-Okay."

"First of all, I'm sorry about tonight. Lilly didn't mean any harm, and I'm glad you got the message from your mother. But in some ways, I feel responsible. That sort of thing happens around me. It happens a lot."

"Mediums interrupt your dinner dates?" I asked.

"Things happen. There are crows watching out for

you, there are ghosts in your yard and messages from the other side, there are crazy drunk guys swimming in your pool in the middle of the night. That's because of me."

"Why?"

He gripped my hands. "I'm connected to more than just the world you can see, the world right in front of us. And if you're around me, you're connected to more, too. I mean I think you are anyway, Taylor. But with me it's present all the time—that's the way my life is. And if you're with me, that's the way your life is, too. It has upsides and downsides."

"Go on."

His dark gaze searched mine. "Can I kiss you?"

I sat up straighter. "Sure, but... Why right this second?"

The muscle in his jaw jumped. "Because you might not want to after I tell you everything, and that'd be a big regret for me—if I never got to kiss you."

I took his face in my hands. "James Champlain, stop talking like that. I can tell you, one-hundred-percent, that I will want to kiss you no matter what you say. So here." I pressed my mouth against his.

I meant to only give him a quick peck, but our lips lingered against each other. I shivered, fire and ice zipping down my spine. I released him before it got out of control. "Go on." I shooed him over toward his seat. "We can really kiss after you talk."

He winced. "But you might not want to stay."

"Aren't we making all the big promises tonight?" I asked. "I *promise you*, on my life, that I'll stay. I'll stay and I'll kiss you."

He relaxed and smiled for a second, the tension leaving his big body. But by the time he sat down and faced me again, his brow was furrowed. He checked his watch. "Here goes nothing."

I sat back, waiting for him to go on.

"When I told you I've had the power for a long time, that's the truth." James grabbed his beer and put his feet back up on the coffee table. "And it's also the truth that I wasn't born with it. I was alive—existing—for a long time before I got my light. I'm older than I told you. I haven't been completely honest because it wouldn't have made sense to you, and it would've freaked you out."

I made sure to keep breathing. "How old are you?"

"Let's just say that there's more than a three-year age gap between us. But I think this is one area that we definitely need to baby-step. Would it satisfy you if I told you that I was much, much older than you?"

"You don't look any older than twenty-one."

He nodded. "That's because I stopped aging then— actually, at seventeen. But I look a little older than seventeen because I've lived a hard life, some of these years. It took a toll on my physical appearance."

"So if I was a sophomore, you'd be a…what? A senior in college?"

He shook his head. "Let's not do the math. Trust me, okay?"

I gripped my water. "Just go on. Tell me everything—tell it to me all at once."

"Okay." James blew out a deep breath. "Before I got my light, I was something else. I lived a different sort of life than the one I lead now. It's not something I'm proud of… I did a lot of things I'm not proud of. But I know now that there was a reason for all of it.

"My family is like me. Actually, I *was* like them, but now I've changed into something else."

"James?" I interrupted. "You need to start using your words. Nothing that you just said means anything—just be straight up with me. Josie and Dylan know, right? They know what you are?"

He nodded.

"Then tell me just like you told them."

"Josie's the one who told Dylan." He blew out a deep breath. "And I *had* to tell Josie, because I was rescuing her."

"From what?"

"From dying." James gave me a long look. "One of my kind attacked her, and I had to save her."

One of my kind. I clutched my water.

James drank some beer, then continued. "My family is supernatural. That's why we have so much money and so many properties. My father understands business, but he's had the advantage of watching the world economy develop over…a very long time. So his investments have been able to grow an incredible amount. He started his own business and it's been successful, to say the least. Nelson Champlain is a name that people recognize and rely on, but the joke's on them—they think my father's the third in a generation of investors, but he's the first. He's the only."

"He's lived for how long, exactly?" For some reason, asking specifically about his father made it easier to talk about.

"Hundreds of years."

My head pounded. "But how do you hide it from people? Your father's famous. I mean, I'd never heard of him, but people who watch the stock market know who he is. How does that work?"

"We have an excellent lawyer," James said. "He understands our needs because he's part of our community. Over the years, they've faked my father's death several times. His children have always been hidden from the public eye. If you look online, there's only a few pictures of our family, including my father. He operates his business remotely, only doing video or telephone conferencing. Before we had all this technology, he used to say that he had a health condition that prevented him from attending big meetings, so he always sent a proxy, someone loyal to our family.

"We've learned to operate covertly, hiding our true identities. That's why we have houses all over the world and haven't been back to Dawnhaven for so many years. We choose places that are either remote or have a seasonal population so it's easy to remain undetected. We cycle through the properties, waiting until the people we knew from each community die out. Because we don't age. My father doesn't age—he looks exactly the same as when he was here last, two decades ago. But I've never been here during the summer season, so the island was one of my choices this year. We have everything planned out, who lives where and when, with some variables thrown in for personal preference. We really have it down to a science."

"So when your father lived here before… You were alive? But no one knew you were alive?"

He nodded. "That's right. My father's a master at deception and planning. I was probably living at our estate in New Zealand while he was here, pretending to be someone else. I don't remember specifically—it all blends together."

"So why are you here now? Why are you letting people know that you're a Champlain?"

"I told you that I have feelings, strong ones—premonitions." James shrugged. "I had a wicked premonition that I should come to Dawnhaven this summer. And now I know why." His gaze tracked to my face. "I've been looking for you for a long time, Taylor."

I swallowed hard.

"But now I've scared you."

"I—I'm not scared. It's more that I'm nervous." I licked my lips. "But I need to know: what are you?"

"In my first life, I was a vampire." He drained his beer. "And now... Now I'm something else."

26

EXTRA

I DIDN'T MOVE. I couldn't speak.

"Damn," James said. "I should've kissed you when I had the chance."

I shook my head. "It's o-okay. Just go on. *Please.*"

He looked out at the water. The sky was dark now, the sun sunk below the horizon. "Not all the stories about us are true. I was born a vampire—that's what I am biologically—I wasn't turned. Both of my parents were born that way, too. Biological vampires *do* age, and for the first years of our lives our growth tracks that of humans. But once we hit puberty and grow into our adult bodies, the aging process continues only incrementally. For a year to show on our face, we have to live twenty. Or in my case, some hard living can age us, but only slightly.

"In order to protect us, my parents sequestered us when we were younger. My brother was always a little wild. But I was a good child, and then when I was older, a good student. I followed the strict rules of our kind. We prize secrecy above everything else. For years I never left my family's remote compound, and I only drank donated blood. But once I was of age, my parents sent me off to live on my own and to see the world. That's also part of our upbringing, our initiation. It's tradition.

"Much like a teenager sent off to college, I indulged myself when I was on my own—except that my indulgences had real consequences. I hurt people. I was reckless with my powers. With all of our wealth and anonymity, I abused my position for a long time."

"I can't picture you like that," I said. "You're *good*. I can see it in your eyes—you're a good person."

James stared out at the water, his expression dark. "I wasn't always like this."

"That makes you human, not a monster," I said softly.

He took a deep breath. "I *did* always try to drink from people who allowed it. But like with so many things, some people want you to prey on them because they're hurting inside. So when you hurt them on the outside, it matches. It's an ugly cycle, and I'm ashamed to admit that I was a part of that."

"People knew what you were?"

"Some," James said. "There are some who seek us out. They're secret keepers. But most people don't know that vampires exist, and the survival of our species depends on it. Our interaction with humans is a delicate balance. That was part of what I learned during my time abroad.

"I met other vampires, all from a variety of backgrounds. Everyone chose their own path—some chased humans for sport, some were in monogamous relationships with a human. Some of them had chosen to altogether forgo drinking direct from the source. These vampires had formed business relationships with medical companies who supplied them with donated blood. My family had a similar arrangement, but it was with a private provider a company my father had set up himself.

"I tried living like that again for a while, surviving strictly from donations. But I couldn't stop thinking about drinking directly from humans. It's addictive. It's pleasurable in a way that nothing else is for our kind."

In a remote corner of my brain, it occurred to me that maybe I should be afraid of him. But I didn't feel that way. I sat there, waiting for him to go on.

James continued, "So even though I lived 'clean' for years, I went back to it. I couldn't help myself. But this time was different, because I knew better. I *knew* I had a choice, and that I was making the wrong one. I started to hate myself. I started to punish myself, but I couldn't stop the addiction, and I couldn't stop the pain. It was this endless cycle of feeding on people and then hating myself for it afterward—it was hell on earth. And then because I was in agony, and wanted to punish myself, I started making even more terrible choices." He turned to look at me. "So after living like that for a few years, I prayed to God to die."

My heart broke for him. I couldn't imagine James in such a dark place. "*Can* vampires die?" The word tasted funny, acrid, on my lips.

He nodded. "There are only two ways. Starvation, which takes a hundred years, or a stake through the heart. That's the one thing popular culture got right. But most of the other things aren't true. We can come out in the day, we can go into homes without being invited, and we most certainly do not turn into bats."

James got up and grabbed another beer.

I watched him open his IPA, trying to make sense of it all. "But wait—vampires can eat and drink regular food?"

He nodded. "Not all of us do, but we *can*. It's encouraged, so that we fit in. But it doesn't sustain us. Only blood does that."

"But if a vampire didn't have blood, it could still live

for a hundred years before it starved to death." I couldn't wrap my brain around it, but I wanted to make sure I had the facts straight.

"Right. So as I didn't feel as though starving myself for one hundred years was my best option to end my miserable existence, I started looking for someone to stake me. I found a professor in Eastern Europe who'd studied folklore, legends, and my kind. And then I set about terrorizing him. I'm not going to go into details— you'd never look at me the same again. But I was desperate. That's my only defense. Desperation will drive you to crazy things.

"I made sure the professor knew who—*what*—was chasing him. I gave him time to mount a defense. And one night when the moon was full, just for added ambience, I attacked him in his home. I only bit him a little. It was feeble on my part; I could've taken him in a heartbeat. Instead, I let him overpower me with silver— which does nothing to our kind, but he didn't know that. Once he thought he had me under control, he staked me. I thought my prayers had finally been answered."

"And then?"

James blinked at me. "And then I didn't die."

"So…" There was so much to process, I didn't know where to begin. "What does that mean?"

He shook his head. "I'm not sure, but it was the beginning of something new."

"Are you sure this professor actually got your heart?" I asked.

"Ha. Yeah, I'm sure. At first, we both thought I was dead. I was immobile. The professor was curious—he kept my body to study me. So instead of abandoning me somewhere, he moved me to his lab. You know those stories about vampire hunters—the ones where they have all this gear, and they make slaying vampires their life's work?"

"I guess so."

James nodded. "Those are based on this guy. He went bonkers with me—testing my skin samples, examining my teeth, taking blood from me. It was kind of wild. I had to keep an eye on him for years after I left, just to make sure no one actually believed that he'd encountered a vampire."

"But what *happened*? He staked you, he's got you in his lab and he's performing experiments on you... But you weren't dead? You knew what was happening?"

"Like I said, I was immobile at first. I *thought* I was dead, but I was still feeling things, still having thoughts. I figured maybe I was experiencing the next circle of hell by being trapped inside my body while the professor made a voodoo doll out of me. But after three days, I could move again. I wiggled my hands and my feet, and the rest of my body's sensations returned after that. But one thing was different—I felt no hunger. I wasn't sure what that meant…

"Luckily, the professor couldn't stay with me all the time. I planned my escape. Back on the streets, I was lost. The wound in my chest healed perfectly; it was as though nothing had ever happened. I wondered what the whole thing meant. I'd wanted to die so badly. At first, I believed it was God's punishment for all the wrong I'd done. Because I hadn't died, did that mean I was even more damned than before?

"I roamed the streets day and night, pondering what had happened. But then one day I felt the sun shining on my face, and…I don't know…I guess I sort of started to wonder if I was still here for a reason. Like maybe there was a purpose for me. Something more." James shrugged. "I hadn't ever considered the reason for my existence before, but I started looking for signs to guide me toward whatever it was.

"My parents, my father in particular, was in awe of what had happened to me. He's lived a long time—he's one of the oldest vampires in existence. He'd never heard of one of our kind surviving a staking before. He believed, as I do, that there's a reason I'm not dead."

"So?" I was ready to jump out of my skin. "What's the reason?"

Finally, James smiled—*my* smile, the one I'd come to know and love. "It's kind of hard to explain. I should probably just show you. C'mon. There's too many people down here to use my light, but the Tower's safe." He stood and motioned for me to follow him back to the truck.

It was full dark now; we drove slowly past Becky's house. All the lights were on. I still had some time before my curfew, time to hear more of this strange tale. I didn't know how I felt about what James had told me— I'd save sorting through my feelings for later. For now, I needed to get as much information as possible.

"What happened after that—after you woke back up and went back to society?" I asked. "Did you start craving blood again?"

"No, never." James shook his head. "I've only eaten regular food since that time, but I don't know if I actually need to. But I like it, so I do it."

"Do you *ever* crave blood? Like, the way a vegetarian might occasionally crave meat, even if they'd never eat it again?"

"No. Actually, there's only been one time since I was staked that I smelled blood and it appealed to me."

"When was that?"

"When you got into my truck with all those scrapes from the rose bushes." He glanced at me. "It was weird. You smelled *yummy.*"

I swallowed hard. "Yummy as in, you wanted to suck my blood yummy?"

"Taylor." James went to reach for my hand but stopped himself. "You're safe with me. I haven't drank a drop of blood since that night with the professor."

"How long ago was that?" My voice was hoarse.

He blew out a deep breath as he turned down the Tower's drive. "A hundred and fifty years ago."

I felt dizzy. "Oh. Wow."

"I told you," James said, "baby steps."

We pulled down the long drive and parked. The house was dark. "Where is everybody?"

"They went to dinner at Patrick's. His family's up for the week." Patrick's mother owned the second-largest home on Dawnhaven, a mansion overlooking the ocean on the opposite side of the island. "So we have the place all to ourselves."

My stomach flipped, and James winced. He leaned back against the seat of the truck. "I don't mean to scare you, Taylor. I'm so sorry."

"I'm not scared." I looked above my head. "What does my aura say?"

"It says you didn't expect to be dating a former vampire."

I tentatively reached for his hand. "I'm not afraid of you." It was the truth, the crazy truth.

"But you *were* worried, all of a minute ago, that I wanted to drink your blood."

I shrugged. "Can I get a pass for that? 'Cause I'm pretty sure I handled it pretty well, all things considered."

He laughed. "Yeah, you did."

I should be terrified, in shock, something. But instead I felt strangely calm—the way I felt once I'd learned my mother was dead. I thought I'd be hysterical, but I hadn't reacted that way. I'd known it was coming. Once the news finally arrived, it was like I could stop holding my breath, waiting for the sky to fall.

And now the sky had fallen again.

But James was still sitting next to me. I moved closer to him. "I owe you something."

"What's that?"

I put my hand on his face and gently stroked his cool skin. "You don't remember?"

His gaze burned into mine. "Oh, I remember."

The look he gave me—*oof.* There was so much hope, so much longing on his face. I felt as winded as when he'd knocked me and Drunk Guy off balance.

THE EQUINOX PACT BOOK 1: AWAKENING

"I just didn't want to hope…" James shrugged. "Because then, you know. I'd have something to lose."

I brought my face closer to his. I could feel his breath on my cheek. The cab of the truck was suddenly very, very hot.

I'd promised to kiss him, but I didn't know where to start. I kissed his cheek. Then I put my lips against his. He sighed and sank his hands deep into my hair. James pressed his mouth against mine gently, pulling me closer against his powerful chest. I leaned into the kiss, my lips exploring his full ones. I wrapped my arms around his neck, getting closer. Our tongues connected, and I felt a zip of electricity all the way to my core.

"Oh!" I pulled back.

To my horror, James laughed.

"Why are you laughing at me? Was it that terrible?"

"Taylor, *no*." He stopped immediately, his expression turning dead serious. "It was amazing. *You're amazing.* I was laughing because I could tell you felt what I was feeling—that spark. And I knew you were startled."

An image flashed in my mind: James putting his hands on the pool water and turning it an electric white-blue. "Was that… Did you just *shock* me?"

"No." He stroked my face, gazing deep into my eyes. "That was just us. That's what we feel like together."

"Is that normal?" I asked.

"You're asking me?" James smiled. "I have no idea."

"I'm sure you've kissed plenty of girls before."

"Not really." He shrugged. "But more importantly, I've never kissed you before. That was…incredible."

"It was." I wanted to go back and try some more, but we didn't have much time. "Are you going to show me your light?"

"Yeah. C'mon." James hopped out of the truck and I followed him out into the dark yard. "I'm going to walk toward the trees, but you stay there. I'll show you a couple of things, but none of it's dangerous. It might startle you, but you're safe—I promise. Okay?"

"Okay." I was shaking, anxious, excited and afraid to see what he could do.

Once he reached the edge of the forest, he said, "I realized a couple of things early on in my second life." All of a sudden, he was standing right in front of me.

"Ah!" I took a step back.

James gripped my hands. "I could move *fast*. Faster than even the vampires." He dropped my hands and reappeared back near the trees. "See?"

"Wow. Are you…" What was the word? "Teleporting?"

"Nah." But his voice came from behind me, in front of the house. "I'm running." He said this from back near the forest.

"That's crazy."

"I know." James stood in front of me again. "But it comes in handy, especially if I'm checking on my girl-friend in the middle of the night."

I smiled in the darkness, rather broadly. *My girlfriend.*

"And here's my light." James took a step back, then stood perfectly still. A bluish-white light appeared all around him, outlining him, then traveled through him in swirls. It was, of all things, pretty.

"I can use it to see in the dark." He ran back to the forest, touching a tree and lighting the giant fir all the way up. It blazed brighter than any Christmas tree.

"There are some fun things I can use it for, too." He appeared to toss a ball of light up into the sky, and it made a glowing, electric-white cloud above us. After a moment it popped, showering hundreds of glowing snowflakes all over the yard. One touched me, and it warmed my skin.

"That's amazing."

"Thank you." James stopped glowing and he walked toward me. "But I should get you home."

"No." I groaned. "I have more questions."

"I know." He laced his fingers through mine. His hand felt perfectly normal, no trace of any supernatural spark. "But if I haven't scared you off yet, I guess there's plenty of time to answer them."

"Do you promise?"

"Yes." He stopped walking and wrapped his arms around me. We stood in the middle of the lawn, the ocean whooshing against the sea wall, a thick blanket of stars stretching overhead. "We're making all the big promises tonight, remember?"

I leaned up and kissed him again, silently making another promise to him. I made it with my heart.

"Taylor." He said my name against my hair. "Thank you."

I held onto him for dear life.

27

COLD WATER

JAMES WAS HELPING Patrick's family move furniture from the mainland to the island, so we didn't have plans the next day. I felt oddly empty as I poured myself a coffee and stood in the quiet kitchen. My dad was at work. Becky had taken Amelia to sailing lessons, then was going off-island for yoga.

The house was too quiet. The hours before my shift stretched out before me, long and boring, a vivid contrast to my date the night before.

I'd lain awake in bed for hours going over every single thing that had happened. I still felt a little numb, probably in shock from everything I'd learned. Vampires were real. All the stories, all the books and television shows, were right. And although James was no longer technically *just* a vampire, he was a supernatural being.

He'd gone all Elsa from "Frozen" on me last night and made it snow electric-blue sparks. Not to mention the fact that I'd also gotten a message from my dead mother at dinner... The world was not what it seemed. There was more to it lurking below the surface, just out of sight.

It made my head hurt. I needed a brain break.

I checked my phone and was thrilled to see a text from Eden. *Six hours until work*, she wrote. *Wanna go hang by the pool?*

I immediately said yes, then rushed to get my things. Now that I knew vampires were real, the Haven Club and its well-dressed members seemed much less scary in comparison. As long as I had Eden and we could sit side-by-side in our loungers, we'd be fine. We could order burgers and those herbed French fries. *Yes*. I felt better already.

I smiled as I threw on my bathing suit and my nicest T-shirt, then brushed my teeth and put on a little mascara. I glimpsed my reflection in the mirror—I didn't *look* any different. But I was. I had a *boyfriend*. Who happened to be an ex-vampire.

Who I happened to be in love with.

Having never been in love before, I would've questioned the feeling—but it was overwhelming, crystal clear. I knew it from my gut: I was in love with James. I loved him fiercely, with my whole heart.

Still, there was a tiny voice inside my head, a trickle of unease, making me wish that maybe my feelings weren't so strong. It wasn't just about James's being supernatural, though that was certainly part of it. The ugly ear worm that Amelia had planted twisted inside me, wriggling its way into my thoughts. *A guy like that's never gonna actually date you.*

But he was. Not only was James dating me, he'd made me feel as though he had real feelings for me, serious ones. That was part of what was troubling me. Had he chosen me—to confide in, to date—because he thought I'd be…an easy mark? I was pretty much alone. My mom had died, and I didn't really have anybody but my dad, who was beholden to Becky.

This particular worry wasn't a huge stretch from my original discomfort. Even without his powers, James was from another world. He had more money than I could hope to earn in ten lifetimes, multiple gorgeous homes, and the economic freedom to do whatever he wanted, whenever he wanted. I was a nobody from a shitty neighborhood. When you looked at it that way, I had nothing to offer him. No equality could exist in our relationship. And now he'd shared that he was supernatural…

Everybody was laughing at you and all you did was smile.

Was I missing something? Had James chosen me for the wrong reasons?

Thank God the doorbell rang. I hustled from my room, eager to leave my thoughts and the memory of Amelia's ugly words behind.

"YOU DIDN'T TELL me the food was this good." Eden scrounged up her last fry and stared at it accusingly. "How have I lived on MDI my whole life and never eaten here before?"

I shook my head. "Your parents never wanted to join?"

"Oh please." She snorted. "My parents would never pay a membership fee for a pool when we live on an island. They'd tell us to pack a sandwich, go jump in the ocean, and be happy about it. They're not exactly fancy."

Eden peered over the top of her sunglasses at the other members lounging by the pool. "Who *are* these people, anyway? I feel like maybe I've waited on some of them at the restaurant, but I don't actually know any of them. Which is weird, because I know everybody."

I wrinkled my nose as I scanned the well-dressed, mostly senior crowd, with a couple of young mothers and their toddlers mixed in. "My dad said it's all people with old money who're members. I guess maybe they just keep to themselves."

Eden adjusted her bikini straps and settled into her lounger. "They've been holding out on us. Those fries were to die for."

"I know, right?" I dug a tube of sunscreen out of my bag. "Do you want some?"

"Nah, the sun's not strong. We're lucky it's even warm enough to sit out here."

"True." It never got hot on MDI, which was one of the things I loved about it. "So... How did you leave things with Patrick?"

She pulled her sunglasses down on her nose and looked at me. "You know that if I show you mine, you totally have to show me yours."

"Uh... Okay?"

"Fine." Eden put her sunglasses back up. "I like him. He's nice, he's handsome, he's smart. He comes from a good family."

"So what does that mean?"

She shrugged. "It means we're hanging out."

"What's going to happen with your boyfriend?'

"Brian? Ugh, I don't know. We've been dating for a whole year, and he's pretty serious. But I don't know if

I'm ready to be, which is why I wanted to see other people this summer."

Eden sighed. "Who wants to meet the guy they're going to marry this young? I mean, I want to go and live my life. I want some adventure. Brian was already talking about the future, like when we'd get a dog together and what city we'd live in after graduation and blah, blah, blah. I was like, slow your roll, dude. I'm twenty-one." She turned to face me. "Do you know what I mean?"

"Mm-hmm."

"No I mean *really.* Do you feel like that, or are you ready to settle down with Prince Charming?"

"I don't know. I can't exactly settle down when I'm a senior in high school." I took a deep breath. "But… Can I tell you something?"

Eden leaned in closer. "Hell yes."

"I really like him."

"No." Eden faked shock. "I couldn't tell!"

I giggled. "Stop it."

"I couldn't tell he really likes you, either." Eden motioned around the pool club. "He bought you a membership here, he bought *me* a membership here, he's taking you out on his boat, throwing parties and taking you to fancy dinners. You've both got it bad."

I sighed. "I hope so. I hope it's not just me."

"It's not. I can tell just by looking at him," Eden said. "He's serious about you."

I wished I could tell her everything, about Drunk Guy and my mother and the existence of vampires.

"He does seem serious. But…" Even if I didn't need it, I rubbed some sunscreen onto my arms for something to do. "I guess I don't know *why*. And I'm not looking for a compliment, I'm just trying to figure it out. James has everything. He could be with literally anybody—even an actress or a model. So I guess maybe part of me feels insecure about it, like I'm missing something. And Amelia said I was an idiot for thinking I'd ever be his girlfriend."

"Amelia's a total bitch. She's just jealous," Eden said quickly. "But I get what you're saying. It's hard to trust somebody who's that good-looking and that rich. You'd think he'd be a player, right?"

"Right. I mean, I don't *think* he is. But part of me wonders if I'm being naive."

"I think it's smart to look at the big picture like that —that's the opposite of being naive, if you ask me. You gotta consider all the angles. But I'm a pretty good judge of character, and I think he's genuinely into you. What does he say? Have you talked to him about it?"

"A little. And he said all the right things. He said he

likes me for the same reason I like him—because of who I am."

Eden grinned. "That's so cute."

My cheeks heated. "Why?"

"Because you guys are *adorable*. And just because I'm not ready to find the one and settle down doesn't mean I'm against true love. I'm all for it."

I fidgeted with my bikini straps. "I am too, but…"

"I'm sure it's scary. You've been through a lot." Eden nodded. "But go with your gut, Taylor. If your gut says this could work, trust it. Don't be afraid to let something good into your life."

"But what if it's too good to be true?"

"Remember those French fries? *Those* were too good to be true—and yet, they were." She grinned at me. "It's like my dad always says, seeing is believing. Just keep your eyes open, you'll be all right."

"Thanks. Hey, you want to jump into the pool?"

"I say we use that old water slide. That will give everyone something to talk about!"

Eden and I made our way to the opposite end of the pool where the ancient, enormous water slide loomed up above the water. Just like she predicted, everyone stared. We *were* the only ones under twenty-five, both of us in bikinis. "Do I have anything hanging out?" I nervously adjusted my top as we reached the narrow stairs.

"No, but you might after you go down this. So hang on." Eden eyed the top of the slide and started to climb. She waved from the top, grinning. Then she whooped as she flew down the slide and splashed into the pool.

I felt eyes on me as I swallowed hard and climbed up. I wondered if the toddlers ever attempted the stairs, which were painfully steep. I was a little dizzy when I got to the top. Eden treaded water in the pool, waiting. "C'mon, the water's not even freezing!" For northern Maine, that was about as much as I could hope for.

I held my nose, closed my eyes, and whooshed down the side. I came up spluttering. "You lied—it's *totally* freezing."

"Ha, I know. And way to hold your nose. That's what my mom does!" Eden swam for the side. "Maybe we should just dry off and order more fries."

I followed her and climbed up the ladder. "Sounds like a plan."

Heading for the safety and warmth of the club towels, I wrapped my arms around myself. But a familiar voice stopped me in my tracks. "Taylor?"

"Becky?" I turned around, shivering and dripping. "Hey."

She had her aviators on, a big straw bag over her

shoulder. Gina and Sylvie were behind her, setting up chairs.

Becky peered past me. "Is James here?"

"No, it's just me and Eden."

"Oh." But Becky looked confused. "So how did you get in?"

She didn't have to say it—I could tell she was wondering if I'd used her account. I shivered more violently. "I have a membership now. So does Eden. James got them for us."

"Wow." She forced a smile. "That was generous."

"Yeah, it was. I have to go get a towel, okay? The water's freezing."

She nodded. "You girls have fun."

I hustled back to our side of the pool and wrapped myself in two towels. Eden was similarly cocooned. She'd already put her sunglasses back on and had resumed her position on her lounger, even though she was covered in terrycloth from head to toe.

I climbed onto my chair, shivering. "Becky's here."

"Yay," Eden said sarcastically. "Becky's my favorite."

I sighed. "I don't think she likes having me in her territory."

"Tough. I heard she's having the Friend of the Island gala down at the Tower. There's no way James would have offered that if it weren't for you. She owes you big time."

I watched Becky as she set up her lounger. She carefully arranged her towel, then pulled off her cover-up, revealing her toned abs in a tasteful navy-blue bikini. Sylvie and Gina sat on either side, either gossiping or talking about window treatments. Or both.

I frowned. "We'll see."

Eden pulled her sunglasses down just far enough to give me a look. "You remember what I said—seeing is believing."

I nodded. "I'll keep an eye out."

She laughed. "With a stepmother like that, you need eyes in the back of your head."

"That's true." I laughed too. "So... Do you want to order more fries?"

My friend grinned at me. "Is the sky blue, Taylor Hale?"

SOFTENING

EDEN and I left the club soon after that. We needed to get ready for work, but also, I couldn't relax with Becky and her friends so close by. In sharp contrast to earlier that morning, I was relieved to find the house was empty and quiet.

I took a quick shower and threw on my uniform. Grabbing my apron, my pad and a pen, I left as soon as I could. The sun had climbed in the sky and felt warm on my face. Waitressing was hardly my favorite activity, but I was still glad to go to work. Being busy was the best thing for an anxious mind. Plus, it kept me out of the house.

Josie was setting up the bar when I punched in. "How was the club today?" she asked.

"Good, but the water's *freezing.*"

"I know, right? You think all those rich people could afford a water heater, but I think they're too set in their ways."

I stared folding napkins. "How was your day? Did you help move Patrick's stuff?"

"Yeah, his mother went a little crazy with the antique-ing." Josie smiled. "Poor James was a sad sack all day without you. We did three trips to Pine Harbor, but he was like a puppy dog. He kept looking over at Crowley Cove, hoping to catch a glimpse of you."

"No sir."

Josie stopped cleaning glasses. "*Yes* sir. Dylan and I were teasing him—we've never seen him like this. He's a basket case."

I bit my lip. "Really?"

Josie stared me down. "You really don't need to play dumb anymore. He told us that he told you—he's into you."

I nodded. "He did."

"So?" she asked. "Do you feel the same way?"

I sighed. "Of course I do."

"So why do you look like that—all traumatized? Oh." She narrowed her eyes at me. "He freaked you out with everything. He told me about that, too. It's kind of a big deal that he confided in you."

"I know—and that's not it, I swear." I shook my head.

"I've just never had a boyfriend before. I'm worried I'm doing it wrong."

"Trust me, you're not. And if it makes you feel any better, I've known James for a long time and he hasn't dated anybody since I met him. I've never seen him like this before. He's probably just as worried as you are—in fact, I know he is."

My heart lifted. "Really?"

She shook her head. "You say that a lot. Go on and fold your napkins. I'd never lie about my friend, okay? This is serious business."

"O-Okay." I went back to folding before I really got on Josie's bad side, and then she'd make me wait for my drinks all night.

"New Girl, come in here!" Elias called.

I went into the kitchen and he looked me up and down.

"You look good…something's different."

"I'm not covered in spilled drinks?" I jiggled some sugar packets. "I don't have that panicked expression in my eyes because I can't find the hot tea bags?"

"Maybe." He chuckled. "I heard you were at Bebe's last night, and back at the Haven Club today. You're making the rounds!"

"Ha." Everybody on the island always knew everything. "I guess so."

Elias eyed me. "Are you happy?"

I nodded. "Yeah. I like it here."

"Good. I'm rooting for you. Tell James to have another party, okay? I could get used to hanging out down at the Tower. I want to see another one of those sunsets."

"He's hosting the Friends of the Island gala soon—do you want to come to that?"

"Are you kidding me? That's *the* party of the summer. Can you get me a ticket?"

"Sure." I would ask James, not Becky. "I'd like to have my friends there."

"Thank you." He smiled. "Now go and get your station ready, and don't take any food without a ticket!"

The restaurant started to get busy. As usual, the bar filled up first with fishermen who'd finished for the day. I'd worked enough shifts so that I'd gotten used to the rhythm of the Portside. I was definitely more comfortable. The hostess sat one table in my station, then another. I took drink orders, followed by food orders, and I did not panic. I did not look at the drinks when I carried them on trays. I did not take food from the line without a ticket. I even served a Cosmopolitan without freaking out.

"Look at you! You're doing great," Eden said when she hustled past me. "You're not even in the weeds!"

I laughed, but it was true: for the first time since I'd started, I was on top of all my orders.

But then the hostess sat a new four-top in my section: Marybeth, her husband Donnie, Gina and her husband. My stomach dropped. Not only would they order Cosmopolitans, they'd scrutinize me for negative things they could report back to Becky.

"Hi guys." I mustered up a smile as I approached their table, pad in hand. "How are you tonight?"

To my surprise, Marybeth gave me a megawatt smile in return. "We're great, Taylor! This is my husband, Donnie. And you remember Gina, of course. This is her husband, Russell."

Everyone smiled pleasantly, as if they were...happy to see me?

"Did you have fun at the club today?" Gina tossed her thick dark waves over her shoulder. Her perfume rolled over me, making my eyes water.

"Yes." I smiled so hard my face hurt. "It's really nice there."

"They need to heat the water, though. I keep telling the board, but they won't listen. They're all about tradition." Gina's blazing white teeth flashed as she smiled. "But I'm glad some of the younger people are coming this summer. It makes it more fun!"

"Great. Thank you." I had no idea what to say. Did Becky agree with them, or were they going rogue?

"Oh, and Becky gave me James's message," Gina continued. "Will you please tell him I called the architect and he's *ah*-mazing? He's going to get started on our plans next week!"

Her husband winced and Gina elbowed him play-fully. "Aw, it's going to be okay. He promised it wouldn't be *that* expensive." But Gina winked at me. It was absolutely going to be that expensive.

"So Taylor, how do you like working here?" Marybeth asked.

I gaped at her. I'd met Marybeth seven or eight times over the years, and this was the first time she'd ever asked me a direct question.

"I like it a lot. The owner's really nice, and so's the kitchen staff."

She kept smiling. "Ah, that's nice. I'm glad you're happy. You deserve it."

"T-Thank you."

"So, can I order a Cosmopolitan?" Marybeth asked. "And can you ask Josie to use fresh lime juice? I don't like all the crap that's in the bottled stuff."

I took the rest of their drink orders. When I went to the computer, I noticed Becky and Sylvie sitting at the bar having wine.

"Hi." I smiled at them but kept my distance.

"Hey Taylor." Sylvie smiled at me, the cat inspecting a particularly juicy canary. "Nice to see you again."

It took a full second for Becky to follow her friend's lead and smile. "You're certainly making the rounds today, aren't you?"

"Um, yep." I was relieved to turn away and punch my order into the computer, but then I had to go and wait at the bar. "Where's Dad and Amelia?"

"They were having some one-on-one time." Becky's tone made me feel guilty, as if she were accusing me of something—like robbing her daughter of a father.

"Great." I smiled tightly, bracing myself, as Josie scowled at the computer.

"Fresh lime juice?" she grumbled.

"Yes, please." I prayed that she didn't complain further, and also, that she hurried up. I didn't want to stand at the bar two feet away from my step-monster and her silver-haired viper of a lady friend.

The restaurant door opened again, and James sauntered in, followed closely by Dylan. His face split into a grin when he saw me.

I grinned back.

"Earth to Taylor," Josie said. "We interrupt your voyage on the love boat to inform you that your drinks are ready. Get them out of here, I've got orders piling up."

"Okay." But I didn't stop smiling.

Becky and Sylvie noticed, of course. Their gazes traveled from me to James and back again.

I put the drinks on the tray and went back to Marybeth and Gina's table. I somehow didn't spill a drop of their cocktails. They kept chatting as I took their order, and even though I had a feeling I would pay for it later, I smiled and talked more than I usually did.

I felt disapproving eyes on me, but I ignored the sensation. I wasn't doing anything wrong. Becky's friends were being nice to me, but that wasn't my fault. And just because my dad had bought me a dress and James had invited me to join his club—that didn't make me a bad person.

Another four-top was seated in my section, making it full, and I literally couldn't worry about Becky anymore. I had to focus on my tables.

When I went back for my next round of drinks, James and Dylan had taken the corner seats at the bar and Becky's scowl was long-gone. She and Sylvie were talking with them about the gala. "We're fully insured, of course," Becky said. "We can handle all of the staffing concerns—I can even have them sign NDAs if that's something you're interested in."

"Shouldn't be necessary." James smiled at her politely. "If we enforce the no cell-phone rule there shouldn't be any issues."

Becky held up her phone. "Do you mind if I take a quick picture? I can send it out in the announcement."

"Sure." James smiled as Becky's flash went off.

"Thanks." She smiled at him, her eyes sparkling.

"No problem. Will you excuse me for a moment?" He turned to me. "Hey Taylor—there you are."

"Hey yourself." I shrugged, but I couldn't stop smiling. "Here I am." I wasn't sure what the policy was, but it seemed ill-advised to kiss him while I was working. But it almost physically hurt to be that close but not touching after I hadn't seen him all day.

"Two questions." James leaned closer. "Can I drive you home tonight?"

"Yes," I said immediately.

"Great." He grinned, flashing the dimple. "And: do you want to get up super-early tomorrow and go up Cadillac Mountain in time to see the sun rise?"

"I'd love to."

"Nice. I'm finally going to get to see my girlfriend again."

Out of the corner of my eye, I saw Sylvie give Becky a look.

"I'm glad you two are reunited, but Taylor, can you

get these drinks out of here?" Josie put her hands on her hips. "I've got seventeen more orders coming up."

"Of course." I hastily picked up my cocktails and made a beeline back to my station.

The rest of my shift passed quickly. At some point, Becky and Sylvie left. So did James and Dylan. I didn't even have time to say goodbye—as soon as my tables turned over, the hostess sat me more parties. By the end of the night, I'd made over two hundred dollars in tips.

Eden counted her large pile of cash at the wait station. "Tonight was awesome—I hope it stays this busy for the rest of the summer. If this keeps up, I might even get a single at school!"

"Tonight was really good," I said. "I didn't even spill anything."

"I told you so. It's easier once you know what you're doing."

The restaurant door opened, and James came in.

"Ah, it looks like your chariot's arrived." Eden winked at me. "See you tomorrow."

I grinned at my friend. "Can't wait." And then I practically ran to James. It'd only been hours, but it felt like weeks.

29

SHAKY

JAMES KISSED my cheek and I lit up. "You seem happy," he said.

"I am." I grabbed his hand as we went out to the dock. "I had a good night tonight. I didn't screw up any orders. I didn't even get yelled at once by the cooks!"

He laughed. "You're a pro."

I felt like skipping down the pier because I was next to him again. "How was your day?"

"It's was good, but it's better now."

"Me too." We reached the parking lot and found his truck, then faced each other in the semi-darkness. "Eden and I did have fun at the pool, though—thank you again. We even tried the water slide."

"Really?"

"Yeah, it was scary but sort of fun. I don't think it gets used a lot."

"Probably not. I'm glad you guys braved it—I would've liked to have seen that." James leaned closer, and a familiar heat kicked up between us. "I thought about you all day."

"Me too."

His face hovered above mine. I raised my lips to meet his. Everything stopped. I'd never known a moment, a touch, could be so powerful. Nothing else mattered. He deepened the kiss and I pressed against him, relishing the feel of his big body.

"Hey you two—get a room!" Josie chuckled as she made it to her jeep.

"Ha ha," James said. We broke apart but he wrapped his arms around my waist, pulling me close against him.

"Seriously, though. Can't you find a better place to make out? It smells like fish guts out here." She waggled her eyebrows at us before she jumped into her car and sped off.

James wrinkled his nose. "She's kind of right about that."

I sniffed the collar of my polo shirt. "It could be me, too. I served lots of lobster dinners and clams tonight."

"It's not you." He kissed the tip of my nose. "But I should get you home so you can get some sleep. If you really want to go to Cadillac tomorrow, we have to leave my dock by three-thirty in the morning."

"Woah, okay. But I'm in." I hopped into the truck. Setting my alarm for three a.m. would not normally be appealing, but it meant I got to see James that much sooner.

"Good." He pulled the truck out and drove the five hundred or so feet to the edge of Becky's driveway. He idled for a minute before he spoke.

"Last night was great, but…" James sighed. "I feel like it was too much on you."

I shook my head. "It's not the kind of thing you can prepare for, but I'm fine."

"I'm sure you have more questions."

"I do."

He reached over and took my hand. "Want to talk about it tomorrow?"

"Yeah. That'll give me some more time to process."

He leaned over and kissed my cheek. "I wish you didn't have a curfew. It probably makes me sound like a weenie to say it, but I really missed you today."

"You're not the only weenie." My heart thudded in my chest. "I missed you, too."

"I want you to know something." James looked down at our hands. "I'm… I'm serious about you. About this."

I breathed in sharply.

"But it occurred to me that maybe you'd be questioning that."

I nodded, feeling jittery. Could James read my mind, not just my aura? "A little."

He stroked the back of my hand with his thumb. "I told you the truth last night—I didn't decide I liked you based on anything other than hanging out with you," he said softly. "And I've never told anybody about myself, my background, before. Dylan, Josie and Patrick know because of...circumstances. I wouldn't have involved them otherwise."

"What circumstances?"

He nodded. "I'll tell you the whole story, I promise, but not tonight. I *had* to tell them—but you're different. I wanted to tell you because it's important to me to be honest. You should know who I really am and what you're getting into. But you're also younger than me, and you haven't seen as much of the world. I just feel like I laid a lot out on you yesterday. I don't want you to think that I'm trying to push things too fast or take advantage of you."

I opened my mouth and then closed it, trying to gather my thoughts. "Part of me's worried that you like me because..." How could I say this?

James waited.

"Because I'm alone," I blurted out. "Because I don't really have anyone."

"Yeah." He winced. "I get that."

"I'm not trying to accuse you of anything," I said weakly.

James squeezed my hands and looked into my eyes. "It makes sense that you'd question it—my feelings. Even though to me, the reason I'm serious about you is obvious. You're the most amazing person in the world."

"Ha." I shook my head. "No I'm not. I'm average on a good day."

"That's not true," he said softly. "In my eyes, you have everything to lose from this, and I have everything to gain."

"That doesn't make any sense. The opposite is true."

James leaned back against his seat. "I'm dangerous. It's selfish of me to want to be with you."

"The way I see it, you're the one with something to lose. You're trusting me with your secret." I hesitated, wanting to say more.

The muscle in James's jaw was tight. "And you're worried I told you because you don't have anywhere to go or anyone to go to. So my secret will be safe."

I nodded. "I don't want to believe that, but I have those thoughts. Because... Why would you have gotten close to me otherwise?"

"I told you the truth because I want you to know me. Because you're important to me." James reached up and brushed the hair back from my face. "Would you believe me if I told you that from the moment I first saw you, I knew you were the one?"

"James." I wiped at my face. "That's crazy."

"Is it any crazier than the fact that I'm a vampire who survived being staked—the only one of my kind? Or that I can shine a blue light from my fingertips? Listen... I've existed for a long time. But the truth is, I've never felt this way about anyone before. I meant what I told you about my gut feeling about coming to Dawnhaven this summer. It was for a reason. You're the reason, Taylor."

His steel-gray gaze pierced mine. "I love you. It's so simple that it's complicated."

I swallowed hard. "I love you too."

The smile that lit up his face—it was pure joy. "You do?"

I pointed above my head, to the aura that was visible only to him. "Duh. I'm guessing you've known for a while."

He shrugged. "I hoped. I didn't know for sure."

"Liar." But I leaned over and kissed him.

He searched my face when I leaned back. "You're better? Just like that?"

"I guess so." I could choose to believe the bad things,

like the stuff Amelia said. Or I could listen to Eden—who said to listen to my gut, and to trust what was right in front of my face. "Plus, Josie said she's never seen you like this. She said you're a basket case over me."

"Oh, great." He laugh-coughed. "That's not embarrassing or anything."

"Ha—yeah, sorry," I said. "I mean, I'm *still* afraid. Not even as much about the stuff that you told me, but more because I feel the way I do."

"You don't have to be afraid." James looked me straight in the eye. "Not of that."

Through the driver's side window, I saw someone watching us from inside the house. I checked my watch—it was almost curfew. "Ugh, I have to go." I kissed him quickly, too quickly, and then climbed down from the truck. "I'll see you at three?"

He nodded, watching me head down the driveway. "I literally can't wait. Love you, Taylor."

I stopped walking and beamed at him. "I love you too, James." I practically skipped down the rest of the drive.

Edgar cawed at me from a nearby tree. "Goodnight Edgar."

He cawed again.

I went into the house, grinning. But Becky was standing right inside the door. One hand was on her hip,

THE EQUINOX PACT BOOK 1: AWAKENING

the other clutched an almost empty glass of wine. Her mascara was smudged a little under her eyes.

Uh-oh. My smile disappeared. "Hey Becky."

"Hey Taylor." The words were laced with something, like two bottles of wine and her own personal brand of acid.

"Everything okay?" I looked past her, hoping to catch a glimpse of my dad.

"Did James just drop you off?" Becky was so waspy, she only slurred a little.

"Yep. We're going to hike Cadillac tomorrow to see the sunrise, so I'm going to head to bed. We have to get up early, really early." I was babbling, but the way she looked at me made me nervous.

"Come on and talk to me for a while." She motioned toward the couch. "We should catch up."

"Okay?" I felt like I was walking the plank as I followed her to the living room.

She sank down into the couch and that's when I could tell—Becky was about an eight drunk. I did not, by any means, believe that alcohol was the devil. But I knew from past experience that Becky could turn particularly evil when she'd had more than her fair share of sauvignon blanc.

"So." She blew a stray lock of hair off of her forehead.

"You missed something tonight—something that's never happened before."

"Oh?"

"Your father took Amelia's phone away." Becky looked at me expectantly, like I should know all about this.

"How come?"

"He said she was giving him a hard time about you. He said she crossed the line." She snorted. "I got her phone back, of course. He had no right to do that—she was just trying to express her feelings. You can't punish her for that."

I wisely kept my mouth shut.

"You know, Amelia's really having a hard time this summer. And I don't blame her one bit." Becky looked at me, but it took a second for her eyes to focus. "You've kind of been in her face since you got here—in all of our faces."

I shook my head. "I'm not trying to be."

"Ha, well. You don't know any better, coming from your background and all. I'm sure it feels good to finally get some attention."

"I-I'm not looking for attention. I'm just trying to follow the rules and get through this year."

"Oh please." Becky slammed her wineglass down on the side table. I was surprised the stem didn't break off.

"What I *am* tired of is the act—you're not some innocent hick!"

"I'm not pretending to be anything."

She snorted. "You might have your father fooled, but I know for a fact that James Champlain wouldn't be sniffing around you like this unless you had him in a tight pussy grip. Give me a break. A boy like that's got no interest in a girl like you, except for sex. He's gonna use you until someone better shows up on the island, which by my count is about any second."

"Wow Becky, tell me how you really feel."

She jabbed a finger at me. "*That's* what I mean. Your attitude! You should be grateful that we took you in, but you just act like this is all yours for the taking. You are trash, Taylor. You can take the girl out of the cesspool, but you can't take the cesspool out of the girl. He gets you and that Lambert girl a membership to the pool when you've got *no* business being there. You're going down the waterslide in your skanky bathing suits from Walmart, making a scene. It's *so* embarrassing. I can't believe I have to put up with this." Becky started to shiver. "Martha freaking Stewart's a member there!"

She shivered more violently, and I sighed. I suddenly felt tired, tired of adults who acted like children. "Are you going to puke?"

"N-n-n-no."

I froze. *N-n-n-no.* She suddenly sounded just like Drunk Guy. "Becky, are you okay?"

She jittered on the couch. It seemed to happen all at once. Her movements turned spastic, then increased in speed. She started moving so fast I couldn't make out her face—it blurred. Becky's body jerked and her arms flailed, knocking the wineglass onto the floor where it shattered.

"Becky!"

"W-w-w-w-w-what's h-h-h-h-h-appening to m-m-m-e?" She stood and staggered toward me.

I screamed and ran toward the door.

"C-c-c-c-ome h-h-h-h-ere." She reached for me.

"Dad? *DAD!*"

I heard thumping on the stairs and then my dad was running through the kitchen. "Taylor, what's the matter?"

At the sound of my dad's voice, Becky stopped seizing. Her eyes rolled back in her head. Then she passed out, crumpling to a heap on the floor.

STARTING SOMETHING

BECKY DIDN'T MOVE, and I couldn't tell if she was breathing. "Does she need a doctor?"

My dad lifted her up off the floor. Careful to avoid the broken glass, he went and gently put her on the couch. He opened her eyelids and peered at her pupils, then checked her pulse. "I don't think so. Everything seems okay."

There was a knock on the door and I almost jumped out of my skin.

My dad cursed. "Who the hell is that?"

"It might be James—he just dropped me off." I opened the door. James was out on the front step, a stricken look on his face.

"Is everything all right?" he asked. "I heard yelling."

"I think so." I glanced back at my dad, who glowered at me.

"Now really isn't the right time for company," he said.

"Right." I nodded at James. I felt jittery, a marionette whose strings were being rattled. "We've got it covered."

He gave me a long look. "Okay. See you tomorrow."

I closed the door gently, and found my father sitting on the edge of the couch. Becky was limp beside him, passed out. Dad stared straight ahead, maybe at the wall, maybe at nothing. "I told her I can't take this kind of crap anymore."

"Which kind of crap?" I asked cautiously.

His big shoulders slumped. "The drinking until she passes out kind. You girls don't need to be exposed to that." What he didn't say, but hung in the air between us, was that he'd never been able to handle my mother's drinking. And she wasn't even bad while they were together—the bad came later.

"Does it happen a lot?"

He shook his head. "No. It used to be bad when her parents were still up here, but she hasn't done it in a long time." He brushed the hair off Becky's face. She looked peaceful, her chest rising and falling rhythmically.

I went and got the broom and a dustpan, sweeping up the tiny shards of glass. "She was pretty upset with me." I didn't dare look at my dad.

"Yeah well. She's more upset with me."

I didn't stop sweeping as I said, "I don't have to stay, you know. Aunt Jackie said it was fine if I wanted to come back. I think she liked having me around." I did her laundry and cleaned the bathroom.

"Absolutely not. Honey, please don't say that ever again." My dad looked like he might cry. "You're my daughter, my flesh and blood. If you feel like you need to leave, I'm going with you."

"Dad." I stared at him. "Don't say things like that. Becky and Amelia are your family—I'm not going to blow that up. We'll be fine… Won't we?"

He took a deep breath. "There's going to have to be some changes around here."

"I'll do whatever you want," I said quickly.

"Not you." Kyle looked back down at Becky. "You should probably get going to bed," he said after a minute.

"Yeah—about that. I'm supposed to go off-island with James early to watch the sunrise from Cadillac."

He sighed. "Fine. But please don't share any of this with him. Tell him she's sick, or something."

My dad forgot that this sort of thing was squarely in my wheelhouse. "Don't worry, Dad. I got it."

THREE A.M. COULDN'T COME SOON ENOUGH. I barely slept. I turned off the alarm on my phone before it even rang, then dressed for colder weather—long pants, a heavy sweatshirt, and a vest. I brushed my teeth and threw my hair up into a ponytail.

I was waiting outside when James drove down the driveway.

As soon as I climbed into the truck, he pulled me tight against him and kissed the top of my head. "I was so worried about you. Are you okay?"

"Yeah. I'm fine. I'll tell you everything, but can we go?" I wanted to get away from the house, as far from Becky as I could.

We drove down to the boathouse in silence. The pier was dark; mist hung over the water. James used his phone as a flashlight as we climbed down the ramp and onto the dock. I climbed onto the boat first, diligently securing my life jacket against my chest. He quickly undid the ties, hopped on board, then pushed us off from the dock.

I sat in the chair next to him as he turned on the

lights and started the motor. He maneuvered the *Norumbega* out into the harbor.

"So what happened?" His voice was quiet.

"Becky had too much to drink last night." I shook my head. "She kind of went off on me, but that wasn't the bad part. She got so upset that she started shaking, stuttering—just like Drunk Guy."

James gripped the wheel. "Can you be specific?"

"I mean, that's pretty much it. One minute she was yelling at me, the next minute she started shaking. It was the same—she looked like she was having a seizure, but she moved so fast she was almost blurry." I shivered. "And then she started coming toward me, but my dad came downstairs. Then she just passed out."

He blew out a deep breath as he navigated between several boats. "What did your dad see?"

"Nothing. She was on the floor by the time he got to us."

"I feel like this is my fault." James cursed. Even in the semi-darkness, I could see his face was pale. "Actually, I know it is."

"What do you mean?"

He shook his head. "Drunk Guy…Adam… And now Becky. I think something's happening."

"Something *what's* happening?"

James stared straight ahead, facing the darkness of the water. "We've started something. Or I have."

"*What?* Tell me what you mean."

"You said that some of the locals thought I was starting a cult at the Tower."

I froze. "I never said that. I never used the word 'cult.'" I'd been careful not to.

"Right—you said they thought what I was doing down at the Tower was strange—the chanting and the meditation. Josie's the one who told me some people were saying we were a cult."

"Why are you talking about this?"

James exhaled. "I don't know."

"Yes you do."

"We're not a cult, not by any means. But when we get together—just me and my friends, and also when we have a larger group over—it's powerful. Like I said, you can feel it." He glanced at me. "But I feel something even more powerful when I'm with you."

"Um… I feel something too, but what's that got to do with Becky freaking out?"

He gripped the steering wheel. "I think we're doing something to her."

"Bugging her?" I asked.

"Worse than that. Usually when something's shaking, it's because its foundation is coming loose."

I crossed my arms against my chest. "I need coffee. I don't know what you're talking about."

"I think I've made a terrible mistake," he said.

"What?"

He looked at me, a stricken expression on his face. "I never should've started dating you."

RISE

I NEVER SHOULD'VE STARTED DATING you. I felt as though he'd punched me in the gut.

"Oh." It was the only word I could get out.

"No—wait. Wow, I'm messing this up." James stopped the boat and grabbed my hands. "It's not that I don't want to be with you—I want that more than anything."

I didn't say another word. I couldn't; I was holding my breath.

"Taylor, please." He pulled me against him and buried his face in my hair. "I'm just worried that I've put you in danger. I don't know what to do."

"Can you start with not breaking up with me?" I still felt like I couldn't breathe.

"I won't. I could never." He kissed the top of my head,

my cheek. "I'm sorry I said that. But I would do anything for you—and anything to protect you. If I've started something, and put you in danger…"

"Started what?" When he didn't answer, I pressed my face against his warm chest. "I don't understand what's happening. I don't understand why they were shaking like that."

"I don't either. Not for sure."

Something in his voice made me feel like he might have an idea. "But what do you think it is?"

"Something might be happening to the balance." He scrubbed a hand over his face. "But I'm not sure. I need to think it through, okay?"

The balance? I had no idea what he was talking about, but I let it go for the moment. "Okay." I didn't have to tell him that he'd scared me by what he'd said; as if to reassure me, he kept his hand firmly on my thigh for the rest of the dark trip to Pine Harbor.

The sky had brightened a little, making it easier to maneuver into the bay. Once we docked the boat, James grabbed his backpack and helped me onto the pier. We went up to the full parking lot and he stopped at a big black Yukon with tinted windows, parked right next to Becky's SUV.

"You know what I just realized?" I asked. "I've never been on the mainland with you before." I hadn't ever seen his real-life car; I was used to the rusty old truck he drove on the island.

"Hopefully this will be the first time of many times— infinity times."

"You don't have to say that." We climbed into the car and I fastened my seatbelt. "I *was* worried you were breaking up with me, but... I've recovered. I think."

James didn't start the car. "Can you forgive me for saying that?"

"Sure, but that's not the problem. The *problem's* that you thought it. I want to know why."

"Because both of these incidents have revolved around you." James watched me carefully. "Nothing like this has ever happened to you before, right?"

"Right. Of course not."

"I think it's my fault. By being in your life, I'm bringing danger to your doorstep. It's in your pool, it's in your living room..." His expression turned desolate as he looked away, and he didn't say anything else.

He started the huge car and backed it out. After a minute, we were on the deserted roads of Pine Harbor, heading toward Acadia National Park. An image of Becky flashed in my mind, her face blurry from the speed of her movement. *Ugh.* Would she remember anything about last night when she woke up?

"I haven't been in the park in a long time," I said. I

wasn't sure if I was trying to change the subject or just babbling because James had gotten so quiet. "What's so special about Cadillac Mountain?"

"You can see the sunrise here first, before anywhere else in the country."

"Cool." I tried to sound upbeat.

James pulled over at the OneStop, the only convenience store for miles. "Be right back." He was gone for all of five minutes before he returned with two large cups of coffee and a bagful of donuts.

"Thanks." I didn't say anything else. I hadn't known James long, but my gut told me he might be a little bit like my dad. When Big Kyle was upset, you had to give him some space to process. What was it my grandmother used to say about him? *Still waters run deep.* It took time for the fully-formed thoughts to bubble all the way up to the surface.

I comforted myself with my cream-filled coffee and a donut covered with pink sprinkles. When James still didn't talk, I helped myself to another one, chocolate glazed. By the time we pulled into Acadia National Park, I was stuffed with donuts and fully caffeinated. It was just past four a.m., the sun still below the horizon. James maneuvered the Yukon along the twists and turns of the narrow roads. We passed bikers and hikers, all with headlamps on. "Wow, it's crowded for so early."

"A lot of people like to come out and see the sun come up." James shrugged. "It's one of the big draws of the park." We drove further and he turned off an exit for the Cadillac Mountain trail. There were a lot of hikers parking and getting out in the base's parking lot, but James continued up the road. "We don't have time to hike the trail."

"Maybe some other time?" I hoped I didn't sound too freaked out or needy. Or both. But a trace of panic still squeezed my chest. I still stung from his words: *I never should've started dating you.*

James glanced at me. He didn't bother looking above my head, but he sighed. "I told you I didn't mean it like that."

"Can you just tell me again how you *did* mean it?"

"I meant that I was selfish when I started this with you. I didn't think about how you might get hurt."

My chest squeezed tighter. "Does that mean you're rethinking things?"

"No, it means I'm pissed at myself. Okay?"

I nodded, hoping he'd have his coffee and a donut soon. He sure was grumpy.

We wound our way around the twisty road, climbing higher and higher up the mountain. Finally we reached the summit. The parking lot was filled with cars, and there were people starting up a trail. "C'mon," James said. "We can go out on the eastern summit this way. There's a great view."

We climbed up a well-worn path that led to the top of Cadillac. There were other people at the top, families with children wrapped in blankets, seasoned hikers with ski poles and full gear, other tourists and couples. Everyone was taking pictures with their phones, and for good reason. The view was majestic. The summit was made of large boulders, with grassy ledges in between. The ocean spread out beneath us, and you could see the islands in the distance.

James pulled a light blanket out of his bag and spread it out on the cold rock so we could sit. "There's Pine Harbor," he said, pointing to an inlet where you could see tiny white dots which must've been boats. "There's Spruce Island." From here, the island looked like its only inhabitants were trees. "And there's Dawnhaven."

Our island seemed impossibly small from here, incapable of holding all the magic and mystery it certainly possessed. "It's so pretty."

"Look, here it comes." James threw his arm around me and pulled me close as the sun peeked up over the edge of the horizon. Everyone clapped and cheered, then a hush fell over the gathering as the sun made its glorious climb above the water. Crazy colors—pinks and blues and oranges—streaked the clouds as the sun began its ascent.

I couldn't stop smiling. "It's so beautiful."

James kissed my cheek. "I'm glad we got to see it together."

I leaned against him, his strong body, his warmth. "Me too."

I let the hope and the love bubble inside me. Maybe they could evict the panic that still gripped my chest.

32

WHO COULD STAY

JAMES STILL DIDN'T TALK MUCH on the drive back to Pine Harbor, but at least he seemed more relaxed. I didn't push him. I was certain that there was more to the strange encounter with both Becky and Drunk Guy than I was aware of. James had shared so much with me already—eventually, he'd come around and tell me what he was thinking.

I just had to wait.

We pulled into the parking lot and he turned to me. "Do you have tonight off?"

"Yeah. I have a double tomorrow." That would be a first for me.

"I was thinking we could all have dinner down at the Tower—you, me, Josie, Dylan, and Patrick. Does that sound like fun?"

"Yeah." We hadn't had much of a chance to just hang out. "Can I ask Eden, too?"

"Of course." He hopped out of the car. "Do you mind going to the market with me? I need to pick up a couple of things for dinner."

"Not at all. Are you going to cook?" I arched my eyebrow. I couldn't exactly picture James in his kitchen.

"Why're you looking at me like that? Of course I'm going to cook." He offered me his arm and I took it as we started up the hill toward Main Street. "What's your favorite dinner?"

"Um…" I blushed, embarrassed. James probably ate duck confit on the regular but Bebe's was most definitely the fanciest restaurant I'd ever been to. I often encountered things in Becky's refrigerator that I didn't recognize, Roquefort cheese and veggie burgers that looked like they were made from meat and something called white truffle butter. Not that Becky ate butter.

"Chicken Parmesan, I guess?"

"Are you asking me?" James made a face. "Or is that your favorite?"

"Yeah, I like it. I like anything with pasta."

"Then I'll make pasta. And Chicken Parmesan. Sound okay?"

"It sounds great."

We made it to the top of the hill and walked along

the quaint Main Street in Pine Harbor. There was a real estate office, a bank, a gas station, and a bagel shop. I saw the sign for the Aqua boutique at the opposite end of the road. The market sat in the center, prime real estate for the town's one little grocery store. Everything seemed so normal, a quaint Maine summer morning, but now I knew better…

James took his grocery shopping more seriously than I expected. He inspected bunches of lettuce before choosing some. He squeezed tomatoes and smelled bell peppers. He had very specific instructions for the butcher. He bought the Italian brand of pasta, super expensive fresh breadcrumbs and herbs, along with two bottles of red wine that cost seventy dollars apiece. He didn't even blink at the price.

He motioned to the gourmet pints of ice cream in the freezer. "Want to cheat and buy dessert?"

"Sure." I was petrified he'd ask me to help cook—I could make a decent breakfast but little else.

After grabbing five pints of ridiculously priced organic ice cream, we went to stand in line. I started fidgeting. James gave me a long look. "Are you worried about something?"

"No." But I bounced my knee. It was stupid but checking out at the grocery store made me nervous. Growing up, my mother had never paid attention to what was in the cart. We rarely had enough money to cover our purchases. Then she'd have to go through and choose what to discard, a process that always seemed to take too long as I stood by her side, silently mortified as the sales clerk and bagger looked on.

When I was older, I went to the store by myself and always carefully tracked the cost of everything. Still, checking out unnerved me. Waiting while they scanned each item, watching the total, counting and recounting the cash in my wallet... I knew James had enough money for what was in our cart, even the insanely expensive wine—of course he did. My jangled nerves were just an ingrained response.

James smiled at the cashier as we checked out. He paid with a black credit card. The cashier's eyes bugged out when he saw the card, but he didn't say anything. We carried our groceries back down to the parking lot, but instead of heading down to the boat, James opened the Yukon's trunk. "Let's put them in here for a minute. I'm not ready to go back."

We deposited the bags and he took my hand, leading me to a food truck parked nearby. "We need lobster rolls, stat."

"You're still hungry?" I asked.

"You're not?"

Even though it was still early morning, he ordered us

each a lobster roll, a bag of chips and a soda. Then we sat on a nearby bench, watching the boats dock in the harbor. The little town was waking up.

"What's with you and grocery stores?" he asked.

In spite of the two donuts I'd eaten, I was already halfway through my lobster roll. It was served in a buttered, toasted bun. The whole thing was insanely good. "Nothing really. It's embarrassing."

"Given everything we've been dealing with, I'm pretty sure I can handle it."

"Yeah…" I took a deep breath. "But wait. Don't we have more important things to talk about?"

"This is important. You're important."

I eyed his sandwich. He'd eaten every bite. It seemed to have made him talkative, albeit not in the direction I'd been hoping for.

I sighed. "My mom used to take me out shopping with her when I was younger. She had a habit of trying to spend money we didn't have—like, she'd put more gas in the car than we had cash for. She'd turn the heat up even when our account was about to be disconnected. But the grocery store was the worst. Every time we went, we had to put stuff back. She didn't keep track of how much everything cost, and she couldn't argue her way into keeping stuff we couldn't pay for. Not for lack of trying."

"So you used to get embarrassed," James said.

"Of course I did. I guess it's stupid, but I felt like people thought there was something wrong with us because we were poor." Becky's words came back to me: *you can't take the cesspool out of the girl.* "I just kind of react when I have to check out. I can't help it—it makes me nervous."

He gave me a long look. "I'm sorry."

"Eh, it's okay. The past is in the past. I just need to remember that."

James leaned back against the bench. "What was your mom like, anyway? I feel like we haven't talked about her that much."

"She was…" I took a deep breath. "It's hard to talk about her without talking about her addiction, you know? That wasn't all she was, but I feel like that's what I ended up dealing with the most."

"Did she always have issues?"

I shrugged. "When I was younger I guess I didn't realize how much she drank. It wasn't that bad until after she and my dad split up, that much I remember."

"What happened to them?"

"They were really young," I said. "They had me before they'd even gotten a chance to know each other. Their personalities were *not* a good match. My dad doesn't yell, and it takes a lot to get him pissed off. But she pushed his buttons, oh boy. And the thing with my mom was, she couldn't let it go until she got a reaction. So even though she knew it was going to end badly, she felt like she'd won if she got him to yell. That was the goal."

James winced. "That's tough."

"Yeah, it seemed better for a while after he left. I don't remember much. I was pretty little."

"Can I ask you something?"

I nodded.

"I don't know your dad well, but it doesn't seem like he'd leave you in a bad situation," he said. "It seems weird to me that you stayed with your mom. He seems like he'd fight for you."

"You're right. He did," I said. "But he didn't know the extent of what was going on. She hid it pretty well. My mom wouldn't let him see me for a long time, so when I was ten, he took her back to court. He had legal visitation but it's kind of hard to enforce if my mother never showed up when she was supposed to, you know? He was going to go for full custody but there was Becky and Amelia... I didn't want to live with them. I covered for my mom for a long time, but then when things got really bad, I told my dad. I had to."

"So things with Becky weren't good from the beginning." It wasn't a question; it was a statement of fact.

"She could never accept the fact that he had another kid. It's not like he hid it from her; he told her from day one. But they were up here, and I was down with my mom, so I think it made it easy for her to pretend I didn't exist. She never came down with him to see me. She never met my mother—not even once. I used to come up here every summer for a few weeks but she said that was too hard on Amelia, so since I've been in high school I only come up for a weekend usually. My dad would come down to Mass to see me during the year, but it's far. It was hard for him with work, and I had a part-time job on the weekends, so..."

"What happened with your dad when things got worse with your mom this year?"

I played with my ponytail. "He started emergency custody proceedings, and I told the lawyers from the state that I wanted to move in with him. They take that sort of thing into account once you're older. But then she overdosed before it ever went before the judge."

James rubbed my back.

"You know, she never talked a lot about her family or her childhood. My Aunt Jackie doesn't either. I think they had it pretty rough." I stared at the boats. "Want to hear something funny?"

He nodded.

"When you were telling me about your past, about

how you felt about yourself when you were…using, for lack of a better word," I said, referring to him going back to drinking from humans, "it reminded me of my mom. She wasn't a bad person at all, and I don't think she ever meant to be mean. Difficult yes, but not mean. She just wanted attention and love. But she never seemed to get what she needed, or it wasn't enough, and so the drinking and then the drugs kind of numbed that, I guess. But she hated herself for it. That was the worst part—the guilt. She felt so bad about what she was doing to both of us that she needed to numb more. It was a vicious cycle, like you said."

"It's a terrible place to be." James looked out at the water. "Sometimes I think people who have problems like that are operating at a higher frequency than the rest of us. It definitely has its perils."

"What do you mean?"

"People like your mom feel things more sharply. Life is hard when you're like that—there are lots of pointy edges to run into. If you don't have a thick skin, even little bumps can hurt like hell. I think that's why people use. They're trying to protect themselves from the pain."

"I think that's true. I always thought my mom was trying to self-medicate, but it just made things worse." I swallowed hard. "So it was amazing to run into Lilly the other night, even though it was crazy. I really feel like my mom's at peace now. It was almost like I could hear her voice." For all her troubles, my mother did try her best to love me. It wasn't perfect, but it was something. "I feel it in my gut... She's okay now."

"And she said you have people watching over you." James nudged me. "She's right about that."

"You can't watch over me if you break up with me."

"Taylor, please." His shoulders slumped. "Do you understand that would hurt me more than it would hurt you? I'm just worried—I'm worried I've put you in danger."

I leaned against him. "Then protect me."

"I will." He kissed the top of my head. "I promise. I'll protect you forever."

33

GLIMMER

FOREVER. I held the word close in my heart, hoping it was true.

We were quiet as we loaded the boat with groceries and drove back to the island. Instead of docking at the boathouse, James drove directly to the Tower.

The massive white house rose up before us. Its tower shined, windows glittering, a beacon keeping watch in the bright sky. The tide had come in, so the sea wall was barely visible. The waves rolled onto the rocky shore. There was no one out on the deck; the estate looked quiet, isolated and impenetrable.

"Don't we need the truck?" I asked. We'd left it down by the boathouse.

"I'll have Dylan or Patrick grab it later," James said. "I

want to keep you out of Becky's sight for as long as possible."

"How come? Are you going to have to use your light on her and erase her like Drunk Guy?"

He pulled the boat up alongside the dock, his mouth settling into a grim line. "I might have to. I don't know."

My phone buzzed and I checked it—it was a text from Eden. "Oh, bummer. Eden can't come to dinner. She has to work tonight."

"That's too bad." But James sounded distracted.

I looked up to see what was bothering him. Edgar was in the yard, hovering near his loot. "Is everything okay?"

"I'm not sure." James put down the grocery bags and started toward the crow.

I left everything on the boat and ran after him.

Edgar was picking at something in the lawn with his beak. There were tufts of grass around him that he'd plucked from the earth. Something glittered in the dark dirt he'd exposed.

"What is that?" I asked.

James crouched down and faced the crow. "You okay?" he asked him.

In response, Edgar rapidly blinked his eyes and started picking at the grass again.

"What's this, buddy?" James reached into the dirt and

pulled out a necklace, platinum with a small aquamarine pendant.

I crouched next to him. "That's Amelia's necklace."

Edgar blinked at us as James ran the chain through his fingers. "I'm afraid you can't keep this," he told Edgar. The crow blinked again.

The aqua gemstone winked in the sun. "Can you ask him if he brought it from Becky's?"

"It doesn't work like that—we can't communicate specifically." James nodded at the bird. "I'm gonna take this as a sign, though. Good work."

When James rose, I asked him, "What do you mean? A sign of what?"

James slipped the necklace into his pocket. "Like so many things these days, I'm not sure."

Edgar flew back up to the trees and sat there, watching us. His stare seemed accusatory—we'd taken away his shiny new treasure.

I was going to ask James more questions, but he'd already started back toward the dock.

———

Josie and Dylan left a note—they'd gone off-island for a hike but would be back that afternoon. Patrick was still down with his family, so James and I had the Tower to ourselves. It was the first time I'd been in the house since the solstice party. Although it had only been a few days, so much had happened that it felt like much longer.

Without the throng of people and throbbing music, I got a better feel for the place. The living room furniture was dark wood, with upholstery patterned in crimson and deep navy. I could see why James had called it "museum-y"—everything was immaculate, but it seemed too imposing to ever be comfortable. Still, the ceiling soared above, reflecting the sunlight that poured through the windows. There was a pack of cards and an abandoned seltzer can on the coffee table, along with a remote control for the giant flatscreen tv, small indications of normal life.

James stood in the kitchen, which faced the driveway, unpacking the groceries. I wandered in, taking in the view from the windows above the sink. The beach stretched out to the left, all the way down to the tiny cabins where Drunk Guy had stayed with his friends. The driveway and the grounds were straight ahead; if anyone came down to the house, you'd see them with plenty of warning. The room was floor-through, so the side opposite the kitchen fronted the ocean. The view was breathtaking. Across the narrow channel, the tide crashed against the shores of Moss Head. The tiny green island gleamed like an emerald in the middle of the sea.

I opened James's refrigerator and started putting groceries away. His fridge would give Becky's a run for its money. It was huge, with shelves you could pull out, and was stocked and organized so well I was almost afraid to add things. "You've got enough food in here for the apocalypse," I joked.

James chuckled. "I might not need it, but I'd rather not find out."

"But do you *get* hungry? Does your stomach growl?"

He frowned. "I don't think my stomach's *ever* growled. Hmm. Maybe I do have a few flaws."

"Ha ha. But do you ever crave normal food?" I asked.

"Not exactly—not physically, I guess." James looked thoughtful as he set the tomatoes in the windowsill's sun. "But I love food, so I think about it a lot. I don't skip meals if I can help it—I like having a schedule, maintaining order to my days so I feel like I'm part of the 'regular' world. Meals help with that."

"Do you sleep?" I asked. It hadn't even occurred to me.

"No, I can't." He shrugged. "Remind me to show you the library here—we have them at all of our houses. I usually read while everyone sleeps, sometimes I watch tv... TV's gotten *really* good lately."

"Yeah." I would ask him about his favorite shows later. Now that he was answering some of my other questions, I didn't want to stop. "Um, do you still…" I'd been wanting to ask him something since he'd told me about himself, but it seemed rude.

"What?"

"Do you still have fangs?"

He nodded. "They didn't fall out when I got staked, so yeah."

"Do you ever use them?"

He motioned to the package of chicken on the counter. "I don't exactly need them for chicken parm."

I wrinkled my nose. "Would you show them to me?"

He sighed. "They're not a party trick, Taylor."

"I know, I'm just…curious."

"I haven't used them since the night I was staked," James said. "I made a promise to myself that I'd never harm anyone again."

"Okay, okay." I held up my hands as if in surrender. "I'm not trying to get you to break your vows to yourself, or anything. I just wanted to see them."

He frowned, but after a second he said, "Fine. But if it freaks you out… I told you so."

I nodded and stepped closer, both eager and a little afraid.

James watched me, probably taking my aura's

temperature. Then he opened his mouth jerked his head, like a genie granting a wish. Two large, pearly-white fangs appeared where his canine teeth had been.

I rocked back on my feet. "Holy shit!"

James jerked his head again, and the fangs disappeared. "Did you think I was kidding?"

"No, but I've never met a vampire before. That was really something."

James laughed and shook his head. "*You're* really something."

"So, what're we going to do all day?" I hoped he'd say something promising, like telling me all his secrets or making out. Or preferably both.

"I need to call my father to update him on what's been happening," James said. "And then we can start prepping for dinner. Okay?"

"Okay. I can put the rest of this away while you call him, if you want."

"That'd be great." He kissed my cheek and then disappeared into the house, probably to make a secret call from the bat cave or something.

I sighed, then started adding more groceries to his pristine refrigerator.

JOSIE AND DYLAN returned sooner than I'd expected, and I tried not to pout. James had been on the phone with his father for what seemed like hours. I'd occupied myself by texting Eden, then my dad. I asked him about Becky.

She's okay, he texted back. *Doesn't seem to remember too much. Def hungover. Bad headache. When will you be home?*

I wanted to type *never.* I wanted to type *I was afraid of Becky even before this* and *PS, Amelia's a douche.* Instead, I typed, *By curfew.* Red heart emoji.

When James returned, he was quiet again. We immediately set to work making dinner. There was no making out. There was no confessing secrets or sharing conspiracy theories.

"What did your dad say?" I asked him. I was careful to keep my voice down because Dylan and Josie were in the living room, catching up on their phones after being out for the day.

"He's concerned." James stirred the pasta. "Which is...concerning. It takes a lot to rattle him."

"He's rattled?" I didn't know exactly how old Nelson Champlain was, but I guessed it was old enough to have seen pretty much everything. "That doesn't sound good."

James started slicing fresh mozzarella. "It's not."

James's rusty old truck drove down the lane. "Ah, that's Patrick. Good. Dinner's almost ready."

I bounced my knee, agitated. "We're not going to talk about all this?"

"We are." James took the chicken from the oven, ladled some sauce onto the cutlets and placed the mozzarella on top.

When he didn't say anything further, I grabbed the placemats, silverware and linen napkins he'd set out. I headed into the dining room, which had a gigantic table, twelve chairs and a huge stone fireplace. A crystal chandelier hung from the ceiling; the style was definitely more Italian Renaissance than Maine beach cottage.

"Want some help?" Dylan popped in and took some of the silverware. Her hair was pulled back into a high ponytail and she wore gray sweats and a T-shirt. Somehow, she looked even more gorgeous than usual.

Josie followed, putting wineglasses around the table. "Dinner smells so good." Like Dylan, Josie wore joggers and a plain white tee. She looked like she'd just left an Athleta photo shoot.

"I love it when James cooks. We're in for a treat." Dylan beamed. "So how are you, Taylor? How was the hike this morning?"

"It was great. The sunrise was so pretty. Where did you guys go?"

"Josie bullied me into hiking the Beehive Trail in the park." Dylan's nostrils flared. "I almost died five times."

"No you didn't, you big baby." Josie laughed. "The views were worth it."

"Worth more than my life?"

"No... But almost." Josie turned to me. "Hey, is everything okay with you?"

"Yeah." I smiled. "Why?"

"You're giving me a vibe." Josie's gaze flicked over me, up and down. "I think something's going on."

"You and your conspiracy theories," Patrick said as he came in. He put two bottles of wine on the table. "You never quit. Hey, Taylor." He grinned at me. "Eden had to work tonight, huh?"

When I nodded, he said, "Bummer. I'm trying to impress her so she'll dump that other guy."

"You're incorrigible," Dylan said. "Trying to steal someone else's woman!"

"They're on a break." Patrick waggled his eyebrows. "It's the perfect time to make a move."

"So much drama, so much drama." James came in, bearing a platter of sliced tomatoes covered with mozzarella cheese and fresh basil.

He set it in the center of the table and Josie rubbed her hands together. "I love it when you make dinner."

James scoffed. "You act like I never do it. I make dinner practically every night!"

"Not lately." Josie poured herself a glass of wine and passed the bottle to Patrick. "Lately you've been *busy*."

"Oh boy." My cheeks heated. "Here we go."

Josie had a sip of wine. "I'm not complaining."

"It sounds like you're complaining." James smiled at her. "But I'm used to it."

"Stop. Are you going to sit down, or what?" she asked him.

"I'm going to bring everything out so we don't have to get up again," James said. "We have a lot to talk about."

Josie wrinkled her nose. "Like what?" But James was already back in the kitchen. "I told you—something's going on!"

James came back with the chicken and a large bowl of pasta. We passed everything around, loading our plates. Once everyone had served themselves, Patrick said, "Thanks for dinner. This looks awesome."

"You're welcome. But... It's not just dinner." James sat back in his seat. "It's a meeting."

The others went collectively silent for a moment while I looked around, confused. "A meeting?"

"Yeah." James frowned. "First of all, you guys need to know that I told Taylor everything about me. I didn't tell her *everything* everything, but she knows about me."

Dylan's jaw dropped but Josie looked smug, as if she'd already guessed as much.

"Second," James continued, "I think some things have been set in motion—things that need to be dealt with as soon as possible. Even my dad said so."

"Your *dad*? Oh Jesus." Josie held her hand out. "Give me back that wine right now!"

BRIEFED

"WHAT SORT OF MEETING? What's been set in motion?" I asked, while everyone avoided eye contact with me—Dylan twirled her pasta, Patrick cut up his chicken, and Josie poured half the bottle of wine into her glass.

"I'll try to explain the best I can. It's complicated." James took a deep breath. "To start with the rest of you guys: I haven't shared everything that's been going on."

"You're telling me." Josie scoffed. "If you've called your dad, things are already out of control!"

"Can I talk, please?" James speared a bite of his food while Josie glared at him.

"Go on." Josie tilted her glass in my direction. "But you might want to give Taylor here a little intro, because her eyes are about to bug out of her head."

"I haven't had a chance to tell you everything yet."

James turned to me. "Dylan, Josie and Patrick aren't just my friends. We're also like-minded—we believe a lot of the same things about the world. We see things the same way."

My mouth might've gaped open, I wasn't sure. "What does that mean?"

"We made a pact. We work together to protect the balance."

"You mean we're *supposed* to work together." Josie eyed him over her glass. "Seems to me like you've been going a little rogue lately."

"I don't understand." I shook my head. "What balance? Like your tattoo, or something? I don't know what you're talking about."

"It's complicated, but at a basic level, yes—like my tattoo. We're concerned with balance in the world, and the intersection of that balance. You know I've lived for a long time. From what I've seen, I believe that things are shifting, changing for the better. These guys believe that, too."

"Wait! Are they…" I peered around the table at everyone. "Are they *you-know-what's*?"

Patrick raised his eyebrows. "You-know-what *what's*?"

"Are you vampires?" I asked.

"No," Patrick laughed. "None of us are vampires.

Only James, and technically, I'm not sure that he qualifies as one anymore."

"I don't think there are clear rules on that," James said. "But no, Josie, Dylan and Patrick aren't vampires. They're not straight-up humans, either. I'll let them explain. Patrick, do you want to go first?"

"Sure. And Taylor, take it easy. You already know about James, so what the rest of us are going to tell you won't be totally crazy. Just relax."

I nodded then stuffed a bite of pasta into my mouth. Stress-eating carbs was one of my well-developed coping mechanisms. I was happy there was plenty more spaghetti.

"I'm not a vampire, but my mother is," Patrick said. "My father was human."

"So—wait." I turned to James. "There's another vampire on the island?"

He nodded. "Patrick's mother is an old friend of my father's. We're the ones who told them about Dawnhaven."

I looked back at Patrick. "But I thought your mom was some sort of tech mogul. Doesn't she own part of the WNBA?"

Patrick nodded. "That's right. In this iteration of her life, she's working in the biotech sector, helping to develop vaccines to help combat the spread of disease.

And she's also really into basketball. She likes to mix things up. And don't worry, she only drinks donated blood."

"Oh, I wasn't worried. This is all just sort of a shock." I examined Patrick, who looked pretty normal to me: he had handsome, even features, dark skin and sparkling, kind brown eyes, and his cornrows were fitted with blue and white beads. "So you're a supernatural, too."

"Not exactly." He sat back in his seat. "Even though my biological mother's a vampire, I wasn't born with any powers. I might live a little longer than a regular human, but with my kind, it varies."

"Y-you're kind?"

He nodded. "I'm not the only one born from the union of a vampire and a human—hardly. There's a fair amount of us in the world. But we're all unique. Some are vampires, some aren't. Some have other special powers or live longer than normal humans, some don't. There's all sorts of variety and combinations. No two of us are exactly the same."

I felt like the world was splintering around me, breaking into new patterns and reforming right before my eyes. "What other sorts of powers can you have?"

Patrick looked thoughtful as he rattled off a list. "Some can run really fast, some are telepathic, some don't need to sleep. But not me. I'm pretty basic."

"So… Your mother's a vampire, your father was human. Can it work the other way around? Can human women have children with vampire men?" My cheeks heated, and I refused to look in James's direction. Not for any particular reason.

"Yes." Patrick nodded. "And it's the same thing—some of those kids are vampires, some aren't."

"Huh." I pushed the pasta around on my plate with my fork.

"You're asking for a friend, huh?" Josie eyed me over her wine glass. When I grimaced, she said, "Aw c'mon Taylor. I'm just giving you a hard time."

"I know." My skin still felt flushed. "So what about you? What's your special…background?"

Josie cleared her throat. "I'm a witch."

I almost choked on my spaghetti. "What?"

"That's right—Dylan and I are both witches." Josie tilted her glass in Dylan's direction. "That's how we met, at a Brooklyn Coven meeting."

Dylan winked at her. "The universe had a plan for us."

"Sure did." Josie grinned at her, then turned back to me. "You don't have to look so scared. We don't fly around on broomsticks, or anything. We can do spells. We can do manifestations. We can make potions."

"Oh." I blinked. "Like, love potions and stuff?"

"We don't ever make love potions, even though that's usually our number-one request," Dylan said. "We don't believe in interfering with free will."

"Some basic witches will do them." Josie frowned. "But they're the same fools who keep frog eyes in jars and put Satanic symbols on their walls. *Wannabes.*"

"We're going to need some spells soon," James said.

Dylan sat back in her chair. "Okay. But I think it's time you told us exactly what's going on."

James took a deep breath. "You guys know that Taylor's mother passed away recently, right?"

They nodded.

"A few nights ago, Taylor woke up in the middle of the night because someone rang her doorbell. She thought she saw her mom in the yard, something I confirmed when I went down there and lit the property up. I could see traces of her mother's aura, but it disappeared quickly because of the nature of the visit."

"What do you mean?" My four new favorite words.

"When a spirit makes contact in this world, you can see traces of their presence. But it's fleeting—it evaporates," James explained, then turned back to the others. "Then we saw Lilly Burke out at Bebe's the other night. Do you remember her—the medium? Her wife's name is Maeve. They own the psychic shop in Bar Harbor."

"Yeah, we know the Burkes," Josie said, "we've hung out with them a few times. Maeve's been over here."

James nodded. "Lilly had a message for Taylor from her mother. She said that for as long as Taylor's been on the island, her mother's spirit was persistent in asking Lilly to reach out with a message. So Lilly ended up at the restaurant by herself the other night, not sure why—but it wasn't just a craving for tapas. She told Taylor that her mother is at peace." James reached over and squeezed my hand.

"So this was strong," Patrick said. "It was clear, direct contact from the other side."

James nodded. "But I didn't tell you what happened in between those two incidents."

Josie emptied the wine into her glass.

"Do you remember I told you that there was a guy here who was bothering Taylor out on the deck?" James asked. "He showed up at her house a couple of nights ago. He tried to drag her into the woods."

"Oh my god!" Josie slapped the table. "Why didn't you say anything?"

"I haven't really had time." His gaze, a little guilty, flicked to me. "I've been…busy."

"Tell us the whole story, go on. What happened?" Patrick asked.

"I got down to the house just in time. Adam was

dragging her out into the woods. He wasn't...normal. But it wasn't because he was drunk or high—there was something else wrong with him. He was shaking. But not *just* shaking—it wasn't human. It was something else."

"It looked like he was having a seizure," I added. "But it was too fast to be a regular one. He was shaking so fast he was actually blurry."

James nodded. "I used my light on him and knocked him out for a minute. Then I cleaned the rest of the yard up, removing all traces of his aura. He left the island the next day—we saw him heading down to catch the mailboat and he didn't remember what happened. He didn't even recognize Taylor. I zapped him pretty good, I guess. So I thought it was over."

"But?" Josie asked.

"But..." James took a deep breath. "Becky was waiting for Taylor last night when I brought her home, and she did something similar."

"I knew that bitch was crazy!" Josie said. "Not just regular old white-wine nasty. *Crazy.*"

"She's not crazy," I said. "I mean, I don't think she is. But she was really, really upset with me. She'd been drinking, and she went off about how I was invading her space and ruining her family. Then she started shaking. It was the same thing—at first, I thought she was having a seizure but then she started moving so fast that she looked just like Adam did. Then my dad came down the stairs and I don't know, she just passed out. I talked to him earlier—he said she doesn't remember anything."

"It's not like she'd tell him she's some sort of freak!" Josie scoffed. She turned to James. "You're not still serious about hosting the gala down here, are you?"

"They started sending out the invites." James shrugged. "It'll be fine. It's better to keep Becky happy, don't you think?"

Josie mumbled something before drinking more wine. It sounded like a string of colorfully strung-together expletives surrounding the words "crazier than I thought."

"C'mon you two—stop bickering. We need to figure this out." Dylan sat forward, inspecting me. "Have you ever experienced anything like this before, Taylor? Any contact with spirits or anyone exhibiting symptoms like the ones you just described?" She suddenly sounded every inch the chemical engineering student I'd forgotten she was, attempting to analyze the available data.

"No." I shook my head. "It's only happened since I've come to the island."

Josie, Dylan and Patrick went silent, eyeing each other across the table. James pushed what remained of his food around on his plate. "What?" I asked. "Why is everybody looking like that?"

When nobody responded, I threw up my hands. "Seriously? You're not going to say anything?"

James finally looked up and smiled, but it was forced. "I think it might mean that you're tipping the balance, a little bit."

"Me?" I decided to eat the rest of the pasta, all of it, right then. "That's the craziest thing I've ever heard, and you guys have told me *some seriously crazy shit.*"

James reached over and patted my hand. "Remember when I told you I'd never felt like this about anybody before?"

Josie, Dylan and Patrick stared.

"Y-Yes."

"I think there might be some consequences to that," James said. "Big ones."

IF I KNEW IT ALL THEN

"UM, CAN YOU EXCUSE ME?" I abruptly pushed back from the table and ran outside.

My head pounded. I gripped the edge of the deck, watching the dark waves crash over the rocky shore over and over again. What did James mean? The balance was shifting, I'd impacted the balance...there were big consequences to something or other.

It occurred to me, not for the first time, that perhaps all of this was a dream. Or that maybe they were all lying to me.

But there were James's fangs, and the blue-white light. There was my mother's spirit ringing the doorbell in the middle of the night, and the message from Lilly. There was the strange way both Becky and Adam had shaken. Those things couldn't be faked—this wasn't a movie. It had all happened, and it had all happened to me.

I wandered off the deck and out onto the beach, heading away from the Tower. I needed a minute. I needed a day, a week, a year, to process all the strange things that I'd encountered. Spirits were real. Witches existed. Vampires dwelled in both the day and night and drank human blood. Vampires and humans could even have babies together, oh my.

I staggered down the rocky beach and found some dry sand. I sat down, crossing my legs, and stared out at the sea. The waves crashed, one after another, and then rolled back out. There were so many things to think about, but my mind went stubbornly blank.

"Hey." James followed me down onto the shore. He took off his flip-flops and made his way through the cool sand. "Is this seat taken?"

I motioned for him to join me.

"Too much all at once, huh?" He sat close, our shoulders touching, as he stared out at the water.

I sifted some sand through my hands. "It wasn't all at once. We've been baby-stepping through most of this. But I didn't even guess this—about the others, I mean. I thought they were humans. It never even crossed my mind that they weren't."

"Well, they are human." James squinted out at the water. "But there's more to it."

"Yeah." I continued to play with the sand. The way it felt against my skin, silky and cool, soothed me. "I keep trying to understand what you just said, about the balance, but I can't. It doesn't make any sense to me."

"I'm sure it doesn't." He raked a hand through his thick, coarse hair. "It's difficult to explain."

"Do you think you could try?" I asked. "Otherwise, I think I might go crazy."

"Of course." He squinted out at the water. "I guess maybe a good way would be to think about the equinox. We just celebrated the summer solstice, right? That's the longest day of the year, when the sun stays with us for the most time. Then there's the winter solstice, which represents the 'death' of the earth, when it goes to sleep and rests before its rebirth in the spring. Different groups all over the world have celebrated the equinox for centuries. But what they represent to me, personally, is balance."

I stretched my legs out. "Between the seasons?"

"Yes, but also, between dark and light."

I stared straight ahead. "But you're not just talking about daylight savings, are you."

"No." James shook his head. "The thing with the equinox is, it represents the consistency of balance. No matter what else has changed in the world, in our existence, the relationship of sunlight and darkness hasn't changed. It's constant."

"Okay..."

"Consistency in balance is key," James continued. "I could get into a whole physics dissertation about the laws of balance—"

"Please don't," I moaned, "I already took physics."

My teacher, Mr. Whistler, used to pace the front of our class, drilling the laws of physics into our heads. A-student that I was, I dutifully memorized them. But they didn't mean anything to me, not in real life. I mean, I understood the basic laws of motion and relativity, but I didn't understand why I had to regurgitate them on our final exam. What was the point?

I traced a line in the sand. "I remember Newton's Laws—I can quote them word-for-word. I just had my final a few weeks ago."

"Okay, so what was Newton's first law?"

"Seriously?" When James didn't say anything, I sighed. "An object at rest stays at rest. An object in motion stays in motion. They'll continue with the same speed and in the same direction unless acted upon by an unbalanced force.'"

"I knew you were an AP kind of girl." James nudged

me. "Since you studied Newton's laws, then you also know that an unbalanced force causes *acceleration*. Hold onto that thought for a second."

He didn't say anything else for a full minute, letting his words sink in.

Unbalanced force. Acceleration.

"What are you saying—I mean, what are you saying that you *aren't* saying?"

James stared out at the waves. "I think maybe we started some sort of acceleration."

My head was starting to throb again. "Acceleration of what?"

"Change. I think there are big changes happening."

I rubbed my temples and he sighed.

"Let me explain to you why I believe this. Stay with me, okay?"

He patted my back then continued. "As someone who's had experience with real darkness, I know the beauty of light. But it's my belief that you can't have one without the other—that's what I mean when I talk about balance. So light and dark, winter and summer, spring and fall.

"Like with the seasons, sometimes the hard parts— the darkness—seems like it lasts longer than the light. Winters can drag on forever. There are days when you forget what the warmth of the sun feels like. But you *know* that it shifts over time, and changes again. You can depend on it. It's all part of a cycle that's been going on since the beginning of time."

I nodded. "I'm from New England—I understand a long winter. And I get it about darkness and light. What I don't understand is what you're saying about an unbalanced force and acceleration. You're going to have to explain that to me and do it slow."

James blew out a deep breath. "My father thinks I'm the beginning of something, because I'm the first."

I nodded, waiting for him to continue.

"To our knowledge, I'm the only vampire in existence to survive a staking. I'm also the only one who has these new powers, my light. We've never seen anything like it before. So my father thinks that I've transformed from darkness to light, and I don't disagree with him," James said. "Once my new life started, I began to notice a difference in the world. For a long time, I thought it was just me—that things had changed because *I'd* changed. And to a certain extent that was true, because I was seeing everything with new eyes."

He picked up a rock and skimmed it across the water. "I saw more kindness, more generosity. I saw people actually wanting to make the world better through their own actions. It wasn't something I'd experienced before."

"Do you think that's because you were a vampire? And your existence had been really different before that?" I asked.

"No, it wasn't just that. I still associated with some of the same vampires, and I didn't change my habits that much, aside from no longer feeding on humans. But from what I saw of the world, it was like both vampires and people were waking up, or something. I don't know." James shrugged his big shoulders. "I started to see more of the light, less of the darkness."

"So what does your father think about all this? He believes that you're the beginning of something...but what?"

He coughed. "He thinks I'm an...." The last word was muffled by yet another cough.

I blinked at him. "I'm sorry?"

"He thinks I'm an angel."

No more blinking—I just stared.

"Ha. I had a feeling you'd react like that."

I looked above my head, for whatever color my aura was betraying me with. "Like what?"

He skimmed another rock. "Like I'm crazy."

"I've accepted that you're a former vampire. I think I at least deserve some credit."

331

James seemed to consider that. "Sure. But now you have to get to the next level."

"So... Vampires, witches, mediums, ghosts... And angels?"

He nodded. "That's what my dad thinks, anyway. He said the only being that could dwell in this existence that was formerly immortal, and then became immortal-undead, has got to be an angel."

"An angel." I turned the word over in my mind. All I could think about were wings, and halos, and little cherubs bouncing on clouds. "Huh. So since you've saved me twice, does that make you my guardian angel?" I joked.

James frowned as he dug through the rocks around us, looking for a good one to skim.

"James." I watched him, but he wouldn't look at me. "Do you think you're my guardian angel?"

He shrugged. "Would it be any crazier than any of the other stuff I've told you?"

I opened my mouth and then closed it. *Yes. No.* "I don't know anymore."

"That's fair," he said.

I suddenly, overwhelmingly, wanted to go to bed. Unable to process any more, my mind was begging for the 'off' button. "D'you think you can drive me home?" I asked weakly. "I'm pretty tired."

James looked vaguely hurt. "Sure."

I didn't want to make him upset, and I didn't want to go home and face Becky, but my brain was like a sponge that had been dunked in a bucket. *Immortal. Undead. Angel. Acceleration.* I was overflowing. If I was going to turn into a puddle, it was best to do it in private.

REAR WINDOW

I TOLD James I'd meet him at the truck, but I'd left my phone inside. I headed up on the deck, but I heard an argument coming from inside the house. I cracked the door, then hesitated.

"Taylor might not want you to do that," James was saying, but Josie interrupted him.

"She *definitely* doesn't want to get assaulted for the third time in a row, so I'm doing my sage!" she yelled.

"You need to calm down." James's voice was strained. Apparently, Josie wasn't the only one who needed to cool off.

I went in, grabbing my phone off the table in the living room, and found them facing off in the kitchen. "What's going on?"

"I'm coming down tonight to burn some sage in your

yard," Josie said. "And the next time Becky leaves, I'm going to need you to call me. I need to burn some in the house, too."

"Burning sage—what does that do?" I asked her.

"It's called 'smudging.' It's an old remedy to clear out bad spirits," Josie said. "I just take some fresh sage, bundle it, and then burn it. The smoke purifies the air, detoxifies it."

"Okay. If you think it'll help, thank you. Please do it." I turned to James. "Did you tell her about the necklace?"

"No, I completely forgot." James pulled the chain from his pocket; the aquamarine pendant winked in the fading light. "We found this in the yard today when we got back from Pine Harbor—it's Amelia's. Edgar had it out in the grass."

"Oh. Ugh, ugh…" Josie started pacing the room, shaking her head. "This isn't good."

"What? What's wrong?" I asked.

"This." Josie took the necklace from James and lifted it up. "There's so much weird stuff going on. The pot's being stirred. And the fact that this necklace showed up down here means something—but I don't know what, and that worries me."

James looked a little pale, the muscles in his face taut. "I had the same thought."

Josie clutched the necklace. "Okay. Dylan and I are

going to get to work on this. Taylor—we'll be in your yard tonight, but don't come out. We'll be quiet. No one will even know we're there. But can you call me tomorrow if you know Becky's going out? I need to get in the house as soon as possible."

"Of course."

James motioned for me to follow him. "C'mon, I'll take you home."

I said goodbye to Josie and followed James outside, down the deck and out to the truck. We drove over the bumpy gravel in silence, not touching.

"Are you..." James frowned instead of finishing his question.

"What?"

He shifted uncomfortably in his seat. "Are you *mad* at me?"

"No." I leaned back against the cool interior. "I'm just exhausted. I need to think about all the stuff you told me tonight, but it's like I can't get my brain to work. I just want to go to bed."

He didn't say anything, just drove slowly as we reached the road.

"I'm sorry if I hurt your feelings." I turned to look at him. His mouth was pulled down, his eyes were dark.

"You didn't." He stared straight ahead when he said,

"And I understand if this changes the way you feel about me."

"It doesn't."

"Even though there are consequences to it—ones that can put you in danger?" he asked.

"No. Nothing's going to change how I feel." I leaned forward as we pulled into the drive. The lights were on, and I could see my dad, Becky and Amelia through the windows. It looked like they were watching television. "But speaking of danger, how do you think I should deal with Becky tonight? D'you think she's going to spazz out on me again?"

James put the truck in park. "I think you need to stay away from her but do it so it seems casual. Same with Amelia. We want to keep Becky happy, on an even keel, so tell her we're confirmed for the gala and that I'm pulling out all the stops. Then say you're not feeling well and head straight to bed."

My pulse was suddenly racing. "Okay."

"Taylor." James waited until I looked at him to continue. "I'll be watching over you. You don't have to be afraid—I'll protect you, no matter what."

I nodded, then reached over and kissed his cool cheek. "Good night."

He reached up and put my face in his hands, then

gave me a long look before he reluctantly released me. "Good night."

I took a deep breath as I got out of the safety of the truck and headed inside to Becky's. "Hey, you're home early," Dad said, a smile on his face even as he surreptitiously inspected me. "Everything okay?"

"Yeah, I'm just really tired from hiking this morning." I forced a smile at them. Amelia was slouched in an armchair, legs dangling over the side, her phone in her face. Becky was sitting on the couch with a throw on her lap, drinking what looked like herbal tea. "How are you guys?"

"Great." Becky gave me a bright, fake smile.

Amelia yawned. "Fine."

"I have a double tomorrow, so I'm just going to head to bed. Becky, James wanted me to tell you that he's excited about the gala and he's going all out for it." I fake-smiled extra hard so maybe she wouldn't attack me again.

"That's awesome! And Taylor, sorry about last night. I don't remember much, but your dad said I was pretty out of it. I took one of my allergy pills before I had a glass of wine, and it really affected me." She raised her mug of tea toward me. "I won't make that mistake again."

"I'm glad you're feeling better. See you guys tomorrow." Under normal circumstances, I would hug my dad goodnight, but I didn't want to risk Becky's ire.

I raced upstairs to my room and locked the door behind me.

It was early, probably too early to go to sleep. I took a shower, put on my favorite pajamas and brushed my teeth. Then I climbed into bed and just sat there.

My limbs were heavy, but my mind was restless. I grabbed my book off the nightstand, but I couldn't focus on the words. I picked my phone up, saw there were no new messages, and put it down. I wanted something, anything, to distract me from the buzzing in my head. But I knew there was no relief in sight. Time would be the only thing that would help the panic-loop of tangled thoughts subside. *Angels. Vampires. Witches. Balance. Consequences.*

I closed my eyes and tried to focus on my breathing.

Not being much of an athlete eventually saved me; I was so physically tired from last night waitressing and our little hike that morning, I eventually drifted off to sleep. Strange images met me in my dreams, a glimpse of my mother in the darkness, Adam emerging from the pool, Becky's wineglass smashed on the floor. I woke up briefly and rolled over, blinking at the clock. It was two-thirty a.m.

I lay there for a while, unable to get back to sleep. I

checked my phone: a text from James, five minutes ago. *Are you up?*

Yes, I texted back.

There was a tap on my window.

I jerked in my bed, startled, as my phone buzzed again. *It's me. Sorry.*

I exhaled deeply and went to the window, sliding it open. James was crouched on the nearby roof, his face outside the screen. "Hey—I'm so sorry I scared you. I guess it's my day to be an idiot."

"What are you doing here?" I whispered.

"Josie and Dylan are smudging the yard, so I came down with them."

"How did you get up there?"

I could see the ghost of a smile on his lips. "I climbed."

To my knowledge, there was no way to scale Becky's huge house to get onto the roof. "On a ladder?"

He shrugged. "It's more like I jumped."

"Ah." I looked around my room, wondering if it was safe to let him in. My bedroom was above the kitchen, on the other side of the house from everyone else. "Do you want to come in?"

"Are you sure you want me to?"

"It's a new day—so stop being an idiot." I grinned as I

slid the screen open and James wriggled through. He landed in a surprising heap on my floor. "Are you okay?"

He pulled himself up into a seat. "Are you *laughing* at me, Taylor?"

"No." But my shoulders shook. "I just figured you'd have some supernatural way to have a cool entrance."

"Yeah well." James stood up. "I'm more human than I seem sometimes."

"So Josie and Dylan are out there?" I went and peered through the window, but it inconveniently faced the rear yard. I inhaled deeply; there was a woodsy, smoky scent wafting through the air.

James nodded. "They're going to smudge the woods around the house, too, just to be safe."

"What does the sage do?" I asked, as I closed the screen and relocked the window.

"It cleans out old spirits, and traces of spirits."

"So…it works kind of like your light does?"

He nodded. "But smudging is a tried-and-true remedy that's been used for centuries."

"They're double-checking your work?" I teased.

"Something like that." He raked a hand through his hair and shifted on his feet. "Are you sure it's okay that I'm in your room?"

I reached for his hand, melting a little because he

seemed the slightest bit unsure of himself. "I'm happy you're in my room. Do you think it's safe?"

James nodded. "If anyone wakes up, I'll be long gone before they ever get here."

"So…" My heart swelled. "Does that mean you can stay?"

He squeezed my hand. "Only if you want me to—and I swear it's to talk to you and protect you, not to try to get into your pants, as our old friend Adam would say."

I grinned at him in the semi-darkness. "Then sleep over."

"Your wish is my command. By the way, cute pajamas."

"Ha. Thanks." My cheeks heated. My pjs consisted of multicolored striped bottoms and a T-shirt emblazoned with a smiling rainbow.

I went and sat on the edge of the bed, unsure of what came next.

James slid out of his flip flops and flopped down next to me, making himself at home. He picked up a lock of my hair and ran it through his fingers. "Did you get any sleep?"

"A little."

"Do you feel any better?"

I sighed. "Not really, but only because I still don't

understand everything that you told me. It's like I can't think it through."

He nodded. "But you *do* already understand, Taylor. You know about unbalanced forces."

"I guess so." I laid down next to him and stared at the ceiling. "In physics, an unbalanced force is a force that can move something. It can *accelerate* something because there's no equal force pushing back against it. Right?"

"A-plus." James rolled over and looked at me. "Here's how I think this applies to us. Like I told you, when I transitioned from being a vampire, I saw the world in a very different way. I saw that more people were waking up—and by that, I mean seeing beyond what was right in front of their faces. They were waking up spiritually, and as I left my despair from being a vampire behind, so did I."

"Okay. That makes sense so far. At least, the part about you does."

"Like I told you, my father thinks my change in and of itself fundamentally shifted things because I left the side of dark and joined the side of light."

I nodded, even though he was nudging up on the part I didn't comprehend.

"Since I've met you, I think things have changed even more." He brought my hand to his lips and kissed it. "It's true what I said—I've never felt this way about anyone in my existence. I know it was fate that brought me to the island this summer, that brought me to you."

Shivers rippled down my spine, and as if in reassurance, he kissed my hand again.

"But since we've been together, activity has kicked up around us. Josie said it best—the pot's being stirred. I feel like we're in the eye of a storm. I've always been around the supernatural, seen the unseen in the world. But this is different. These are 'regular' humans who are acting out. It's not something I've ever experienced before."

"But why?" I whispered. "I don't understand what you and I have to do with anything other than us."

James took a deep breath. "I think because I love you, and you..."

"And I love you," I finished for him.

"And you love me," he reached out and tenderly stroked my face. "I think that's impacting people around us. I told you what I thought of Becky—that she can't see anything that's not right in front of her face. What I mean by that is, she's not awake. She sees labels and money and houses and status as something real, other than what it really is—a distraction."

"A distraction from what?"

James continued to stroke the hair from my face.

"Her spirit. Her mortality. Nature. The suffering around her, and the beauty."

"That's pretty deep, James."

He chuckled. "I've had a long time to work on my philosophical side. But the point is, maybe she sees our relationship as a threat to her world order. Because she only sees what's on the surface of things, and we violate her sense of right and wrong. Does that at least make some sense to you?"

I nodded in the darkness. Why she cared, I couldn't understand, but I knew she did. Becky didn't want me to be with James, even though it was convenient for her fundraiser. She wanted me to stay in my place, in my efficiency apartment, far from her sight.

"I think because I'm a supernatural, this has riled her up in a way that she might not even be aware of. A fundamental way. So back to our physics lesson—when things are in balance, things stay in place, or stay moving like they always have. When there's an unbalanced force—like maybe, you and me—there's acceleration. Things happen. Things *change*. And because of that there might be pushback. There might be a scramble from some other force to restore order, to restore balance."

"So you think the fact that we're dating has caused a shift." I stared up at the ceiling, seeing little dots play in front of my eyes in the darkness. "You think there are consequences to it."

He nodded. "I think we're seeing them now, like what happened with Becky."

"So what do we do?" I almost asked him if we should break up, but I didn't want him to say yes, so I fell silent as I waited for his answer.

"I think you should go to sleep, and that I should figure it out." James kissed my cheek, then pulled the blankets up to my chin. "We can talk more tomorrow. My father had some ideas—I'll talk to him again. But for now, it's my duty and my honor to protect you, Taylor Hale."

My exhaustion from earlier crept up, along with an overwhelming feeling of relief because James was there. Things were crazy, but I felt so safe with him near. "Thank you... I love you." The words still tasted funny on my lips, fresh and new and filled with a raw, wild hope.

"I love you, too."

With James watching over me, I fell into a deep, dreamless sleep.

TOO FACED

"SOMEONE'S COMING," James whispered in my ear. "I'll be out on the roof." Before I'd even really woken up, he was gone.

Early morning sunlight streamed into the room. I squinted at the clock: five-forty-five a.m.

There was a knock on my door. "Taylor?" Becky called. She jiggled the handle.

I'd forgotten I'd locked it. I crept to the door, heart pounding. "Is everything all right?"

"Yeah…" She sounded slightly confused. "Why is your door locked?"

I took a deep breath. James was outside, but he would protect me. Somehow. "Old habit, I guess."

She tried the handle again. "Open up."

"Um, I'm not even dressed," I lied. "Can we just talk later?"

"I want to talk to you *now*."

It was scary Becky. What I *didn't* know if it was scary-shaky Becky.

"O-Okay." I unlocked the door and opened it a crack. Becky stood on the landing outside, fully dressed in her workout clothes, hair up in a high ponytail.

"I thought you said you weren't dressed." She eyed my rainbow pajamas with vague disgust, as though they might be contagious with something vile, like a Walmart vibe.

"Is there something you want to tell me?" Becky asked. Her voice was laced with an unspoken accusation.

"Um…" An image of her seizure-like episode flashed in my mind, but I shook my head. "I don't think so?"

She crossed her arms against her chest. "Amelia's missing the necklace we got her for her birthday. The one with the aquamarine. Do you know anything about that?"

"No, I haven't seen it." Wait, was she asking if I'd seen it, or if I'd *stolen* it? "When did she lose it?"

"Oh, she didn't lose it." Becky took a step closer. In the early morning sunlight, the smattering of freckles across her nose made her look wholesome, as if she might pour me an iced tea and set out a plate of homemade biscuits. "Someone took it from her room. They left her jewelry box open on her dresser."

"That's terrible." My cheeks heated. Could Edgar have come into the house and taken Amelia's necklace? I highly doubted it, even with all the craziness I'd experienced lately.

Becky's ice-blue eyes narrowed as she waited for me to say more, possibly to confess my guilt. "You don't know anything about it?"

"N-No." I was the worst liar ever.

"Taylor." She took another step closer, and I held onto the door tight in case I needed to slam it in her face. "There's only one person who would've done this."

"I didn't touch it, Becky." My chin wobbled a bit, like the time my French teacher accused me of cheating on a quiz. I wasn't guilty, but the allegation still made me feel dirty.

Becky's smart watch must've buzzed or something, because she glanced at it and cursed. "I have to go. You better not be l-l-l-lying to me Taylor." She shook briefly for a moment, her face turning into an incomprehensible blur. It stopped as quickly as it started.

Once it subsided, she blinked at me, that familiar scowl on her face. "What are you staring at?"

"Nothing."

"I'll deal with you later." With a toss of her ponytail, she huffed down the stairs.

I closed the door, relocked it, and sank back down on my bed.

"Hey—I saw that. I would've come in, but she stopped so quick." James came back through the window feet first. He landed and stared at me. "Are you okay?"

I stared at the floorboards. "I don't know."

"It's not safe for you here anymore."

I put my hands in my face. "What do you expect me to do?"

He knelt before me. "Come and stay at the Tower. I'll keep you safe, Taylor."

"It's not like I can explain this to my dad," I said. "What am I supposed to say? 'Becky's having some sort of spiritual meltdown, and my boyfriend the guardian angel thinks it's safer if I stay with him.' That's not exactly going to fly with Big Kyle."

"I'll think of something. It's going to be okay, I promise." He went still for a second then said, "Your dad's waking up. I should go."

With a quick peck on my cheek, James climbed back out the window, leaving me alone with my swirling thoughts.

"Hey!" Eden gave me a big smile when I got to work, but it quickly turned to a worried frown. "Everything okay? You look a little…tired."

"Yeah, I am." I scrubbed a hand over my face.

She waggled her eyebrows. "Did you stay up late making out with James?"

"Not exactly. He made me dinner, though. It was pretty good." I filled up the water pitchers, remembering the few things I could safely share with Eden. "Patrick was asking about you—he was disappointed that you couldn't come down last night."

She shrugged. "A girl's gotta work."

"I think he really likes you."

"Yeah…. About that." She sucked in a deep breath. "Brian called me yesterday."

"How did that go?"

"Not great. I told him I'd met someone and he flipped out."

I started stuffing sugar packets into the ramekins. "I thought you agreed to date other people this summer."

"We did, but I'm the only one who's doing it." Eden grabbed a bag of coffee and started measuring it and dumping it into a filter. "He didn't actually think I'd go through with it, so he was pretty upset."

"Ugh. I'm sorry."

"It's okay. But he threatened to come up here—he said he wants to see me, so I remember how good we are together."

"Wow. He's serious, huh?"

She winked at me. "I guess I'm hard to get over. Anyway. We're both on a double today, so let's try and have some fun, okay? I don't want to think about stupid boys for the next seven hours."

I grinned at her. Stupid boys weren't what I was avoiding, but I still craved a distraction. "Deal."

Before I went back to check the specials, I remembered that I hadn't asked for a gala ticket for Elias. Before I got any tables, I quickly texted James and asked him if it would be okay. He texted back *yes* immediately, so I sailed into the kitchen, happy to have some good news.

"Hey New Girl." Elias greeted me with a smile. "Word on the street is that you have your first double today. Jenny must think you're doing all right if she put you on the schedule for that."

"Thank you. It's definitely getting better." I grinned at him. No matter what else was going on, the fact that I was not as much as a disaster at waiting tables made me feel pretty good. "Hey, I just wanted to let you know—I got you a ticket to the gala. I didn't want you to think that I forgot."

"Yes, Taylor! Way to come through—I already pressed my suit. I could get used to having celebrity friends." His face split into a grin. "This doesn't mean you can take food without a ticket, though!"

Thankfully the restaurant was busy for lunch, and the waves of customers spilled over into dinner. My station filled and emptied, then filled again. I found that I could use shorthand, making it easier to take my notes, and that balancing things on a tray had gotten slightly less terrifying. The day passed in a blur, with no sign of James, Josie or the others. A different bartender was working today, a retired fisherman named George. He smiled and nodded when we picked up our drinks, then got back to chatting with his cronies at the bar.

By eight p.m. the hostess started seating parties in other people's sections, not mine and Eden's. "They do that when you work a double, so you can go home earlier." Eden yawned. "That's fine by me—I'm ready to pack it in."

"Me too." I checked my phone. My dad had texted me an hour ago, saying they'd driven the boat over to Pine Harbor to grab a late dinner and pick up some groceries. *Good.* I immediately texted Josie, to let her know that the house would be open for probably another hour. Maybe her sage would eradicate Becky's strange shivering.

One could only hope.

Eden dropped me off at my driveway, and Josie pulled up a minute later. "I'm going to park down at the dock and walk up, so my jeep's not here. Be right back—thanks for letting me know."

I waited for her, staring up at the blanket of stars overhead. There was a slight breeze, swaying the tips of the firs. I wondered if Edgar was around, or was he asleep? Did crows sleep? And then I wondered again how he came across the necklace. Josie interrupted my musings a minute later as she strode up the driveway, a bag slung over her shoulder. She followed me inside.

"They went to dinner about an hour ago, so I don't know when they're coming back." I flicked on the lights in the living room. "We probably don't have that long. Is James coming down?" I hadn't heard from him all day, which was weird.

Josie started digging through her bag. "Nah, he's been on a call with his dad for the past hour. Are you in withdrawal, or something?"

"Ha ha." But I felt a little mopey. "I just haven't talked to him all day."

She found what she needed and pulled it out—a bundle of fresh, stalky green herbs, held together by multiple loops of twine, a lighter, and a flashlight. "Hold this." She handed me the light.

"Why do we need it?"

"In case they pull in the driveway and we're up their bedroom—I don't want all the lights on, do you?"

"No."

Josie got straight to business. She held the herbs, lighting the bushier end. The sage immediately began to flame; Josie blew on it so that it didn't burn, only smolder. The smoke curled up toward the ceiling, its pungent scent filling the room.

"Here we go." Josie went through the living room, waving the sage like it was a duster in corners high and low. She swung it above the couch, back and forth, the smoke settling down on the cushions.

"They'll be able to smell it, huh?" I asked.

"Actually the scent disappears pretty quick. I'll move as fast as I can so it won't be so bad."

Josie worked quickly. I followed her into the kitchen, where she waved the sage over the appliances, around the refrigerator, and over the sink. Next was the dining room. Again, she made sure to smudge all four corners of the room and then the center. She headed up the dark stairs, so I clicked on the flashlight and followed her. I hadn't been up to this wing of the house at all so far this summer, so it felt strange.

"Which room is Amelia's?" she asked.

When I pointed to the right, she marched in with her sage. Josie moved swiftly, working her way around the room. She hovered over the bed, making sure the smoke hung in the air over Amelia's color-blocked bedspread.

Josie headed into the bathroom, smudging it quickly, then I followed her out to the landing. She led the way with the sage, a smoky torch against the darkness. We headed into my old bedroom, now the guest room, Josie working quickly in the dark. I stayed close, inhaling the smoky scent of the sage and silently praying that it worked some kind of miracle.

"Here we go." Josie stood at the threshold of the master bedroom. Once she crossed over, she shivered. "Oh yeah. There's some bad juju in here."

"There is?" I didn't want my dad to get hurt, or to be around any bad juju, whatever that meant.

"Yeah, I can feel it—it's like a chill." Josie shivered again, then rubbed her arms and started smudging with renewed vigilance. She waved the smoking bundle of herbs in the closets, over the dressers, the window, the rug, all four posters of the bed. She was similarly thorough in the master bath, even climbing inside the tub and going around the toilet.

Once she'd finished, she stood up straight. "There.

That should do it. Let's get out of here, okay? I don't want you to be on Becky's bad side."

I laughed weakly as I followed her down the stairs. "It's a little late for that."

Josie grabbed her bag, careful of the still-smoldering sage. "Walk me out?"

We headed outside and I took a deep breath of the cool nighttime air. "It feels better around here." It was like having fresh, clean sheets. Nothing had been wrong before, exactly, but you could still sense a difference.

Josie inhaled deeply and nodded, looking back at the house. "James told me what happened this morning. Becky thinks you took the necklace."

I sighed. "I don't understand how it got down to the property."

She bounced her knee. "Dylan and I took a look at it —it's some sort of magic. But we're not sure what kind."

"Magic?"

"Yeah." Nervous energy rolled off her in waves. "Edgar didn't just randomly find that necklace. Where I come from, there's no such thing as a coincidence."

"Speaking of where you come from..." I had so many questions, and not enough time to ask them. "How long have you been a witch? Is it like being a vampire—are you born that way?"

"I think so. Not everybody agrees with that, but I

knew I was a witch since I was a little girl. I could make things happen, and I saw things that other people couldn't see."

"Do you mean spirits? Ghosts? Are you a medium, too?"

"No, I don't consider myself a medium. But I was always aware that there were things that I could see that weren't visible to other people. I had an aunt who was like that, too. And my grandma. They both had the sight. They recognized it in me early, and they raised me to respect it."

"So you've been practicing witchcraft since you were a kid."

"Yeah." Josie answered my question, but her focus still seemed to be solely on the house.

"So how long have you actually known James? He told me how he met you, you know."

She finally tore her gaze from the house and raised her eyebrows. "He *did*?"

"Yeah. He said that a vampire had attacked you, and that he saved you."

"Did he give you any more detail than that?"

I shook my head. "Am I missing something?"

"Hell yes, you are. But I'll leave it to him to tell you." She went still for a second. "I hear a car—I'm going to run. See you tomorrow."

Before I could properly thank her, she was gone. I raced back into the house, heading up to my bedroom before my dad, Becky and Amelia came in. Becky's appearance at my door that morning had scared me, as had her quivering.

I wasn't ready to face her again. Not even close.

38

PROTECTIVE

Before I even turned on the light, I locked the door. When I turned around, James was sitting on my bed.

"Oh my God!" I clapped a hand over my heart to stop its wild lurch.

"Ugh, I have to stop doing that to you." James looked sheepish. "Sorry—I texted. You didn't see it?"

I took a couple of deep, calming breaths before I answered. "I didn't have a chance to check my phone."

"Ah. Next time, I'll wait until you text me back."

"Next time?" I went to the bed and wearily sank down.

"You said your dad would never agree to let you come stay at my house, so here I am. Your protector. I'm not leaving you alone again."

"That's sweet, but..." I looked down at my rumpled

polo and chowder-stained shorts. "I'm sort of disgusting."

"Hardly." He leaned up and kissed me, his lips lingering near my throat. "Although you *do* sort of smell like fried haddock.

"Ew, give me a minute." I headed toward the bathroom, then stopped. "Are you sure this is safe?" I suddenly remembered to whisper. My dad, Becky and Amelia had come in and were rummaging around in the kitchen, probably putting groceries away.

"It's absolutely safe. If I hear anything, I'll hide. No one will see me unless Becky goes off again—in which case, I'll shield you."

I sighed in relief. I really didn't want to be alone with her. "Thank you."

His eyes sparkled. "It's my pleasure, roomie."

Warmth bloomed in my chest as I took a shower, hopefully scrubbing the scent of fish and chips off of me. I brushed my teeth carefully, then put on a clean T-shirt and a pair of sweats. It would be nice to have something super cute to sleep in, but aside from my pilled rainbow pajamas, this was it. It would have to do.

James didn't seem disappointed when I returned. His smile was huge, dimple winking, as I climbed onto the bed.

"Hi." It felt awkward, and awesome, to have him there.

"Hi." He laced his fingers through mine. "I missed you today."

"I missed you, too." I faced him and we grinned at each other. "So...how was your day?"

"It was productive, I think. I had a long talk with my father. He said he wants to meet you."

"Oh. Wow." The idea of meeting *the* Nelson Champlain, gazillionaire-hedge-fund owner and ancient vampire, seemed more than a little bit intimidating. "What about your mom? You never talk about her."

A shadow crossed James's face. "We aren't very close."

"Oh. Is it okay for me to ask why not?"

"Of course, but it's difficult to answer." He rolled over onto his back. "Let's just say that we've had our differences over the years. We don't see eye-to-eye on a lot of issues."

His answer was hardly illuminating, but I sensed that he wasn't willing to share more at the moment. "So... Is your dad coming up here?"

He shook his head. "He can't, not with all the locals still around. Maybe when it's fall, or maybe we could go out there instead."

My heart stuttered. "Out where?"

"He's in Oregon right now. We could visit him there, or maybe Hawaii."

"Um." I laughed. "I can't picture my dad letting me go on a vacation with you. He'd probably rather ground me for the rest of my life."

James turned to look at me. "Aren't you turning eighteen in September?"

"Y-Yes."

"Once you're eighteen, you don't need his permission."

I leaned up on my arm and stared at him. "What are you saying? I'm going to be a senior at MDI. I can't just take off."

James's gray-blue gaze pierced mine. "But what if you needed to, in order to be safe?"

I shook my head. "You're keeping me safe. Isn't that enough?"

His gaze darkened. "I don't know, but I'm not willing to risk you to find out. If Becky keeps showing signs like this, me sneaking into your room every night isn't going to be enough."

"Do you think you should zap her?" The thought had crossed my mind more than once that day.

"Maybe. But I don't know what it will do to her—I don't want to erase you from her memory completely, and I'm worried that I might. Because if she attacks you again, my power will be strong. I won't be able to control my reaction, at least... I don't think I will. I've never been in this situation before."

"When have you used your light, aside from Adam? In what types of situations?"

James put his hands behind his head, causing his large, pale biceps to bulge. "I've only used it on people, and vampires, a few times. And only in extreme circumstances. If I'm very upset, it can be dangerous."

"Can you kill someone with it?" I asked.

He frowned. "Probably. My light can't kill a vampire, though. It can seriously wound them, but not destroy them. Only one hundred years of starvation or a stake can do that."

"Speaking of vampires..." I tilted my head as I looked at him. "You told me you met Josie when a vampire was attacking her. I asked her about it tonight—she said there was more to the story."

"Huh?" He pretended to not know what I was talking about.

"She said there was a *lot* more."

He shook his head. "I dunno. Hey, c'mere." He pulled me in for a kiss, then nuzzled my neck.

I moaned, relishing the feel of his scratchy face against my sensitive throat. Then I realized that he was trying to divert my attention away from what I'd asked.

"Hey." I reluctantly pulled back. "Can you tell me what she meant?"

James stared at my mouth. "Wouldn't you rather do this?"

"Yes, of course I would. But stop staring at me like that! Use your mouth to *talk*."

He flopped back on the bed, a grumpy expression on his face as he stared at the ceiling. "I thought Josie was all about keeping my secrets. Now she won't shut up."

"She burned her sage all through the house. She's trying to help me," I reminded him. "Also, she said she felt something in Becky's room. She said it made her shiver. Not *shiver* shiver, but it made her cold."

He nodded but didn't say anything.

"Anyway, I'm the one who brought up the attack. I was asking about her past."

James scowled. "I bet she left out quite a bit."

"Oh, I'm sure she did. She said you should be the one to tell me."

He exhaled in a hiss.

"So?"

"Are you sure you want to hear this?" he asked.

"Yes. I want to know everything."

He turned to face me. "When I found her, there was a vampire feasting on her. She was about to die, or maybe he was going to turn her. I don't know."

I sat up. "Woah—we haven't talked about being turned. You can do that?"

James nodded. "We have to drink enough of a human's blood—almost all of it. Then we can secrete another compound which starts the change. But not everybody survives the transition. It's pretty brutal."

"But vampires who are turned... Do they have the same powers? Are they immortal?"

His gaze flicked to me, then back up to the ceiling. "Yes. But like I said, not everyone survives the process. It's very, very dangerous."

"H-Have you ever turned anybody?"

"No. And I never would, Taylor. I don't believe in it. If you're born human, you should stay human. Changing someone violates the balance, in my opinion."

"But you changed," I said softly.

He shook his head. "That's not the same. That was nature—no one *did* anything to me to make me what I am."

I trailed my finger along the comforter, my brain racing along with the new information.

"Don't even think about it." James's voice was stony. "I would never, *could* never, turn you. Don't go all Bella and Edward on me—it's not like that, not at all."

"Like what?"

"Romantic. If I tried to turn you, you would probably

die. Do you want that on my conscience for the rest of my existence?"

"Of course not." I frowned. "But would you do it, if you had to? Like, to save me? Or to save someone else?"

He sighed and rolled over, his back to me. "I don't ever want to have to make that choice. I've seen it for myself. It's terrible, and it goes against what I believe in: the natural order."

I gently prodded his back. "I'm not asking you to turn me. I was just curious. You can understand that, can't you?"

"I guess." He waited a minute before he rolled over and faced me. "But can you understand that I don't ever want you to ask me to make that choice? I couldn't live with myself, Taylor."

"Okay, okay." We could figure out the logistics of our vampire-human relationship later. The ramifications of my mortality and his lack of it weren't things I'd even begun to consider. "Back to Josie. Will you please tell me the story?" He was already agitated, it was probably better to just get it over with.

His gray eyes were mesmerizing. "Remember when I told you my brother was dead?"

The turn in the conversation startled me. "Of course."

"Well... I wasn't being technical. When I said he was

dead, I meant, he was dead to *me*." The muscle in his jaw jumped. "He's the one who attacked Josie. That's who I saved her from: my brother."

I stared at him. "You mean he's still alive?"

He shrugged. "Last I heard. He's been banished from our family. That's one of the reasons my mother and I don't get along. She doesn't think I'm on the 'right' side."

"Which side is that?"

"Her side." His scowl deepened. "She's sort of a... vampire supremacist."

"What?"

"She thinks vampires are a superior race and humans are our playthings, blah blah blah."

I couldn't imagine James being related to someone like that. "What does your father think?"

"He used to be like that. It was a long, long time ago. So they have their differences, and in some respects my mother feels betrayed because he's changed his vision of the world. He supported me about my brother—it was his decision to cast him out. My mother won't ever forgive him for it. But they've been together for centuries, and hopefully they'll stay that way. My father's a big believer in keeping your friends close and your enemies even closer. It would be dangerous if my mother went out on her own."

I swallowed hard. "Oh."

James laughed, but it was without humor. "I guess you're even less excited about meeting my parents now."

"It's not that." I laid back against the bed, taking his hand in mine. "I just don't want to make things any harder on you."

"You're not." He squeezed my hand.

"So your brother…" I hesitated. "What's his name?"

"Luke." He spit the word out.

"Why did Luke attack Josie?"

"He thought she smelled good. And because he knew she was a witch." He shook his head. "If I know my douche brother, he wanted to turn her into a vampire to see if she'd have any special powers."

"Would she?"

He shrugged. "I don't know, and I don't intend to find out. I saved her that day. But I also almost destroyed my brother, and I ripped my family apart. It wasn't a good time."

"Were you close to him before that?"

"Off and on." He stared at the ceiling. "When Luke is good, he's very very good. When he's bad, he's the biggest douchelord of them all."

"Where is he now?" I asked.

"Don't know. Don't care." He looked at the clock. "I think it's time we ended our Q-and-A session. My human girlfriend needs to sleep. It's good for her immune system, all the better to fight off her crazy stepmother."

"Ugh," I said.

"Ugh's a good word for it." He tucked me in, turned off the light and kissed my forehead. He rolled close to me, his big body keeping me warm through the blankets.

"Good night Taylor. I love you."

I giggled. "I could get used to this, you know. My hot guardian-angel-protector-slash-bodyguard keeping watch over me every night."

"You *better* get used to it." He snuggled against me. "Because I'm not going anywhere. Not ever."

39

THE ALTAR

I MADE sure I was up extra early the next morning in an attempt to leave the house before Becky got up. There was an extra bonus: I woke up in James's arms. "Hey." Wary of possible morning breath, I was careful not to talk directly to his face.

He kissed the top of my head. "Good morning."

I peeked up at him. "How are you?"

"Excellent. I enjoyed watching you sleep all night. Do you know that your eyes don't close all the way? It's *adorable.*"

"That's not true." I clutched the comforter to my chest. "My eyes do so close!"

"No they don't," he whispered wickedly. "And neither does your mouth. Like I said: *adorable.*"

I groaned. "You might get banned."

"Nah," James squeezed me in for a hug, and I felt his muscles ripple around me. "You'd be lonely without me."

"That's probably true." James loomed over me, and I couldn't help but stare at his mouth. I was eager to kiss him, to feel those strong arms wrap tighter around me...

James flashed the dimple. "See something you like?"

"Of course I do." I sighed and rolled away from him. If Becky got up early again, I'd have to face her. I had no intention of letting that happen. "But I wanted to get up so I could get out of here soon. I don't want to see Becky."

"I don't blame you. Do you want to come over? I'll make you breakfast, and I can tell you more about what my father said."

"That'd be great."

With the sunlight streaming through the windows behind him, James was lit up, either an angel or a Greek god or a super-hot model. He smiled broadly. He'd probably read my aura, which was likely panting for him.

James kissed my forehead before he left. "I'll be waiting outside."

I floated on air for a moment, then snapped back to reality. I hastily got dressed and brushed my teeth. I hustled down the stairs and scribbled a quick note for my dad, who would be leaving for work soon: *Got up early. Going to hang out with James today. I'm working later. Love you!* My chest squeezed. I hadn't talked to my dad much since Becky had freaked out; I hoped he didn't take it personally.

But my desire to see Big Kyle was outweighed by my fear of Becky. I also had no desire to see Amelia. Was she the one who thought I'd stolen her necklace? I wouldn't put it past her.

I was happy when I made it outside, the chilly Maine morning air bright and bracing against my cheeks. James stood at the end of the drive, grinning at me. It'd only been a minute, but I practically ran to him. "Where's your truck?"

"Around the corner." He didn't stop staring as I approached.

"What?" I looked down at myself. "Are my eyes or my mouth still hanging open?"

"No." His smile broadened as I reached him. "It's just… You're cute."

Warmth bloomed in my chest. "So are you."

He held out his arm for me. "I know."

The island was still sleepy as we slowly drove down to the Tower. "Don't give Josie a hard time about what she told me, okay? Because she didn't actually say anything. And I think I'm just getting on her good side— I'd like to stay there, thank you very much."

373

"Fine."

"So what else did your father have to say?" I asked. "Does he agree with you about your whole physics spiel, about the acceleration?"

He raised his eyebrows. "It's a spiel, now?"

"You know what I mean."

James looked thoughtful as he pulled the truck down the drive. "He agrees that something's been shifted. But he's also always thought that the island had a certain vibration to it, something that you don't find a lot of in other places."

"The *island* has a vibration?"

He nodded. "He thinks it's a crucible for magic. He said he felt that way when he first visited here, so many years ago. He knew there was something special about it —I mean, look around, it's basically nature at its best. I personally haven't been many more places that are more beautiful than Dawnhaven, and I've traveled all over the world."

I looked at the rose bushes, scratching the sides of the truck. They were stunning, perfect, as was the whole island. There was also something mysterious about Dawnhaven, but... "Does he really think it's magic here?"

"Not exactly. It's more like he thinks it's a fertile environment for magic, if that makes sense. Hey—

what's going on?" He pulled past the Private Property sign to the clearing. Josie and Dylan were out on the lawn, waving us down.

James's face was a pale mask.

"What's wrong?"

"I don't know—but let's go find out."

Josie and Dylan waited, tense looks on both of their faces. "We found something," Dylan said, "and it isn't good."

James gripped my hand. "What happened?"

"We need to show you—follow us." Josie started toward the woods and Edgar cawed at us from his perch on a nearby tree.

"Morning, Edgar," James said, and the crow followed our group into the forest.

As soon as we crossed into the trees, I felt a chill. It was noticeably colder in the shadows from the firs, almost a different season altogether. The sun didn't penetrate the canopy. The forest floor was cool and mossy, the tree trunks still damp with dew. "Where are we going?" James asked.

Josie glanced back as she trekked through the woods. "Dylan's been coming out here the past couple of mornings real early to go for a walk. Today Edgar was squawking something fierce—he led her deeper into the forest."

Dylan nodded. "He wanted to show me something. Did you know there was an old well out here?" she asked James.

"Yeah, but they sealed it up years ago. They drilled a new one closer to the house."

Dylan maneuvered through the trees. "Well, someone opened it back up."

Icy needles of fear jabbed down my spine. "We're seriously going down into an abandoned well?"

"We're not going into it," Josie said, pushing a branch back. "We just want to show you what we found."

James stopped. "You can go back to the house, Taylor. You're safe there."

"It's fine." But I didn't object when he pulled me closer.

We walked for another few minutes until Dylan said, "Here it is." She stopped near a small clearing. In the center was a concrete cylinder, about three feet high. Its concrete lid was laid to the side.

"Who the hell moved that?" James asked as we got closer. "It's not exactly light."

"We're not sure who opened it," Dylan said. "But look inside."

Edgar cawed as he landed on a tree nearby. He blinked at us, and at the open well, in rapid succession.

Josie and Dylan grabbed each other's hands as they

got closer and peered inside. "This is seriously creepy." Josie's voice echoed off the interior.

"Let me see." James dropped my hand as I hung back. He looked inside the well. "Oh shit."

I wasn't sure what had made him curse, so I went and looked. "Oh my god!" Inside the dark well someone had strung a net—it looked similar to the netting found inside a lobster trap. On it was what looked like a memorial. A memorial to Amelia...and *James?*

There was a large, framed picture of Amelia in the center of the net. It looked like her most recent one from school. The portrait was surrounded by several objects of hers that I recognized: one of her old teddy bears, an infinity scarf, and a designer-label headband she often wore. There was also a burned-out candle and a large photograph of James, printed out on what looked like copy paper, stuck inside a frame.

It was the same picture Becky had taken the other night at the bar.

The strange collection sent shivers through me. "What *is* this?"

"It's an altar." Dylan crossed her arms against her chest. "We use them for spells all the time."

"An altar? What does it do—what does it mean?"

James took his phone out and took a picture of the

odd assembly while Josie said, "An altar's used for magical purposes—spells, manifestations, or worship."

I took a step back. I didn't want to be anywhere near the well. "Who would be worshiping out here at a creepy old well?"

Dylan frowned as she stared down at the objects. "Whoever made this might not be worshiping here. They might have chosen this place when they asked for a manifestation."

"A manifest-what?" My mouth had gone dry.

Josie stared at the well. "A manifestation is a wish that comes true."

I looked back at the pictures of Amelia and James, placed side by side. I opened my mouth and then closed it: I had no idea what to say.

COUNTDOWN

THE REST of the morning passed quickly. As promised, James made breakfast, but I barely ate. He, Josie and Dylan discussed the memorabilia at the well and the various rationales behind it, but we all knew the truth.

Becky had made that altar.

Did she want Amelia to go out with James? That thought didn't make much sense. Amelia had just turned fourteen, and she was Becky's only child. I knew for a fact that Becky was strict with her daughter about boys —Amelia wasn't even allowed to date yet. So what was with those photos...did Becky want her daughter betrothed to the island's resident hot billionaire? I couldn't exactly picture it.

Still, Becky thought the sun rose and set on Amelia. Maybe she believed that she was simply a better candidate to someday date hedge-fund royalty. She was probably right about that.

"It must be where Edgar got the necklace." Josie put a fresh cup of coffee in front of me. "He was trying to tell us about the well."

James nodded. "I wonder when Becky put everything there."

I dumped cream into my coffee and stirred it, then stared at the swirls.

"Taylor?" James nudged me. "You okay?"

"Oh, I'm great. My stepmother not only hates me, but she's having these weird seizure things, she's almost attacked me twice, and oh yeah—she set up some sort of pagan altar because she wants you to date my fourteen-year-old half-sister. Best day ever!"

He laughed, then abruptly stopped. "Yeah… It's a lot."

I shook my head. "The thing is, that altar is *so* not Becky. The weirdest thing she's into is hot yoga, and maybe the occasional green smoothie. She's color-inside-the-lines *normal*."

Worried that I'd offended them, I quickly said, "Not that you guys aren't normal. But do you know what I mean? Her idea of a good time is a trip to Portland to go to a spa and then hit Nordstrom Rack. I can't picture her out in the middle of the woods, erecting some freaky altar in an abandoned well."

Josie, Dylan and James exchanged a look, but didn't say anything.

"Don't *do* that! Tell me, whatever it is. Just say it."

"She might be under the influence of something that's outside of her normal character." James sat forward. "It's like the shaking—she might not be in control of it, or even aware that it's happening."

I blinked at him. "You think she built that altar and she doesn't even know about it?"

"It's possible." James nodded. "She could be reacting at a fundamental level to changes in the balance. She might not have any idea that these things are happening to her, or that she's doing them."

"That could be true, but remember—she also hates Taylor," Josie said. "She hates her a lot."

I held on tight to my mug. "Gee, thanks for the reminder."

"It's true," James agreed. "She's always had a hard time dealing with Taylor and been jealous of the relationship she has with her dad. But I think the fact that Taylor and I are in love has—"

"Woah woah *woah*," Josie said. "Did you just use the L-word?"

James sighed. I wasn't sure if it was possible, but the faintest blush seemed to creep over his cheeks. "Yes Josie. I just used the L-word."

Josie turned to me. "Are you using it, too?"

My face felt hot. "Y-Yes."

Josie and Dylan gave each other a look, but this time I didn't ask what it meant. Instead, I busied myself by staring at my coffee, cheeks flaming, while James continued.

"Back to what I was saying before I was interrupted by my best friend, who apparently has the social IQ of a seventh-grader." James sat forward in his seat. "My guess is that Becky's riled up in a way she's not even aware of. She's unhappy about Taylor being here this summer, obviously. But I think our relationship has stirred up something deeper inside of Becky—it goes against her sense of justice. Which brings me back to the altar. It looks like she thinks Amelia should be the one with me, not Taylor. I think on some subconscious level she thinks Taylor is stealing something that should have been hers."

"That's *crazy*. Amelia's fourteen!" I put my face in my hands, letting his words sink in. "But you're right—Becky might not even remember making the altar. She accused me of stealing the necklace with a straight face. If she put those things into the well, and I think she did, she probably doesn't remember it."

James nodded. "It's like I said before—I don't think she's awake. I mean spiritually awake, in touch with

THE EQUINOX PACT BOOK 1: AWAKENING

what's going on inside of herself... I don't think she's aware of what's going on. So these things could be happening to her, and she's not even in control of them."

I shivered. "So what do we do?"

"We have to cancel the gala." Josie put her hands on her hips and faced James. "You cannot have that crazy bitch and all her friends running around down here, all drunk and dressed up. It's a recipe for disaster."

"I'm not going to cancel." James's voice was firm. "The fact that I'm hosting the fundraiser makes Becky happy. Becky's less dangerous when she's happy."

"I don't know." Josie shook her head. "I don't think you should let her down here—she's dangerous."

James shrugged. "I'd rather keep an eye on her. After this weekend, we can reassess how we deal with her."

Dylan and Josie looked at each other.

"What?" James sounded irritated.

Dylan sighed. "We're just worried that you're being a little too confident. We haven't dealt with something like this before, and I don't know...that altar gave me the willies."

"Me too," Josie said. "It's the same feeling I had when I was in Becky's room. Chills, and not the good kind."

"I don't think I'm being overconfident when I'm dealing with a human, particularly one who's unconscious. I've lived for thousands of years—it's not my first rodeo. I'm not afraid of Becky." James tilted his head in my direction. "Plus, I have the proper motivation to keep the situation under control."

Josie raised her eyebrows. "I know that. But don't let your L-word, overprotective-immortal mode blind you to the fact that this is something you've never dealt with before, and it could be dangerous! That's all I'm saying. I've never come across someone who makes an altar because they're under some sort of internal spell. That's some crazy shit, if you ask me."

"Fair enough." James nodded. "But it's nothing I can't handle."

Josie muttered something to herself as she and Dylan left the room. It sounded suspiciously like *stuck-up stubborn asshole vampire.*

James and I spent some time cleaning up, then walked the beach. We didn't talk much. A thick silence settled between us, but it didn't feel uncomfortable. He was lost in his thoughts; I was mired in mine. We headed back inside and watched a movie, some documentary about a rock climber who scaled these amazing cliffs with nothing but his hands. It was interesting, but my mind kept wandering back to the strange altar in the woods. I couldn't get Amelia's smiling portrait out of my mind.

I checked my phone; it was creeping into the early

afternoon. "Hey, I should probably head home to get changed soon." I didn't want to leave the safety of the Tower, but I couldn't skip my shift.

James watched me carefully. "Are you sure you want to go?"

I nodded. "I need to work."

"If you need help, I can—"

"No. Please, I have to go." I hopped to my feet. "I appreciate the offer, but I need to take care of myself. You can protect me with your non-sleeping and your magic light, but I'm used to paying my own way."

"Okay." He looked like he wanted to say more, but he stopped himself.

It was bad enough that there was no equilibrium in our relationship. It had also begun sinking in that James could be in danger because of *me*. Becky had been out on his property, doing juju and making an altar in his woods. He was already protecting me twenty-four-seven. I didn't want to be any more of a burden.

He must've caught my train of thought. He squinted at the space above my head. "You okay, Taylor?"

"Yeah I'm great." I forced a smile. "Do you mind giving me a ride?"

THE NEXT FEW days passed in a blur. Fueled by panic, I launched a carefully orchestrated, full-court campaign of familial avoidance. When I wasn't working, I was at James's. I started bringing my uniform with me every morning, changing at the Tower before my shift. I texted my father several times a day, assuring him that I was fine. I faithfully obeyed my curfew.

I barely saw my dad, Becky and Amelia. Each night when I got home from work, I claimed to be tired from so many busy shifts in a row. There was only time to give my dad a quick hug before I escaped to the safety of my room. Becky didn't have a chance to accost me about the necklace, and Amelia could only scowl in my direction.

That worked for me. In spite of my fear, I was excited, thrilled when I got to my bedroom, because James waited for me. After a make out session that was always too short, I fell asleep in his big arms. I knew Becky couldn't hurt me because he was near.

Part of me worried that James's constant presence, his protection, was making me soft. That was probably true, but I didn't want to change a thing. I'd been on my own my whole life. Having James watch over me acted like a drug; I couldn't get enough of him, his soothing presence. I rushed to my room less because I was afraid, more because even though I'd been with him most of the day, I wanted more. Lying in bed with him, wrapped in his arms, I was able fall into a deep, peaceful sleep.

I tried not to worry about my eyes being half open. Or my mouth. But each morning, James didn't seem bothered by anything I'd done. He greeted me with a smile, a reassuring kiss, and my favorite—pulling me close against his powerful chest. He'd hold me for a few precious minutes, the heat spreading between us, as I wrapped my arms around him too.

He always told me he loved me before he climbed out the window. His steel-gray eyes held me captive, then released me before I was ready.

Once he'd gone, even though I knew I'd see him minutes later, I ached.

I'd thought I'd been in love with him before. But that week solidified it—my feelings were turning into something else, something deeper. I couldn't imagine ever being away from him. No matter what had happened with Becky, I didn't want summer to end. Every time I said goodbye to James before work started, I felt like I might cry.

Thursday night was my last shift before I had the whole weekend off. Even though my freedom was in sight, I'd hated saying goodbye to James. I felt a little mopey as I tied my apron around my waist and organized my notepad and pens.

Eden inspected me. "You've got it bad," she said. "James literally dropped you off down here two seconds ago, and you look like you need your blankie. What's up with that?"

I shrugged. "I have to check the specials," I mumbled as I escaped to the kitchen. I didn't need to tell her she was right: I *did* have it bad.

"What's up, New Girl?" Elias asked. He narrowed his eyes at me. "Hey—what's the matter? You didn't have a fight with that handsome man of yours, did you?"

"No." I glumly wrote down the specials.

"Then what's your problem?"

I fake-smiled at him. "Nothing. I'm fine."

What was I supposed to tell him—the truth? *I'm so in love with my boyfriend, I can't stand to be five feet away from him.* That made me a stalker. That made me pathetic.

My phone buzzed and I eagerly read a text from James. *Counting the minutes until I see you again.* I grinned, then headed back to the wait station.

I wasn't the only one who had it bad, thank goodness.

41

TOXIC

EDEN PREDICTED IT, and she'd been right: we had offi-
cially hit the busy season. The restaurant was packed
non-stop. As soon as one of my tables cleared, another
party sat down. Everyone was in vacation mode,
ordering lobster dinners, cocktails, desserts, bottles of
expensive wine. Before I knew it, I had over two
hundred dollars in my pocket and my shift had ended.

I had the next two days off; the gala was Saturday
night. I'd promised James I'd help him get the Tower
ready even though he'd hired a party planner, caterers
and servers. We both knew the truth. It was just another
excuse to give my dad, another reason for us to be
together.

One more sleep before I could spend the entire day
with James. I headed into the house, relieved that the

living room lights were off. I'd worked late. Everyone was probably already in bed. Eager to be reunited with James—in my bed—I rushed inside, intent on heading up the stairs. But Amelia waited in the kitchen.

"You're home late." Her voice was laced with accusation, her pretty face scrunched into its usual disapproving sneer. "Ew, you smell like a lobster trap."

I took a step back. "Sorry about that. We had a lot of tourists tonight. I served a ton of lazy-man lobsters."

"Gross." She tilted her head as she inspected me. "Mom said she asked you about my necklace."

I nodded. "I didn't take it, Amelia. I wouldn't do something like that."

"You probably hocked it so you could pay for the pill." Her sneer deepened. "Unless you're not even on it, 'cause you're trying to get pregnant with a billionaire's baby."

W.T.F. "Amelia?" I took a step closer—let her smell me, that was the least of her worries. "I don't know what slimy corner of the internet you've been hanging out in, or maybe you've been watching the Kardashians for too many seasons, but you need to back off. Don't say things like that. I would never do that, I would never even *think* about doing that, but I'm more worried about you and how your brain works. There's something wrong with you."

She laughed so hard she snorted. "There's something wrong with *me*? You're a homeless ho-bag who lives in my house and eats my food. You stole my necklace from my room."

"I told you, I didn't steal it."

"Yeah right." Amelia's cheeks burned bright pink. "It just so happens to be the necklace dad gave me. Of course you took it—you're jealous he has a daughter he can claim in public. Not some unwanted skank-baby whose mom was a fucking welfare hooker *junkie*."

Hot, angry fire shot through me. "You don't talk about my mother like that."

"What're you going to do," Amelia asked in a taunting, sing-song voice, "steal something else from me? And then go blow your boyfriend so he'll bully me?"

I clenched my fists together. "I'm going to smack your ugly, fat, nasty face."

"Hey hey hey, what's going on down here?" My father was suddenly in the kitchen, standing between us.

"Taylor said she was going to hit me." Amelia's face screwed up, like she was about to cry.

Dad eyed my fists. "What's going on, Taylor?"

Ratting out Amelia had never worked in my favor before, but I wasn't going to let this one slide. "She called mom a junkie."

"Well it's true." Amelia's about-to-cry act vanished for a second. She sounded like a triumphant tattle-tale.

Dad winced. *"Amelia."*

"Yeah it is true," my voice rose, "but she wasn't a 'fucking welfare hooker,' which was the other thing you called her."

"I did not."

"Did so."

"Girls." Big Kyle got directly between us, looking from Amelia to me and back again. "This is not okay. Amelia—apologize to your sister right now."

Amelia gave him side-eye. "She's not my sister, and I'm not apologizing to her. She stole my necklace and she's lying about it. Go get Mom. She needs to hear about this."

Kyle stared at her. "I'm not getting your mother, and like it or not, Taylor is *absofuckinglutely* your sister. You will not speak to her that way. Now you apologize, or you can shut your mouth, go to bed and be grounded."

"Pfft, Mom won't ground me for this. She gets it. You can't see that Taylor's a faker, and a liar, and a *thief*, but whatever." Her voice shook. "You want to choose her over me, you do that."

"I'm not choosing between you—" Before he could finish, Amelia stomped out of the kitchen.

Dad turned to me, his lips set in a grim line. "You're punished, too."

"What? I didn't do anything!"

"I *heard* you. You said you were going to smack her, and you said some other pretty nasty stuff, too."

I took a step back from him. "She deserved it. Did you hear what she said about mom? It wasn't the first time, either. I usually try to ignore her, but she pushed me too far tonight."

"You're grounded," he said calmly. "For the weekend."

"The gala's this weekend—I can't miss it."

My dad didn't often get mad. He just got quiet, which was worse. In all honesty, I was floored that he'd used the f-word with Amelia—I don't think I'd ever heard him say it before.

He was silent for a second before he said, "Don't push me, Taylor. Now go to your room. We can discuss this in the morning." He turned on his heel and was gone.

And I just stood there, my hands still clenched into fists, feeling angry and very, very much alone.

EVEN JAMES in my bed couldn't make me feel better. I told him what had happened, and he tried to comfort me, but nothing could stop the blood from boiling in my veins.

I rolled away from him, needing space, needing sleep. But Amelia's words replayed in my head, over and over again, a toxic loop on repeat. Even though I tried to relax, I clenched my hands into fists again. I wanted to smack that sneer right off her face once and for all...

"Are you sure I can't do anything?" James sounded not only pissed, but helpless.

"Unless you can zap Amelia's personality out of her, I don't think so. I'll be fine. I just need to sleep, okay?"

"Okay." He kissed the top of my head and turned onto his back, letting me rage in private.

I tossed and turned for a while, but eventually, fatigue from my long shift won out. For the first night in many nights, I began to dream. At first, it wasn't unpleasant. James and I were walking on the beach near the Tower. He turned to look out at the water and I moved away, picking up rocks from the shore.

I found Amelia's necklace buried in the sand. I turned to show it to James, but he was gone. The aquamarine pendant winked in the sunlight as I turned it over in my hand. Then, in the way of dreams, I wasn't on the beach anymore.

I was in the field near the Tower, walking toward the forest.

Hundreds of crows sat in the trees, cawing at me. The cacophony rose as I entered the dark forest, brushing the heavy branches from my face. I held my hands out, pushing my way through, trying to keep the trees from stabbing me.

The well was up ahead. I knew I had to see it.

"Taylor?" There was a voice, an echo, coming from the well. Was someone down there? I rushed forward and peered inside, but the altar was gone. It was dark; there was nothing to see except for a swirling, inky blackness, and it was as quiet as a tomb. I held the necklace above the opening and let go. It was like dropping something into the abyss: I never heard it land.

"Taylor?" It was my mother's voice, coming from the bottom of the well.

I furiously looked through the gloom for her. "I thought you left!" All of a sudden, a spotlight illuminated the darkness: my mother's face was visible below. She didn't look frail anymore, she didn't look sick. But she wasn't smiling.

Her face shifted, like one of those cheap toys I had when I was a little girl—a kaleidoscope? It changed and then changed again, switching faces. Each different face stared up at me. Though they were different, they all wore the same expression: afraid, pleading. First it was Becky. Then Amelia. Then Eden. Then…me.

I heard something—the heavy concrete lid sliding across the top of the well. But I could still hear my mother's muffled voice from inside. "Taylor? *Taylor?*"

I sat up, breathing hard.

"What was it?" James brushed the hair back from my face. "You're shaking."

"N-nothing. Just a dream." I lay back and pulled the covers up to my chin, sweat chilling on my skin. I rolled away from him.

But it wasn't nothing, and I knew it.

42

THE VISITOR

I WAS STILL awake when the sun came up.

James rolled over and propped his chin up on his hand. I stared, mesmerized, at his enormous, pale bicep. "Do you think you'll be able to get out of being grounded?" he asked.

"I don't know." My mouth felt dry. "My dad's never punished me before. He was seriously pissed."

James grimaced. "If you can't come to the gala, I'll cancel it. I'm not leaving you down here by yourself while I host some stupid party."

"You can't do that." I tore my gaze from his bicep and looked him in the eye. "Becky would seriously freak."

"Spoiler alert: she's probably going to freak out anyway. You know first thing Amelia's going to do this morning is run to mommy and rat you out."

I sighed. "I know. I should probably get up and deal with it."

"Okay." He hugged me and kissed the top of my head. "I'm going to get moving. I'll be outside if you need me, okay? If I sense any trouble, I'll be here before you know it."

He kissed me goodbye and climbed out the window.

I stared at the ceiling, feeling miserable. All I'd wanted was to spend the next two days with James uninterrupted. Now the empty hours stretched out before me, lonely and impossible. How was I supposed to stay here, when Amelia said those things to me? How was I supposed to go down and grab breakfast when both she and Becky hated me so much? I remembered exactly what Amelia had said: *You're a homeless ho-bag who lives in my house and eats my food.* The thing was, except for the ho-bag part, it was true. I had no home. I *was* eating Becky's food.

I felt sick, even as my stomach growled.

I would never understand why they hated me that much. Or how they could care so little about my feelings that they were capable of saying such horrible things. I'd gotten nasty with Amelia last night, and I was ashamed of myself. I wondered if either of them ever felt bad about the way they treated me... But signs pointed to no.

I'd learned the hard way that people didn't always do the right thing. Maybe they couldn't, I mused. Maybe they just couldn't help themselves.

I dragged myself out of bed. My dad would already be gone; it was just us girls. I didn't want to eat their food, but the restaurant wasn't open yet. Plus I was grounded. I didn't know what that meant, really, but as my stomach growled again, I knew I had to brave the kitchen. Then I'd spend the rest of the day in my room if I had to.

Downstairs was surprisingly, blessedly empty. I worked quickly, shoving a bagel into the toaster oven and making myself a cup of coffee. I dumped cream in my mug, slathered cream cheese onto my bagel and was about to retreat when the front door opened. It was my dad and Becky, both fully dressed, their cheeks ruddy. It looked like they'd been out for a walk.

"Hey, hold on a minute." My dad's face looked puffy, as if he hadn't slept much. "We wanted to talk to you."

"Okay. But—why aren't you at work?"

He kept his hands stuffed into the pockets of his navy fleece vest. "I needed to talk to Becky about what happened last night."

Becky had been watching, but she stepped forward with a surprising, tentative smile. "I heard you and Amelia had an argument."

She wasn't being mean. She didn't seem angry. "Y-yeah."

"It wasn't an argument—Taylor tried to hit me." Amelia clomped into the kitchen in a pair of pajama short-shorts and a yellow tank top. "She said I was *fat*."

"I didn't say th—"

"Girls." Big Kyle's voice held a warning. "That's enough."

"Amelia honey, it's okay." Becky gave her a sharp look. "Your dad and I talked about it, and we don't think that you should be punished. *Either* of you."

"What? This is just so you can have your stupid freaking fundraiser!" Amelia screeched. "She said I have a fat face, mom! I can't freaking believe this shit!"

"Amelia." My dad stepped forward, all six-foot-five of him. "Do not speak to your mother like that."

"What're you going to do? Oh wait—*nothing*! Neither one of you! You're freaking blind, and mom, you're selling out your own daughter so you can get drunk in some slutty cocktail dress that's too young for you, and that *no one* cares you're wearing—especially not dad! While the ho-bag lives her best life and eats all the freaking bagels she wants!" She stomped out of the room.

Becky followed her. She paused as she passed me. "She'll be all right." Like I cared. The fact that Becky was being so polite to me, and had obviously gotten my punishment lifted, only made matters worse.

My dad and I faced each other. His mouth was set in a grim line. I had a sip of coffee before I asked, "I guess us not being grounded wasn't your idea?"

"I think you should be punished, and so should your sister. This kind of behavior's not acceptable and you know it."

Shame heated my cheeks. "You're right. I shouldn't have gone after her last night, but I lost it. I'm sorry."

"I accept your apology, but you know better. You're older. You have to be the mature one." He scrubbed a hand across his face. "But... I didn't know how bad it was. I can't believe the things that're coming out of her mouth. She's *fourteen*. Where the hell did she learn to talk like that?"

I wanted to suggest that either Becky's broad use of foul-language or perhaps Amelia's unfettered access to her iPhone might have something to do with it, but I didn't dare. "I think she's just upset. I'm sure it's hard having me move in here so suddenly. It's not like anybody planned on it."

My dad's shoulders sank. "That's true, but you should be getting the opposite of the treatment you're getting. She should be nice to you, not nasty."

I shrugged. "Like you said, she's fourteen. Sometimes stuff like that doesn't compute when you're that age."

"You're too young to sound that old." He gave me a long look. "Anyway, you're not grounded. As long as you're in by curfew you're free to go. But I want you to promise me something."

"Okay. What?"

"Be careful," my dad said.

"What do you mean?"

"I don't know." His bushy eyebrows knit together. "You ever just get a weird feeling?"

"Yeah Dad. I do." I went and hugged him, which was like hugging a boulder.

He patted my back. "You'll be all right. I've got you. You're still my little girl."

"I know." My voice wobbled a little and I ducked out of his arms. "I'm gonna go and get dressed, okay? Eden and I are going down to help at the Tower."

"Okay, honey."

I felt his eyes on me as I disappeared up the stairs, and I wondered if any of this was really okay.

Mrs. Lambert made us an early lunch, oven-roasted

turkey, cheddar cheese and local hot pickle relish on thick, crusty bread.

"What the heck are you wearing tomorrow night?" Eden asked, as she dumped some more chips onto our plates.

"The dress my dad bought me last week. It's sort of plain, but it's pretty. It's definitely the nicest thing I have."

She nodded. "I think I might wear the dress I wore to the semi last year. It's dressy, but I think that's okay, don't you?"

"Definitely. Want to show it to me?"

"Sure. I'll go grab it." Eden grinned and she jumped up, red curls bouncing. She came back a minute later with a white lace cocktail dress. It had spaghetti straps and a black satin bow at the waist.

"It's gorgeous." I beamed at her. "Patrick's going to freak!"

We did that thing girls did in the movies—we clutched each other's hands and jumped up and down for a second. Then I ruined the moment by saying, "Wait. Didn't you say Brian was threatening to come up here?"

"Ugh, yes. He called again last night. I told him it wasn't a good time. I hope he finally got the message."

"You could do the humane thing, and just break up

with the poor kid," Mrs. Lambert called from the living room. "Instead of stringing him along with this 'see-other-people' nonsense."

"Thanks for eavesdropping, and for your opinion," Eden hollered back, "but I've got it under control!"

She blew out a curl from her forehead. "You ready to go? The gestapo won't leave me alone about Brian, and I'm tired of listening to it."

"Sure." Eden didn't seem amused, but I chuckled as I finished my lunch, and made sure to thank Mrs. Lambert on the way out.

Eden let out a low whistle as we made our way down the Tower's drive past the Private Property sign. "Somebody's going all out."

"Woah." There were several trucks parked in the lot. A bunch of workers were in the yard, setting up an enormous tent. "I didn't know he was getting a tent—it looks like the setup for a wedding."

Eden scrunched her nose up. "That's because you've got weddings on the brain."

"Stop it." We hopped out of her truck and were greeted by Josie and Dylan, who were both pulling buckets filled with fresh flowers from one of the truck beds. "D'you need help?" I asked.

"Here, you can take this." Dylan handed a bucket to Eden, and they headed up to the deck.

Josie pulled another bucket out and handed it to me. It weighed about ninety pounds. "I didn't know James was getting a tent," I said.

"James is going full-out." Josie shook her head as we watched two guys wrangle one of the tent's stakes into the ground. "Wait till you see the inside of the house—they've been moving everything around. He had a bunch of new furniture barged over. I even found him ironing a *suit* this morning."

"Seriously?"

"I'm dead serious." She gave me a look. "I heard Amelia gave you a hard time last night."

"She used some colorful language—I think my favorite was when she called me a 'ho-bag.' It was endearing."

"Yeah, she's a national treasure." Josie laughed. "The apple doesn't fall far from the tree, I guess. By the way." Josie leaned closer and lowered her voice. "Dylan and I went back to the well yesterday. We put a protective spell around the altar."

"So wait. Did you take it apart?"

"No, we didn't touch it. When you don't know what kind of magic someone's used, it can be dangerous to try and disassemble it. The spell we used acts more like a bubble. Nothing can get inside it, but more importantly, nothing can get out."

I let out a deep breath. "I don't know exactly what that means, but it makes me feel better."

Josie nudged me. "We got you. It's going to be all right, as long as we can get through this weekend. I know it's your family and all, but I feel like we've invited the devil to dinner."

"James feels pretty confident that this is the right thing to do. I don't know, but then again, this is sort of outside anything I've ever dealt with." I hesitated. "Speaking of family... James told me more about what happened to you. With his brother."

Josie started lugging her bucket toward the house. "Yeah, I heard."

I struggled to keep up with her. "I hope I didn't get you in trouble."

"It's fine." She shrugged. "His brother's crazy. I knew Luke for years before he tried to turn me—I should've known better and stayed away from him, crazy-ass vampire."

"Oh. Were you two...friends?"

Josie cleared her throat. "Something like that."

When she didn't elaborate, I asked, "Are Lilly and Maeve coming to the gala?"

She narrowed her eyes at me. "Yeah. Why?"

"N-no reason. I just had a weird dream last night. I wanted to talk to Lilly about it."

"There's a lot of weird going around." Josie gripped her bucket as we climbed up the stairs. "And I don't like it."

We worked around the house for hours, cleaning, organizing the bright new living room furniture, setting up a parquet dance floor in the tent, putting out tables and chairs. Eden and I filled flower vases until our fingers went numb. Even though James had hired a bunch of workers to come down and set up, all of us were busy.

James and Patrick passed through the kitchen where Eden and I were working. James stopped to kiss me on the cheek. "Thanks for your help. I'll pay you in pizza later."

I grinned at him. "Sounds good."

"Hey, is that the delivery guy?" Patrick nodded toward the window. A rusty old Bronco was bumping over the rocks. It looked suspiciously like the car that had been parked at Eden's house all summer, one I'd thought was too broke to drive.

Eden peered out the window. Disbelief crept over her features. "Oh crap."

"What is it?" I asked. "Isn't that one of your cars?"

She crammed her last rose into a vase, then wiped her hands off on her jeans. "That's Brian. I can't believe he came down here."

LEIGH WALKER

"Wait—*Brian*, Brian?" Patrick followed her out the door.

A young man hopped out of the Bronco, looking around, the muscles in his jaw taut. He was six-feet tall, with a wiry frame and thick, wavy hair pushed back from his face. We watched as Eden ran down from the deck and approached him. Her hands were on her hips, her face almost as red as her hair. I couldn't tell for sure, but it seemed like she might be yelling.

Brian reached for Eden, but she jerked away. His face crumpled, then reassembled itself. His new expression was clearly pissed.

"I'd better get out there." James headed for the deck and I followed close behind.

"Is that your frickin *boyfriend*?" Brian shouted, gesturing at Patrick, who stood a few feet behind Eden.

"It's none of your business, because I told you—we're on a break this summer!"

"That's not actually a thing, Eden!" Brian raked his hands through his hair, making it stand up wildly. "You don't take a break when you're in a relationship with somebody and you frickin *love* them!"

"Hey, is there a problem here?" James came even with Eden. Luckily, he was strategically dressed in a tight-fitting black T-shirt which showcased his broad chest and enormous arms. Patrick, also tall and muscular, stood behind him. His big hands were curled into fists.

Brian's eyes glittered as he faced James. "There's no problem, except that my girlfriend's sleeping with someone else."

"I am not." Eden lowered her voice. "I haven't been with anybody like that, not that it's your business. I'm sorry, Brian. You should go."

"I'm not leaving the island without talking to you." He sounded as if he might cry.

"Go on and drive to my house. I'll be there in a little bit." When he hesitated she said, "Go *on*."

He climbed back into the Bronco and sped off, dried gravel flying up behind the tires.

Eden turned back to Patrick and James. "Sorry about that. I guess I better go talk to him."

"Are your parents home?" Patrick asked protectively. "I can come with you."

"No, it's okay. My dad was just getting back from fishing. Don't worry—Daddy has his rifle, but Brian wouldn't hurt a flea. He's just upset. I'll see you guys later, okay?"

I followed Eden to her truck. "Are you all right?"

"No." She smiled weakly. "I really hate it when my mother's right."

43

HIGHER LOVE

LATER, when I was eating mushroom and black olive pizza, Eden finally texted me.

I broke up with him, she wrote. *He took the mailboat back to Pine Harbor. Not sure why I'm crying, but whatever.*

I went out on the deck and called her. "I'm sorry you're upset."

"Bah." She sniffled, then blew her nose. "I should've just done it while we were still at school. I was being a chicken, hedging my bets. I just feel shitty about it, I guess. He was so upset."

"Well—he has good taste in women. I'm sure it was hard to hear goodbye.

"Hah. Thanks. Good women who string him along, just like my mother said." She blew her nose again.

"Does Patrick seem okay? He's texted me like six hundred times."

"Yeah, he's good. He's probably just worried about you."

"Well, I'm fine. I'm going to go to bed early, get up and go for a run, then wait all day for the party to start."

"Do you want to come back down?" I asked. "There's pizza."

"Not tonight, but thanks." Eden sounded a little raw. "I'll see you tomorrow, okay?"

Patrick was all over me when I went back inside. "Is she okay? Did he leave? What'd she say? Is she coming down here?"

"Woah, easy," I chided him. "She's fine. Brian left. But she doesn't want to come back down tonight, she's going to bed early."

"Hmm." Patrick stared out the window at the ocean.

"Do you really like her?" Dylan asked. "Or is the thrill gone if she's actually single?"

Patrick pointed at me. "You can't say anything, okay?"

"I won't." I looked at him expectantly. I would *totally* tell Eden if he said he wasn't into her—she deserved to know.

He sighed. "I really like her. Like, *really* really. Like, I want to transfer to Bates like her."

Dylan grinned and tucked her legs beneath her, so she was sitting cross-legged on the floor. "Who knew my two favorite bachelors would find love this summer?"

James reached over and rubbed my shoulders. "Yeah, who knew?"

Josie grabbed another slice of pizza, one loaded with artichokes and sliced tomatoes. "So what's everybody wearing tomorrow night? I have one serious gown, so that's going to be it for me."

"I've narrowed it down to a couple different dresses," Dylan said.

James played with my hair. "I have my suit."

"Same," Patrick said.

I cleared my throat. "All I have is that black dress my dad gave me. Is that all right?" I asked James. I mean, how dressed up could you get on a tiny island in northern Maine?

"That dress is great, but actually..." James cleared his throat. "I ordered something for you. It came in yesterday." The glitter in James's eyes told me he'd picked out a dress he really liked, which made me more than a little nervous.

Everyone stared as I croaked, "Oh?"

"Yeah." James leaned forward, closer to me. "You'll look stunning in it."

"Stunning. Really." I put two more slices of pizza on my plate. Stunning wasn't exactly a word that I had a lot of experience with. I stuffed more pizza in my mouth as James watched me, frowning.

"What's the matter?" he asked.

I couldn't answer. My mouth was full.

"I can't read auras, but I do read girl, so I'll translate: you're a stalker," Josie explained. "That's like a fifty-shades-of-grey move, a billionaire buying your high school girlfriend a sexy dress."

James made a face. "Who said it's sexy?"

"Duh," Josie said. She nudged Dylan. "Go on, ask him what it looks like."

"What's it look like?" Dylan asked innocently.

"Classy," James insisted. "Even her dad would approve."

"Oh yeah." Josie started laughing so hard she almost choked. "Her dad's going to *love* the fact that you spent four-thousand dollars on a dress for his seventeen-year-old daughter."

At that, I put down my pizza. "Four thousand *what?*"

James waved me off. "It wasn't four thousand."

"Six," Josie taunted.

"Enough." James stood. "Taylor, do you want to see it? I don't think it's too revealing." He tugged at the collar of his shirt. "But we should be sure. Your dad wouldn't like it if it was."

I accepted his hand and followed him up the stairs to his room. We hadn't spent a lot of time there, but of course it was nice. The room faced the ocean. The waves crashed against the sea wall as I sank down onto the huge bed, made out of dark, intricate wood.

"I swear it's not sexy." But James looked worried as he went inside his walk-in closet and wrestled with a garment bag.

I swallowed hard. "How much did it cost?"

"It doesn't matter. I've had more than one lifetime to amass a fortune. If I want to spend money on a dress for you, it's not a big deal." James brought out the dress on a hanger. He looked so proud, and worried, that my heart almost burst.

"Oh… Wow. It's beautiful."

I'd never seen a dress like that in person before. It was strapless, pale pink, with some sort of overlay—perhaps tulle—that made the knee-length skirt full. The dress sparkled as James held it out; it was as if someone had sprinkled the perfect amount of stardust on it.

"I'm glad you think so. I got you shoes and earrings to match."

"What?" I asked, overwhelmed. "How did you know what sizes to get?"

"You know when you're asleep, with your eyes and your mouth half-open?" James grinned. "I checked out your closet."

I glared at him, but only for a second. I went back to ogling the dress. "It looked like something an actress would wear on the red carpet."

"Does that mean you like it?" James sounded hopeful, and like he was trying to not sound hopeful.

"I love it. It's incredible. But…" I winced.

"It's not sexy. I mean, I don't *think* it's sexy." James held the dress up next to him, inspecting it. "Is it sexy?"

"No, it's not." By any standard, the dress was classic. Even though it was strapless, it wasn't low-cut. More than anything, the word I'd use to describe it was *pretty*. "It just looks like it cost a small fortune. I can't accept something like that from you. What if I spill something on it? What if I trip?" Both of those scenarios were painfully likely.

James hung the dress back up in the closest. He came and sat next to me. "Money doesn't mean anything to me, Taylor. I literally don't care about it."

"Only someone who's a gazillionaire has the luxury of saying that."

He took my hands in his. "That's absolutely true. It's not something I've ever had to worry about. My dad has a printing press. If we're ever in danger of running out of cash, which isn't likely, he could just make more."

I had a "Charlie and the Chocolate Factory" moment, when the kids realize that there's candy everywhere, all the time. "Are you serious?"

He nodded. "I'm not saying that to impress you. It's just so you have some perspective. We give away millions of dollars every year to charities. I'd give it all away, honestly. But we have to keep our properties to stay safe."

James brushed the hair back from my face. "The dress is yours if you want it. The fundraiser's formal, so I just wanted you to feel comfortable. Your other dress is perfect, though. I love it."

I pointed at the closet. "It's not as nice as that. Even *I* can tell the difference."

He held my face between his hands. "Honestly? You could wear a paper bag and you'd still be the most beautiful girl in the world. I mean that."

My heart did a somersault. "That's sweet."

"It's not just sweet." He kissed my jaw. "It's true. Every time I look at you, I don't know. It's like you undo me."

"Ha." But I stopped laughing as he trailed kisses along my jaw and down my neck, making my heart thunder. I wrapped my arms his shoulders, relishing the feel of his big body so close to mine.

"I feel the same way." I didn't want to tell him the truth, which was that I ached for him. I ached right now, even though he was kissing me.

"You do?" James's voice was husky. His steel-gray eyes bore into me. "Because I knew I was in love with you, but it feels even stronger now. Every time I have to say goodbye to you…"

I stared up at him. "I feel the same way. It's ridiculous."

"Is it?" His dimple peeped out. "Because I was thinking it was sort of awesome."

I grinned at him. "It's awesome *and* ridiculous." I tentatively placed my lips against his. James was the first guy I'd ever kissed and even though I felt comfortable with him, I still felt shy making the first move.

Clearly, my shyness wasn't necessary. "Mmm." James sank his hands into my hair and deepened the kiss, pulling me even closer.

When our tongues connected, electricity zipped straight to my core. I climbed onto his lap, kissing him back, fisting his thick hair with my hands.

"Woah, okay." James exhaled deeply and sheepishly pulled away. "I need to put myself in time out."

"Why?" The question came out a little sharp. I felt

like a child whose favorite toy was being unfairly taken away.

"Because I'm getting out of control." James scooted over on the bed.

"That's okay," I said eagerly.

"No it's not."

"Why is it that..." I frowned, tracing a line on the comforter between us. This was not an easy subject to broach. "Why is it that we haven't done anything besides kiss?"

James seemed perplexed as he glanced above my head. "You think I don't want to be with you like that?"

I shrugged.

"Are you crazy, Taylor?" He shifted his pants uncomfortably. "*Of course* I want that. You don't need to read my aura to tell, either."

"Ha. Okay." My cheeks blazed.

"I just want it to be the right time for us. Don't you?"

I nodded. But lately I felt like every time we were in bed together was the right time. Or in his truck, or on the beach...

"Trust me, I want to be with you more than I've ever wanted anything. And when I say anything, I mean it— it's way worse than when I used to crave blood. And I used to crave it a lot. A lot a lot." He shook his head. "But

I've waited this long to find you—I'm not going to rush things. You deserve better than that."

I tossed my hair over my shoulder. "Um, what if I don't want better than that? What if I'm good?"

He reached for my hand and pulled me a little closer. "You deserve everything, including our first time being perfect. Not when your family's asleep in the same house, not in my truck, not in the field, not on the beach —although all of those have certainly crossed my mind —and not tonight while our friends are downstairs and could totally hear us. I love you, Taylor. I've been waiting for you for centuries, and you've been waiting your whole life. It's not something we should take lightly. When we're together for the first time, I want it to be romantic and perfect. I want it to be incredible."

"O-okay." How could I argue with that?

He leaned closer and waggled his eyebrows. "Doesn't mean we can't make out for a while."

"Ah. I love you," I said.

"I know." He brought his lips close to mine. "And I love you, too."

44

LIKE A PRAYER

THE NEXT MORNING I woke up early. James gave me a quick kiss before leaving; he had to get back to the house to keep getting ready. The gala was that night. I was excited, I was nervous, I had all sorts of butterflies. I'd never been to a formal party before and had little idea of what to expect.

There was also the fact that I'd have to deal with Becky, her viper friends, and my venomous half-sister. *Yay!*

I took a page from Eden's playbook and decided to go for a run. I laced up Becky's sneakers, which were already beaten and stained from working at the Portside and headed out into the chilly air. The early morning fog still clung to the lawn. I glanced at the pool as I passed it. I'd vowed to take a dip, but after Drunk Guy had polluted it, I couldn't bring myself to get psyched enough to jump in.

Plus, it was freezing. The island was mostly always freezing.

I pulled my sweatshirt over my hands and started power-walking. Maybe I'd work up to a run. But power-walking was a thing, wasn't it?

I started down the road, past the mini golf course with its creepy, moldy teddy bear, the run-down store, the abandoned school. There were no signs of life. Even the birds were quiet. It seemed ominous, like the island was holding its breath. My own breath was coming in little puffs; even though it was summer, I could see it. Shivering, I decided to pick up the pace. Running a little wouldn't hurt me, at least I hoped it wouldn't.

I took the road heading toward the Tower, even though I had no intention of running all the way down the private drive. The residential neighborhood was quiet—the fishermen had already gone out on their boats for the day. The foggy mist wet my cheeks and my hair. Dew clung to the grass and weeds that lined the sides of the street, making them tip over, heavy and full. When it was foggy like this, the sun usually burned through at about ten a.m. Once that happened, the plants would spring back to attention. The bees would come out, humming while they did their work.

But that would happen later. For now, the only sound was my pathetic huffing and puffing. I reached the end of the road before I knew where I was. The tiny rental cabins surfaced from behind the fog, where Drunk Guy had stayed with his friends. The cabins looked abandoned and creepy in the morning mist, the windowsills covered with thick, springy moss.

I shivered, then turned around and ran back up the street.

I had to stop after a minute. I panted, holding onto the stitch in my side. Forget sprinting, running, or even power-walking—I'd be lucky if I made it home alive.

The unpleasant thought was chased away by a more unfortunate reality: at the top of the road, Becky and Sylvie sprung from the fog, dressed in their workout clothes. Becky held weights in each hand, pumping her biceps as she and Sylvie aggressively power-walked toward me.

For an instant I considered running away, hauling ass down to the Tower where I'd be safe from them. But as the cramp pricked my side, and they gave me an unfriendly wave, I knew I was trapped. "Hey," I called as they inevitably drew closer. "I was just out for a run."

Sylvie arched an eyebrow at me. "So why aren't you running?"

I rubbed my side as we reached each other. "Cramp."

"You can run through those, you know." Sylvie really was a bitch.

"Yeah, maybe I should do that." I smiled stupidly as they both looked me over. Neither seemed impressed by my frayed hoodie, thin gray sweatpants and Becky's ill-used white sneakers.

Becky had on running tights and an expensive coral athletic jacket, her hair pulled up into a high ponytail. She wore no makeup, but those mink eyelashes were genius, giving her ice-blue eyes a thick, doe-like fringe. Sylvie didn't have false eyelashes, but she'd already put on a heavy layer of mascara. She was perfectly put together in an immaculate, cropped sunshine-yellow sweatshirt and camouflage leggings. They both looked as though they'd stepped out of an athleisure catalog, one of the super-expensive ones.

"Are you ready for tonight?" Becky asked.

Her friendly tone once again caught me off balance. "Y-yeah. James has the house in amazing shape. He had new furniture barged over yesterday, and the tent's been set up. It's going to be an incredible party," I babbled.

"This must be *such* a treat for you." Sylvie smiled at me with zero warmth.

"Yeah," I agreed, even though I didn't know what she meant. I suspected that it was something mean. "James has been great. He's happy to host the party. Wait till

423

you see all the flowers he ordered, they're amazing. We're going to put some of them out in the tent, it'll look really pretty. Speaking of the tent, it's so cool. There's even a dance floor." *Stop babbling, please.*

"Yeah, we're going to head down there to check it out. You don't think James would mind, do you?" Becky asked, her tone still chummy.

"N-no, of course not."

"Great." She smiled brightly. "We won't go up to the house or anything. We just want to see the setup."

"Okay, see you back at the house." Cramp be damned, I was going to sprint home so I could hide from her.

"Hey Taylor," Becky called, "I forgot to ask—what're you wearing tonight? Do you need anything? We're not the same size, but…"

I licked my lips. "James got me a dress."

"Oh." A shockwave rippled across Becky's face, immediately replaced by a tight smile. And then for one instant, her face got blurry. It happened so fast, I might've imagined it.

Sylvie didn't seem to notice anything, she just stared at me.

"That was nice of him. See you later," a non-blurry Becky said.

"Yeah. See you."

As she and Sylvie headed down the street, I whipped out my phone to text James. *Went for a run. Saw Becky and Sylvie—they're on their way to check out the tent. Do you think they'll go to the well?*

No, he wrote back immediately. *I don't think she remembers anything about it. It's okay.*

My heart pounded in my chest as I replied. *She shook a little. I mean, I thought she did.*

My phone rang and I was so freaked out I almost dropped it. "Is she still near you?" James asked, his voice tense.

"N-no. They're walking down to the Tower."

"Go home. *Now.* I've got this." He hung up before I could say more.

I ran all the way back to Becky's house, cramp be damned.

———

I PACED MY ROOM, waiting to hear from James. Finally I gave up and texted Josie.

It's fine, she wrote back. *Becky's just walking around like she owns the place.*

What about the well? I asked.

It's under control.

I paced some more, until James texted me an hour

later. *She's on her way back to pick up Amelia. It went fine. She's going off island—but stay in your room until you're sure she's gone.*

Becky came home a few minutes later. I heard her go into the kitchen. "Amelia?" she called. "Let's go honey, we have an appointment!"

I breathed a sigh of relief when they left the house soon thereafter. The truck tires crunched over the gravel in the driveway, and then I had the house to myself.

I found a note in the kitchen. *Amelia and I went off-island to get mani/pedis! :) See you later.*

I crumpled the note and tossed it in the trash. Of all the insane things I'd experienced lately, the fact that I was vaguely hurt they hadn't invited me was the most ridiculous.

I called Eden. "Want to do our nails?"

"Hell yes." Her voice still sounded thick, as though she had a cold or had been up all night crying. "I was just going to call you and ask you the same thing. I have a mud mask, too. And my mom made muffins. You want to come over?"

Warmth bloomed in my chest. "Yeah. That sounds awesome."

"Good." Eden sounded relieved. "Today's going to drag, isn't it? It'll be so much better if we hang out."

I grinned as I hung up the phone and raced upstairs. Eden's invitation was just the reminder I needed. Forget Becky and Amelia. Forget Sylvie and her stupid arched eyebrow. Forget the altar, if possible, and my strange dream about the well. Forget the blurriness and the shakes. There were so many good things in my life now, way more than there were bad. I had Eden. I had James. I had my dad.

That was something. That was everything.

EDEN and I spent most of the day together. Her eyes were a little puffy. She showed me some old pictures of her and Brian, but she didn't seem too sad. We painted our nails. We did a mud mask. We gorged ourselves on Mrs. Lambert's delicious homemade blueberry muffins.

With her help, the hours passed pretty quick. I got several texts from James. He was happy I was spending time with Eden. He said that the Tower was ready, and that the work crews had done a great job.

Finally, it was time to get dressed. Eden did my hair, meticulously twisting her flat iron over my unruly locks, reforming them into smooth, beachy waves. Then she insisted on doing my makeup, what she called a "smoky eye," blush and glossy pink lipstick. When she stood

LEIGH WALKER

back and admired her work, she pronounced me perfect.

I texted my dad. *Going to get ready at James's—my dress is there. See you soon!*

In his usual wordy style, he texted back *ok.*

James came to pick me up, happily accepting a muffin from Mrs. Lambert. She refused his invitation to the gala—his third, he reminded her—because she had to fish the next morning. She winked at me as I headed out the door. "You have fun tonight, Taylor."

"I will, Mrs. Lambert. Thank you."

James held my hand as we drove over the bumpy rocks that led to the Tower, but he was silent.

"Is something wrong?" I asked.

"You already look so pretty it hurts," he admitted.

I nudged him. "Stop."

"You stop." He grinned at me, his dimple peeking out, as he clutched his heart. "I'm telling you, it hurts me right here."

I shook my head. He was so ridiculous.

The house was in an uproar when we arrived. Last minute touches were being handled in the tent. The large band—which included a brass section, and whose members were dressed in tuxedos—was doing a sound check. The tuxuedoed wait staff hustled, filling water pitchers and polishing silverware. The catering staff was set up on the deck, with enormous tables set out with heaping platters of food. There was a huge beef tenderloin, salmon, lobsters, towers of mussels and what I assumed was caviar. Thirty bottles of Veuve Clicquot graced the top shelf of the bar.

Josie met us on the deck. She was stunning in a one-shouldered black satin gown, her makeup shimmery and perfect. "Hey Taylor." She smiled at me, then frowned at James.

"What?" he asked.

She jerked her thumb at the champagne. "All that cougar juice is a recipe for trouble, if you ask me."

James smiled. "I didn't."

I stepped forward. "You look beautiful, Josie."

"Thanks, but you two better get ready. I have a feeling people are going to show up on time. There's no fashionably late tonight—there's nothing else to do around here, and some of these people have been waiting to get down here for decades." She cursed and pointed at the yard, where a well-dressed driver was parking a beat-up SUV. "See? Here come some fools now! It's ten minutes early!"

"C'mon, we should hurry." James led me through the bustling house. We were so busy dodging staff, I only glimpsed how beautiful everything looked.

"The house looks so nice," I said, as he pulled me up

the stairs. "Everything seems perfect."

"I think so. Even Becky approved, when she was here earlier."

"Did she seem okay?" When he nodded, I said, "Maybe I imagined the shaking. It happened so fast, I might've."

"You're not imagining things. She was definitely agitated when she got down here, but she perked up when she saw everything. That Sylvie's something, huh?"

"Yeah. I'm super excited to see them tonight."

"Ha." James closed his bedroom door and smiled at me. "Are you ready? I put all your things in the bathroom, you can change in there. I'll put my suit on in my closet—no peeking." He winked at me. "We'd better hurry, though. If I leave Josie down there by herself for too long she'll be pissed."

"Where are Dylan and Patrick?"

"They went to pick up his mom."

We headed into our respective rooms. I gasped when I saw what James had left for me: the blush-pink gown hung behind the door. There were dainty sandals, delicate gold, with a small, manageable heel. I blushed as I examined the lingerie he'd bought me—pale pink lace. He'd even chosen jeweled chandelier earrings, the perfect complement for the gown.

I blinked back my tears. If I ruined Eden's smoky eye, I'd never hear the end of it.

I worked quickly, zipping up the gown and fastening the shoes. Everything fit like a dream. I put the earrings on, then shook my beachy waves over my shoulders. I almost didn't recognize myself in the mirror: I looked like a princess.

James waited for me outside. His suit was dark navy, and he wore a crimson tie. His mouth gaped open when I walked out.

"Oh wow." I stared at him, ogling how handsome he looked in a suit. "You look gorgeous."

"Taylor. Woah." He sank down onto the bed and put his hand over his heart again. "I'm immortal, but you're killing me."

"Ha—stop it."

"No way." He shook his head but never tore his eyes away from me. "Not ever."

"We should get going, shouldn't we?" I asked softly. All I wanted to do was stay in his locked bedroom and run my hands up and down his broad, besuited chest.

"Wait—one quick thing." He whipped out his phone and stood up, coming and putting his arm around me.

"You look so beautiful, I want to remember this night forever." He snapped a picture. "And you know I mean that literally."

45

THE GALA

THE PARTY WAS in full swing by the time we arrived downstairs. James gave Josie side-eye as she stood in a corner, clutching a bottle of Veuve.

"What," she said, not bothering to make it sound like a question.

"The whole bottle, Jo?"

"Can't let the cougars have all of it." She held the champagne protectively against her chest. "They are in *rare* form tonight. Look out. By the way Taylor, you look stunning." She slipped away as Becky, Sylvie, Gina and Marybeth clicked into the living room.

The cougars were in rare form, indeed.

Marybeth wore a form fitting, floor-length, fringed black gown, her ample assets displayed to their full advantage. Sylvie wore a structured fuchsia gown with a

Mandarin collar, her short silver hair swept back from her face. Gina wore red, the bodice of her billowy dress plunging to her navel.

But Becky was clearly queen for the day. Her layered, champagne-colored gown was perfect against her pale skin and hair. The bottom portion of her dress was metallic, strapless, and skintight. The overlay was sheer and one shouldered, giving her the appearance of a goddess. Her blonde hair hung in calculatedly loose waves down her back.

"Are you ready to talk to them?" James whispered.

I felt as though we were about to face a well-dressed firing squad. "I guess so."

He held my hand as we went to greet them, but I stayed tucked a little behind. "Good evening, ladies. You all look lovely."

The response was swift and coddling.

"Aw, thank you James!"

"Love the suit!"

"Your home is ah-mazing! These views are to die for!"

"The party is flawless," Becky said, grinning. She'd never looked so triumphant. "The other board members said this is the best fundraiser we've ever had. I can't thank you enough."

James flashed the dimple. "It's my pleasure. It's for a good cause."

I peeked out from behind him. "You look so pretty, Becky. So do the rest of you ladies."

"Let's see your dress," Becky said gamely.

James nudged me forward. Even though the heels were small, I almost tripped as I showed them the full silhouette.

"Oh my goodness!"

"You look like an actress!"

"That color…wow. It's so flattering on you."

"Is that a *de la Renta?*"

"James got it for me," I said by way of explanation.

Becky looked me up and down. Only a bobble, a tremor, of distaste passed over her features before she wrangled control of herself. "You look beautiful." The way she said it, I knew she was telling the truth. I also knew that it cost her to say it.

"Where's dad?" I asked, eager to change the subject.

"Oh, he's outside with Amelia." Becky leaned closer, catching me off-guard. "I don't think he's in a great mood. Can you check in on them?"

"O-of course. Excuse me, ladies." I hurried out to the deck, eager to be away from them while being careful not to twist my ankle. James stayed behind, the perfect host, answering their questions and offering to fetch them drinks.

There was already a throng of people outside on the deck enjoying the last of the day's warmth. The band's music floated up from the tent. I spotted Elias and Eden together, standing in the same spot we'd claimed at the solstice party. Elias wore a linen suit, and Eden was radiant in her white lace dress. "Hi, guys!" I hugged them both.

"Holy crap!" Eden's eyes bugged out. "That dress is amazing!"

"It was on the spring runway!" Elias gaped at the tulle skirt. "Do you know what it retails at?"

I shook my head. "Don't tell me. I'm already petrified I'm going to ruin it." I grinned at him. "You look so handsome—you clean up really nice."

He lifted his champagne flute to me. "So do you, New Girl."

I hugged Eden again. "You look beautiful. Thanks for hanging out with me today, it was fun. It was a good day."

"It *was* a good day." She squeezed me. "Now don't get me all emotional, this isn't waterproof mascara!"

"Have you guys seen Amelia or my dad?" I asked, scanning the crowd. "Becky sent me out here to check on them."

"I saw Amelia, all right." Elias had a big sip of champagne. "What I *didn't* see was her dress."

"What do you mean?"

"Um…" Eden gritted her teeth. "She looks like she's wearing something made out of dental floss."

"Huh?"

"Over there, nine o'clock," Elias said.

I searched for Amelia and my dad. When I saw them, my jaw dropped. "Oh my god—you weren't kidding about her dress."

Elias finished his champagne. "I wish I was."

"Okay… I'm heading over there. Wish me luck."

"Good luck," they said in grim unison.

I needed luck. I could only see Amelia from the back, but I could see almost her *entire* back. Her dress—what there was of it—was a micro-mini, strapless, white and banded. Each strip of white fabric was juxtaposed with some sort of nude panel that made it look like she was half-naked. Her tanned skin shone against the fabric. She wore four-inch spiked high heels, the likes of which I'd never seen before in Maine. Her hair had been blown out stick straight. From the back, she looked like a thirty-year-old Victoria's Secret model.

My dad wasn't looking at her. He clutched a whiskey and stared out at the water, fuming.

"H-hey." I reached them and did a double take when I saw Amelia's face. She'd had lash extensions put on, and wore heavy makeup, including dark maroon lipstick.

"What?" She scoffed at me. "Are you going to give me a hard time, too?"

"No, not at all." I smiled tentatively at my father. "Hey dad."

He didn't turn around. "Hey."

"Can I get you guys anything? There's lots of appetizers..." I motioned helplessly at the buffet table behind us.

"Nah." Big Kyle took a long sip of whiskey.

Amelia tossed her hair over her shoulder. "I can't really eat 'cause of my makeup."

I nodded. We hadn't had a decent conversation in so long, I barely remembered how to talk to her. I racked my brain, trying to find something neutral but polite to say.

"Your mom looks pretty."

She ducked her head. "Yeah, that dress cost a thousand dollars. Yours is nicer, though."

I took a deep breath. "James got it for me. I really don't know anything about dresses." There was an awkward pause before I said, "Your dress is really unique. Where did you get it?"

"Mom ordered it for me online. It was the only one I wanted."

Dad snorted, still staring straight ahead.

"Nice." I had no idea what else to say to her. "Dad, do you want another drink?"

He clutched the glass so hard, I was surprised it didn't shatter into the ocean below. "Sure."

"Okay."

"I'll get it." He brushed past me before I could claim the excuse to flee.

Amelia watched him go, a pronounced sneer on her face. "He needs to calm down."

"He cares about you, that's all." I took his place at the railing. "You're his little girl."

"Right." Her scowl deepened. "He's been acting like I'm the biggest whiner ever since you came up here. I can't do anything right."

"I'm sorry. And I'm sorry about how I acted the other night." I meant it. "I'm sure this has been difficult for you."

She shrugged, looking old and impossibly young at the same time. "Whatever. You can't change the past, right?" Her eyes lit up as she saw some people her age down on the beach. "Hey, those are my friends! Tell dad I went to hang out with them. See ya." She tottered down the deck but was smart enough to take off her heels before she climbed over the sea wall and braved the beach.

Dad came back once she'd gone. "Amelia went to see her friends." I nodded at the congregation of kids on the beach. One of them had set up a speaker and they were blasting music, competing with the wafting sounds of the band.

He shrugged his big shoulders and settled in, hanging over the rail. "Great. They can see her, too—all of her."

"Dad." I winced. "C'mon, you shouldn't say things like that."

"Oh I know—I'm not supposed to comment on her appearance. I'm supposed to support her, no matter what." He scrubbed a hand over his face. "But she's fourteen years old. If her dad's not looking out for her, who is?"

We blinked at each other.

"Becky bought her that dress. She got those damn eyelashes glued onto her in Bar Harbor today." He drained half his drink in one sip. "I will never understand that."

I shrugged. "Amelia said that dress was the only one she liked. And she's been begging Becky to get lash extensions. You know how it is—she's persistent."

"She needs a parent. Persistence be damned." He

glared out at the water, then turned to me. "How are you doing?"

"I'm fine." I smiled at him. "I don't like parties, but I'm fine."

He nodded. "I don't like parties, but I'm *not* fine. How about that?"

"That's okay." I felt sorry for him, overruled as usual. "That's totally okay."

A FEW HOURS LATER, almost everyone at the party seemed to be an eight drunk. I helped the wait staff in the tent, clearing dishes and refilling waters. The band had finished for the night and a deejay had taken over, playing raucous dance hits. I darted between bodies gyrating on the dance floor and wedged myself between people screaming conversations at each other. Becky and her pack of vipers commanded a large portion of the parquet floor, boogying, shimmying, and generally making asses of themselves. It was good that Amelia was still down on the beach. She would've been horrified to see Becky and her friends dancing to "Single Ladies."

I escaped the tent and took a moment to stare up at the blanket of stars overhead. *It's almost over*, I reminded myself. Becky seemed happy. The altar in the abandoned well seemed like a distant memory, something from a dream that couldn't hurt me.

I took a deep breath, then headed into the fray on the deck. People still swarmed the bar and the buffet table, eating, drinking, taking pictures. Inside the house was a similar scene—wall to wall well-dressed, buzzed people shout-talking at each other and taking selfies.

I searched for Maeve and Lilly. I still wanted to talk to Lilly about the dream I'd had the other night. The couple had arrived late—something about their kids fighting—and had been locked in conversation with some local artists ever since. I searched the room, and finally found them hiding near the cheese boards.

"Everything okay?" I asked.

"Oh Taylor—you're a sight for sore eyes!" Lilly immediately drew me in for a hug. "This is my wife, Maeve. Maeve, this is Taylor. Remember I told you I met her at Bebe's?"

Maeve was tall with thick, auburn hair. She clasped my hands. "Of course. Your mom's the one who made contact. It's nice to meet you. Wait—act like you're talking to us about something wicked important." She leaned down, staring into my eyes and clutching my hands.

"Okay?" I didn't dare look around as Lilly leaned in, too. "What's going on?"

Maeve's green eyes got big. "You know Melinda Braeburn?"

"The professor?"

She nodded vigorously. "She's stalking us—I don't want her to come back over here. She's been hounding us for the past two hours to do some sort of psychic booth to raise money for the island gallery. She's *so* annoying. She thinks we're show ponies or something! People don't realize that sight doesn't work like that. You don't feed a quarter in my meter and then I spit out some kind of prediction."

Lilly leaned in closer. "Melinda's always been a pain in the ass."

"Oh, that's too bad." I wasn't sure I still wanted to impose on them by asking about my dream.

"You need something, honey." Maeve didn't ask me, she told me. "Go on and tell us. You're no Melinda, I can tell by just holding your hands."

I sighed. "I had a weird dream the other night. My mom was in it."

"Go on." Lilly watched me carefully. "Did she say anything?"

I shook my head. "She called my name, that's all. But she was calling it from the bottom of an abandoned well."

Maeve and Lilly looked at each other.

"What? Does that mean something?"

"Tell me the whole dream," Lilly said gently.

I left out the details about Becky and the altar, but I told them about the well in the forest. "She was down there in the dark. I could see her because there was some sort of spotlight. Her face kept shifting, changing to other people's faces. The last face was mine—and then someone closed the well. I could still hear my mother, though. She was still inside, calling my name."

They looked at each other again.

"You're starting to freak me out with that." I pointed between them. "Do you have any idea what the dream means?"

Lilly tossed her dark hair behind her shoulder, her lips set in a grim line. "When I saw you at the restaurant, your mother made it clear that she was at peace. She indicated, and I felt, that she was leaving this realm for the other side because she knew you were going to be okay. If she's still here—reaching out to you from what sounds like some sort of trap—it means that something went wrong."

"Like what?"

Maeve gripped my hand. "A dream like that means there's something going on in the subconscious. That's probably what the well represents. Your mother's spirit wants to protect you, Taylor. She's down there fighting something."

"O-oh." I suddenly felt dizzy.

"Taylor?" Eden suddenly appeared at my side. Two hectic spots of color flushed her cheeks. "I'm so sorry to interrupt."

"What's wrong?"

She'd been dancing with Patrick and her skin had a sheen to it, but her expression was stricken. She held up her phone. "My mom just texted me. She said Brian came back and took the Bronco. He's on his way down here."

"Oh crap."

"Oh crap is right." She sounded miserable.

We left Maeve and Lilly, running to the kitchen to look out the windows. Beyond the tent headlights appeared, coming down the drive. Eden shook her head. "I bet that's him. I gotta go talk to him—tell him to go the hell home. *Again.*"

"Let me come with you," I said.

She shook her head. "No, I've got this. He needs to understand, once and for all, that I meant what I said. It's over."

I stepped in front of her so she couldn't leave. "Are you sure it's safe?"

She looked me straight in the eye. "Yes. Brian's upset,

but he would *never* hurt me. He's gentle—I wouldn't go out there if he wasn't. I have my phone, okay? I'll text you if I need backup."

"O-okay." But I felt a pit in my stomach as I watched her maneuver through the crowd, white lace swishing.

I wasn't sure why, but I suddenly felt like I might cry.

DOWN DOWN DOWN

JAMES, Josie and Dylan came into the kitchen a minute later. Josie shook her head. "I told you not to buy all that booze. I think I just walked in on an episode of Wife Swap out in the parking lot."

James winced. "It's a little out of control."

"Hey." I tugged on his sleeve. "Brian came back— Eden's outside talking to him. She said it was okay, but I'm worried."

He frowned. "I thought he left yesterday."

"Yeah, he did—he took the mailboat. But I guess he came back."

He nodded. "C'mon—we should go check on them."

Josie and Dylan followed us out. We elbowed our way through the throng on the deck and made it to the still full parking lot.

James looked around. "Where are they?"

"There." Josie pointed past the tent. Two figures stood near the edge of the woods. I caught a flash of white—Eden's dress.

We started toward them, but my dad's voice boomed from nearby. "Taylor! Come here."

I squeezed James's hand. "Make sure Eden's all right. I'll be right there."

I peered through the dark parking lot until I saw my dad. He was holding Amelia up, his arms wrapped under her shoulders. "She's in bad shape."

Amelia's head lolled to the side.

"Oh my god—is she sick?"

"She's drunk." Kyle hoisted her up, but she slipped again, as if she were about to pass out. "I've got to get her home. Can you let Becky know?"

"Of course. Do you need help?"

Amelia started to cough, then cry. "Dad... Everything's spinning." She retched and threw up all over his shoes.

He cursed, then picked her up and started for the truck. "Go find Becky—make sure she gets a safe ride home. "

"O-okay." I hustled for the tent, the last place I'd seen my stepmother and her friends. Marybeth was slow dancing with her husband, her head pressed against his chest. "I'm so sorry to interrupt, but where's Becky? Amelia's sick, I need to let her know."

"Huh?" Marybeth's head popped up. She looked half asleep. "I think she's in the back."

The tent had mostly cleared out. A few stragglers like Marybeth remained on the dance floor, and there were still some groups seated at the tables. The back of the tent was pretty dark. I searched for Becky, but Sylvie stepped in front of me. "Where do you think you're going?"

Sylvie was almost a nine drunk. Too bad she hadn't passed out yet. She glared at me, her hands on her hips.

"I need to find Becky. Is she back here?" I peered past her to the dark corners of the tent. There were some couples in the shadows, but I couldn't make anyone out.

"That's none of your business." Even hammered, Sylvie had an edge.

"My dad sent me to find her—Amelia's sick." When I went to walk by her, she blocked me again.

It was my turn to put my hands on my hips. "Bitch, you best get out of my way."

"What?"

"You heard me."

Sylvie gasped as I shoved past her. She didn't understand. Confrontation was not in my nature, but my best friend was dealing with a possibly crazy ex-boyfriend, my half-sister had just thrown up all over my dad's shoes, and I was seriously tired of this stupid party. Sylvie would get over it. And if she didn't, boo fucking hoo.

I marched to the back of the tent, inspecting the lip-locked and groping couples. Finally, in the way back of the darkest corner, I found Becky. She wasn't alone. Some guy was grabbing her ass as she rubbed herself furiously against him.

"Becky!"

She turned around, lipstick smeared, chest heaving.

"Dad wanted me to tell you that he took Amelia home. She's sick—drunk. She puked all over him." My gaze traveled past her, to the handsome man she'd been making out with. I quickly looked away.

"You need to get a ride home. I guess you're all set with that?" I turned on my heel and hustled away before I said more.

"Taylor, wait—"

Becky grabbed me, but I shook her off. "I don't want to talk to you," I said. "Tell it to your frickin boyfriend."

"Taylor!"

She chased me out of the tent, Sylvie close at her heels.

I didn't look back. I couldn't. My fists clenched together as I marched out onto the grounds, looking for

Eden and the rest of them. "James?" I called, but the music was too loud. I looked around, but they were nowhere to be seen. They must've gone into the woods. I ducked into the dark trees, relieved to at least get the hell away from Becky and Sylvie.

"James?" I called again. I could hear voices up ahead —someone was yelling. I saw a light and stumbled toward it. My dress was going to be ruined, but I had to make sure Eden was okay. Maybe I could pay James back, give him all the tips I'd been saving...

I made it to the clearing, recognizing where I was at once—the site of the abandoned well. James, Josie, Dylan, Eden and Brian were there. Both Dylan and Josie had the flashlights from their cellphones on, lighting the space. Eden and Brian faced each other. James stood by at the ready, his big shoulders tense as if he were about to spring at Brian.

"What's going on?"

Eden glanced at me. "Go back to the party, Taylor. Brian here's just drunk. We've got it taken care of."

"I'm not drunk." Brian's voice was thick, desolate. "I came back here to bring you home with me. And now you're turning it into some big goddamned deal, surrounding yourself with these people like I'm some sort of threat. You know me better than that, babe. This is crazy!"

She pointed at James. "They followed me out here because they heard you yelling. They were worried about me, and for good reason. You're drunk as a skunk! I had to drag you out into the woods so you wouldn't make a scene, but you won't shut up. I told you, we're through. I'm sorry if it hurts. But stop acting like a crazy person because you're not!"

"What's going on?" Becky and Sylvie burst into the clearing. I'd never seen Becky look so used up. Her hair had a twig in it, her eyeliner was running down the sides of her face, and her dress was twisted the wrong way. Sylvie panted beside her, pale as a ghost.

"Nothing, Becky." James smiled at her, but his tone was sharp. "You and Sylvie just go on back to the party. We've got it handled—these two were having an argument. It's no big deal."

Becky blinked from Eden to Brian, and then back again. "You're having a fight?" Her words were slurry.

"Don't worry about it, Mrs. Hale." Becky fake-smiled at her. "Everything's okay."

Becky swayed on her feet and jerked her thumb at me. "Taylor and I were having a fight. She ran away from me. I need to talk to her."

"No you don't." I crossed my arms against my chest.

"What did you say to me?" A trace of Becky's usual indignation crept into her tone.

I stared at her. "I said, you don't need to talk to me. Didn't James ask you to go back to the party?"

"Y-y-es." Becky shook a little, stuttering, as she answered.

My eyes locked with James. He went closer to Becky. "I don't think you're feeling well, Mrs. Hale," he said in a soothing tone. "Can I bring you back to the house? I could drive you home."

While James was distracted with Becky, Brian closed the distance between him and Eden. He faced her, her back to the well.

Dylan and Josie edged closer to them. "Stay away from her," Dylan warned.

But Brian ignored her. "Eden Baby," he said, "please just talk to me. I know you don't mean what you said. You haven't thought it through."

He reached for her and she pounded his chest, pushing him back. "Yes I have, dammit—you just don't want to listen! No means no! I told you I don't love you anymore and I meant it!"

"Yes you do." Brian started crying. "Don't say that—I feel like I'm going to be sick."

"C'mon Brian." Eden sounded like she was crying, too. "Don't make this so hard."

"You broke my fucking heart."

Brian reached for her again but this time, James leapt between them. "Don't touch her."

Sylvie leaned toward Becky. "Did you see him jump like that? Am I seriously that drunk?"

"I saw it. James." Becky staggered closer to the two men. "How did you do that?"

He didn't look at her—his gaze was trained on Brian. "I work out."

"You're s-s-s-special," Becky scary slurred. "I knew it. Sexy, rich and *special*." She stared at him, drunk eyes wide, chest heaving. "You're perfect. I think someday you should marry my little girl. Amelia's s-s-s-special too, much better than Taylor-Trash."

"I think it's time you went home and passed out, Mrs. Hale," Eden said pointedly. "Probably way past time."

As if she'd slapped, Becky's face jerked in the direction of my friend. "Speaking of trash—don't you take that tone with me." Her tone was sharp, refocused. She jabbed a finger in Eden's direction. "You and this fool deserve each other, out here fighting in the woods like rednecks. Fucking Lambert whore."

"Don't talk to her like that!" Brian whirled on Becky, his eyes wild. "I will literally rip your throat out if you disrespect her!" He lunged toward Becky and she laughed, sounding delighted.

"T-t-t-told you." She started to shake. "T-t-t-rash."

Everything happened at once. Brian swung at Becky and they collapsed against each other, struggling. Sylvie ran into the woods, screaming for help. James lit up with white-blue light like he was conducting the electricity. Josie and Dylan threw down their phones and scrambled to back James up as he headed for the fight.

But Becky was moving fast—incredibly fast. She shook so quickly she was a blur, and Brian became a blur with her. She appeared to be dragging him around the clearing. Wrapped in her embrace, I couldn't even see where he was. Every once in a while, they stopped spinning. It was like an amusement park ride where it paused for a second, just long enough to showcase the rider's terrorized faces.

Brian was on the ride of his life, and he couldn't get off.

James swore as he chased them back and forth. He shot several beams of light at the blur, but Eden screamed, "I don't know what you're doing, but stop! You'll kill him!"

All of a sudden, Becky appeared with Brian right in front of Eden. She grinned at them. "Enjoy the trash chute."

She went to throw Brian at Eden, but James hit her with a burst of light. It shot Becky forward—Brian flew from her arms directly into Eden's chest, and they tumbled backwards into the well. Eden screamed as they sailed down into the darkness.

Becky collapsed onto the ground, convulsing as white-blue light sparked through her.

I rushed to the edge of the well. It was pitch-black inside. "Eden—*no!*" My voice echoed off the walls with no answer. "Help! James, help them!"

He crouched on the edge of the well and jumped—but sprung back out, as if he'd been repelled. He stood up and was about to try again when Josie said, "Hold on! The spell, remember?" She grabbed Dylan's hand and they gripped the edge of the well, chanting.

"What the hell are you doing?" But intent on their chant, they ignored me. "Eden? *EDEN!*" I screamed, sobbing, as Josie and Dylan finished.

"Go," Josie told James. *"Go!"*

He immediately dropped into the darkness, lighting it up. What I saw made me retch on the ground right next to Becky.

Eden was at the bottom of the well. Brian lay on top of her, his back facing us, his neck at an odd angle. They were both motionless.

"Eden, no. No." I sobbed, sinking down onto my knees. I wasn't big on praying, but I begged God that she wasn't dead. I begged God that she would be okay, that all of this was somehow a mistake.

James carried Brian out first. He lay him on the ground and Josie and Dylan descended on him, checking his pulse and murmuring to each other. James went back for Eden. When he carried her back up, her eyes stared off into the distance, not moving.

I felt like my heart was being ripped out of my chest. "No. *Noooo.*"

James put her down and I went to my friend, weeping over her. "Please no. Eden. No..."

"He's gone," Dylan said softly as she closed Brian's eyes. She moved over to Eden, taking her pulse. None of us breathed. "It's weak. Thready." She looked at James. "I don't think she'll make it off-island, even with an airlift."

"What? No." I shoved Dylan off of Eden. "She's okay. She's got to be okay." I kept babbling, shivers coursing through me. I put my hands on Eden's cool forehead, brushing the red curls from her alabaster skin. "No. She can't die—James. *James.* Do not let her die!"

His skin pulsed with blue light, but it slowly faded. "I can't help her," he said miserably. "My light can't fix what happened to her."

"Then turn her." I didn't even know where the words came from, some deep dark part of me. "You have to turn her!"

"Taylor." He looked anguished. "I can't do that. I don't even know if it would work—"

"You have to try. *Try!* You can't just let her die, this is our fault! Please." I burst into hysterical sobs. Tears streamed down my face. "Please don't let her die, she's so young, she wanted to get a single dorm room this year, she was saving her tips to go to Paris—"

I collapsed into sobs over my friend, holding her and crying onto her. She was so cold. She wasn't moving and she was so, so cold.

"Taylor." James sounded as if his heart was breaking. "Taylor, get Becky out of here. I'll see what I can do. But you have to go home."

I sat up, wiped my face and looked at him. His steel-gray gaze, so familiar and dear, had turned dark. Desolate.

"Go home," he said again.

I didn't wait for him to tell me a third time.

DYLAN HELPED me carry Becky back to the party. Josie stayed behind with James.

"What are we going to do?" I whispered. I felt numb.

Dylan hoisted Becky up. "Take the Jeep and bring her

home—she can't hurt you after James zapped her like that."

"I mean—what are we going to *do*?"

Dylan's dark eyes filled with sympathy. "I don't know. Josie and I will cast a spell so that people don't remember anything weird happening. I'll go and find Sylvie first. I'll make sure I trace anyone she's talked to. We'll take care of it."

"What about Brian?" I couldn't bring myself to say Eden's name.

She shook her head. "I don't know. People knew he was down here—Eden's mom knew. We can't hide the fact that he's dead."

I felt sick to my stomach as we reached the edge of the grounds. "Should we wake Becky up?"

"Nah, people will just think she's passed out. Let's get her to the Jeep." We dragged Becky through the parking lot.

"I don't understand something," I said, careful to keep my voice low. "Why couldn't James get into the well until you reversed your spell? Nothing stopped Eden and Brian..."

Dylan sighed. "I think that's because Becky's the one who pushed them. She was the one who opened the well. Maybe she still had some magical control over it that trumped what Josie and I did."

"Does that mean… What does that mean?" I hoisted Becky up. "What sort of power does she have?"

"I don't know," Dylan said. "I've never encountered something like this before. But she's got some sort of magic."

We fastened the seatbelt over Becky's inert form, and I hugged Dylan, clutching her hard. "Thank you." I started crying again. "Please make sure James is okay. And Eden."

"James will be fine." Dylan held my arms and looked straight into my eyes. "I don't know about Eden—I don't know if he can do anything for her. I don't want you to have false hope."

"O-Okay." Hysteria bubbled in my chest, but it would have to wait. I needed to get out of there, to get Becky home. Dylan needed to go and find Sylvie.

We said goodbye, then I floored the Jeep and tore down the drive.

All the lights were on at Becky's house. I could see my dad pacing the living room. I looked over at Becky, either asleep or knocked out in the passenger seat. She looked peaceful. She looked serene.

I slapped her across the face, hard.

"Ow. The fuck?" She blinked her eyes open. It seemed as though her eyelids were heavy, they kept drooping down.

459

"We're home." She'd never remember me slapping her. I fought the urge to do it again.

She grunted and tried to undo her seatbelt. I finally did it for her, then went around and opened her door. Thankfully my dad came out. I didn't want to touch her ever again, unless it was a touch that hurt.

"Taylor." Dad rushed to my side and hugged me. "You okay?"

"Yeah. Becky's in rough shape, though."

"Huh?" She blearily opened one ice-blue eye. It focused on her husband. "Oh hey."

"Jesus, Becky." Kyle picked her up and carried her into the house, muttering to himself.

I leaned against the Jeep, unable to move.

A loud caw came from a nearby tree. I couldn't see anything, but I knew who it was. "Edgar. Go and tell James I made it home safe."

I heard the sound of his wings beating through the darkness, but it gave me no comfort.

I trudged into the house and went straight to my room. I hung up the dress. It was dirty, the beautiful tulle skirt torn in a couple of places. I took off the lacy underwear and stepped into the shower. I stood under the water, but there was no relief, no escape from my thoughts. Every time I blinked, the image of Eden, her eyes staring blankly off into the distance, crowded my mind...

I crawled into bed and stared at the ceiling. I could hear cars outside, people leaving the party and finally going home. I wondered what James was doing. I wondered if Eden was dead. And if she wasn't, what that meant...

I must've drifted off to sleep, because I sat up with a start. James was at the edge of my bed, hunched over, his face in his hands. "James?"

"It's done." His voice was hoarse, broken. "I brought Eden up to the Tower. But I don't know if she's going to make it."

"You turned her?"

He wouldn't look at me. "I drank her blood, almost all of it. And I secreted the serum. I don't know if it's going to work."

"Thank you. Thank you." I wrapped my arms around him from behind, but his whole body tensed.

"Don't thank me. It's my fault this happened."

"No it's not. It was an accident—you were trying to stop Becky. I saw the whole thing."

"It doesn't matter." He slid out from beneath my touch and went to the window. He still wouldn't look at me. "I called the police about Brian. I told them I thought he'd jumped into the well to kill himself

461

because he was so upset about Eden. I had to bring his body back down there." His voice broke. "The police are coming over by boat—I have to get back to the house."

"Oh, James."

He hung his head. "I don't know what to tell the Lamberts about Eden. She could die tonight."

"Let's not tell them anything yet. She might make it. She could make it." The words came out all in a rush.

James still wouldn't look at me. I felt sick.

"James?"

He stared out the window. "I have to go."

I jumped out of bed and went to him, clinging to him. "I'm so sorry. I didn't know what to do. I'm sorry I asked you to do that."

James was frozen, immobile, beneath my touch.

"I don't want my friend to die. I'm so sorry. I love you. I'm sorry."

"I'm sorry too." He wrapped his arms around me for a moment, one precious moment, before he broke our embrace. "And no matter what happens, you need to know something. I will always love you, Taylor."

He was gone before I could ask what that meant.

EPILOGUE

LAST NIGHT I dreamt I was on the island again. I'm down near west beach, at the Tower. It's been a while, but it looks the same. It can't be—I know this. But in the dream, I choose to ignore the facts.

I stand in the field at the end of the drive. The crickets chirp in the high grass as it sways, swept by the ocean breeze. Toward the water the enormous mansion looms, white and empty, its tower outlined against the darkening sky. The waves crash against the rocks. The ocean rumbles, buzzing in my ears.

I want to go inside the house more than anything. I want to see who else is here. But as I start up the steps, something, some dim awareness, tugs at me: *Go back. Leave.* I should never have returned. But in the way of dreams, my limbs are heavy, and I'm slow to follow instructions. The only thing that's fast are my thoughts. They whizz, chasing the truth, reaching for the edge of the memory of what happened to this place. It eludes me, slipping around the corner, just out of reach...

I jerk awake, first stunned by the sunlight streaming through the unfamiliar windows, then grateful for it. In the sun, it's safe to think about the big white mansion on the island.

I turn and stare at the empty space next to me, and my sense of well-being evaporates.

Some things are never safe to think about.

I pad down the hallway to another room, then open the door slowly. She's awake. She's always awake.

Eden sees me and tugs on the restraints holding her to the bed. "Taylor!" Every day it's the same. She can't remember we've had this conversation many, many times.

I go into the room, careful not to get too close. Her hair is the same, red curls tumbling back against the white sheets. But her eyes are different now. They're steel blue—or is it gray? They seem to change color with her mood.

"Taylor." She stops struggling for a moment. "What's going on? Why am I here? Why am I tied up like this? Let me go!"

"I c-can't." I lick my lips. No matter how many times I say no, it still breaks my heart. "Not yet."

"Taylor, let me go *now*!" This time it's a roar, an unearthly one, and I'm relieved that there aren't any neighbors close by.

"I can't." I keep my voice firm. "But I'll be back with some breakfast in a minute."

"Wait—*wait*!" Now Eden sounds like herself. Her pretty face screws up as she thinks. "I have to ask you something."

"Okay." I brace myself.

"I remember a couple of things, but it doesn't make sense." She stares around the room, her gaze coming back to rest on her restrained wrists. "Taylor. I remember the woods. I remember the well—I remember what happened to Brian. I remember it."

"I know. I'm so sorry."

"But I don't understand." Eden stares at me hard, then her gaze trails down her own body.

"If I'm dead...how come I'm still alive?"

Vampire Royals

The Pageant (Book #1)

The Gala (Book #2)

The Finale (Book #3)

The North (Book #4)

The Siege (Book #5)

The Realm (Book #6)

The Uprising (Book #7)

The Crown (Book #8)

Vampire Kingdom Trilogy

The Trade (Book #1)

The Pact (Book #2)

The Claim (Book #3)

The Division Series

ABOUT THE AUTHOR

Leigh Walker lives in New Hampshire with her husband and their three children.

In her pre-author life, Leigh had many different jobs. She worked in advertising at *Boston Magazine* and was a copy editor at *Chadwick's*, the women' fashion catalog. She was also a barback, waitress, barista, receptionist and lawyer. She has degrees from Suffolk University School of Law and the University of New Hampshire.

Right now she's doing what she loves most—being a full-time writer and sports-mom!

Outside of writing and family, her priorities include maintaining a sense of humor, a steady caffeine intake, and a busy Netflix schedule that includes Grey's Anatomy, Cheer, and Chris Rock's "Tamborine."

She loves to hear from readers! Email her at leigh@leighwalkerbooks.com, and sign up for her mailing list at www.leighwalkerbooks.com.

www.leighwalkerbooks.com
leigh@leighwalkerbooks.com

ACKNOWLEDGMENTS

First of all, thank YOU for reading this book! I hope you enjoyed the story. I truly loved writing it and I can't wait to share the next book, *Promised*, with you.

I have to thank my mother, without whom I literally wouldn't be here. Do you have a wonderful mother, or a special person who has always loved and supported you? I do. I recommend hugging them and saying thank you. Thank you, Mom, for always being there through thick and thin. Thank you for being a great grandmother, too. We all love you. Thank you to my Dad, Alec, who is the best father and grandfather that anyone could ever ask for. You're the gold standard.

Thank you to my wonderful family in Maine. I love you all!

I would like to thank the crow that was standing

outside of Cumberland Farms in the summer of 2019. It was so big, it was like a puppy. I watched it as it took several rocks it had stashed and moved them to another (hidden) location nearby. This led me to do research on crows. I read some amazing stories about these birds, and also learned that crows could count. Thank you, crow! I keep looking for you. You are amazing and I hope you are well. Maybe you've moved onto greener pastures than Cumby's.[1]

Finally, thank you to my ride-or-dies: my husband, Bob, and our children, Carter, Max and Graham. Love makes you humble, and in this case, love keeps you in the kitchen, cooking and cleaning, so that you are forced to take breaks from your writing. (My writing. You get what I mean.) What's more humbling than living with a bunch of dudes who don't want to talk about your swoon-worthy angel-reformed-vampire hero and your obsession with crows? Nothing I can think of. Thanks for keeping it real, guys. Maybe someday one of you will make dinner. Maybe. Either way, I love you all. Thanks for being my reason.

---

1. AS I LIVE AND BREATHE...THIS IS SO CRAZY! Today is February 24, 2020. I wrote these acknowledgements weeks ago —I haven't even finished writing the book but I wanted to write these words of thanks! BUT TODAY I SAW THE CROW AGAIN—ONLY HE'S NOT A CROW, HE'S A RAVEN! My kids

think I'm NUTS but I got out of the car at Cumberland Farms and fed him a donut. Then I went inside and the women working there told me THAT HIS NAME IS EDGAR. I AM NOT KIDDING YOU!!! So Edgar the Crow was named after Edgar the Raven BUT I DIDN'T KNOW THE BIRD FROM CUMBERLAND FARMS WAS NAMED EDGAR WHEN I NAMED THE CROW IN MY BOOK EDGAR. God works in mysterious ways, you guys! I'm like James—always on the lookout for signs. Thank you Edgar! :)

Made in the USA
Middletown, DE
13 January 2021